Tequila and Tea Bags

Laura Barnard

Sofie,
So lovely to meet you!
Love + Laughs
Laura Barnard

Published in 2014 by FeedARead.com Publishing

First Edition

A CIP catalogue record for this title is available from the British Library.

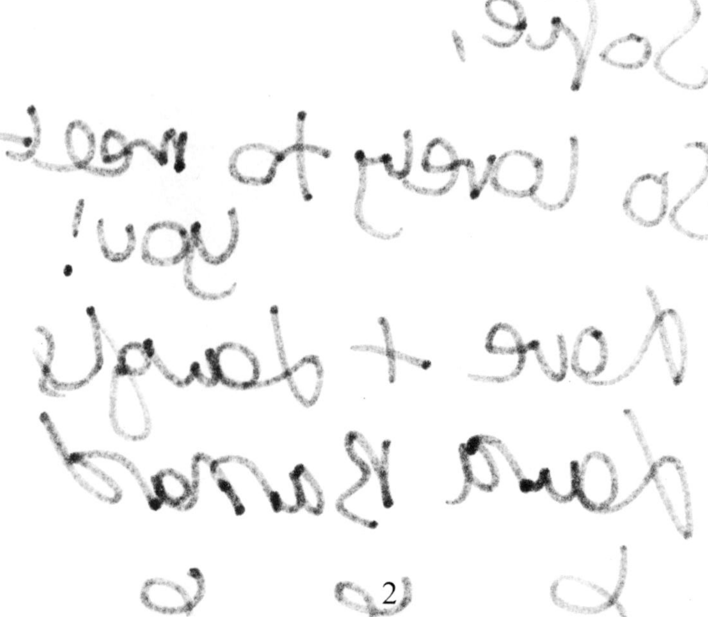

This book is dedicated to my daughter Betty. I love you with all of my heart.

Chapter 1

Sunday 28th September

I wake up and try to open my eyes. My eyelashes are sticking together from the previous night's mascara, thus reminding me I'm not following my new skincare regime. I peer around the room as my stomach grumbles, wondering if I've got a cereal bar I can eat. Making tea seems like far too much effort right now. The lurid green walls aligned with posters of naked women tell me I'm not home. I sit up and soon realise I *too* am naked. The duvet is dirty and crisp to the touch, as if it hasn't been washed in years. It smells of cheesy feet and cans of lager. Eugh!

In the words of Britney Spears, *oops I've done it again*. Well done, Rose. I jump out of bed, sudden panic racing through my veins. Where is he? I pull last night's green mini dress on as I draw back the curtains, hoping it will give me an idea of my location. Only a brick wall greets me. Where the hell am I? What if I've been abducted? The last thing I remember is Janey and I getting into the new club in town. Then…nothing. Shit. Don't panic.

I grab my bag and sling it over my shoulder, choosing to carry my shoes. It'll make it easier to sneak out. I stand by the door, my heart thumping, and I take a deep breath. As long as I act confident I'll be just fine. I slowly pull it open, making myself jump with the large screech it sends out. Pull yourself together, Rose.

I walk through a narrow grey corridor and follow the sounds of raucous laughter. My stomach bubbles with fear. What if it's Russian gangsters? What if I'm now a sex slave? I'll do anything for a kebab when I'm drunk. Maybe I went too far. When I round the corner I spot three guys sitting around, and eating what looks like cold pizza. Luckily, they don't seem Russian. Well, there's no Russian vodka on the table and they're not wearing furry hats. That's all I know about Russian people.

'Morning,' the one with brown eyes and dyed blonde hair says to me.

'Hi,' I say, kicking myself as my voice trembles. Act confident, God damn it. 'Thanks for last night, but I've got to go.'

I look around at the other faces. One of them is actually gorgeous. Black hair and green eyes. Yum. The other has light brown hair and grey eyes. He seems a bit shorter, but still good looking. At least I haven't lost my taste.

I smile and head for the door.

'You can't go without saying goodbye to Barry,' the one with brown hair says with a sly smile.

I begrudgingly turn slowly around to look at the other two. Crap. Which one is Barry? I feel sweat forming on my forehead as I look from face to face, wishing one of them would help me. I smile weakly, pure, hot humiliation spreading over my body. Why am I such a drunken slut?

'Were you going to leave without saying goodbye?' a deep voice says from behind me.

I swivel round to face a man of about five foot six, who is at least twenty stone. His face is sweaty, as if just standing up is too much effort for him. *Barry?*

'Yeah, Baz,' shouts the brown haired one with a grin.

This is Barry. Dear God, what is wrong with me?

'Um…I'm just in a real rush.' I smile apologetically, trying to keep the revulsion from my face.

Get the hell out of here, Rose!

'Come here and give me a kiss.'

Before I have time to pull away in disgust, his big pudgy hands grab my face and pull me in, crushing his fat lips against mine. They taste of salt and vinegar crisps. *Eugh.* I yank my head away before he dares stick his tongue in.

Why him*? Why?*

***

As I walk the last few steps towards my house I notice Mum's car in the drive. Great. More drama. I unlock the door and creep into the hallway, cursing as my dirty feet leave marks on the beige carpet.

This whole house is beige. My parents are beige. Boring and *normal.* The idea of being stuck here with them on a Friday night is enough to send shivers down my spine. Even worse than the idea of spending it with Barry.

'Rose?' she calls out from the beige sitting room.

I sigh, already agitated. 'I'm going to bed, Mum,' I shout, annoyed by her already. She's so bloody whiny!

'Come here, please,' Dad shouts, his voice stern.

Shit. He's here.

I huff loudly as I drag myself in, now deliberately dragging my feet on the carpet in an attempt to stain it. Their faces are strained. Dad's glasses are on the edge of his nose, his greying hair uncharacteristically ruffled. Mum's face is tear-stained, and she hasn't bothered to clear the mascara from under her eyes. How bloody dramatic.

'We've had enough of this,' dad says, his face the colour of a post-box. Calm down, old dude, you'll give yourself a heart attack.

God, they're dull as dishwater.

'Well *sorry* for having a life,' I snort. 'Maybe you should try it sometime.' I lean on one hip in an attempt to show defiance.

'You can't keep doing this to your mother.' He points to her as if I don't know who she is.

She sniffs dramatically. God forbid my poor tragic mother has to do anything but watch her pathetic soaps. Jesus, they treat me like a teenager. Is it any wonder I stay out as much as possible?

'I'm twenty-three,' I spit out. 'I can do what I want.'

He takes a deep breath. 'We've enabled you to live this lifestyle long enough. No more. We've decided it's time for a change,' he declares, pushing his glasses up his nose.

Here we go again. Another lecture about being responsible.

'You're going to live with your cousin Elsie in Yorkshire.'

'Wha…what the *fuck?*'

***

Monday 29th September

As we drive through the leafy village, passing the sign for Belmont Leaf, I look at the small, old brick houses. They all have pastel coloured front doors and perfectly trimmed bushes, as if they're done with nail scissors. And it's so quiet! All I can hear is the gravel under the car. It's unnerving. I feel like I'm driving into Midsummer Murders, and we all know how that normally ends. I look out of the window and wonder which house is Elsie's. I haven't seen her since I was seven, and even then I remember her as a bore. Too scared to jump off the garden shed roof. What a pussy. I might have broken my arm, but at least I was up for an adventure.

'Here we are,' Dad says, pulling in, a strained smile on his face.

I don't know why he's acting upset. This should be the happiest day of his life. Getting rid of me. I've only ever been an inconvenience.

I shift in my seat so that I can get a good view. This house is even smaller than the others, with only one small window next to the front door. The door is painted a pastel green and a gold bird knocker hangs from it. Along the picket fence are little signs; 'Welcome to our Home' and 'Smile, it's catching.' Oh God, what kind of person has Elsie grown into? A hippie? I could have asked Mum and Dad on the drive down, but I was too busy sulking. Mature of me.

Suddenly the door swings open and a small woman about the same age as me comes running out, her arms wide.

'Welcome!' she screeches, her wide set blue eyes nearly bursting out of her chubby heart shaped face.

I stand out of the car and try to take her all in. She's got bobbed brown hair which seems to fall in crazy, untamed waves. Hasn't she heard of a straightener? She's wearing a high collared peach dress that falls just below the knee and what seems like no makeup, apart from some Vaseline on her lips. Is this chick a librarian? She's dressed at least twenty years older than she is.

'Rose!' she cries with such alarm I jolt. 'You look so different! What is with the pink streaks, *girlfriend*?'

She is clearly not the type of girl that goes about saying 'girlfriend'. It sounds so unnatural coming from her. Especially with her accent. I actually cringe on her behalf.

'Hi,' I say reservedly. 'Are you Elsie?'

'Of course, silly!' she giggles. 'Or should I say *roomie*!' She grabs me and forces me into a bear hug. She clearly has no boundaries when it comes to personal space.

'I like your necklace,' I smirk, looking at her pearls. I'm so tempted to crack a joke about who in this village gave her the pearl necklace that is around her neck, but I have a feeling it would be lost on her. She seems naïve.

'Thanks!'

I was right.

Before I can protest, she's pulling at my arm, dragging me into the house. Dear God, this chick's excitable. She's giving me a headache. She's stronger than she looks. The sitting room is tiny, about the size of an average box room back home. It's got a small two-seater sofa shoved against one wall and a TV against the other. I suppose that's all you need. Our sitting room at home has four large sofas in it and a table and chairs. Not that we ever use them.

The walls are painted a mellow yet warm green and she has pictures all over the place. Most of them are of a grey cat with massive green eyes. How weird. There's one taken a few years ago with my Auntie Susan. It must be five years since she's died from a sudden heart attack. One thing catches my eye immediately, and I suddenly question how it wasn't the first thing I saw. A large crucifix hanging from the wall. We're not a religious family. *Are we?*

'Try to make yourself as comfortable as possible!' she bellows, as she struggles up the stairs with my suitcases.

I'm not going to bother unpacking them. As soon as my parents go then I'm off. She must have some money around here somewhere. I just need to get to it, book my tickets, and then I'll be off to Mexico to be a club rep with Janey. Seeing her leave without me was heart breaking. It really will be as easy as that.

***

Chapter 2

Tuesday 30th September

When I wake up the next morning the chirping birds seem to be mocking me. *Okay,* I want to shout. So I couldn't escape last night. But my God, she never leaves me alone! She's constantly checking up on me; asking me if I'm okay, do I want a drink. She even offered to tuck me in last night! My own mother isn't this courteous.

'Morning, sunshine!'

I jump and pull the covers over my face in fear. I turn towards the door, sure she must have burst in, but she's not there. I'm hearing this through the paper thin wall. Is she talking to me?

'Morning birds! Morning clear skies! What a beautiful God given morning!'

Oh my God, she's actually talking to things. I'm living with a nutter.

'Morning, Marbles.'

She's clearly lost hers.

The door swings open to reveal her in unflattering beige flannel pyjamas. 'Morning, Rose,' she beams, bursting through the door, making me jump back in fear. I make sure the purple gingham duvet is covering me. Especially as I sleep naked.

'We've got an action packed day ahead of us!' She grabs the curtains and pulls them back, letting the autumn sun in. Ugh, she is so annoying.

I give her a fake smile. 'Thanks, but I actually planned to chill out today. You know, get used to my new surroundings.' I stretch to emphasize my intentions.

'Don't be boring, Rose!' she exclaims. 'Today we're going to do some charity work at the local care home.'

Charity work? Is she *mental?*

'Jesus Christ!' I snort. 'You won't find me wiping other people's arses. What are you, a nun or something?' I chuckle at the idea.

She smiles, but this time it's tight and her body is stiff. 'Actually, I *am* training to be a nun. Now I'll meet you downstairs in five minutes, and I'm not taking no for an answer.' She turns and pulls the door closed behind her.

What the fuck?

'Oh, and Rose?' she says, sticking her head back in while my mind is still reeling.

'Y-Yes?' I stammer, still in shock. A fucking *nun?*

'Please don't use the Lord's name in vain. Thanks.'

Its official – Elsie's a nutcase.

I hear her bound down the stairs, already singing 'All Things Bright and Beautiful'. What the hell is wrong with her? I'm now afraid for my well-being. What if she stabs me in the night with her crucifix because she thinks I'm a sinner?

I swing my legs out of the bed and stretch my arms above my head. It's going to be hard to fake enthusiasm.

Thud!

What the hell was that? I look around, trying to work out where the sound came from. Did I imagine it? Is this house leaking some sort of crazy gas?

Thud!

Is it the wall? I look at it, trying to decide if I should walk closer. I'm a little scared. What if the room's haunted? It *is* an old house.

THUD!

Okay, this time I know it's the wall. My headboard actually shook. Is the neighbour…having sex? My eyes light up at the idea. We must have young next door neighbours. God, I hope he's a fitty that I can drool over.

I press my ear to the wall and press my hand over my other ear, trying to suppress a giggle. I can hear muffled voiced.

'Will! I! Am!' she shrieks.

'Oh, Fergie,' a male voice coos on another bang. 'Oh, Fergie!'

'That's it,' she screeches, her voice getting louder. 'Mix your milk with my coco puffs!'

'Dirty bit!' he shouts as a final loud thud hits the wall, ending their session.

Did I really just hear that? Are my neighbours Fergie and Will. I. Am. from the Black Eyed Peas? Do they have a hidden country retreat in the UK that no one knows about? But then, I thought Fergie was married. And their voices did have Leeds accents. Are they…ew, are they role playing? That's so bloody random. I laugh to myself, covering my mouth so they can't hear me. What pervy little neighbours I have! At least someone's getting some around here.

***

By the time Elsie's old Cotra pulls up outside the vast grey building, she's told me her life story. She likes to talk; it's exhausting. She turned to God after Auntie Susan passed away, feeling there was no one else she could count on. *Hello,* doesn't she have any friends? From there it seems they've brainwashed her into thinking she needs to 'do God's work', and she claims one night an angel visited her, telling her she must dedicate her life to helping others, that it was God's plan. Sounds like too many Sambuca's to me.

From there she's somehow in training at her local church. It sounds like slavery to me. I've never trusted religion; all that stuff about heaven and hell. It always sounds like they're threatening you, and I swear half the people attending church are only there because they're terrified they'll be struck down otherwise. And an angel visiting you? All a bit too far-fetched for me. I'd probably believe aliens before that.

'This is it,' she announces fondly, staring up at it through the windscreen.

I look up at the building, with its crumbling plaster and chipped window frames. This can't be the nursing home she was telling me about. Old people can't live here; they'd die of pneumonia.

'Obviously it would be a lot smarter if they had more funding,' she says, noticing my looks of despair, 'but it's council run and they're low on donations lately.'

Low? I'd be surprised if they've had *any* donations.

She practically skips out of the car. I trudge along after her begrudgingly. We walk into the building to meet a stark grey hallway, the lino clicking under my biker boot heels. This place looks more like a morgue. There's an old wooden desk left unattended, which I'm guessing is their version of reception, although there isn't a computer in sight. Don't tell me they rely on pen and paper? This is like stepping back in time!

'Come on,' she smiles, tugging on my arm like an excited child. 'I'll introduce you t' residents.'

I allow her to tug me into what seems like a large sitting room, the carpet containing so many flowers I feel dizzy. Immediately the smell of urine hits me, followed by the smell of dust mites. I look around to see a crowd of old people sitting on high backed chairs that look extremely uncomfortable. Some are sleeping with their mouths wide open, dribble falling out of their mouths, while some others are chatting amongst themselves or reading magazines with magnifying glasses. One by one they stop what they're doing and turn to stare at me.

It's like a horror film.

'Ey up everybody,' Elsie sings. 'I'd like to introduce you to my cousin, Rose.'

They look me up and down disapprovingly for a moment before going back to doing their previous activities. Well, that was friendly. Not.

'Aren't they lovely?' she coos, as if she is looking at a nursery of new born babies.

'Yeah,' I laugh, before realising she's not joking. 'So are they dying or what?'

A small crowd of old men turn with fear on their faces.

'Sssshhh!' Elsie whispers. 'No, they're not dying.' She turns back to the men. 'No one is dying,' she clarifies with a smile.

'So what do you *expect* me to do?' They're all so gross looking. I hope she doesn't expect me to touch them.

'Well, our events coordinator has left, so could I leave you to entertain them?' She widens her eyes innocently.

'Entertain them?' I gulp. 'What do you want me to do?'

'Just that,' she smiles while backing out of the door. Why is she so eager to leave?

'But, Elsie…wait!' I shriek, attempting to run after her.

She's out of the door before I get a chance to stop her. Fuck. I turn round to see old people with expectation on their faces. What the hell am I going to do? Some even put down their magazines.

'Well?' says a grey haired elderly lady. She's got a neck like a turkey. 'What are you going to do to entertain us?'

'Err…..' Think Rose, think. 'Tap dance?' I suggest, completely out of ideas. I *literally* cannot think of one sensible idea.

'She sounds like the Queen,' one of them giggles.

I feel like the new girl at school.

'Yes, do some tap dancing!' a lady with brown hair in perfect rolled coifs says, clapping excitedly.

'Don't be silly, Betty!' the grey haired woman snaps. 'She's not going to tap dance.'

The way she spits it back to this Betty makes me suddenly furious. How dare she speak to her like that? It's just mean. It's like an elderly version of Mean Girls.

'She might,' Betty retorts, crossing her arms. 'Mighten you, love?' She looks up at me and winks. The sparkle in her eye makes me giggle. I bet she was trouble sixty years ago.

Before I know it I'm tap dancing. Not that I've ever tap danced in my life, but I'm banging my heels on the floor and doing jazz hands.

'See, Ethel?' Betty says in triumph. 'What did I tell you?'

'Now, now ladies,' a man with grey hair and half of his face drooped says. Is he having a stroke? Should I call someone?

'Well,' I blow some hair out of my face, 'now that's over, what now?'

'How about our soaps?'

***

Well, this is easy. There I was thinking this looking after old people lark would be a nightmare, but here I am sitting on a chair painting my toenails. They all seem to be glued to the TV while they watch repeats of Coronation Street and something called Doctors. Anyone would think they weren't allowed to watch TV or something. It's hilarious. I can see why Elsie likes volunteering here. It's a breeze.

I'm just wondering whether I should give my nails another coat when the door clicks open. Must be Elsie checking in. She'll be so impressed with me. I look up to find a tall guy in his late twenties with olive skin and shaggy brown hair, looking furious.

'What the hell is this?' he asks the room, his fists clenched at his sides.

Peggy jumps up and switches off the TV. They all look guiltily back at him, as if they are children caught in the biscuit tin.

Who the *hell* is this dude? And why is he so angry?

'Well?' he demands. 'Where the hell is Elsie?'

He looks over and finds me. I shrink into my seat and try to swallow down the panic. He glares at me unapologetically. His hair is cut short at the back and sides, but the top layers are jaggedly cut, giving it lots of texture and height. His glare is terrifying though. I kinda wish I wasn't barefoot at the moment.

'Oh…um… She left me in charge,' I mumble. Why the hell do I sound scared of him? I don't want this guy to think he's affecting me at all. Arrogant prick.

'And you *are*?' he asks, irritated, his pale green eyes alive with hatred.

'I'm Rose.' I jump up and hop over to him, still with my toenail separators in. I put my hand out for him to shake, but he just stares back at me in disgust. Alright mate, they're toenail separators. Chill out.

'Jesus,' he breathes out, pinching the bridge of his nose. 'Since the incentive programme we're getting in all sorts,' he says quietly, but not quietly enough for me to not hear. 'Elsie isn't supposed to leave volunteers on their own. She knows that.'

'No!' I jump, scared he'll tell Elsie off. 'I'm her cousin….so she probably thought….I was responsible.'

Come to think of it, Elsie is kind of nuts to think that of me. The whole reason I'm up here is because I apparently can't be trusted.

'Well, she was clearly wrong,' he says, pointing at the TV.

I stare back disgruntled. 'Sorry, but are we looking at the same thing? That *is* a TV we're looking at, right? Not a crack den?'

He stares back with complete contempt in his pale green eyes. I feel the iciness of it touch my soul. 'TV is *not* a suitable activity. You're supposed to be doing things to stimulate the resident's minds and bodies.'

Jesus, what kind of prison is he running here?

'She didn't mean any harm,' Betty says, standing up. 'I suggested it and I'm NOT sorry.'

What a spunky old bird. I *love* her.

'Of course you suggested it,' he says, sighing heavily. 'Who else?' he mutters sarcastically, rolling his eyes.

'So who are you?' I ask, folding my arms and resting on one hip in what I hope is an aggressive gesture.

'I'm William,' he says with no hand held out. 'Friends call me Will.' He studies my face and seems to be taking in my choice of hair colour. 'You can call me William.'

I retract, my mouth dropping over, completely shocked by his rudeness. And he hasn't even looked at my boobs. What a freak. I am *not* used to this kind of reaction from men.

'If you're here for this incentive thing, you can kiss goodbye any chance of me signing off your time sheet.'

Who *is* this arsehole!? Who made him king of the kingdom?

'What incentive thing are you even talking about?'

He smirks. 'So you're honestly telling me you're not here for the council incentive? You're not trying to volunteer the most hours so you can get a free holiday?'

'Holiday?'

I could get to Mexico. I could meet up with Janey. She told me the job was in the bag as long as I could make it there. I could get everything I want.

'Actually…yes, yes I am.'

***

So I've found out the skinny. Basically their council is so desperate for volunteers to work in the care home that they've come up with this incentive programme. The person who clocks the most hours this month wins a holiday of their choice. It's bloody made for me!

When I get home I borrow Elsie's laptop, assuring her it's for research, and log onto Facebook. Well, once I've held the router out of her bedroom window. Apparently the village's connection is dicey. Proving to me we're at the end of the world.

I open up a new message and type to Janey. Its bloody hard one-handed.

Hey hunnie,

So I've arrived in this twee little village and met Elsie. She's worse than I remember – all preachy and self-righteous. I'm clearly not going to survive here.

Anyway, GREAT NEWS – it looks like I'm going to be able to get my way to Mexico! Have to do loads of volunteering, but you wait, at the end of the month I'll be able to join you and we can be the best club reps ever. Save me some men!

I flick through her page and find photos of her first night out. There are gorgeous men, cocktails and sun. I NEED to get there.

***

I walk down into the tiny sitting room two hours later, feeling like I could climb the walls. I've never been so bored in my life. She doesn't even have a TV upstairs. Just the one in the sitting room. I find her on the sofa reading the bible while stroking a grey cat I recognise from the photos. I mean, really? The bible?

'Hey, hun,' I say cheerily, pulling all the strength of my face muscles to smile.

'Alright,' she smiles, looking slightly suspicious.

'So… Is there a pub or something around here? There must be some kind of night life?'

It can't just be fields and fields of nothing. God, just thinking about the isolation makes me feel suffocated.

'Of course, silly!' She giggles. 'We should go!' She jumps off the sofa and starts putting her boots on. The cat hisses in protest. 'Oh, I forgot, this is Marbles.'

Oh, that makes sense. That cat glares at me.

'Let's go.'

Well, that was easy. Maybe she's not such a bore after all. I put a quick swipe of lipstick on and grab my coat and boots.

We walk the short distance in awkward silence. When we walk into the pub I glance around at the few middle aged couples sitting on burgundy stools, nursing pints of bitter and wine the colour of cat piss. *This* is the only night life? Dear God, kill me now.

Elsie smiles at the barman, a balding man in his late forties with a ginormous forehead. She grabs at my arm and practically skips to the bar with me.

'Nah then, Phil,' she beams. 'I'd like you to meet my cousin, Rose.' She actually places me in front of him like I'm on show. To be fair, I probably give her some extra cool points, which I'm positive she needs.

'Nice to meet you, pet.' He briefly smiles, looking stressed as he dries some glasses.

'You too,' I say quickly, already gagging for some alcohol to make this disastrous life move seem a little more entertaining. 'I'll have a southern comfort and lemonade. And Elsie…a lemonade?' I turn to her.

'Actually,' she says, rolling her eyes, 'I'll have a red wine.'

No way! The Virgin Mary drinks?

'Of course, ladies,' he nods, setting about getting them for us.

'You drink?' I ask, completely taken aback. 'I didn't think nuns drank?'

She smiles and it looks strangely mischievous. 'Well, I'm not a nun *yet,* and anyway, they have communion wine, don't they?'

I get a quick insight into what fun Elsie would be like. I *have* to release her. Was she joking when she said she was becoming a nun? Surely they're all holier than now.

'So anyway,' I grin, feeling now is the best time to broach the subject. 'What's with the neighbour's and the loud sex?'

She looks back at me confused, her eyes creasing so much she almost looks a bulldog.

'What on earth are you talking about?'

'Oh, come on,' I giggle. 'I know your room's not attached to theirs, but you can't be deaf. They were fucking so hard the walls were quacking!'

'Rose, don't be so crass,' she snaps. 'And anyway, you must be mistaken. Those neighbours are Mavis and Bernie. They're in their early sixties. Hardly the type to quake walls.'

No way. Horny old guys? You've got to give it to them; they're keeping their marriage alive. I'm weirdly impressed. But still more horrified.

'I know what I heard.' I smile smugly.

'Well, don't be spreading vicious gossip like that around here.' She lowers her voice to a whisper. 'She owns the bakers.'

'Ooh, I can imagine the headlines now. Local baker caught with husband's hands on her buns!' I roll my eyes. 'Hardly front page stuff, Els. And anyway, it's not a vicious rumour.'

'Whatever, Rose,' she says harshly. 'Please remember that this is a small village. Any lies of yours will follow you around.'

Lies? She thinks I'm lying? Why the hell would I lie about something so random? God, you lie about eating the last fruit pastel when you're seven and you're branded a liar for life.

She turns to Phil, clearly trying to change the subject.

'You seem stressed tonight, Phil.' she enquires. She's always been far too nosey. Even as a seven year old she insisted she asked my neighbour why a different man's car, other than her husband's, was parking in their drive.

'I am, pet,' he nods. 'That damn Rachel keeps calling in sick and I've worked all day without a break.'

My ears perk up. He needs a barmaid? I could get a little job here and get some spending money. Buy some little bikinis. I saw a red polka dot one on Asos that I know would look hot on me.

'I could work for you,' I blurt out, immediately sticking my boobs out.

He looks back warily. 'Do you have any experience, love?'

Do my boobs have *no* effect in this village?

'Well, obviously,' I laugh. 'Loads of it.'

Although I'm sure drinking in lots of bars and dancing on them probably doesn't count, but he's not to know that. He still looks unconvinced.

'I've worked in all of the top bars and clubs in London. Plus, I've done loads of promo work.' I look around at the domino players. 'I could really get this place jumping.'

That's not a complete lie. I have worked in them, but as a dancer or one of those annoying girls who sells shots to drunk men while they ogle my boobs and try to grab my arse.

'Really?' he asks, cocking his head to the side.

Elsie looks at me questionably and I smile my brightest, most confident smile.

'Well, then you're hired,' he sighs, throwing the tea towel over his shoulder. 'As long as you can start now.'

I jump up onto the bar and swing my legs over it. He raises his eyebrows and opens the bar hatch, as if to show how unnecessary that was. Oops.

He quickly runs through the till with me, as if I'm launching a space ship, and I try to memorize how he pours the pints of bitter. It really doesn't look that hard.

'Right', he says. 'Here comes your first customer.'

I look up to see a God of a man walking towards the bar. He's got dark brown hair which falls into messy loose curls around his face. He's got stubble that looks like he hasn't shaved in about a week, and he's wearing a checked shirt with baggy jeans. Oh my God. He looks so rough and dangerous. *Swoon!*

'Nah then,' he smiles. 'You're new.' He cocks his head to one side as if challenging me, a mischievous smile on his face.

I can't help but copy the gesture. 'Yep, I'm Rose.' I smile, lifting my hand up to awkwardly wave at him. He grabs it and kisses the back of my hand, shooting tingles through my stomach.

'Pleasure to meet you, Rose,' he says slowly, eventually letting go of my hand. 'I'm James.'

And I'm in love.

I notice Elsie roll her eyes and sink a lot of her wine.

'What can I get you?' I ask as seductively as I can, leaning in, very aware that my boobs are pushed together. God, if he asked for a quick shag I'd be out of here in an instant.

He smiles as if knowing this. 'I'll have a pint of bitter ta, Rose.'

God, the way he says my name is so sexy. He really pronounces the R.

Concentrate, Rose. Try to remember how to do this bitter malarkey. I grab a pint glass and start pumping the beer out, just like Phil did. Only it seems really foamy. Really fucking foamy in fact. Okay, don't panic. It'll calm down. I look up to gauge James's reaction, but he's looking a bit concerned. Okay, keep pumping. It's overflowing into the tray underneath, but it's still so bloody foamy! What the fuck is wrong with it?!

I place the pint down in front of him as confidently as I can. He looks back at me in amusement.

'On second thought, I'll have a Becks. A *bottle* of Becks.'

I grit my teeth and roll my eyes, grabbing one out of the fridge and practically slam it down in front of him.

'And one for your beautiful self, Rose,' he says, clearly worried I'm offended.

I should refuse just on principle, but I could do with a drink.

'Thanks, I'll have a Bud,' I reply, quickly taking one out of the fridge, flipping the lid off and gulping a few sips.

'You like Bud, then, huh?' He chuckles. 'That's what I'll call you,' he declares. 'Rosebud.'

Oh great, a fucking nickname.

Elsie rolls her eyes again, seeming a bit tipsy now. 'I'll have another red wine while you're at it,' she declares, thrusting her glass into my hand.

Steady on, Elsie. She'll be saying twenty Hail Mary's before the night is up.

When I've filled her up and James has gone outside she beckons me over, hunching over as if she's about to confess a secret.

'Rose, don't be thinking James is fit or anything,' she warns, almost slurring. She's a cheap date.

'But he *is* fit.' My eyes light up mischievously just at the thought of him.

'I know, trust me I know. But he's trouble. Everyone in the village knows about him. He has a *reputation*, if you know what I mean.' She raises her eyebrows as if to hammer home how serious she is.

'You mean he's a good shag?' I ask, taking pleasure in the way Elsie grimaces when I say shag.

'I mean,' she says sternly, 'that he's bad news. Trust me, stay away.'

Sounds like fun to me.

***

Chapter 3

Wednesday 1st October

I walk up the hill to the care home, completely out of breath. I would have thought all those years of dancing would have left me fitter. I look down at the village below. From up here it looks idyllic. I know most people would probably love a view like this; the endless fields, the blue sky and the old brick cottages, but it just screams dull to me. It's too green, too boring. Plus it smells of cow shit.

'I'm chuffed you're showing so much enthusiasm towards volunteering,' Elsie beams, seeming completely unphased by the hike we've just endured. I'm sweating out of every orifice.

I roll my eyes. 'Yeah, I just love helping people,' I drool sarcastically. 'And how do I get involved with this whole incentive thing?'

'Oh, you heard about that,' she says with suspicious eyes. 'Here I was thinking you were just enjoying it.' She smiles smugly, as if reading my thoughts completely.

'Yeah, right,' I grin.

We walk into the grey dull hallway of the care home. God, this place looks more depressing every time I come here. Only this time the reception desk is manned by a little blonde girl who can't be more than fifteen. She's got huge eyes and big lips. She reminds me of a fish.

I think of the potentially tortuous day ahead. Well, it'll be tortuous if that Will dickhead is here. I force a smile on my face and trudge through to the desk.

'Alright, can I help you?' the young girl smiles, eyeing me up and down suspiciously. Or maybe she's just looking normally. With those eyes I can't tell. She looks over my outfit of hot pink jeans, black hoodie and biker boots. I was wrong. Definitely judgemental.

It occurs to me that she's my competition. She must be volunteering here too. How unfair that she's got the cushy job of receptionist when I'm stuck entertaining.

'Just volunteering again. Is William about?' I ask casually, flicking through a leaflet on how to spot signs of dementia.

'He's in't lounge,' she says while standing and leaning on one hip.

I narrow my eyes and look back at her with contempt. This little bitch is not going to steal my flight to Mexico. I'll die before she wins it. Probably just wants to go to Disneyland. The teeny bopper. Minnie and Mickey have nothing on Mexico.

I say goodbye to Elsie, who heads upstairs to do some cleaning, and wander into the lounge looking around for him. I find him chatting to Peggy, dressed in light blue worn jeans with a V-neck jumper over an open collared white shirt. I can't help noticing that the sleeves are pushed up to just underneath his elbows, exposing his bronze muscly forearms. I shake the thought out of my head quickly. I must still be thinking of James. I need to get some and soon.

I take a discreet deep breath, not wanting him to see I'm affected, and walk over to him. I know he sees me behind him, but he deliberately ignores me and carries on talking to Peggy as if I don't exist. What a bloody arsehole. With a flash of irritation I cough discreetly. Half of the residents turn around to stare at me. Maybe it wasn't that discreet.

'Ah, Rose.' He smiles insincerely with revulsion in his eyes. 'Back again.'

'Yep, that's me. Eager to please,' I deadpan, my face cold and unsmiling.

His forehead creases as he frowns. What the hell did I just say? Did it sound like a sexual innuendo? What is wrong with me? He's probably already heard of my reputation as a tart.

'Well, I'll need you to complete an official form for the council incentive, but in the meantime you can start work. The hallway needs re-painting.' He turns back to Peggy, chatting again as if I'm not here. As if he didn't just ask me to paint the friggin' hallway.

'The hallway?' I blurt out.

Paint? Me? Does he think I'm a painter and decorator? Surely he's mistaken. I thought I was the entertainer. The job of a clown sounds far better suited to me.

He turns back around. 'Yes, the h-a-l-l-w-a-y,' he says slowly, as if I'm stupid.

I feel my jaw tense and my blood boil. What a prick. I hate being made to feel stupid. People assume just because of my cool hair and killer body that I'm some bimbo, but the truth is that I got A's and B's in my A-Levels. Just because I can't bear to keep a job in a boring as fuck office, people assume I must be a little thick. I think they're the thickos for staying in a dumb job they hate. Where's the logic there?

'Where's the paint?' I ask, without moving a muscle. I don't want him to think I'm unable to do it. I'm up for the challenge. I'll show him. I'll show this little prick.

'There should be some in't garage.' He turns immediately back to Peggy, obviously dismissing me.

My fists clench and I feel actual steam coming out of my nose. Who *is* this guy? I hate him. I turn and start for the door, choosing to ignore his rudeness. I'll only say something I'll regret and I can't afford to be fired from this stupid job. I need that flight to Mexico. Just keep thinking of the sunshine.

I'm almost at the door when I hear it.

'Rosie! Rosie!' he calls.

I feel my blood boiling under the surface. I feel so hot I'm sure I could beat the temperature in hell right now. I *hate* when people call me Rosie. My name is not Rosie, it's Rose. I turn slowly to see him waving me back over. Like I'm some puppy. I take a deep calming breath. Keep cool, Rose. Don't go ballistic. But it's like trying to reason with the hulk. My body is already reacting.

I storm back over to him, blood pumping through my veins. He looks up and starts slightly when he sees me. I must look as furious as I feel.

'My name is Rose. Not Rosie. Please don't change my name without my permission. It's very rude. Unless you're happy with me calling you Willy?' I finish my tirade, slightly out of breath, to realise that I've gathered quite a crowd. Did I just call him Willy? Oh God.

William is looking at me, his eyes glowering with fury. I've humiliated him in front of the old people and I'm not even sorry. The guy's a douche.

'My sincere apologies, Rose,' he snarls sarcastically. 'Now get back to work.'

***

'Can you believe that arsehole?' I practically scream to Beth, the little fish girl from reception. I've roped her into helping me check out the paint situation in the garage. I kind of told her William said she had to help. Which isn't a *massive* lie. She's okay when you start chatting with her. At least she's young enough to also find living in this village shit. She wanted to hear all about London. I was vague, as Watford is definitely no London.

'I'd say it sounds like a normal misunderstanding to me,' she shrugs.

The poor girl has no idea how men work. They're going to walk all over her.

'Misunderstanding my arse,' I snort.

I pull open the garage door and look at the mess of half used paint cans whilst trying to ignore the smell of dry rot. I swear if this was a real company health and safety would be all over this.

I run my hands over the paint pots, checking the colours. There's one with the same horrible grey colour it's currently painted, but there's also lots of little pots of different bright colours. I wonder when these were last used. It seems such a waste, especially when you look at the ugly grey. It's so depressing. No wonder William's in a bad mood all the time if this is what he's looking at. Maybe I'll do something a bit different. The residents deserve to smile, especially with that cock William hanging around annoying everyone and spoiling their fun.

'What are you thinking?' Beth asks, worry in her eyes.

'You just wait and see,' I grin.

***

I stand back a couple of hours later and marvel at my job. I might be sweating like a bitch, have splatters of paint all over my vest top and have not eaten or had a drink in hours, but I think it looks amazing. I've done a beach mural with red and white striped beach chairs, a dazzling blue sea and some of those annoying seagulls to make it look realistic. Only I had to paint them grey because I ran out of paint. I hope it doesn't ruin it.

Beth doesn't seem convinced. She says it's okay, but I'm sure it's because she's jealous of my talent. Probably scared I'll get praised and given loads of extra hours. Her trip to Disneyland is looking more unlikely by the second. The reception phone rings and she goes to answer it while I congratulate myself. I don't think I've ever been prouder of myself, which is weird I suppose.

'Rose, Will wants you to see him in his office,' she announces as she puts the phone back down.

'Will? He lets you call him Will?' This bothers me more than it should. What the hell have you got to do to be friends with someone? Not that I even like him. But still, I suppose I'd like the option.

'Aye, why?' she shrugs, as if it's no big deal.

Maybe he's just got something against Southerners. What a fucking racist.

I get the directions from Beth and storm upstairs, ready to tear myself a Yorkshire pudding. Or something. I really need to work on my Yorkshire insults.

The door to his office is open so I let myself in, slamming the heavy door behind me. Only he's on the phone. Well, that's anticlimactic. He looks up in shock, then annoyance. He places a finger in the air as if to halt me.

My good manners make me obey, but I roll my eyes to show what a dick I think he is. Again, he's treating me like a dog. I'm eager for a fight, but the longer I have to wait the more I'm losing my steam. Maybe I'm over reacting. I shuffle from foot to foot nervously.

'Okay. Ta very much,' he says into the phone before he finally hangs up the phone.

I take a deep breath, suddenly uneasy. He leans arrogantly back in his swivel chair. He must think he's a king in his little office. Idiot. You wouldn't be such a big fish if you lived down South. You'd just be an arrogant prick.

'You wanted to see me?' I cross my arms over my chest and lean against the wall. I can play cocky too. Even if I feel like a bundle of nerves inside.

'Yes.' He smiles smugly. 'I'm completing your council incentive forms and I just want to confirm a few things with you.'

'Oh.' He's actually helping me. I relax myself a minute, realising I've been tensing my shoulders. Try to play nice.

'So I need your full name, as it appears on your passport. I already know your first name is Rose.' He stops to smile sarcastically. 'But what's your surname? And do you have a middle name?' He picks up his pen, waiting.

Shit. He needs my full name. Well I've only gone and shot myself in the bloody foot haven't I? Why did I make such a bloody fuss about him calling me Rose? This won't make him like me. I guess I better get used to calling him William.

'Well…my middle name is Catherine and my surname is Chapman.'

Do I really have to tell him my first name according to my passport?

'Okay, great. If you can just fill in the other few details here.' He hands over the form and I fill in my date of birth and the other few things before signing. I hold it, delaying handing it back to him.

Jesus, I'm going to have to just bite the bullet and tell him. How mortifying. I close my eyes and pray that he'll go easy on me.

'Um…well…my name is Rose, but…' I look at the floor, ashamed. Why did I have to cause such a scene?

'But what?' he asks, irritated, raking his hands through his hair. No wonder it's so messy if this is how he treats it.

'Well....I suppose my official name...according to my passport...is Rosemary,' I whisper, staring at the floor.

After an extended silence I look up to see his mouth dropped open slightly. He quickly tries to recover himself, before leaning his elbows onto the desk, joining his fingers together.

'So, let me get this straight. Your real name is Rosemary, not Rose?' he clarifies, his eyes dancing with amusement.

'Yes,' I nod, swallowing the lump in my throat. Stand strong Rose. Don't show him you're embarrassed. That's what he wants.

'But you still felt you had the right to protest to me calling you Rosie? Even though you actually shortened your own name.' He smiles smugly, enjoying this. Sick, sadistic bastard.

I sigh, defeated. 'Everyone calls me Rose. I've always been called Rose, never Rosemary. I don't even know why they called me it in the first place.' I attempt a laugh, as if to show how this could even be funny. He doesn't join in.

'Well, *Rosemary*, it seems we're going to have to live to your rule. I'll call you Rosemary for the rest of your placement.' He's smiling now. Outright smiling; completely unembarrassed at subjecting me to this humiliation.

'Please don't,' I beg shamefully, placing my palms on his desk, hoping my boobs are pushed together inside my vest top. 'I hate it. Don't you hate being called William?'

'Nah,' he shrugs, leaning back in his chair, his eyes confused.

'Really? William is such an arrogant name,' I blurt out before I can stop myself.

'Arrogant name?' His eyes narrow on me, and I feel my blood turn to ice. Whoops.

'Err...well, you know, like Prince William. Your parents obviously thought they were giving birth to royalty.' I snort with laughter. I'm greeted with more silence.

'You can call me Will, if you *must*,' he says, seeming no friendlier. 'But please stop offending my parents' choice of name for me. Especially with a name like Rosemary. I *hardly* think you're in a position to judge,' he chuckles.

I curl my lip in rage, but feel a smile tugging at my face. It annoys me and I try desperately to supress it. I don't want him to think I find him amusing. I think he's a twat.

'Nah then,' he says, abruptly standing up. 'I assume you've finished painting the hallway?'

I nod, still trying to keep the smile from my face. He'll think I'm a loon.

'Well then, lead the way.' He extends his arm, essentially dismissing me from his office.

The walk downstairs is awkward to say the least. Even though I was supposed to be leading the way he seems to keep stride in front of me, his long legs making ample work of it. Every few steps I have to do a little skip to keep up with him. I hope he doesn't notice. He doesn't try to engage in any conversation and the longer the silence goes on the harder I want to giggle. I wonder if there is an actual object stuck up his arse.

He walks to the bottom of the stairs and I smile proudly, presenting my masterpiece with open arms. His face drops.

'What the fuck is this?' he whispers, rubbing his eyebrow wearily.

'It's my painting, *obviously.* I painted the hallway, just like you asked. Remember?'

Why does he look so stressed?

'I asked you to repaint it, not make it look like a fucking baby crèche!' I jump from the aggression in his voice. What is his problem?

'Baby crèche? How fucking dare you? It looks damn better than the shitty grey that was there before.' I lean on one hip, fully ready for a show down with this tosser.

'Please don't swear, Rose. The residents might hear you,' he berates as if I've just used the c-word.

'What? So you can fucking swear and I can't?' This guy is so infuriating. Visions of me strangling him to death flash in my mind. I'd do time to finish this arsehole.

'You'll have to re-paint over it,' he says in a tense voice, rubbing his forehead. 'We're trying to prove t' residents that this is a responsible, caring environment. Not somewhere to drop the baby off while you get your nails done.'

Hurt and resentment rises in my chest.

'You are such an arsehole!' I scream, unable to stop myself.

He narrows his eyes at me and grips my arm, pulling me over to one side. I'm fucking livid. How dare he drag me around like this? Man handling a woman! Who is this wife beater? I realise Beth has been watching the whole thing and I'm mortified. It only makes me more furious.

I hear some of the residents walking out of the lounge, probably on the way to bed. I can't look at them though. I can only glare at Will and his hand still on my arm.

'Get your fucking hands off me!' I throw his hand off and elbow him in the stomach. He doubles over straight away, the wind knocked from him. 'If you *ever* fucking touch me again I'll do that to your dick!'

I'm glad I used to do martial arts. I always wanted to be a ninja. Well, a teenage mutant ninja turtle, but I soon learned you can't live your life being bossed around by a rat. Now I've got the theme song in my head!

Teenage mutant ninja turtles. Heroes in a half shell, Turtle power!

'What...' He's still out of breath from the punch. 'What the hell is wrong with you?' He looks up at me and he genuinely seems hurt, not just physically.

I sigh loudly. 'Look, I'm sorry, okay.' I cross my hands over my chest. 'But you don't just grab someone like that, at least not in London. Not without expecting some sort of comeback.'

I can pretend I'm from London for this. It makes me sound tougher.

'Okay!' he shrieks. 'Look, I *am* sorry. I didn't mean to cause you any harm. Trust me, I'm ashamed to think you could imagine that I could hurt you, or any woman for that matter. I'm not like that, I swear.' He looks genuinely pained, his hands up in defeat. I actually feel sorry that I overreacted. Well, maybe slightly.

'Okay, apology accepted.' I nod, still choosing to keep him on my shit list.

'Wait a second. Why am I apologising to you when *you* punched *me* in the stomach?' he asks, bewildered.

'Because you were wrong,' I answer immediately.

He sighs heavily. 'You still need to re-paint the wall.' He looks towards it, shaking his head. 'Look, even the residents find it amusing.'

I look over to see that it's attracted a small crowd. There's Zimmer frames everywhere. I pout, stupidly upset. I put some real hard graft into this and everyone's just ridiculing it. I walk up to them, ready to stand up for myself. I was just trying to perk the place up for them, the ungrateful tossers.

'Don't worry ladies and gents,' Will says, 'the wall will be back to normal tomorrow.'

I shoot him a glare. What a waste of my day.

'Why the heck would you want to do that?' Betty asks, looking back at it fondly. 'It's wonderful.'

'Aye. Reminds me of Blackpool beach when I was younger,' Alfred says. 'Me and Doris used to go there for our holidays.' He smiles sadly at the memory. He never smiles unless he's talking about Doris.

'No, no,' Ethel disagrees. 'It's clearly Clacton. I used to work there as a nurse in my twenties.'

Will looks at me, bemused, raising his eyebrows questionably. He turns back to the residents. 'So…are you telling me you guys *like* this?'

'Aye, we love it,' Peter cheers. 'Don't we everyone?'

They all murmur appreciatively.

'Well done, Rose!' Betty cheers, jumping on a chair to do a celebratory dance.

'Get down!' Will shouts.

They seem to grab me into an embrace all at once, kissing me on the cheeks.

I feel myself choking up. As if I have the love of forty grandparents, when I didn't even have one growing up. They all died before I was born. Well, I definitely didn't expect this. I turn to Will and smile smugly before leaving triumphantly.

***

God, working in this pub is boring. Probably even worse than the care home. At least there you can chat with them, even if they do repeat themselves fifteen times. I discreetly pour myself a shot of vodka and down it. Getting drunk has to be the only way to get through this.

'Oh my God, you're the girl from London!' someone shrieks from behind me.

I turn to see a teenager with tousled dark brown hair staring at me, her brown eyes almost as wide as her grin.

'Sorry…and you are?' I ask, not amused. She could be crazy.

'Oh, of course.' She flicks her hair over her shoulder. God, it's glossy. 'I'm Megan. I'm Phil's daughter and your new best friend.' She beams back at me.

'Excuse me?' I scoff. The last thing I need is a teenager following me around.

'Don't deny me this!' she begs dramatically, hanging on my arm. 'I haven't left this village my whole life. At least be my friend and tell me how to be cool.'

'Okay!' I shout, throwing off her arm.

Jesus, she's persistent.

Just then the door swings open, bringing with it a sharp gust of wind. I shiver and hope my nipples haven't reacted. They react far too easily to the weather. I'm basically Karen from Mean Girls. I can tell when it's going to rain.

I look up, doing my best to feign interest, when the God that is James walks in, all messy curly hair and smouldering sexiness. He's wearing Levi's jeans and a leather jacket over a white t-shirt. Jesus, he looks like a modern day Danny Zuko dressed like that. Yum.

'Hey, Rosebud,' he grins. It's almost as if he's snickering at me.

'Hi James,' I say, narrowing my eyes at him suspiciously, not quite understanding him at all. Northerner's are weird.

'I'll have a beer. A *bottle* of Becks.'

Ha ha bloody ha. I feel nervous all of a sudden, which I HATE feeling. Especially being made to feel that way by a man. It's so derailing. I'm normally drunk when I chat to hot guys.

I hand over his beer with a shaking hand.

'Thanks, Rosebud.' He smiles, his deep dark brown eyes glistening with mischief.

I smile despite myself. God, he's hot. He takes a sip and starts rolling up a cigarette. Even the way he licks the Rizla papers makes me want to rip his clothes off and do the same to his entire body. He nods at me before going out the front door to smoke.

I should stay here and wash some glasses or something. Maybe go over to the old men playing dominoes and start chatting. But I *want* to go outside and see James. Maybe I should go collect glasses outside. I mean, we're hardly rammed in here. And we can always do with more glasses, right?

I straighten myself up and push my boobs out. I walk outside and quickly go to the other side of the benches, away from him. I don't want him to think I'm following him or anything. It's bloody freezing. For once I wish my nipples didn't always react so quickly to the cold. They actually sting. I cross my arms over them

Shit. There's only one glass to collect. Well, I look ridiculous. I glance up at him and notice he's watching me. I feel a shiver go through me that has nothing to do with the cold. He's just so bloody sexy. His eyes are lit up from the orange cigarette tip and he's looking right at me with a sly smile on his face.

'Alright, Rosebud. Follow me out here did you?' His smile spreads up to his eyes.

'No,' I say as sexily as I can. I attempt a giggle, but it comes out more as a fog horn noise. Sexy. Real sexy, Rose. This is so much easier when I'm drunk.

‘Come here,’ he says, sticking his fag into his mouth and reaching out with both hands. He looks at me, his eyes twinkling, as if daring me to walk into his arms. God, he’s hot. He’s making me stupid.

I look at the floor for a second, sizing up my options. He might just be taking the piss. I might just fall into his arms, only for him to laugh and shout ‘only joking, dickhead!’ I have to play hard to get. Regain some control.

‘I’m not just going to fall into your arms, you know,’ I say, raising my eyebrows, my hand on my hip. ‘I don’t know what kind of Lothario you are in this tiny village, but you don’t impress me.’

He coughs out a laugh, completely taken back. ‘Really?’ he smiles cockily, as if he doesn’t believe me. He throws his cigarette into the road without putting it out. How inconsiderate. How sexy.

I raise my eyebrows again and shrug. ‘Believe it, baby,’ I scoff, striding past him, sashaying as best I can.

He grabs hold of my waist and pulls me back into him. I try not to look up at him, but I just can’t help it. I look into his liquid chocolate eyes, still smirking at me, as if I’m the most amusing creature in the world.

‘I don’t believe it, *baby*,’ he smirks. ‘I think you’ve got the hots for me.’

The way my heart races tells me he’s right. I take a calming breath, trying to look indifferent.

‘You’re wrong,’ I whisper, my voice giving away how much of a liar I am.

I look into his eyes, glittering in the darkness, as need and desire start to push me to the edge.

‘Let’s see’, he grins, leaning into me.

Before I know what’s happening I’m leaning into him too. We’re millimetres away from each other’s lips. It’s as if he’s daring me to resist. My breath is getting heavy and I can feel his on my lips. The soft stir of his breath is seducing me. Hypnotising me.

Fuck it. I lean in and push my lips against his soft ones. He kisses back reverently, turning it quickly into a deep sexual kiss, our tongues entangled in a dance. A moan escapes my lips before I can swallow it back down. I feel him smile against my mouth. I hate the power that gives him. His hands cup my bum, before he slides one hand down the back of my jeans, twirling my lace knickers in his hands. It's enough to jolt me back to reality.

What am I *doing?* It's doing all of this stuff that got me in this bloody village in the first place. I'm such a slut.

I push back abruptly, placing my hands on his chest. God, it physically hurts to leave those lips, but I have to. He smiles cheekily, as if he finds it amusing how I can't resist him.

'Well, I should get back to work.' I turn around quickly and take a deep breath.

'Wait.' He pulls me back by my arm.

'What?' I ask, rolling my eyes. It's clear he just wants to sleep with me, and I need to go now before I do. It's so bloody tempting at the moment.

'Come t' zoo with me,' he says, his face serious.

'Wh…what?' Is he serious? I stare at him, my eyes probing for the truth.

'Come t' zoo with me,' he repeats. 'I'll call you.'

'Of course you will,' I say sarcastically, backing away from him.

He doesn't even have my number. I walk back into the pub, kicking myself for being so stupid. Again.

Chapter 4

Thursday 2nd October

I can't stop thinking about James. Sweet, sexy, sure of himself James. He's just what I need in this boring village to liven things up. Not that I don't find Betty hilarious. I've taken a real shine to her. She's just got so much spunk for an old lady. She's been telling me about swing music in the forties and how she travelled around Paris, but I can't concentrate. I'm too preoccupied thinking about James' lips. Them spreading red hot kisses down my naked, panting body.

Will comes walking into the main lounge, ruining my midday fantasy. I feel him before I see him. It's like he has his own pretentious air, making me realise he's here even before I've seen him. He's got a young redhead with him who looks no older than Megan. I should ask if she knows her. She's not so bad I suppose. We spent a lot of last night gossiping about how fit James is. Something Elsie would never do with me. Especially after she warned me off him.

'Rosie!' he calls, smiling falsely.

I tense my jaw. Little bastard. I know he's trying to look nice in front of this bird when only I know calling me Rosie is an insult. I hate him.

I smile begrudgingly and walk over, my hands on my hips. 'Yes, Willy?' I smile innocently, batting my eyelashes.

He visibly straightens, his eyes narrowing harshly on me. I smile back, leaning on one hip. Two can play that game, dick.

'This is Violet. She's a new volunteer here. Can you show her the ropes?' It sounds like a rhetorical question. I'm sure of this when he starts walking away.

'Sure,' I smile although I'm sure he can't hear me. He's almost out of the room.

She's got a pale oval face with light piercing blue eyes. She doesn't seem to wear much make up, but as I get closer to her I see she's got foundation on that's hiding her natural freckles. A real red head. It's a lovely dark chestnut colour. I wouldn't mind a few streaks of that through mine.

'Oh, you're that new girl from London!' she giggles excitedly. Again, not exactly, but I ignore it. 'The whole village is talking about you.'

I lean more on my hip, glaring at her. Is she stupid? What the hell does she mean by that?

I'm glad when I spot Will staring at her strangely from across the room. I wonder if he has heard. He meets my eye and winks at me. It's so shocking to me that I stumble slightly, my mouth gaping open. I quickly try to recover myself, but I can't stop looking at him, my cheeks redden with embarrassment. Why on earth would he wink? It makes me feel ridiculously girly. Is he *flirting* with me? Do we have an inside joke going on that I'm oblivious to?

He walks over, scarily calm, keeping intense eye contact with me the entire time. It's so unsettling. He's such a weirdo. It's like he finds joy in making me feel uncomfortable.

'So, if you could help the residents get ready for bed?' he asks, nodding at me. He smiles assuredly at Violet before walking off.

'So what's the deal then?' she asks, looking around at the old people with disgust. 'We don't, like, need to do proper caring for them, do we?'

I look at her face of revulsion. I probably had the same look when I started. Now I don't even notice the piss smell. She won't last five minutes here. The idea comes to me immediately. I know how I'm going to get rid of this one. She's a wimp and a girly girl. I've already been told by Elsie that this home is just for old people who need some supported living. There are only a few special people that have care givers come in separately from the council. But Violet doesn't know that.

'Of course we do,' I smile. 'We have to do everything. Bed, baths, the lot!' I exclaim, throwing my hands dramatically in the air.

'Huh? You're joking, right?' she asks, her body recoiling in panic.

'Nope.' I turn around to the residents and clap my hands, trying to impersonate a cheerful Elsie. 'Right everyone, bossy pants Will wants everyone to get ready for bed. Come on.'

Betty giggles and some others roll their eyes. It must be shit having a young girl like me telling you when you have to go to bed. I mean, these people could be my great grandparents. Imagine living to a ripe old age only to be bossed around by children. It's unthinkable.

They all begrudgingly start closing their magazines and the sound of them creaking as they attempt to stand fills the room. They're cute really. We start helping them up and herding them up the stairs.

Violet still looks on the edge of hysteria. 'But, I mean…we don't clean up their poo, right?' She looks petrified at the thought of it. This really is too hilarious.

I try to keep a straight face. 'Of course we do.'

Her forehead creases up and she grabs a strand of her hair, twiddling it around her black painted nails. 'I don't believe you,' she argues, her face apprehensive.

'Don't then,' I snap sarcastically, walking past her. Who the hell is she to doubt me?

I walk into Betty's room and slam the door behind me. 'Are you okay, Betty? Do you need help getting changed?' Anything to be away from Violet a bit longer.

'Aye, I'm fine, my love,' she says stripping down, seeming completely at ease with me. She pulls on her pink nightgown. 'Come here and tell me how you've been settling in t' village.'

A calming peaceful feeling comes over me and I realise how much simple affection I'm missing in my life. Mum and Dad have never been huggers.

I grin, realising I haven't had a chance to gossip with anyone yet. I'm so bloody isolated, and Janey still hasn't returned my Facebook messages. I'm sure she's just busy having an awesome time.

I grab a chair and drag it over to her bed. 'Well, according to Violet, the whole village is talking about me.' I grimace jokingly.

'Of course they are.' She smiles kindly, her brown eyes lighting with affection. 'They don't see beauty every day.'

I smile shyly, feeling my cheeks redden. I wish I had a cool grandma like her, or any grandparents for that matter.

'Well, anyway, I've made one friend. Do you know James?' Just saying his name gives me the butterflies.

'Oh, I do,' she grins. 'Gorgeous lad, isn't he?' She winks naughtily.

'He's alright.' I grin, remembering James's rough hands all over me. Not that I've heard from his since. The zoo my arse. Maybe I came off as too easy. God knows I am.

'You know I courted his grandad?' She smiles fondly, a memory obviously playing in her mind.

'No way!' I shout excitedly, clapping my hands together. 'Tell me *EVERYTHING*.' I lean back, ready for a gossip.

'Maybe another day, love. I'm shattered.'

I'm ridiculously disappointed, but then I look at her face and see that the lines around her eyes seem deeper tonight. And she's a little pale, but that's probably because she's halfway through taking her make up off with a face wipe. God, she really cakes it on.

'Okay, goodnight.' I give her a quick peck on the cheek before tucking her into bed, inhaling her talcum powder scent. She's so cute; I want to adopt her. I've never even wanted to look after my own mother like this. Especially when she gets one of those pathetic headaches.

I walk into the hallway and bump straight into Violet. She already looks hassled, the hair around her face tousled as if she's twirled it to death. Perfect opportunity to throw her off the edge. I bite my lip to try and stop the evil smile trying to break out on my face.

'Violet, have you checked on Peggy? She can…' I lower my voice to a whisper, 'have bad bowel problems.' I try desperately not to smile and instead look firm.

Her face contorts. 'You *can't* be serious. I know you're lying about this, you know.' She crosses her hands across her chest defiantly.

What a snarky little bitch. I knew I didn't like her. Anyone who denies their freckles is hiding something.

'Oh, really?' I snarl, my hand on my hip. I can play bitch too. 'Well, I guess I'll just have to prove it to you, won't I?'

I march into Peggy's room, a grim determination on my face. She looks up from her Bella magazine, her eyes alarmed. 'Ey up, Rose. Something wrong?'

'No, no!' I shrill, waving my hands frantically. Perhaps too frantically. I stick them to my sides in an attempt to look sane. 'I just want to use your bathroom.' She's one of the few people here with an en suite.

I sit on the pink toilet and think seriously about what I'm going to do. I know it's insane, but it's the quickest way to scare her off. Something about her tells me she's a hard bitch who is determined to win. She's so close to the edge, all it would take is a little shove.

I grab one of the grey cardboard trays they keep in case someone's sick and squat down over it, closing my eyes. Just think of Mexico. The guys, the sun, the beach. Each person I get rid of gets me closer to that plane ticket. It's just a bit of poo. We all do it. Don't think about how despicably gross you are.

I walk out of the room to find Violet leaning against the wall. Already slacking on the job. Her face changes when she sees me carrying the tray. I thrust it at her and watch as her face repels in horror.

'Wha…what…the hell is that?!' she shrieks, her face already sweaty with panic.

Now, now. You'll be sweating that foundation off if you keep on.

'Hey, if you can't handle looking after these residents maybe you should stop now, before you waste anyone else's time.' I smile evilly.

She gawks back at me, her eyes red rimmed as if she might burst into tears.

My phone beeps and I pull it out to read a text message from an unknown number. I'm happy for a minute, thinking it might be Janey. She's always losing her phone.

The zoo tomorrow. Meet at mine 1pm, 28 broad street. James x

Oh my God. My stomach flips with excitement as if I've just been dropped on a rollercoaster. He was serious about the zoo. Images of his naked body enter my mind. Oh, how I'd love to lick him. I'm pulled from it when Violet thrusts the tray back at me. Bringing me back to the present. Back to the poo.

'Nah, forget this. I'm out of here,' she squeals.

Mission accomplished.

***

Friday 3rd October

I walk up to his house the next day wearing my tight black skinny jeans that make my pathetically small arse look like it actually exists, converse sneakers, and my black hoodie. I had to seriously scrub it to get the paint out, but that's what you have to do when you've only packed one jumper. I obviously thought I'd be on a beach right now. I think it's the perfect mix between casual and not looking like a tramp. Either way my hair looks fantastic. I always feel more confident when it's straightened perfectly. Although the fact I went over it seven times shows how nervous I am.

I knock tentatively on the door of the white cottage. It looks like all the others on this street, only this one has roses grown around the door. How ironic, I think to myself.

He swings the door open confidently, exposing a toothy grin. 'Hey, Rosebud.'

Swoon! I'm already a goner. I smile as confidently as I can, but I'm pretty sure I look terrified. It's this whole sober thing. It's like a whole new awkward world. Maybe I have a problem.

'You going for the Goth look, or what?' he asks, scanning me up and down. He pulls the side of his lips up, amused.

I look over myself and realise I *am* all in black. 'Oh, you know, just mourning my life,' I snarl sarcastically, following him in. I try to sound cool and unaffected. Instead I sound miserable.

This wasn't the plan. Going into his house, being on his turf. We were going to the zoo. I do *not* want to sleep with this guy. Well, not right away anyway. I stand awkwardly in the hallway, shifting my weight from foot to foot as he walks into the sitting room. I look through and see who I can only assume is his dad drinking a can of beer, watching Loose Women. How odd. He doesn't turn to acknowledge me so I stay where I am. I feel like I'm intruding. James grabs two glasses from the kitchen and runs back out to me.

'Change of plans.' He grins mischievously.

'Huh?' I blink, dazed by his incredible beauty. His white t-shirt is clinging to him in just the right way.

He grabs my hand and starts bounding up the stairs, dragging me with him before I can even question it. I'm too busy thinking about how his calloused hand feels grasping mine. What the hell is this guy doing? Does he honestly think I'm just going to go straight upstairs and sleep with him? I knew I shouldn't have kissed him the other night. I've given him the wrong idea. Or maybe he's heard about my reputation from Elsie. Or maybe he's just a giant man slag who thinks he can bed anyone he meets immediately. What the hell am I doing here?

Oh, who am I kidding? I know exactly what I'm doing here.

He leads me towards what I can only assume is his room. I pull my hand away from his and step back. He seems amused at my futile attempt to resist him.

'I thought we were going to the zoo?' I cross my arms over my chest, knowing my boobs will be pushed together perfectly. I'm trying to hide my fury, but I'm pissed off. I mean, how dare he think I'm that easy? I haven't even had a drink, so if he thinks I'm just going to jump into bed with him he has another thing coming. If I was shit-faced on wine then *obviously* things would be different.

'We were,' he grins, his eyes twinkling, 'but I thought why go t' zoo, when the zoo can come to you?'

He swings open the door to reveal a floor picnic over a gingham red blanket, with different stuffed toys sitting all around it, each with a tea cup and saucer in front of them. A warm fuzzy feeling takes over me, making me feel pathetically girly. Oh my God. This is seriously cute.

'Are you for real?' I ask, trying hard to suppress the giggles.

'Don't go offending Mr Hippo,' he says, looking mock offended and covering the stuffed hippo's ears. 'He's already got a complex about his weight. If you refuse to meet him he'll be devastated.'

He's *too* adorable.

'You are such a dick,' I laugh.

The truth is that I find this ridiculously sweet. I mean, don't get me wrong, I still know his intentions. His bed is too close to ignore, but he bothered to set this all up. Why not indulge him for a little while? It could even be seen as romantic. Hell, it's the most romantic thing that's ever happened to me.

'You've got a dirty mouth,' he grins, leaning forward to brush a haste kiss on my lips. Wow, he's touchy already. 'Come here and let me put something in it.'

'What?'

He bends down and looks into the wicker hamper, pulling out two handmade sandwiches wrapped in cling film. 'Jam or cheese?'

Phew, so he's *not* that forward. Yet. And, okay, so he's no Jamie Oliver, but at least he made the effort. Although I wouldn't mind seeing this chef naked.

'Cheese, I guess.' I begrudgingly accept it before introducing myself to the zebra, lion, panda, and who can forget the hippo? I make sure not to mention his weight.

'Dead tame for wild animals, aren't they?' he says, biting into his jam sandwich.

'Surprisingly.' I nod, taking a can of warm lager. 'What a romantic setting for a zoo.'

'That's what I thought.' He smiles, leaning in to be closer to me. So close I can smell his masculine aftershave. It's a blend between mint, lavender and vanilla.

He's such an idiot thinking he's going to get anywhere with me. Now that I'm calmer there is no way I'm sleeping with him. I've decided it's final. But I might as well have some fun with him.

'Yeah, it's *so* romantic,' I gush. 'I'm actually tempted to take all my clothes off and show the animals how humans have sex.'

He chokes on his lager, a bit dribbling out of his mouth. 'What? Err, I mean…aye, let's get to it.' He puts his sandwich down and jumps to his feet.

'I was joking, actually.' I smirk, loving having the upper hand with him. I get the feeling it doesn't happen often.

'You can't let the animals down like that.' He sounds heartbroken on their behalf. 'I'm afraid, Rosebud, that we're gonna have to educate them, as promised.'

I roll my eyes as he takes my hand and pulls me up to standing. I quickly finish chewing my cheese sandwich, wondering where this is going. Or where I'm going to allow this to go.

'Come on,' he challenges, smirking at me. 'Do you want to break those animal's hearts? I didn't think you were into animal cruelty.' He juts out his bottom lip and pulls a sad puppy dog face.

'Well, I am.' I nod. 'In a *big* way.' I cover my smile by drinking out of the lager can.

'Are you telling me you beat dogs or something?' He looks mock horrified.

'Obviously not!' I hit him on the shoulder, but he grabs my arm before it even makes contact. Wow, quick reflexes. He uses it to pull me closer towards him. I stumble into his personal space, spilling some lager onto his t-shirt. I'm equally annoyed and turned on that he can throw me around like this.

'If I knew you were into animal cruelty I wouldn't have invited you t' zoo,' he says, his voice low and husky, his eyes dancing.

My breathing comes out in a rush. 'We're not at the zoo,' I correct him, my voice raspy with need.

My breathing is heavy and I can't stop looking at his mouth, surrounded by his dark overgrown facial hair. I know it's supposed to look messy, but on closer inspection it looks like it's shaped perfectly. He probably spends ages on it. The thought makes me smile.

'Nah we're not.' He grabs the strings of my hoodie and uses them to pull my face closer to him. My breath hitches at the move, but I try desperately to look unaffected as my lips dangle close to his.

‘I’m not going to have sex with you, you know.’ Even *I* don’t sound convinced. My voice is all raspy and breathless, my chest is rising and falling so dramatically you can see it through the hoodie.

‘That’s fine. I wouldn’t want you to do anything you don’t want to do.’

He pulls at the strings until my lips are only a mere centimetre from his. I look at his deep brown eyes under his bushy dark eyebrows. Oh God. He’s daring me to go the rest of the way. I just know it. And I never refuse a dare.

Fuck it.

I push my lips against his with such force that I almost knock him over. He steadies himself before grabbing my neck, deepening the kiss, pressing me fully against him. The warmth of his body melts the last shred of resistance I was clinging onto. Oh dear. This isn’t going how I’d planned.

***

Chapter 5

Why the hell did I do it? And twice? What is wrong with me?

I lie on his bed, fully naked, trying to collect myself. It's so weird having sex sober. Normally I'd just pass out afterwards, like James did, but now I'm just alone with my thoughts and it's not nice. I mean, don't get me wrong, the sex was good. It was better than good, it was amazing. I've never been with someone before who has so much fun as James. It's strangely addictive. We laughed practically the whole way through it. Thank God we did, as I couldn't take my shoe off, he broke the zipper of my jeans, and I somehow managed to fall off the bed. But the way he laughed everything off made me relax. Hell, I needed it. Without my usual Dutch courage I was practically shaking. I almost felt like a virgin again.

Not that it wasn't wonderful. Just remembering his touch on my skin, the smell of his aftershave, the way he caressed my thighs. God, just remembering it makes me want to go for round three. I have to get out of here while I still can. I jump out of bed and start collecting my clothes from the floor.

He starts stirring, so I quickly throw the hoodie on over my head and scramble to get into my knickers and jeans.

'Alright,' he smiles, his voice sleepy and alluring, his hair completely sexed up. 'Going already?'

'Yeah.' I smile shyly, suddenly feeling self-conscious. Don't be stupid, Rose. This man's seen you naked. 'I'm gonna try and squeeze in a few more hours at the care home.'

His face drops. 'You're volunteering at the care home?' He sounds far more shocked than he should.

'Yeah, why?' I ask stiffly.

Don't I look like the kind of person to selflessly volunteer my time?

He shrugs. 'It probably means you've bumped into my brother.' He yawns, sitting up and rolling his shoulders out, exposing his perfectly formed chest. He's not really muscly, but he's still defined enough to take my breath away.

I try to concentrate. His brother? A stone drops within my stomach, bringing with it a spreading feeling of dread.

'Who's your brother?' I ask, trying to sound vague and uninterested. It's already dawning on me though. There's no one else there of a similar age. No, it can't be him. Please say it's not him.

'Will. You don't know him? Walks around taking everything too seriously, always looks like he's brooding over something?'

Shit. I slept with Will's brother. That's not going to get him to like me anymore than he does already.

'Err, yeah…we've met,' I say in a high pitched squeal, turning to face the wall as I tie my hair back. I turn back around to face him when I feel I've composed myself.

He smiles knowingly. 'Did he piss you off?'

'Kind of.' I shrug, not wanting to make a big deal of it.

'Well, maybe we shouldn't tell him about this. You don't want to give him any more reason to hate you. He doesn't generally get on with my women.'

'Your *women*?' I raise my eyebrow sceptically with a grin on my face.

'At different times,' he shrugs, smiling devilishly.

Oh God, maybe I'm his third woman today. I might not be Mother Theresa when it comes to my bedroom antics, but I don't normally share my men. Thank God we used condoms.

'I just can't find my bra,' I admit reluctantly, scanning the floor for the sixth time.

'Don't worry. I'll find it for you. Get off t' work for my slave worker of a brother.' He slaps my arse before rolling over and going back to sleep. Charming. Glad I caught that one.

***

The walk of shame is never a good one. Especially when its daytime and you've lost your bra and your jeans zipper is broken. I hate walking around, knowing I've had sex. I feel like people can smell it on me. Especially in this twee village. The lack of pollution just makes it all the easier for them to sniff me out. I creep down James's road, careful for no one to see me.

'Look at her!'

I turn around to see a group of teenage girls leaning against a wall, pointing at me and sniggering. Some are smoking and others are drinking from a bottle of cider. Jesus. Damn Yorkshire hood rats.

'What the hell's so funny?' I demand, putting my hand on my hip.

Violet suddenly appears from inside the gang of girls. It only takes me a second to realise she's their leader. Head bitch.

'We're laughing at your slaggy arse. You just slept with James, right?' she asks, pointing at my broken zipper.

'No!' I shout far too dramatically, trying to cover my modesty.

'Please,' Violet laughs cruelly back to her gang. 'From what I've heard she had to move here because she'd boned everyone in London.'

I cannot *believe* the rudeness of her. She was clearly putting on a nice act at the home.

'Piss off, you little bitch,' I snap, turning on my heel and walking hurriedly away, hoping they're not following me.

'And she shovels shit for a living,' I hear her sneer as my walk turns into a slow jog.

Before I know it my jog has turned into a full on sprint. How could I have been so predictable? Sleeping with the village player? I run until I get to our street. Stupid tears are falling down my cheeks. Traitorous, stupid tears. I hit a stone and fall onto my knees, the gravel grazing them. Why is my life so shit?!

I look up to the heavens, to the God Elsie so believes in, begging for some mercy. I close my eyes when the sun blinds me. I open them but shield my eyes. I'm suddenly shaded. I look back up to see a woman's head looking down at me. She's mixed race, with the most beautiful glowing skin I've ever seen. Her afro curls stand around her head like a halo. Is she an angel?

'Need some help?' she asks in a silky soft voice.

I wail some more. I need her help so bad, she could never understand. I'm barely able to nod. I'm too pathetic to speak. I feel arms undermine and then I'm being pulled up to stand on my feet.

'I'm Lauren. Come on.'

She leads me over to the brick cottage next to ours. I'm pushed through her red front door and placed roughly onto her kitchen table chair. I place my head onto the table and moan. She's clearly not an angel. Just a nosey neighbour. Who'll probably tell everyone everything I tell her.

I finally look up and into the stranger's oblong shaped face, her hazel eyes warm and fabulously big, curly hair sitting at attention. She looks maybe early forties. It's hard to tell with her great skin.

'So, you want to tell me what that was all about?' She smiles warmly.

'Err…it's a long, very stupid story.'

She rolls her eyes with a smile. 'I don't know if you noticed, but there's not owt else going on around here.'

I laugh, the grin taking over my face involuntarily. It's probably the first time I've properly laughed since I moved here. Well, apart from during sex with James. Maybe she's okay.

'I just wish I wasn't treated like such an outcast.'

I'm aware how tragic and self-indulged I sound, but I can't help it. That's how I feel right now.

'I wrote t' book on being an outcast,' she scoffs, jumping up and filling up the kettle. 'Try being t' first black woman in the village. *And* I arrived pregnant, minus a father. The old biddies around here were having heart failure.'

I giggle, even though I know it's not nice. That must have been seriously hard for her. Everyone is so clicky around here.

'Yeah, that must have been a bitch,' I sigh, sympathising.

'Aye, so excuse me if I don't feel so sorry for you. Poor little London girl that everyone is interested in.' She laughs to let me know she's only joking.

Everyone is talking about me?

‘I just feel such an outsider,’ I moan, pouting as she gets up to pour my tea, her old fashioned kettle screaming on the hob.

‘I get it, me, I really do. But you need to stop caring what other people think. I did, and it’s liberating. People move on. The gossip moves on to someone else.’ She hands over a tea.

‘Yeah, me!’ I laugh.

‘Really.’ She nods. ‘So stop your Southern bitching and pull yourself together.’ It sounds harsh, but she says it with a smile, so I don’t feel like she’s being a bitch.

I think I may have met my first friend. Well, my first friend who isn’t fifteen years old.

‘Also, sorry, but I don’t drink tea,’ I say apologetically.

Her face retracts as if I’ve slapped her. ‘What? You don’t drink tea? You’re never going to fit in!’ she jokes.

‘Anyway,’ I lower my voice to a whisper, even though no one can hear me, ‘what’s with that old couple having loud sex? You must have heard it, right?’

Her forehead wrinkles in confusion. ‘Old couple. Who?’

‘Mavis and Bernie.’

She bursts out laughing so dramatically that she actually spits on me slightly. ‘Rose, you’re hilarious! We’re gonna get on great.’

Why does everyone think I’m lying?

‘I’m serious. I heard them the other morning. They were going for it!’

She laughs again, as if I’m still playing with her. ‘Rose, you must have heard the TV or something. They’re the sweetest little couple.’

‘Yeah, and the dirtiest!’ I snort. ‘Did you know that they role play Fergie and Will. I. Am.?’

‘Stop!’ she says, doubling over in hysterics. ‘You’re killing me.’

Why the hell does nobody believe me?

I hear the door slam from our house. These walls really are too thin.

‘Elsie’s home. I should probably go.’

I thank her for her help and go back home. Elsie's sat on the sofa eating a chocolate bar the size of my leg.

'What's up, Els?'

'Nothing!' she snaps, her face red and angry.

Wowzas. She can be scary.

'Okay. So we're just ignoring the fact that you're eating that, right?' I can't help but smile even though I know I'm only aggravating her more.

'Can't a girl enjoy some chocolate in peace?!' Her face is practically purple now, but her eyes look miserable, not angry.

'Okay! Fine!' I say, my hands up in defeat.

'It's the church. I found out I can't wear make-up when I become a nun,' she blurts out, looking down at the floor.

'Make up? Why do you care, you barely wear any.' I look at her dewy skin. It's perfect.

'I wear loads, Rose! I just make it look natural. You've seen me first thing in the morning; I'm a pale monster.'

I chuckle. 'Slightly dramatic. So just don't become a nun,' I shrug. Problem solved.

'Yeah, because it's just that easy!' she shrieks, getting up and storming upstairs.

***

Saturday 4th October

Phil's asked me to come in early today to do a bit of cleaning. I have no idea why the normal cleaner can't just get on with it, but either way I'm here at seven o'clock in the morning. I bang on the pub door but don't seem to get an answer. If he's forgotten I'll bloody ring his neck. I despise being up this early.

I remember Megan talking about a private side entrance. I wander around to the fence and realise that at the end of it is a rickety old gate. I look around to make sure Phil isn't already at the pub door, and when I'm sure, I push it slightly with my hand. It falls open without any resistance.

CRACK!

The sound of a gunshot jolts my entire body, sending shock waves pulsing through my stomach. I've dived onto the floor instinctively before I can think of a more sensible option. Something thuds to the floor beside me. Oh my fucking God!

I open my eyes and stare at a dead squirrel. What the FUCK?

I look up to see Phil, naked apart from a pair of leopard print silky boxer shorts with a shotgun in his hands. His beer belly is protruding over the shorts. Eugh. I may get sick.

'What…the fuck…was that?' I scream, stumbling over my words.

'A squirrel.' He shrugs as if it's no big deal.

'I know it was a fucking squirrel! What happened?' I shriek, looking back at the poor dead squirrel.

'I shot it, pet.'

I look back down at it, my mouth agape in horror. He killed a poor little squirrel? How the hell could he do that? Why on earth would he even *want* to?

'Aye. Vicious creatures, love.'

'How can you say that?' My voice breaks from emotion. I must be due on. I'm crying over a squirrel. 'He's just a poor little defenceless animal.'

To this he just shrugs unapologetically and walks off. Hopefully to get dressed. Jesus fucking Christ. This is *not* the way to start a day.

Monday 6th October

Well, thank God for this fling with James. If it wasn't for me sneaking round to his house for a quick shag all weekend I'd literally have nothing to do. I don't care if they're all calling me a slag. I mean, this village is just so boring. I'd rope Elsie into some mayhem, but she's always so busy with church stuff. It's thanks to her schedule that she hasn't noticed me sloping off. I'm pretty sure if God took the time to create her he'd want her to party while she's here.

I am actually kind of glad to be working at the home today. At least it's full of people. Even if they're ridiculously old and wrinkled. It's still noise. The village is just so quiet. It's like I'm just alone with my thoughts, and that scares me. My mind keeps wandering to thoughts of where my life is going and the truth is that I don't know. I need distractions.

I'm chatting with Norman when I hear the commotion. I look around and spot Peggy and Betty going at it. Peggy's all up in her face, pointing her bony finger against Betty's chest. Betty's hardly going down without a fight though. She stands up and squares right back at her. Old ladies fighting? This is strangely awesome.

'No one wants you here, Betty,' Peggy snarls, loud enough for everyone to hear. 'You can't just reappear in this village and expect everyone to fall all over you.'

'Oh piss off, Peggy. You're just jealous that I left this place. You've never done owt,' she spits back.

'I was too busy laying down some roots. Making friends, marrying t' man of my dreams and starting a family. You're only jealous you don't have anyone who loves you.'

Ouch. Low blow, Peggy.

I see Betty's face fall before she quickly puts her mask back up.

'Loves you? Your old man cheated with Florence and your kids moved to Leeds. Hardly the loving family you portray!' she sneers.

Go Betty.

Peggy shoves her hard and Betty falls back onto her chair. Shit. This got violent really quick. Bettys face becomes enraged, a vein on her forehead throbbing. She jumps up, as if she was still twenty-one, and grabs Peggy's grey hair, getting her into a headlock.

Oh my fucking God! This *cannot* be happening.

I run over, trying desperately to tear them apart. They tumble to the floor, rolling around, their skirts up round their waists, their stockings on show. I try to pull them apart, but with no one else helping it's hard. No one else seems to be doing anything. They're just looking on in amazement. To be fair, it's probably the best entertainment they've had in a long time. I'm half expecting them to start chanting 'FIGHT! FIGHT! FIGHT!'

What the fuck am I going to do?

I consider my options. I could run and get Will from his office, but that's bloody ages away. They could have killed each other by then. I frantically think back to any other bitch fights I've witnessed. It comes to me immediately. I remember Sarah and Kim fighting over a guy in Destiny toilets. The only way I got them off each other was to pinch their nipples. Only I'm not sure if I should look at their chests or in their socks.

I jump on them in an attempt to shock them, but I end up rolling around with them until I manage to get to their boobs. I pinch as hard as I can.

'Ah! Ah!' they both shriek, their faces contorting with pain. I've got them now.

I start standing up, dragging them up with me. They suddenly look frail and I feel bad. They are old ladies after all, and I *am* twisting their nipples viciously. How surreal.

'Come on, ladies. There's no need to argue,' I try to reason.

'Why don't you tell *her* that?!' Betty snaps like a petulant toddler.

I thought old people were supposed to be all wise and calm? This lot seems to be reverting back to their teenage years. I let go of their nipples and grab their shoulders instead.

'I only finished what you started, Betty!' Peggy roars, trying to go around me to point her finger towards Betty again. She's a vicious little thing.

'Apologise to each other now or I'm ripping your nips off!' I bark, making Peter and Ethel giggle.

They both pout and grumble sorry at each other.

'Good. Now I think it's best you stay out of each other's way for a while, don't you?' They don't answer, but look at the floor. 'Good.'

I let them go and the crowd starts to break up. It's only when they start to disperse that I see Will standing amongst the crowd. He looks at me, amusement on his face, and winks. What is with the winking? I seriously don't know how I feel about it.

I ignore him and walk Betty towards her room. When we get there I shut the door behind us.

'So are you going to tell me what that was about?' I demand, my hand on my hip.

'She's just a contrary bitch, that's all. She's always been contrary.' She sits on her bed, looking away from me.

'Come on. I know there's more to it than that. Tell me.' I sit down on the edge of her bed watching while she gets changed into her night dress.

'We used to be best friends, but she betrayed me. It's a long story.' She looks out of the window, deep in thought.

'So tell me,' I giggle. 'I've got time. It's not like there's anything else to do in this village.' I wish I had some popcorn.

She smiles, then furrows her brow. 'If I tell you, this can't be repeated to William or James, understood?'

Will and James? What have they got to do with it? Now I'm interested.

'Of course.'

Will and I are barely friends anyways, and James and I don't do much talking, if you know what I mean.

'William's grandfather Thomas and I used to court each other,' she explains, turning to face me.

'Really? And? What's that got to do with Peggy?' I ask in a rush.

'I were madly in love with him,' she smiles. 'Only…when he asked me to marry him I got scared.' She takes a small photo album out of her bedside table and flicks to a well-thumbed page.

'Scared? Of what?'

Was he a big scary bastard or something?

'Of settling down and possibly never leaving this village. I wanted to explore the world, meet new people, and experience new things.'

It sounds familiar.

'So you turned him down?'

'Aye.' She passes over the album and points to a young couple. They're on a kissing post and they look mad about each other. 'I explained that I loved him, but that if he loved me he had to let me go. We parted on good terms and I went off t' London to train to be a nurse. I told Peggy to write to me if he ever got involved with anyone else. I know it was selfish, but I still wanted him to myself. I just needed to get it out of my system.'

'So what? She never wrote to you?'

'She never wrote. After four months I missed him terribly, so I decided to go home to him. Only when I arrived I saw him with Karen. Coming out of the church, married.'

No! Oh my God, poor Betty. She must have been heartbroken

'Karen? Who the hell is Karen?'

'Will's grandma. The lady he married. I was destroyed, so I decided to go off on my travels to get over him. The worst thing was that Peggy was the maid of honour.'

'Why would she do that to you?' I wonder if she was jealous.

'I don't know, pet. I thought we were friends, best friends. Anyway, it was probably for the best. I travelled all around Europe and did everything I ever wanted. But I just can't forgive her for that. So please don't ask me to.'

'I'm sorry, Betty.' It sounds so sad. I can imagine Betty travelling around desperately trying to mend her broken heart, when the one thing she truly wanted was back home without her.

She looks at me seriously. 'Rose, if you ever find love, cling to it. Everything else can be saved for another day, but love is the one thing you'll regret letting go.'

I don't think I'll have anything to worry about.

***

Chapter 6

Later that night I still can't shift the feeling of Betty's story. My shower didn't even rinse away the melancholy feeling. To let the love of her life fall through her fingers like that. And for her best friend to be a part in it all. I don't know how I'm going to be able to treat Peggy fairly now. Every time I look at her face all I'll see is the deceit she showed Betty.

I towel dry my hair and walk into the living room in just my towel. I still can't believe Elsie's bathroom is downstairs, but at least it's clean. I log onto Facebook to check for messages. I've discovered that if I place it on the top of the fireplace I get a weak connection. I still haven't received a reply from Janey when I know she's seen it. My heart aches with longing. There are new pictures all over her page. More nights out, more tequila, more men. God, it looks amazing. Could she be my Peggy? Is she deliberately trying to ruin things for me? No. I shake the thought from my head. I'm just getting paranoid. That's what living in isolation does to you.

A knock at the door startles me out of my moping. I look at the clock. 8pm. Who the hell could that be? It's probably Elsie forgetting her key or something. For someone so God-like she's scatty as hell. She's at some church committee or something. The girl never stops. I'm exhausted just watching her flit in and out.

I swing the door open, barely looking at her. 'Forgot your keys again?'

'Err, no.' I look up, way up, into Will's face. What the hell is he doing here?

'Will!' I shriek. I'm suddenly aware that I'm in nothing but a flimsy white towel. And it's cold. My nipples are perking up to greet him. For *once* could they not react to *everything*?

He rubs his hands together and breathes into them, clearly cold, his burgundy scarf obviously not doing the job. He walks past me and into the lounge without an invite. What the hell is he doing? He's so bloody presumptuous.

'Come in, why don't you,' I say sarcastically, rolling my eyes.

'Sorry, I didn't realise you wouldn't be dressed.' He takes a slow, lazy look over my body. Pervy bastard. I start to feel my cheeks redden as a hot flush takes over me. 'So it seems we may have gotten off on the wrong foot,' he explains, taking his scarf off. Make yourself at home why don't you?

An apology? Is that what he's here for? I didn't think he cared what a little minion like me thought.

'I don't think it had anything to do with me. More to do with you and your head being stuck up your arse.' I look away as I grin. One point to me.

He balks. 'If you could just stop being such a bitch for just one minute I could try to explain.'

A bitch? Did he really just say that? My hands starts to shake at my sides, rage and hurt taking over. How can he call me a bitch? I've been called worse, but it still hurts more that it should. I push my hand through my wet hair and stand on one hip, with my eyebrows raised, challenging him.

He sighs, clearly exasperated with me. 'Anyway, I just wanted to apologise and thank you for breaking up that fight earlier.'

Is this guy bi-polar? I can't keep up. Is he calling me a bitch or thanking me?

'Oh, yeah. Calling me a bitch is a *really* good apology,' I snap sarcastically. 'Thanks for your help, by the way,' I joke accusingly, a grin playing at my lips.

His face lights up with amusement. 'Sorry, but it was far too much fun watching you roll around on the floor with them.'

I try to look pissed off, but I can't hold in the laugh that escapes my lips. 'I didn't realise those kind of things went down with old people.'

He chuckles. It's a beautiful sound and lights up his face. 'Well, our Yorkshire lasses are very passionate.' He smiles, and it's breath taking. It pisses me off that it makes my legs wobble slightly. It's just that I haven't seen him be anything but hostile towards me. I ignore it and smile back. He must share the charming gene with James.

'Have you had a lot of experience with the Yorkshire ladies?' I ask, suddenly wondering about his dating history. He doesn't act like he has a girlfriend.

'Nah,' he says, clearly offended. 'Well, obviously yes, but not loads.' He looks confused and annoyed. 'Anyway, I'm here to say thank you.'

'Well, you've said it.' I bob my head awkwardly, wishing he'd leave. He makes me feel so uncomfortable.

'But I want to show you.' He walks up to me, towering over my face. My breath leaves my body. I have to look up to him, he's so tall. I'm used to being tall at five foot seven, but this is scary height. He must be six foot four at least.

I can almost feel his breath on my forehead. Oh my God. What the hell is he offering here? My palms start sweating and the back of my neck feels hot. Is he going to kiss me? Do I want to kiss him? My heart rate says different to my brain.

'So…what…what…what are you going to show me?' I mumble, my voice raspy, my breath coming out in sharp spurts, making my chest rise and fall dramatically.

Suddenly a box is thrust in my face and I have to stand back so it doesn't hit me.

He grins. 'I'm introducing you to Yorkshire tea.' I look at the box closer and he's right. It's a box of tea bags.

Is he serious? Talk about getting a girl hot under the collar!

I laugh, pushing him away, trying to act like I'm not a hot mess. 'Sorry, I don't like tea.'

He rolls his eyes. 'Elsie mentioned it, but that's only because you've been having shitty southern tea. Our water is far softer. Let me make you a proper brew and I promise you'll like it.'

He looks so hopeful and happy…over tea. It's weird, but kind of endearing. Is this what turns him on? Tea? Is he going to ask me to tea bag him? I laugh to myself at my little joke.

'O…kay. But I should get dressed first.' I back away towards the stairs, his eyes following me, amused. Why does he always seem to be laughing at me?

'You're probably right.' He smiles, with a wink. What the hell do these winks mean? He's giving me a headache.

'Right.' I nod.

I turn around and stub my toe, stumbling onto the first step, and squashing my boob. I shriek from the agony. Not the boob. I go to grab the towel, but it's already fallen on the floor, pooled around my feet.

'Aaaaahhhhh!' I scream, desperately trying to cover myself. What do I cover first? The boobs or the Lulu? Oh dear God! 'Look away! Look away!' I shriek, trying to cover everything at once.

'I'm looking away,' he says, chuckling silently to himself.

I watch him turn his body slightly, his hand up over his eyes. I grab the towel and throw it around myself, running up the stairs as fast as my legs will take me. I rush into my room and close the door behind me, sliding down to the floor. What the hell is wrong with me? Even when I don't want to get naked with a guy my body somehow finds a way. He must have seen. He must have. My boobs are hard to miss.

I pull on some black leggings and a loose grey t-shirt. I grab Elsie's over-sized black and grey cardigan and apply a small bit of make-up. I mean, I know I don't even like the guy, but I still don't want to look like a monster in front of him. Just a bit of blusher, some mascara and some lip balm. Simple for me. There, that looks fine enough. I go to put my boots on when I realise that will probably look weird. I *am* supposed to be in my own house.

I walk down shyly in Elsie's Forever Friends socks. I should really have something more sensible, but I didn't plan on wearing socks with my sandals in Mexico. I look at the sofa, but he's not there. Has he gone home? How long was I up there? Maybe he was offended by my nakedness.

'Will?' I call out shyly, tucking a bit of hair behind my ear.

'In here.'

I smile, but then pull myself together as I walk towards his voice in the kitchen. Why am I even happy he's still here? He's a lordly arse. I find him filling up Elsie's teapot, swishing it around like he's creating art or something. Make yourself at home, why don't you?

'So you're really into your tea, then?' I raise my eyebrows at his swirling to show my amusement.

'Not just me. All of Yorkshire. Hell, most of England. Trust me when I say *you're* the weirdo. I'm just trying to get you to fit in around here.' He flashes another grin and I'm shocked that it sends a warm feeling down in my tummy. He's got a dimple on his left cheek that appears when he smiles. I hadn't noticed it before.

'Maybe I don't want to fit in,' I counter, leaning against the worktop.

'Yeah, I get the feeling you don't,' he smirks.

I tense my jaw. 'What is *that* supposed to mean?'

'God, why are you always so up for a barny?' he sighs. 'We Northerners are so much friendlier than you guys.'

'No, you're not. Especially you!' I shriek, pointing my finger at him. 'You can be downright rude.'

'Really? Because I seem to think I'm making you a brew right now?' He puts the kettle down and smiles triumphantly at me.

I open my mouth to retort something sharply, but then realise he is kind of right. Shit, that's annoying.

'Go sit down and I'll bring it in.'

I skulk into the sitting room and turn the TV on. I make myself comfy on the sofa, with my lugs tucked up underneath me. This feels really weird, listening to Will banging about in the kitchen. I wish Elsie would come home and break the tension.

He walks into the room two minutes later, carrying a tray with a tea pot, two of Elsie's china mugs, a jug of milk and a small plate of chocolate digestive biscuits. He pulls over the coffee table and lays it down.

'So do you like sweet things?' He wiggles his eyebrows suggestively at me.

'Is that some kind of sexual innuendo?' I ask, wondering whether I want it to be.

'Nah,' he laughs. 'I was just asking if you wanted sugar in your tea.'

'Oh.' I face palm myself. I'm such an idiot. 'I do like sweets.' I discreetly try to push the packet of Haribo on the side further out of sight. I don't want him to think I'm a sugar junkie.

'Okay, I'm giving you two sugars.' He makes up my tea, taking a ridiculous amount of time and effort, before handing it over to me. 'Now give it a chance,' he warns sternly.

I turn my nose up at the smell of it, but feel too rude to refuse it. He's gone to all of this effort. I bring it to my lips and take a tentative sip. Is it weird that it actually tastes good? And it seems to calm my running mind. I instantly feel relaxed and cosier.

'Okay, it's nice,' I admit reluctantly.

'I told you!' He grins. God, he's happy about this. He's actually beaming. It's kind of cute.

'You really do love tea,' I laugh, rolling my eyes. The guy needs to get a life.

'Did you know that when tea first came over here it was so high in taxes that none of the working class could afford it? But William Pitt the Younger cut the taxes massively, so smuggling stopped and everyone could enjoy it.'

God, he's boring.

'Were you named after him or something?' I snort, spraying a bit out of my nose. I wouldn't be surprised.

'Nah,' he smiles, 'but I get why you'd think that. I know I'm amazing too.' He sips his tea. 'So did you find out what that fight was about?'

Ah. Now I see his ulterior motive. Nosy bastard thought he could soften me up and then make me spill my guts.

'Err…no.' I look away so he can't see my face.

I won't betray Betty's trust.

'I don't get it, me,' he muses. 'They've always hated each other. There was always a weird atmosphere when my nan was alive too. I wonder what happened with those three.'

'Who knows?' I shrug, taking a sip of the tea, trying to avoid eye contact. I *hate* lying. I'm so shit at it.

He turns to face me fully, tucking his knee underneath him, looking at me sceptically.

'I think you know more than you're letting on,' he challenges.

Shit. I really need to practise lying.

'I…err…don't know what you mean.' My shaking hand makes my china cup clatter as I place it back on the coffee table.

'Anyone ever told you you're a shit liar?' He chuckles, looking at me not with annoyance, but affection.

'Yes, actually,' I giggle. I'm giggling? Did he spike my tea? Why am I acting all weird?

'Well, I suppose it's a good quality. And I'm guessing you'd tell me if I needed to know, right?' he asks, is face flitting back to serious.

'Right.' I nod.

'Well, then it seems I'll just have to trust you.' He lingers his eyes over my face, making me blush again. Why the hell do I keep blushing? I never blush. But then I'm normally trashed when I chat to men.

'Why do you get so uptight at work anyway? Why do you even care so much?' I ask, unable to stop myself. It's weird.

He sighs heavily. 'The only reason I get so uptight about that place is because I want it to be the best. I want the residents to be well looked after.'

That's really nice of him, but he must have ulterior motives. No one can be that nice.

'But why?' I press.

He pauses, obviously considering if I'm worth the truth.

'Because my grandad used to be there. I was off working in Leeds when he died.' I stay silent, hoping he'll continue. 'I suppose I started there because I felt guilty I didn't make it back before he passed. But now I realise how scared those people are. Imagine not being able to stay in your own home because you're too old and thrown into a care home, where no one really gives a fuck.'

I consider it for a second. The idea is abhorrent to me. More the idea of getting old and wrinkly above anything else.

'Exactly,' he nods, pleased that I'm understanding. He probably assumes I'm a dumb ditsy blonde like everyone else. 'I just want to make the home run as well as it can. Those people have supported this village their whole life. It's time for us to look after them.'

Who would have known it? Will has a heart. It's weird. Unsettling almost.

We sit in silence for a while pretending to watch EastEnders. Well, at least I'm pretending. He seems to be genuinely engrossed in it. How bizarre. I can't put my finger on it, but I feel ridiculously self-conscious being here like this. In socks with wet hair. It feels strangely intimate. It's almost more embarrassing than being naked. Almost.

The dun dun dun comes up as the show ends. He stands up. 'I should get off.'

I hope he didn't feel like he needed to stay out of courtesy. Or because he thinks I'm some lonely, pathetic girl.

'Oh, of course.' I stand up and walk him towards the door. I have a niggling feeling he may have seen more than he let on earlier. Maybe that's why he's being so nice to me. He's seen my body and now he wants some of it. Stupid men, run by hormones.

I can't help it, I need to ask. 'So, you didn't see anything back there, right?' I pull on a thread by my wrist. Anything to avoid looking at him.

He pulls on his coat and wraps his scarf around his neck, a smile threatening to break across his face.

'Course not,' he grins.

'Thank God.' I breathe out a sigh of relief, shaking my head at my ridiculous thoughts. 'I'll see you tomorrow.'

'Yep.' He turns to go, but just before I shut the door he stops me with his hand. 'So is that a birth mark or a scar?'

I'm thrown. 'What?'

Oh my God. It dawns on me. He's referring to my right boob. I've got this weird brown freckle that could almost pass as a third nipple. He saw me. He saw me *good.*

'Wha...?' I can't even speak.

He winks, nice and slow, before turning and walking down the road.

I hate him.

***

Chapter 7

Tuesday 7th October

So it occurred to me today that I'm in charge of activities and to date I've planned no activities. That makes me bad at my job, and I don't want to give Will any excuse to whinge about me. Or see me at all. The guy saw me naked. I'd rather not relive that embarrassment.

So I've decided to organise a few things. The most important being a dance I'm going to hold for the residents. They're always telling me about their old music and how dancing was so romantic back in their day, so what better way to stimulate them. Plus, it'll be great exercise. Well, for the ones that can still walk unaided.

I'm just jotting down a few songs that they've told me about when Beth grabs my attention, skipping into the room.

'Got another one,' she sings, pointing towards an impeccably presented, tall yet thin guy around my age.

I assess him quickly, trying to work out if he's competition. Will walks in and shakes his hand, but the new guy seems uneasy. Then he tries to discreetly take out some sanitizer gel to spread on his hands. Bingo. A clean freak.

I rush over, quickly trying to smooth down my hair so he thinks I'm worthy of his time. It doesn't help that I let Ethel braid it into six separate sections. Just seeing Will makes me flush, but I try to ignore him.

'Hi, I'm Rose,' I say, smiling widely. 'I would shake your hand, but…you know…germs!' I grimace, as if the thought grosses me out.

Will looks at me strangely. No doubt still imagining me naked. Pervert.

'I get you!' Eric chuckles, his eyes lighting up as if he's finally met a person who understands him.

'Will, I'll show Eric the ropes.' I link arms with him and start walking him down the hallway.

'If you're sure…' Will calls out suspiciously. I look back to see him scratching his head, confused.

I lead him towards the second resident's lounge which is packed up and covered with dust sheets so that it can be painted. Well, so that it can be painted by someone boring and trustworthy who is just going to paint it one colour. Will didn't necessarily say that, but I know he was thinking it.

'Oh dear,' Eric says, clearly distraught as soon as we walk into the room. 'What's happened here?'

The mess must be killing him.

'We're getting it ready to be sanitised.' I nod as if I know everything.

'Thank God!' he cries. 'Something being cleaned! It's filthy in this place.' He looks around distastefully as if he might catch the plague. It gives me an idea.

'Tell me about it.' I smirk. 'But even now they're only doing it because of the *outbreak.*' I busy myself with adjusting a dust sheet, trying not to smile as this news settles over him.

'Outbreak?' he shrieks, his hand clutches up to his chest. 'What…er, what outbreak?' he asks as casually as he can, even when I know he's already looking for his nearest exit. This idea was genius.

'Oh…well, we're not supposed to talk about it.' I look away again, desperately trying not to let the smile break on my face. I bite my tongue so that my mind focuses on the pain.

'Talk about what? Rose, what the hell happened?' He's almost hysterical now.

'It's no big deal,' I put my hands up defensively. 'Just a few residents that contracted MRSA.' I literally feel his body tense at the word MRSA. 'It's all cool now. They just need to sanitise the home and hope no one else catches it.'

'Oh…so the people are all better now?' His eyes narrow in on me and I realise one is twitching nervously.

I can't resist. 'Well…they're *gone* if that's what you're asking.'

'GONE? Gone? Where?' he shrieks, clearly beside himself with worry.

I lower my voice to a whisper. 'They *passed.*' I do the sign of the cross on my forehead and shoulders, really trying to make it believable.

'They're…dead? They *DIED?*' he asks incredulously.

'Shush! Lower your voice, will you? I'll get fired if anyone finds out.' Finds out that I'm lying, that is.

'Surely the families were informed?' I can almost feel the cogs in his head whirling.

'They didn't have any family,' I sigh, feigning sadness.

'But surely there would have been ambulances called?'

Uh-oh. He's got me there, the bastard. Nothing happens in this village without everyone knowing about it. Think on your feet Rose.

'It was too late by the time we found them. They're…' I lower my voice to a whisper, 'well, they're buried in the back garden.'

His eyes bulge out of his head. 'What? WHAT?'

'Please,' I grab his hands, 'don't tell anyone.' I flutter my eyelashes, trying to look as innocent and afraid as possible.

He throws off my hands, immediately spraying hand sanitizer over them and the rest of his arms. God, this guy is a nutter.

'I have to get out of here! Tell them I quit!' he shouts, running, practically screaming from the room.

Another one bites the dust.

Wednesday 8TH October

'Rose, do you have any idea why all of these volunteers keep quitting?' Will asks me the next day.

I avoid looking right into his eyes. 'Erm…no. They probably just…can't be bothered or something. It's a real sad state of affairs if you ask me.'

'Really?' he challenges.

I make the mistake of looking up into his face. He's looking down at me sceptically. Shit, he knows I'm lying. And he knows how bad I am at it. Quickly, Rose, think of something.

‘So, um…is there anything around here to do this weekend? Or is it still just fields and cows?’

He smiles slowly, relaxing slightly. ‘Actually there is this dressage thing this weekend. You should come. Most people in the village go.’

A dressage? What the hell is that?

‘Oh, okay. A dress thing. So is it like…a fashion show or something?’ I ask, sounding as clueless as I feel.

He doubles over laughing. What the hell’s so funny? I cross my hands over my chest, feeling affronted.

‘No, funnily enough, we don’t have much need for fashion shows in the Yorkshire countryside. I said a dressage. As in for *horses?*’

Horses? What the hell is he talking about?

‘Oh! The dressage for horses! Of course, yeah, I get it.’ I smile confidently, not wanting to look stupid.

I mean, do they put horses into dresses and then parade them around? That sounds…well, it actually sounds pretty hilarious.

‘Count me in.’

‘Okay,’ he nods, rocking onto his heels. ‘It’ll be good for you. Help you make some friends in the village.’

Make friends? Does he think I’m some kind of socially inept prat? Or an outcast? Or…does he think I’m a loner? I couldn’t give a shit if anyone likes me. But what *he* thinks of me…well, for some reason I care about that.

‘In the meantime, no more scaring off volunteers, hmm?’ He grins.

I feel my cheeks redden. He knows. I’m sure he knows. He smirks before turning and sauntering away. Shaking that delicious arse in my face the whole way. Delicious arse? Woah. What am I saying? I need to get me some. I’m starting to fancy Will!

What am I saying? I’m shagging his brother.

***

Later that night I'm trying on dress after dress of Elsie's. She was deliriously excited when I told her I was going to this dressage thing. Apparently it's a big deal in the village and I think she has false hopes that it's my way of trying to integrate with everyone. More like so I don't die of boredom. And if I happen to see James there again…well, so be it. The fact that he hasn't bothered to text me or anything is really not bothering me at all. I mean, why should I be bothered? We just hooked up. But I suppose in a village this small it's hard not to realise when someone's avoiding you. And now I keep panicking that I'll bump into him in the street or something. I mean, how bloody awkward would that be?! Imagine if he just blanks me! And he still has my bra…

I throw another one off, huffing loudly in exasperation.

'Another one! I told you, Elsie. Dresses just don't fit over my boobs!'

I've always had the same problem. If I try to get a dress to fit my boobs then it hangs massively on my arms or works out too long. These manufacturers are too bloody used to all of these skinny minis. Hello, not all of us are the same size or shape, arseholes!

'Well, you can't wear trousers,' she says adamantly.

'Too right. I'll just wear my jeans or something. Or my leather mini skirt with a shirt.'

'Yeah! Leather mini!' Megan sings, indulging in the rest of Elsie's giant chocolate bar. She really won't leave me alone, but the truth is that I'm really starting to love her.

'You will NOT be wearing your mini skirt. This is *not* a mini-skirt kind of event,' she says adamantly

'Jesus, what is it with this dressage?' She shoots me a quick look for using the Lord's name in vain. 'Isn't it just a load of ponies in snazzy outfits?' I chuckle.

She looks confused, before her face splits into a grin. 'You think…that horses dress up? Do you…not know what a dressage is?' She looks to Megan who starts laughing too. They're full on hysterical now. Annoying girly giggles that I want to smack off their faces. I hate being made to feel stupid.

'Okay, smart arse! Tell me what it is,' I challenge, shooting her the evil eye.

'Let me think of how to explain it to you…didn't you see Zara Philips do it at the Olympics?'

'Do I look like someone that kept up with the Olympics?' I was too busy celebrating with the tourists.

She sighs heavily.

Megan sits up. 'Well, Michael McIntyre calls it dancing for gay horses.' She collapses on top of the sofa, barely able to contain herself.

I'm surrounded by nutcases.

'I don't even know why I agreed to go to this stupid thing,' I whinge, throwing myself on top of her.

She stops laughing and pushes me off her. I fall onto the floor with a thud. Elsie leans over me, gripping my shoulders. 'Don't be silly, Rose. We'll find you a dress. Cinderella *will* go t' ball.'

***

Friday 10th October

By Friday I still have no dress. I ordered a few emergency dresses online using Elsie's credit card, but none of them fit. Even she can't believe it as I come out of the toilet, pulling a thumbs down to the last dress which won't go over my boobs.

'It's no use, Elsie.' I shrug, walking back into the lounge. 'I've gone off the idea anyway.'

I didn't even know what dressage is. I'll probably make a fool of myself anyway. I don't want to set myself up to look like a twat.

'What's this?' Betty asks, leaning in, clearly eavesdropping and interested.

'Nothing,' I shrug, not wanting to get into it. Damn boobs.

'It's not nothing,' Elsie snaps. She turns to Betty. 'She's coming t' dressage this weekend, but we can't find any dresses to fit over her gigantic boobs.'

'Shut up!' I hiss, shoving her. 'And stop talking about my tits!'

'Make the most of them,' Betty chuckles. 'Before you know it you'll be tucking them into your socks.'

'Betty!' I can't help but laugh. I hope I'm as cool as her when I'm old.

'Well, lucky for you, I have a solution, my love.' She pats me on my hand.

'Oh?' I'm intrigued.

'Go to my house and get out a chest in the loft with a Rose on the front. Kind of funny, huh, I kept all of my favourite dresses from the fifties. Broads had big boobs and big bums back then. Any of those will fit you. I guarantee it.'

'Wow. Are you sure, Betty?' I gush, feeling strangely honoured…wearing a real vintage dress.

'Go for it, girly. If you've got it, flaunt it!'

***

Saturday 11th October

'Having fun?' a voice says in my ear, their breath tickling my ear lobe.

I swivel round to face Will, looking dapper in a dark burgundy suit, his fitted blazer showing off his wide shoulders. His skinny green tie hangs long against his broad chest. Visions of me letting it slip through my fingers before pulling him to my mouth invades my mind. He's grinning ear to ear as if he can read my mind. What is going *on* with me?

'Yeah,' I just about manage, pulling myself together before I start drooling.

'You scrub up well. Who knew?' He seems genuinely shocked. Rude bastard.

I look down at the red fifties prom style dress that I got from Betty's attic. Its taffeta lined with a tulle overlay, velvet floral designs sown on it. Its red glittery sparkles catch on the natural sunlight. I fell in love with it the minute I saw it. It's stunning but still simple enough to wear to this event. Well, that's what Elsie told me anyways. Either way it fits like a glove and everyone's been staring at me all day. I thank God women were curvier back in those days.

'Yeah. It's one of Betty's.' I do a little twirl, revelling in the attention.

He furrows his brows in concern. 'You know you shouldn't get too attached t' residents, right?'

'What? One minute you're telling me how much they mean to you, the next I shouldn't be too nice. Which is it Will?' His moods are giving me whiplash.

'I just want you to be careful,' he warns. 'I don't want anyone thinking you're treating her favourably.'

God, he's a job's worth.

I roll my eyes. 'Okay, whatever, Will.' I turn back to the dressage. Or as I like to call it, 'gay horse dancing'. I can't actually believe this thing is considered a sport. I mean, we're all dressed up to the nines, trying to keep straight faces, while horses dance to Night Fever. It's ridiculous.

'Sorry.'

I turn to face him in shock. Did he just say that? He's admitting he's sorry? Wowzas.

'I'm just a bit stressed today.' He touches his forehead as if to show how stressed.

'Why? What's up?' I shouldn't care, but I do. Something draws me to him. I think it's because he's James' brother.

He looks at me questionably, as if wondering whether or not to tell me. 'Can you keep a secret?' he whispers.

I shrug. 'I suppose.'

He laughs. 'Don't fill me with confidence or anything!'

'Sorry. Brownie swear.' I nod, holding up my palm.

He leans in a little closer and I try not to notice my heart start to beat faster at his unique scent. He smells so good. Like mint and soap.

'The home's in trouble.'

Not what I was expecting. Although I'm not sure what I *was* expecting.

'We've had our funding cut by the council. We've now got to run with only twenty percent funding or we'll be forced to shut down.'

'What? How the hell are you going to raise the money?' I ask, a little frantic. Does this mean the incentive programme is cancelled? How else am I going to get to Mexico?

'I've no idea. We can't let it close. The home has been open since the war. They decided to leave it open so that local residents wouldn't have to sell their houses, but they've obviously realised how that's not a money maker. We'll either have to raise the money or close down.'

'So, wait. Is that why they've done this incentive programme?' It's all starting to make sense now.

'Yep. Trying to encourage more volunteers.'

'Oh, *Will!*' a female voice sings over his shoulder.

We both turn to face a girl about our age. She's got long, glossy red hair which tumbles into loose curls at the ends and dark brown eyes which seem to be looking accusingly towards us. Her bright red lips pout at me. Who *is* this bitch?

'Alright, hun,' Will smiles; it doesn't fully meet his eyes. 'You should meet Rose.' He turns to me. 'Rose, this is Riley.'

Riley plasters on the nicest and fakest smile ever and shakes my hand, her bony manicured fingers making my hands feel huge and manly.

'So nice to meet you! I've been hearing a lot about you,' she gushes.

I blush, wondering if she means good or bad, but quickly recover. I don't want this bitch to know she's affecting me.

'I bet,' I smile. 'Not much ever seems to happen around here, so I must be big news.'

'Anyway.' She turns to Will and puts her hand possessively on his shoulder. It annoys me more than it should. 'We're going back to Andy's for a drink.'

'Okay. I'll meet you there,' he says coolly, not averting his gaze from me. It makes me feel edgy.

She looks back at me and seems to change, suddenly appearing friendly.

'We should have coffee sometime.' She seems like she genuinely means it. How confusing. I nod noncommittally.

'Actually, Rose now works at the pub, so I'm sure you'll bump into each other,' Will adds, seemingly pleased that I'm making a friend.

'Great,' we both say at the same time. She smiles before walking off. Maybe I judged her too soon.

I wonder who the hell she is to Will? All of that touching. Is she his girlfriend?

'Girlfriend?' I blurt out as soon as she's out of ear shot.

He scrunches his forehead, then grins. 'Ex-girlfriend.'

That's pretty bloody friendly for an ex, if you ask me. There's an awkward pause while I think of something to say.

'So…do you like the horses?' he asks with a shy smile.

Is he…trying to keep me talking? Surely he should be rushing off to that drinks party. I wish he'd invite me. I'm gagging for a drink. I'm just going to go home and have cheese on toast with Elsie.

'They're alright.' I pretend to inspect a chipped nail. They're painted perfectly. I don't have anything else to do around here but groom myself.

He snorts, a smug smile on his face. 'I take it you never had a horse growing up?'

'A horse growing up? No, I didn't grow up in the Little House on the Prairie.' Unless he can count my enormous My Little Pony collection.

He looks offended. 'I had a horse.'

'Of *course* you did,' I nod sarcastically. 'I'm sure King William also had servants.'

He rolls his eyes. 'It's my mum's horse. Well, it *was* my mum's horse.' His tone turns dejected.

'Did the horse die?' I ask carefully.

'No. My mum did.'

My eyes shoot up to meet his steely gaze. Oh holy fucking shit balls. That's it Rose, insult his dead mother. What the hell is wrong with me?

'Shit. I'm sorry.' Could I feel any worse?

'Don't worry,' he says dismissively. 'I still have the horse though. She made me promise.'

Made him promise? She must have known she was dying then. I wonder how long ago she died. Seeing the pain in his eyes, even for a second, before he covers it back up with his proud mask makes me too afraid to ask.

My phone beeps and I take it out of my bra, glad for the distraction.

Hey, sexy bum, fancy round two? I have your bra...

I blush, even though Will can't see what's written. What a booty call. I can't believe James just expects me to drop everything and go shag him. What an arse. But then I realise James also lost his mum. Maybe it's made him afraid to get close to women. It would make sense.

'Although I think I may have to sell her,' he continues.

I look up at him, confused. Sell who?

'The horse,' he nods, as if reading my mind.

'Why would you do that? Surely she reminds you of your mum.'

'She does, but I just don't have the time to look after her. A lady at the stables would muck her out and ride her every day, but now she's moving and I can't afford to pay someone.'

An overwhelming sadness settles over me. The one thing that reminds him of his mum being forced away from him after he promised her on her death bed to keep it. It's too tragic for words.

'I'll do it,' I blurt out, my mouth working before my brain.

'What?' He looks at me suspiciously.

Yeah, WHAT? Why the hell did I say that? I don't want to do that.

'You have experience with horses?'

‘Yeah, yeah,’ I nod, trying not to meet his eye and hoping he doesn’t want me to elaborate.

He looks shocked. ‘That would be…amazing. Ta. You’re sure?’ He smiles, his dimple coming out to greet me again.

‘Err…yeah.’ I should have probably thought about this a little longer, but I can't let him down now. I can't let that dimple down.

‘Great. Do you want to meet her tomorrow?’ He seems excited.

‘Yeah…great.’ I smile. I’m already texting James back.

On my way x

I need him to fuck some sense into me.

Chapter 8

'Fucking…amazing,' James pants, his body still crushing mine into the mattress.

I smile despite my worry. I mean, will I *ever* orgasm? Was I cursed as a baby or something? Did that scary guy that came for Harry Potter come for me instead, but decided it would be crueller to never let me achieve the one thing I want. All I bloody hear about is everyone having them. I can't open a magazine without seeing top ten ways to achieve the best orgasm. None of them work. Not on me anyway. I'm the only girl in the world who's never had an orgasm. But I still enjoy it, don't get me wrong.

'I should go.' I get up and put my bra on quickly, careful for him not to steal it again.

I don't know what it was about this time, but it felt wrong. Maybe it was the fact that I was all dressed up and he couldn't even be bothered to leave the house. He just had to send a quick text and I came running with my tail wagging. How pathetic.

'See you soon,' he says, his arm over his face. He's already starting to fall asleep, his breathing slowing and becoming steady.

By the time I'm dressed and have reached the door I can hear his snores. Why am I such a bloody whore?

***

Sunday 12th October

I walk into the field the next morning, feeling ridiculously self-conscious. I mean, I had *no* idea what to wear, so I decided on jeans, my black hoodie, scarf and Elsie's UGG boots.

'Alright, Rosie!' a jovial voice sings.

I spin around with a glare, ready to kill him, only he looks super-hot. He's wearing a checked flannel shirt with a black padded gilet. He's got a thick red scarf around his neck, which only seems to accentuate his green eyes.

'Don't call me that!' I snap as my cheeks redden. I lower my face to the floor in an attempt to hide it. Why am I being so bashful?

‘Sorry, it's *Rosemary*, right?’ His eyes twinkle in amusement.

I ignore him, choosing to jut out my jaw to show my annoyance instead. He only seems to find it funnier.

‘Come on. Let’s introduce you to Mitsy.’ He grabs my hand and pulls me along after him, almost pulling my arm out of its socket.

It feels weird to have my hand in his, but it's also too comfy and warm for me to object. It’s smooth too, unlike James’ calloused ones. He’s obviously never done a hard day’s work in his life.

‘Are you nervous?’ he asks, glancing back at me, not breaking from his huge strides. I’m practically running after him or I’d be dragged, face down against the grass. I have a feeling he still wouldn’t stop.

He looks back at me again, this time with a quizzical expression. He must think I’m acting weird. I hope my hands not sweaty.

‘Don’t worry,’ he smiles reassuringly. ‘She’s going to love you.’

Ah, he must think I’m agitated about meeting the horse. Come to think of it, I am. I don’t have the first bloody clue about horses. He’s going to think I’m an idiot.

I attempt a deep breath, suddenly feeling as nervous as he described. I stop when I collide with his back.

‘Ow.’ I rub my forehead.

He turns and smiles at me, clearly amused. I look around him to see that we’re in front of a small stable. It stinks of poo. Let’s hope the horse doesn’t smell this bad.

He leads me over to it and goes towards a dark chocolate horse.

‘This is Mitsy.’ She has the brightest blonde hair contrasting it. It's almost as if she’s had highlights. What a bloody gorgeous horse. Who knew they could actually be stylish? Then I look down and see that she’s wearing a onesie. A onesie?

‘Err…why on earth is she wearing a onesie?’ I can't keep the laugh out of my voice.

‘They’re her pyjamas,’ he says, his eyes seemingly serious.

'Horses wear pyjamas?' How weird. '*And* they dance?' I can't help but blurt out.

He chuckles loudly. 'Yep. Just like you and me.' He rolls his eyes. 'Come and say hi.'

I realise I haven't moved and I'm still some way away from her. A quick stab of fear hits my chest, bringing with it a quickening heartbeat. I slowly walk towards her, cautious not to trip and head butt her by accident. That would *really* be a first impression.

I stand in front of her, looking to Will for encouragement. She starts sniffing and making weird noises, her big mouth moving towards me. Shit! She's going to eat me.

'Here, give her a polo,' he offers, handing one over.

I instinctively put it flat in the centre of my palm and shyly offer it to her with a shaking hand. She grabs it from me, her tongue saturating my hand. Ugh, gross. I wipe it on my jeans, unable to hide my disgust.

'She likes you,' he smiles, contentedly stroking her hair.

'She likes polo's more like.' I laugh nervously.

I tentatively reach up to her hair and lightly stroke it, accidentally brushing Will's fingers. My skin burns at the contact. I quickly move my hand away. I feel her skin and the warmth that comes from it is weirdly comforting. She's an actual living little thing. Not so little actually.

'So what's the plan with saving the home?' I ask, trying to quickly get over the awkwardness. I haven't been able to stop thinking about it. Well, in between the sex. Where will all the residents go? Will they be left homeless?

'Plan?' he asks, seeming shocked. He shakes his hand. 'I don't have a plan.'

'Just as I thought,' I nod. 'So I think we should arrange some events to raise some money. What do you think?'

'Okay.' He nods, deep in thought. 'You get the ball rolling on something and I'll support you any way I can.'

I smile shyly. Why on earth do I feel shy? I'm never bloody shy. I look back at Mitsy, the size of her registering to me what a massive chore I've taken on.

'So what exactly do I need to do with this horse?'

***

Why the hell did I volunteer to do this? I don't even bloody like Will and here I am working like a dog, just so that I can look after his horse. For free. In my spare time. What a doughnut. And why I ever thought wearing Elsie's UGGs was a good idea is beyond me. It's so muddy up here, they're bloody soaked. She's going to kill me. I cannot wait to go home and get in the shower. My muscles are so sore and heavy. I don't get how horse riders don't look like supermodels. It's a serious workout.

'Right,' Will says, breaking me out of my destructive thoughts, 'there's only one more thing to do.'

My heart sinks. I literally cannot do another single thing or I might just die here on the floor. My muscles are screaming in agony every time I move. And I have to work at the pub tonight.

'Don't look so horrified,' he grins. 'I was just going to ask if you wanted to ride her.'

'Ride her?' I look up at the giant horse in apprehension. 'I don't know,' I waver. 'Maybe you should just ride her today and I'll do it next time.'

He suddenly turns away from me. 'I don't ride her,' he says sadly. He turns back to face me, his eyes glazing over with some memory.

'Why not?' I blurt out. What's the point of having a horse if you don't ride it?

I wonder if he had a horrific accident and it's mentally scarred him for life. He doesn't seem to have any physical scars.

'I just…I haven't been able to ride her. Since…since my mum died.' He looks to the floor, his hand raking through his wayward hair.

Oh God. He looks so forlorn. I want to hug him, but I pull myself back before I become a complete hippie weirdo that walks around hugging people. That's so far from me. God, am I turning into Elsie? I shiver at the thought.

'Anyway.' He shakes his head and runs his hand over the back of his neck. 'Maybe we should go for a drink. You know, so I can thank you for taking this on.'

Go for a drink? Is he serious?

'Oh.'

Hasn't he seen how disgusting I look? I haven't got a mirror, but it's pretty obvious with my wet UGGs, starting to frizz hair and smudged mascara. He made me cry when I had to pick up the horse poo. God, it was revolting. Although now I've picked up so much of it I almost feel immune.

'Don't sound too excited,' he smirks. 'You'll break my ego.'

Ego? What is he talking about? Is he…asking me out? As in…wants me? As in…likes me? No, I don't think so. That couldn't be possible. The guy's just relished in my agony all day long. Is he a sadist? But he looks so disappointed and his cheeks are turning rosy in embarrassment.

'No, it's just that I probably stink of horse poo,' I laugh, trying to diffuse the awkwardness.

'You definitely stink of horse poo,' he grins. 'But I was going to suggest a shower first.'

My eyes nearly bulge out of their sockets. The thought of Will naked, soaping himself up invades my mind. I can feel my cheeks redden as if he can read my mind. What a dirty pervert I am. I wonder what he's like in bed. Probably just like James. Stop it!

'Not together!' he says loudly, laughing awkwardly. 'Obviously *separately.*'

'Obviously.' I look away, my cheeks burning, one blush blending into the other. 'But…I'm pretty tired. I should probably…you know…I've got work later.' I start backing away, trying to ignore the pull I feel towards him.

'Oh yeah, of course,' he smiles. 'I'm pretty tired too.'

Why is it suddenly so awkward? And why do I feel bad for turning him down? This is all becoming weird. I say my goodbyes and run off as quickly as I can.

The sooner I get to Mexico the better.

***

I lean on the bar later that evening, listening to Trevor reading out the quiz questions. It's a quiz night, teams consisting of six people, desperately trying to work out who won the Eurovision song contest in 1989.

God, this is bloody boring. Plus this endless time to think is making me crazy. I still can't think why things suddenly shifted with Will. I went from hating him and his ridiculous anal, bossy ways to finding out he is slightly normal. And then I don't know what it was; maybe being with Mitsy, seeing him being normal with another creature. It was kind of endearing.

But why did I get so scared when he asked me for a drink? I mean, he was only trying to thank me. Janey and I go for drinks all the time and I don't expect her to jump me. Although she has a few times when she's been truly smashed. The girl's a part-time lesbian.

The truth is I don't even know if Will likes me like that. What am I saying? I *know* he doesn't like me like that. He probably thinks I'm just some silly slut. Maybe he thought I'd be easy and he fancied a quick shag. Yeah, that sounds more plausible. Assuming I'd be up for it.

I'm broken from my thoughts by Phil calling my name.

'Rose, love, it's quiet tonight. I need to pop out to see someone. Can you hold down the fort?' he asks, scratching his nearly bald head.

'Err, yeah, that's fine.' Wow, this guy has trust. I barely know the man, but I suppose that's small village stupidity for you. I doubt a crime's ever taken place here. I've never even seen a police man.

'Good,' he nods. 'Normally I wouldn't leave you so soon, but you've got so much experience, I'm sure you'll be fine.'

Oh crap. My big mouth getting me in trouble again.

'Of course! Thanks. Have a good time!' I shout, sounding shrill and unnatural.

I look around as he leaves. Why am I freaking out? They're all just sitting there doing this stupid quiz anyway.

'We're going to take a quick break for a drink and so you can use the loos,' Trevor says into the microphone, which is completely unnecessary.

Teams start coming up to the bar, all eager to get a drink within the break. Then the football team comes in the front door. Suddenly it's as if there's a stampede at the bar. Everyone wants a drink and they want it now. I try to keep up, but it's hard when they're all ordering four drinks at once.

I'm pouring a Carlsberg when it suddenly comes to a halt. What the hell? I hit the beer tap with hope that it'll start again. Shit, it's run out. I look up, right into the eyes of Will. I start, unsure as to whether I'm hallucinating him.

'Nah then,' he smiles knowingly. 'Need some help?'

I look back pleadingly. 'Err…its run out,' is all I can seem to blurt out. I'm aware I sound like a bumbling idiot, but I'm too hot and flustered to think straight.

'Want me to cover while you change the barrel?' he asks, already opening the hatch to step behind the bar.

Change the barrel? Of course that's what I need to do. Duh. I'm sure it's easy. Right?

'That is unless…' he looks at me questionably, 'you do *know* how to change a barrel, right?'

'Yes!' I shrill, a little too defensively.

I hate how he just assumes I'm an idiot. I mean, I *am*, but that's beside the point.

'Good.' He walks up to a couple at the bar and shoos me off.

I walk into the back and finally find the cellar room. Thank God it's not actually underground, it's just out back. I shiver, the temperature lower than the rest of the place making my nipples zing to attention. The barrels make a weird buzzing sound, so loud I can't think straight. Right, let's assess this.

There are silver barrels all over the place. Some seem to be plugged up to the wall and some don't. I look closely at the wall and see that someone has named them, thank God. I scrutinise the messy handwriting, finally locating the Carlsberg, seeing the weird pump thing is empty. It almost looks like a penis pump. Weird. Not that I've ever seen one, but it's how I imagine they look. I follow the lead down to the barrel and have to think about how I'm going to do this.

I'd call Megan, but she's at a friend's house. That's the problem with being friends with a fifteen year old. Damn sleepovers.

I hold onto the handle, squeezing it and turn. I manage to unplug it easily and throw it to the floor. Success. Now I just have to find a Carlsberg barrel. I find it at the other bloody end of the room. Well that's inconvenient. I go to lift it up and nearly scream from the pain in my arms. *Fuck*, that's heavy. Jesus fucking Christ! There is no way I'm going to be able to lift this. Especially after the workout Mitsy gave me. Maybe I should call Will and ask for his help, but then…I don't want to be all helpless in front of him. I don't want him to think I'm some nit-wit with no idea what I'm doing. Which in reality is *exactly* what I am.

Maybe I could roll it over. That seems more do-able. I push it with all of my strength until it crashes down onto its side. Success! I roll it closer to the wall pump and when I'm happy that its close enough I try to drag it to upright again. Fuck! I need to start lifting weights, but Phil obviously thought I was capable or he wouldn't have left me here, surely? I must just be a wimp. A big, fat, slutty wimp. Come on, Rose. You can do this.

I use all of my inner strength, the strength I imagine I'd have to use if I ever gave birth, and manage to pull it to standing. It hits the floor loudly…trapping my toe underneath an edge.

FUUUUUUUUUUUUUUUUCCCCCCCCCKKKKKKKKKKK!!!!!!!!!!

I fall back onto my arse, the pain too intense to even concentrate on anything. I only manage to hurt my leg further. AAAHHHH! The pain is so over powering that it blurs my vision. I desperately claw against it. It dawns on me that I have to do something to get out of this. It gives me the determination to spring up to a standing position, the pain rushing up my leg, and push it off my foot, cursing all the time. I've broken my toe. I must have broken my fucking toe!

I lean against another barrel and take my boot off. Thank God I wasn't wearing flip flops or Elsie's UGGs. I managed to hide them before I left for work. At least this had some support. Not that it seems to matter. The boot is basically broken; completely crushed. I carefully peel off my sock to see my toe is twice the size and the colour of a beetroot. Jesus! The nail is seriously bruised and there's a little bit of blood. Ew!

I can't help it. I feel it brewing in my chest, the tears filling in my eyes. I let the cry of anguish being held in my throat go and burst into tears. Ugly, snotty tears. Why is life so hard?! I let myself wallow in it for a second. My parents not giving a shit, Janey not replying to my messages, the teeny boppers calling me a slag; all of it. The tears tumble down my cheeks and onto my sore shoulders, desperate for a hot bath.

I need to pull myself together. These people need their Carlsberg. I grab hold of the pump and try to work out what to do with it. I must just…secure it? I'm sure it's easy.

I hobble over to it and attempt to attach it. I've barely tried to press down when beer comes squirting out of it, spraying me in all directions! What the fuck? I pull it away, realising it's all over my top. It's basically see through. Great. Tonight really wasn't the day to go braless. My nipples are like bullets. I take a deep breath and try again, pushing harder this time. More beer squirts out, this time covering my hair and getting my jeans and feet. For God's sakes!

I let the tears take over again, slumping down on top of the barrel. This is hopeless.

'Hey, are you okay?'

I look up through the tears to see Will standing in the hallway. As soon as he sees my face it's like I've crushed him. His whole face contorts in sympathy, as if he can feel my pain. He rushes over to me, bending down onto his knees in front of me in an attempt to look into my eyes, which I'm trying to hide. This is the ultimate humiliation. Crying in front of a guy.

'What's happened?' he asks, his voice soft and sympathetic.

I sob louder. It's too ridiculous to say out loud. I mean, I'm sitting here with one shoe off, my toe the size of the empire state building and my clothes saturated with beer to the point of him being able to see my tits. It's pretty clear I'm having a break down.

'I…I can't…change a…' I break into a sob again, covering my face with my hands.

He pulls my hands away from my face so I'm looking into his caring eyes. 'A barrel?' he grins. 'Yeah, that's pretty clear.'

What a smug bastard.

I hit his strong chest, my weak hands doing nothing to hurt him.

'And…' I sniff, wiping my nose on the back of my hand, very unladylike, 'I crushed my toe!' I realise I'm whining like a two year old, but I can't help it. My life is ridiculous. I'm stupid. I hate myself.

And the worst thing is that I know all of this is my own stupid fault. My own stubbornness. I should have just told Phil I hadn't changed a barrel before, so he taught me before he left. Or I should have taken Will's offer for help and made him come with me.

He stands up and grabs my chin, forcing me to look up at him. I lower my eyes to the side, ashamed. I can't imagine the mess I must look like. I refuse to wear waterproof mascara; it dries out my lashes, so I must look like a demented panda. He waits patiently until I look back at him, our eyes locking intensely. His eyes are such a clear, intense green.

'We'll get some ice for your foot, don't worry. And I'll change the barrel.' He starts to walk over to it, but I grab his arm. Jeez, it's muscly.

'No. Teach me how to do it. I need to learn.'

He raises his eyebrows, surprised. Probably used to princesses who like men to just swoop in and save the day. Not me. I'm mortified.

'Okay,' he nods. He helps me up and hands me over the pump. 'The trick is that you have to press down really hard and then twist, otherwise this happens.' He points to my clothes.

'Yeah, I got that what I was doing was wrong,' I snarl sarcastically while jumping off the barrel. I bite back the scream from putting pressure on my foot.

'Okay, clever clogs. Off you go,' he says, gesturing towards the barrel.

Shit. I shouldn't have been so cocky.

I take a discreet deep breath and attach the pump, trying to hold it down and twist hard, just like he said. Beer fires everywhere, getting Will too. I persevere, thinking it might need to do that a little bit to work. Will pulls his hands up over his head and shouts, and then pushes me out of the way to secure it.

We both stand still in the after math, our breath heaving out of our chests erratically. He's soaked, his shirt clinging to his broad chest. How did I never realise how built he was before? He raises his eyebrow sarcastically. And he has a washboard stomach? Quick, look away!

'Why did you have to take over?' I demand aggressively, deciding that's the best emotion to go with right now. 'Now I'll never know how to do it.'

'Sorry,' he snaps, his eyes like ice. 'I was under the impression that you wanted some beer left *in* the barrel.'

I scrunch my face up in anger, leaning into his face. I could *so* punch him in the nose right now. The know it all bastard. Who the hell does he think he is?

He looks back just as mad, but then his eyes soften slightly, and before I know what's happening he's smiling.

'You're cute when you're angry.'

I'm so thrown off from it I actually stumble, shifting my weight to my painful toe. I wince. Fuck! He grabs my arms to steady me. God, he's got strong arms.

'I'm not cute!' I snap. 'I've never been called cute before.'

'Well, there's a first for everything,' he grins, his eyes dancing with amusement.

He's such a dick.

'*Puppies* are cute. I'm sexy, not cute.' I try to pull a sexy face, but then I remember I have a broken toe, am soaked in beer, and potentially have all of my make up half way down my face. Probably not my best look.

He looks intently over my face, and I'm sure he's going to laugh right in it. Tell me I'm a minger right now and that I should have taken the compliment while I had the chance. But instead something shifts between us. I'm suddenly aware of every sound in the room; the beer taps buzzing loudly in my ear. He's breathing heavier than normal and there's something in his eyes that tells me he's serious about something. What I don't know.

'You're right,' he whispers, his voice smooth like honey.

'Huh?'

I'm right? He's letting me think I'm right?

'You *are* sexy,' he says quietly.

I can't help it; I swoon and look at his lips. I never noticed before how plump and sexy they are and it makes me wonder what they taste like. I'm itching to touch them. I have a feeling he'd taste earthy. Almost dirty. I force myself to look away, already feeling bereft. Get a hold of yourself, Rose.

When I look back into his eyes I realise he's looking at *my* lips. Shit, he's thinking the same thing as me. I lean in, ever so slowly, giving him the chance to reject me. Giving me the chance to laugh it off and say I fell over, only he's moving too, even if it is the speed of a snail. I swallow. Oh my God, we're actually going to do this. This is it. It's happening.

'Err, sorry to interrupt?' a loud voice booms with authority.

We both snap our heads around to the door. Phil's standing there, his arms crossed over his chest. Shit.

'Does someone want to explain to me why the bar isn't manned right now?' He looks over our wet clothes and how close we look. 'Unless I'm interrupting something?' he says sarcastically.

'No!' I laugh, far too forced. 'I…just…it's all my fault. I'm so sorry,' I ramble.

'Rose, I think we're going to have to talk.' He looks seriously pissed. Shit. I know that tone all too well. He's going to fire me. Another job lost.

I need this money or I'll be begging Janey to share her beans on toast with me.

'She's lying,' Will says, his hands stuffed into his pockets.

I turn to him, completely confused. The absolute bastard is ratting me out. He's going to tell him that I've never changed a barrel in my life and that he was a fool to trust me. How could he do this to me? The cold hearted bastard. Jesus, I wonder whether he'll think the same thing and get me removed from the home?

'It was my fault,' he declares.

I stare at him aghast, my mouth almost hitting the floor.

'Really?' Phil smirks. 'You can explain this, can you?' he challenges.

'Yes,' he nods seriously. What the hell can he say to get us out of this? 'I've never changed a barrel before and I begged Rose to teach me. It's not her fault I was absolutely useless with it. She tried to take over, but I kept insisting. I'm really sorry.'

Phil looks between the both of us, sighing heavily. 'Is this true, Rose?'

I look back at Will for confirmation. He does the smallest nod, sure that Phil doesn't notice.

'Erm…yeah. It's true,' I whisper, my voice barely audible.

'Well, we still need to talk. You can't just abandon the bar so that you can teach someone to change barrels. It's very unprofessional,' he chastens.

'Sorry,' I mumble, staring at the floor.

'It's fine. And Will, I thought you would have been more sensible. Don't let me catch you behind this bar again,' he warns.

'Sorry,' we both whimper like children.

He turns to walk back and we follow. I desperately try to avoid Will's gaze, even though I obviously have to thank him for saving my arse. Only now I can't stop looking at his.

Chapter 9

Monday 13th October

The next day I avoid Will like the plague, only wherever I bloody turn there he is. I also don't know if it's the whole saving me/almost kissing thing, but he seems so much more attractive to me. I mean, he was clearly never butt ugly, but he pissed me off so much it was easy to not see it. Not to see his strong set jaw or his adorable dimple under his left eye. Now I can't stop thinking about how messy his hair is and how it always seems to fall to the left side. I can't work out whether he deliberately styles it like that or if it just falls naturally. See what I mean? Why on earth am I obsessing over his hair? It's this village. It's making me stir crazy.

I bound into Betty's room at midday with her lunch. Apparently she's been tired today so she hasn't been down in the lounge. Just chilling in bed watching This Morning. Being old doesn't sound so bad. I'm just glad for the sanctuary. I hand over her tuna mayo sandwich and open up my own cheese and pickle sandwich.

'So tell me,' she beams excitedly, 'how was the dressage?'

'Really good,' I nod, trying to hide the smile on my face. Why do I want to smile like a loon? 'I got to know Will a bit better.'

'Oh, aye,' she grins, raising her eyebrows in question.

'Not like that, you dirty minded old lady!' I scold jokingly.

I hope I'm this cool when I'm old.

'Hey! Less of the old,' she moans, pouting dramatically.

I chuckle and fill her in on the whole thing. Me volunteering to help look after Mitsy and the whole weirdness that was the cellar last night.

'That's what a great dress will do for you,' she winks, clearly pleased with its influence. I'd say she's definitely team Will over James. 'I'm chuffed someone got to wear it again. I always thought I'd pass it on to my daughter one day.' She looks sad for a second, before masking it and biting into her sandwich.

'It *is* a great dress,' I snigger.

'Aye. Last time I wore that it was 1958. My thirtieth birthday. I spent it in Paris.'

She grabs a photo album and shows me a photo of her on that night. She looks unbelievable. Curves like a race car and long dark brown hair, tumbling over her shoulders in sexy waves. She's stood with a good looking older man with a weird moustache.

'Who's that?' I point to the guy. 'And what were you doing in Paris?'

Her life was so bloody exciting and here I am in Yorkshire.

'I went over there to work as a nurse. Had a wild time, let me tell you,' she laughs fondly. 'That's Colbert. He was a senior doctor in the hospital.'

I grin, imagining this young, beautiful Betty wrapping good looking men round her little finger.

'Oh, yeah, play a bit of doctors and nurses, eh?' I ask playfully, raising my eyebrows.

'We did more than that, my love.' Her cheeks pink up, even though she seems anything but embarrassed.

Ew.

'He proposed to me that night. Took me out to a fancy hotel for a delicious meal and then we went for a walk. Asked me to marry him underneath the Eiffel Tower. It wasn't so common back then as it is nowadays.'

He wanted to marry her? Jesus, this woman's had more marriage proposals than Liza Minnelli.

'So, what did you say? Did you marry him?'

'Of course not.' She adamantly shakes her head.

'Why?'

I don't get it. Surely it was a second chance at happiness for her. I can tell she's happy in the photo. I can see it in her eyes. They look carefree and mischievous.

She sighs heavily. 'Because I was still in love with Thomas, Will's grandad. Even after all those years I couldn't bear to settle for second best. Everyone paled in comparison to him.'

'That's so sad,' I blurt out loud.

‘That and he was already married,’ she adds, as if this is no big deal.

‘WHAT?’ I exclaim, nearly falling off my chair.

‘Yes love, I was his mistress.’

‘Betty!’

I can't believe her. I’d never have had her down as the mistress sort. Not that I can judge, of course. My romantic history is hardly a Mills and Boon story.

She rolls her eyes. ‘Oh, don’t get up on your high horse. I’m sure his wife knew. Women just put up with things back then. Anyway, it gave me the push I needed to move onto Ireland. And that’s a *whole* other story!’

Jesus, this woman needs to write a book.

‘What happened in Ireland?’

‘That’s a story for another day, my love.’ She does actually look tired. ‘But throughout all my adventures, I’d give them all up to have married Thomas and lived happily ever after. But it wasn’t to be.’ She looks so forlorn.

‘I’m so sorry, Betty.’

She smiles sadly. ‘Don’t be, my dear. Just don’t make the same mistakes.’

What does she mean by that? I don’t press her as she looks beat, bless her. Being old just seems to zap your energy. I kiss her goodbye and walk back down the corridor.

‘Rose!’ I hear him call. I turn around to see Will walking towards me.

My whole body tenses. Crap. He looks especially smoking hot today in his dark jeans that make his arse look amazing and a light blue shirt, open at the collar, exposing the tiniest bit of chest hair. God, how I’d love to run my fingers through it. His sleeves are rolled up to his elbows showing off his perfect forearms. Focus, Rose.

‘Hi!’ I say, my pitch far too high and unnatural.

‘I’ve been looking for you all day.’ He smiles and I nearly fall over. He’s just too beautiful. How was I ever blind to it?

‘Really?’ My heart rate spikes.

Play it cool, Rose. Why the hell has he been looking for me? He probably just wants me to thank him for saving me last night at the pub. Take all the glory. Smug bastard.

'Yeah. I meant to ask you this morning how it went with Mitsy? I'm sorry I just abandoned you to ride her on your own.'

Oh yeah, Mitsy. Shit, I forgot to let her out this morning! That's not a good start. She must still be in her onesie, poor thing.

'No, that's fine,' I say, laughing it off. 'A lady at the stables helped me.' I try to sound as aloof as possible. The poor bloody horse.

'Still,' he grimaces, rocking on his heels with his hands in his pockets. 'I feel bad.'

Not as bad as I feel. I'm going to be reported for horse cruelty.

'It's fine,' I shrug, feeling worse by the second. 'And thanks for last night. Not just covering for me with Phil, but for tolerating me while I was a blubbering mess.'

Just thinking about what I must have looked like makes me inwardly cringe.

'Don't be stupid,' he grins, popping that adorable dimple. It makes my Lulu tingle, which I know is ridiculous. 'Anyway,' he straightens his face. 'I have an official question for you.'

I gulp, my throat suddenly dry. 'Official?' I ask my voice unsteady.

Oh my God. What the hell could it be? Does he need references or something? *Good luck.*

'O…kay?' I mumble nervously, my pulse quickening.

He bites his lip and looks away from me. 'I bumped into Violet yesterday and I asked her why she decided not to stick around.'

My stomach falls to my feet. Oh shit. Shit being the appropriate word. Why the hell did I *ever* think pooing in a tray would be a good idea?!

'Mmm,' I nod, hoping if I don't speak he won't be able to sense my internal panic. Although I'm sure he can smell the sweat off me.

'Anyway,' he hesitates, running his hand through his wayward hair. 'She said something about having to clean up…poo.' He swallows nervously. 'Do you…know anything about that?' He looks baffled and mortified to even be having this conversation.

Oh, holy fuck. What am I going to do? How could I have been so bloody stupid? In what universe did I think that this would work out? I could always call Violet a liar. Yes, that sounds legible, right?

'She…she must be mistaken,' I stutter. 'I don't remember anything about poo.' It's so hard to keep my voice even. Why am I such a tool?

'Really?' he asks, creasing his forehead in suspicion.

I can feel sweat forming on my upper lip. Keep it breezy, Rose. Keep it fucking BREEZY.

He bites his lip, seeming to consider it. 'She's a very trustworthy girl. You do realise she's the vicar's daughter?'

Oh for *Christ's* sakes. Why did I pick on the vicar's daughter? Of all bloody people.

'Oh, well…it doesn't matter who her father is,' I snap, discreetly wiping my sweaty forehead. 'The fact is she's *obviously* lying. I mean, maybe she's a compulsive liar or something. Rebelling against the whole vicar's daughter thing. I don't know. I'm not a therapist.' I realise I'm babbling, but I just can't stop myself.

He looks back at me distrustfully. Possibly too much, Rose. You frigging idiot. I attempt a confident smile.

'Okay,' he nods, seeming satisfied. I feel my arse de-clench itself. Thank God. 'I believe you. She's Riley's sister so I promised I'd look into it.'

Riley's sister? Shit shit shit! If possible I actually feel worse that he has faith in me. I'm a no good liar. Quickly, think of something to distract him.

'Bingo!' I shout out of nowhere, desperation colouring my tone.

He jumps, his eyes widening in alarm. I was a *little* loud. 'Come again?'

Oh God, I'd love to come just the one time. My throbbing Lulu tells me I want to do it with him over and over again until I'm sore. Oh God, I'm going off track. Focus your slutty little mind!

'I think we should plan some bingo. And…you know, maybe some other events like…an outdoor cinema viewing for the whole village?'

Yes, that sounds viable, right?

He looks surprised. 'That's a great idea, actually.'

Okay, now I'm kind of offended. What, he doesn't think I'm capable of a good idea?

'I know it is,' I say, sounding more affronted than I meant to. I cross my hands over my chest.

'Well, if you need me to come around to brainstorm let me know.'

He smiles before turning and sauntering off, that arse of his practically waving. Oh I will, Big Willy. I will. *Sigh.*

***

Tuesday 14th October

As I lead Mitsy out of the stables the following morning, I can't help but think of the shit storm I'm brewing for myself. Why on earth I had to tell Will that Violet was lying, I don't know. I mean, she's the vicar's daughter for God's sakes. If I wanted to make enemies she's probably the worst person to pick. I'd confide in Elsie, but I'm scared to mention it. I know she'd go mental and take her side. And why shouldn't she? She'd be right. When you put our values up against each other there's just no contest.

I lead Mitsy into the field and tell her to have a good day. I'm really not looking forward to facing Will. Especially if he's had a chance to talk to Violet again. Or Riley. She's probably filling his head with lies. Evil bitch.

I walk straight into a rush of red hair, jumping back to apologise. I straighten myself back up, picking her hair out of my lip gloss.

'Riley!' I breathe, trying desperately to keep some composure.

Speak of the devil and they shall appear. She smiles, her perfect teeth giving her a Hollywood effect. There's just something about her I don't trust. I think that vicar and his wife are breeding devils. How ironic.

'Hey, Rose,' she beams, her brown eyes warm and friendly. 'I was just visiting Mrs Johnson. Her dad just had a heart attack,' she says, answering my unspoken question. She leans in and whispers, 'Too much of the red wine I think.'

I laugh because I feel I should. I know she's trying to be nice, but I'm sure underneath it all she doesn't like me. I just get a vibe.

'Anyway, I was wondering if you fancied a night out soon?' she smiles hopefully, her eyes almost pleading.

Night out? Did she really just say night out?

'You mean down to the Dog and Pond?'

'No,' she laughs, rolling her eyes in a jovial manner. 'I was thinking about going into the next village. There's some fun bars there.'

My party brain wakes up.

'Bars? As in...places that don't also serve a family friendly roast dinner?' I ask, desperation clear in my tone.

'Yep,' she beams. 'I thought you'd be up for it. Someone needs to show you the fun side of living here. Besides, it helps when I get drunk away from my students.' She giggles girlishly.

'Students?' I blurt out.

'Aye. I'm the primary school teacher. Didn't Will tell you?' she asks, confused.

I shrug, nonplussed. She looks more hurt than she probably should. A definite sign she still has feelings for Will.

'Anyway.' She shakes her head as if to pull herself together. 'What about tomorrow night? Elsie can come too.'

I look her over and try to judge her intentions. Worst case scenario she's trying to suss me out and see if I fancy Will. And I still get to leave this village and ingest alcohol.

'I'm in.'

***

I've been at the care home about an hour when I hear it. Pearl's daughter is visiting her and she seems terribly excited.

'There's horses all over the village! They must have escaped from the stables,' she says in distress. 'It's awful.'

Oh my God. I hope Mitsy's okay. How the hell could they have gotten out? Probably some moron leaving the gate....oh *shit.* I did shut the gate, didn't I? DIDN'T I?!

She carries on talking while my stomach takes a nose dive. 'It's mayhem out there. I don't know what they're going to do.'

Shit shit shit.

I swallow down the nerves and try to see through the blind panic. Okay, calm down. It can't be that bad. Pearl's daughter is probably just a drama queen. It's probably just one horse that's escaped. But still…could this be my fault? Really? Think, Rose. Did I lock the gate? Did I do that special knot thing Will showed me? Oh God, I can't remember.

I get my phone out of my pocket and stare at it, contemplating if I can really call Elsie for help. Will she go mad? But then I don't have many other options right now. I dial her number with shaky hands.

'Rose. Are you okay?' she asks, anxiety in her voice. It must be obvious something's wrong. We're in the same building. Why else would I be calling her?

'No.' I gulp loudly enough for her to hear. 'I fucked up.' I cover my face with my hand. 'I really fucked up.'

She sighs audibly, making me feel a million times worse. 'I'm coming to find you.'

***

As we drive through the village all I can see are horses. Fucking horses *everywhere!* I've already spotted three, but not Mitsy yet. Dear God, if she's killed by a car Will won't ever forgive me.

'Fuck, Elsie. What are we going to do?' I throw my head down on the dashboard, hoping I'll knock myself out and wake when this is all over. Instead I just get a headache.

‘Pray to God for a miracle!’ she shrieks, making the sign of the cross against her chest.

If He’s our only help we’re screwed.

‘I was thinking more of something that might actually help us,’ I snap.

Elsie and her stupid God. Why would He have let this happen? If He’s real, He’s got a sick sense of humour.

‘Okay, let me think.’ She touches her hand to her forehead. Her head snaps back, suddenly determined. ‘Get out of the car.’

My stomach drops. She’s cutting me loose? She’s telling me to run away?

‘What? You’re abandoning me in my time of need?’ I plead, sounding as pathetic as I feel.

‘No, you wally. Get out and try to herd the horses. I’m going to go find some of the owners. They should be able to help.’

She leans across me, opens my door and practically throws me out of the car. Her exhaust fumes fill my throat as she wheel spins away from me. I cough and splutter as I watch her leave. Oh fuck. How the hell do you herd horses? Where’s a Collie dog when you need one?

I look around and spot a black horse over by the bramble bushes. It's bloody massive; easily twice the size of me. It could probably kill me with one kick. I have no idea how to get it to come to me.

‘Here, horsey, horsey, horsey.’

It looks back at me as if I’m stupid. I suppose I shouldn’t call it like it's a cat. I take a deep breath and walk over to it cautiously, trying to work out if it's a man or a woman. For some reason I feel like I’d have more chance if it was a girl. You know, woman to woman. I can't see a horse penis, but I don’t know if horses have penises. Do all animals that are male have dicks? Or is it just some of them? I remember our old family dog Champs that used to nosh himself while we were trying to watch Hollyoaks. It was beyond gross. Anyway, focus, Rose. FOCUS.

I put my hand out to it, trying to coax it towards me. Instead it gives one glance at my hand before deciding to bolt, kicking dirt in my face. I try to run after it, but after a few hundred yards decide it's useless. I need something to coax them back home. It seems my charm is doing nothing. What would tempt a horse? What would tempt Mitsy? Oh my God, that's it. I need polo's and I need them now.

I run towards the local corner shop, sweat trickling down my back. I should really do some exercise classes. I'm seriously unfit. I still ache from Sunday with Will. I rush in, tripping over a baby pram wheel and head towards the mints. I use my top to scoop up as many packets as I can carry.

'Got bad breath, love?' the cashier asks, herself eating a smelly tuna sandwich.

I turn my nose up and try not to be sick. Then I realise I have no money. Crap. I left my purse at the home. Not that twenty five pence would have gone far anyway. I look at the cashier with weary eyes, already begging forgiveness.

'I'm sorry. I don't have any money, but…I'll bring it later.' I start backing out of the shop.

'Sorry?' she stammers, putting down her sandwich and wiping her mouth with the back of her hand.

I don't wait for her to question me further. I turn and run as fast as I can out of the shop and down the road, trying to find the giant black horse. It's only when I feel a stitch attack my side and stop for a minute that I realise she's bloody running after me!

'You picked the wrong bitch to steal from!' she screams, holding a baseball bat over her head. 'I came fifth in cross country running!'

Oh, mother of all that is holy! I run faster, my shins aching more with every thud to the gravel. I glance back and she's gaining on me now. My stomach tightens in fear.

I grab a kid's nearby bicycle and throw it behind me. I hear her go down and glance back to see her cursing me, her fall gathering a small crowd. Jesus, I've crippled the bitch. I sure am making a lot of enemies here. And I've only been here a few weeks.

But I don't have time to wallow. I spot the same black horse eating Mrs Casey's front garden daisies. Well, she's not going to be happy. Another enemy.

'Horsey,' I sing, edging towards it very slowly. I'm still so out of breath. 'I've got some *p-o-l-o-s.*'

Its ears instantly prick up. I've got her attention now. This close I'm almost sure there's no horse dick.

'Yes. Lots of lovely *polo's,*' I tease, waving them around.

She trots towards me, making a weird sniffing sound. I give her a polo, her tongue licking my entire hand. I back away a good couple of steps and she instantly follows. It's working.

I've almost got up to the stables when a car screeches behind me, freaking the horse. I turn and see Elsie and two women jump out.

'Bluebell!' one of them shrieks. 'Come here, my baby.'

Bluebell walks straight towards her, love and devotion in her eyes. Well, she didn't need the polo's. I wonder if Mitsy will ever love me as much. I doubt it. She puts a saddle on before jumping up on her.

'Thanks so much, Rose,' she gushes. Elsie obviously didn't tell her it was my fault to begin with.

I look to the other woman.

'Let's separate. Here's some polo's. Do you know how many are missing?' I ask, suddenly feeling beyond exhausted. It's going to be a long day.

'Six escaped in total, but we've already got three back.' Not that she looks happy about it. She obviously suspects me.

'What about Mitsy?' I ask hopefully. Maybe she's already back home, wearing her onesie and watching the drama unfold.

'She's still missing.'

***

I zero in on the white horse. This one seems extra jittery. It seems to want the polo's, but it doesn't trust me. Why would it? I'm a raving lunatic! I still haven't heard anything about Mitsy, and as time passes so does any hope of finding her. If something has happened to her I'll never forgive myself. Hell, Will definitely won't forgive me.

Losing his dead mother's horse a few days after beginning to look after her. I'm such an idiot.

My phone rings, only spooking it further.

'Elsie?' I whisper, not wanting to scare her further.

'Aye, it's me. Mitsy's back. She's safe.'

I let out a breath and realise my whole bodies been tense the entire time. Thanks Jesus!

'Thank fuck. I'm just getting this one. I'm on Cherry Blossom Avenue.' I'm so glad she's safe. It's nearly over.

'Okay. We'll bring the horse coach along.' She sounds just as tired as me.

'Okay, hurry, but be quiet. Any fast movements and I think this one will bolt.' I hang up before she has the chance to respond.

Suddenly I hear a car screeching up behind me. It can't be Elsie. She's just hung up the phone. I look round to see Will in his car. Oh fuck a duck.

'Rose,' he shouts from his window, his face thoroughly unimpressed. 'What the fuck is going on here?'

The horse backs away, seeming spooked by his shouting.

'Shush!' I try to whisper, signalling towards the horse.

'Why is there a horse here?' he shouts, getting out of the car and leaning against the door. 'You realise that's not Mitsy, right?'

'Will, be quiet!' I whisper hiss.

'Why?' It's as if steam is coming out of his ears. 'What the FUCK IS GOING ON?!'

'Neighhhhh!'

I turn to see the horse losing it, throwing herself back, kicking her front legs up in the air. Fuck. I squeeze my eyes shut in fear. When they go back down they land on the bonnet of Will's car with an enormous smash.

Fuck! A whimper escapes my throat.

'Oh my God!' he screeches, throwing his hands in the air.

The horse flies its legs up again, seeming intent on destroying the car.

'Polo's! Give her some fucking polo's!' I throw him a pack, trying to be helpful, but it only hits him on the head. Oops.

'Rose!' he hisses through gritted teeth. He picks them up and starts offering them to the horse, although he's more throwing them at her. Has he never handled a horse before? I push him out of the way and try to calm her. She begins to settle down just as Elsie and Tina round the corner with the horse lorry.

Thank God. They rush over and start to load her into the van.

Will turns to me. 'Rose, can you please tell me what the *fuck* is going on?'

***

Wednesday 15th October

The next morning Will's still not calmed down when he calls me into his office.

'So you let the horses escape, left work without informing anyone, shoplifted from the local shop, and then totalled my car,' he says, listing them off on his fingers. 'Did I get everything?'

I suppose technically he left out me throwing a bicycle at the shop manager, but hey, I'm not going to correct him now. Elsie says it's only a sprain. It'll serve the aggressive bitch right.

'Pretty much,' I nod, trying to ignore the irresistible urge to giggle. I think then he'd really lose it.

He narrows his eyes on me. 'Rose, how could you be so irresponsible?' He sounds just like my dad.

'Sorry!' I snap. 'But you gave me one day's crash course on how to care for horses. I'm not a frigging…vet or something. Or you know…someone that knows about horses.' I sound like a fucking moron.

He breathes out, obviously completely frustrated with me. 'I guess you're right,' he says through gritted teeth.

'Sorry…what?' I stammer. Did I hear him correctly?

He sighs again. 'You're right. I threw you in at the deep end and I'm sorry.'

Wow. Will apologising. This is new. New and *weird.* Although he still looks more pissed off than understanding.

'But that doesn't excuse all of this.' He raises one eyebrow to stare at me.

'I know.' I sigh heavily. I shouldn't really give a shit. I mean, the guy has no real control over me. But then I suppose he does. If he throws me out I won't even be in the running to get to Mexico. And I suppose there's a teeny tiny part of me that wants to please him. Wow, where did *that* come from?

I smile sweetly and discreetly touch his arm. 'I'm sorry.' It normally works.

His arms are so muscly to the touch. You really wouldn't realise otherwise. He comes across as so tall and lean. Images of me licking his inner forearm invades my mind. What the hell?! It's just that I can appreciate a good body. Yes, that's it.

He slumps over the desk, his head in his hands. 'It's fine.' It sounds anything but fine. 'Do you want to do some more horse lessons with me?'

More time alone with him? I don't really think I could handle it. I'm already acting like a loon.

'No, I'm fine. I think me and Mitsy are going to get along just fine. Well, better than you and me anyway,' I joke.

He grimaces and looks genuinely upset. Why would he care?

'Anyway, I should get back to work.' I turn and walk out of his office before he can berate me further.

I go straight to the communal room and sit down next to Betty.

'Nah then my lovely,' she smiles, her eyes lighting up when she sees me. 'Where have you been? Letting more horses out? More shop lifting?' She chuckles heartedly.

It seems the whole village knows what happened. How mortifying.

'Ha ha bloody ha,' I snort, closing my eyes and hoping it will all go away.

'Don't be so miserable, love,' she chuckles. 'You have to be able to laugh at yourself.'

I should be a bloody clown with the amount of times I've had to laugh at myself.

My phone bleeps in my pocket, reminding me I should have it on silent. Another reason for Will to tell me off. I take it out and open the text. It's from James.

Hey baby, fancy another booty call? You know you're wet just reading this x

I smile to myself. What a cheeky bastard. It makes him all the more irresistible to me. I need a distraction right now.

'Who's that?' she asks, peering over, trying to read it. Nosey parker.

'Just James,' I shrug, unable to hide the smile on my face, butterflies fluttering in my stomach at the excitement of him touching me again.

'James Buckley?' she squeaks, her cute face recoiled in horror.

'Yeah, why?' I shrug.

'He's bad news, Rose.' She creases her eyebrows in concern.

'Haven't you heard?' I laugh sarcastically. 'So am I.'

***

Chapter 10

Thursday 16th October

The dance is today. Well, I say dance; I've downloaded a load of old tracks Betty told me about and I'm playing them while a few pathetic banners and balloons are pinned around the room. I persuaded Coral in the flower shop to donate them. They look like she was about to bin them anyway.

It's my only way to redeem myself with Will. I've also thrown myself into organising this bloody outdoor cinema screening. Madge from the library still hasn't gotten back to me about us borrowing the big projector, and apparently I need a licence from the local council so we can use the green on the common. It's such a bloody palaver.

Slowly, one by one, the men stand up (if they can) and walk over to a woman, requesting her hand and asking her to dance. It's so cute I can't help but smile. This is how dating used to be. So dignified and respectful. Not like now, with a creepy guy appearing from nowhere and deciding it's okay to start grinding behind you or James sending me a booty call request. God, how I wish I was born in another time.

Soon almost all of the residents are up dancing to Peggy Sue by Buddy Holly. It's one of the few I know. I start tapping my feet involuntarily.

'May I have this dance?' asks a voice behind me. I turn around to see Will bowing dramatically in front of me.

I raise my eyebrows, but take his hand and let him lead me to the middle of the dance floor. He places his hands on my hips and pulls me close. It's so quick that I have to steady myself by grabbing onto his sides. God, the abs on this man are ridiculous. I can feel them through his shirt. He must work out.

He carefully collects my hands and holds them in front of us. The residents are jiving, but as they can barely move it's a far pared down version. Before I know it he's pulling me around in a circle, before pushing me away from him. I think I'm going to fall, but then he grabs my hand again and pulls me back in.

'Not used to dancing?' he asks with a grin as I step on his foot again.

'Sorry, I didn't realise we'd gone back in time,' I snap, irritated with myself for having two left feet. 'Put on Beyoncé and I *dare* you to a dance off,' I joke, raising my eyebrows jokingly.

'Here,' he offers, putting his feet out. 'Stand on my feet.'

I frown. 'What? Like a child?' I'm highly offended and it's hard to hide.

'Whatever you want to call it,' he says, quickly losing his patience.

How he can flip from silly and playful to moody and intimidating so quickly I don't know.

'But I'll crush your feet,' I mumble.

'Nah more than you're doing now,' he snaps, narrowing his eyes at me. I stand back, ready to push him away, but then realise his eyes have playfulness in them. He's so hard to read.

'Fine,' I snap, stamping one foot on top of his, hard. I see him wince from the pain, but he takes it like a pro. I place the other one on and look around to see if anyone can see us. They're all too busy reminiscing about old times. 'Am I hurting you?'

'Sorry? I couldn't hear you through the crushing pain,' he jokes. 'Please, you weigh nothing. You need to eat more.'

God, he's bossy.

He starts jumping around, light on his feet even though I'm crushing them. He can jive. How random.

'You're joking. I've put on weight since I moved here. I don't get it either as I'm eating less. At home my parents would always leave a massive dinner for me.'

He slows his jumping, although he seems nowhere near out of breath. He has stamina, eh…FOCUS!

'So…what, you're not eating dinners now?' He sounds far too concerned.

'Elsie can't cook, so I'm basically surviving on cheese on toast.' I smile to let him know I'm only half joking. I don't want him to think I'm slagging her off. She's been nothing but good to me.

'That can't be good for you,' he reasons, narrowing his eyes again.

I just nod in agreement. I'm in no mood for a fight. Especially when he's making me so dizzy with all of the twirls.

I attempt a change of subject. 'Will, why don't you ride Mitsy anymore?' I blurt out.

I've been thinking about it and it's weird. Something big must have happened to take such drastic action.

He stops dancing and looks away, as if watching something else happening. Trying to ignore me.

'I saw you the other day,' I press, eager to find out more about him. 'You were itching to ride her. Why not?'

'It's just…' he hesitates, looking away again before locking his eyes with mine intently. They bleed vulnerability. 'She reminds me of my mum too much.' His voice makes it sound like he's confessing to a humiliating weakness.

I've never seen him like this before. I just want to wrap him up, take him home and cuddle him until he feels better. But I reckon I'd look a bit stalker-ish.

'But surely your mum loved her,' I press carefully. 'If anything, isn't it a way to be close to her?'

I'd love to see him ride her. I can see he loves her.

'I can't be close to her, Rose. She's dead,' he says bluntly, swallowing down a lump in his throat.

'You know what I mean.' God, he's annoying.

He's not going to shut me up this easily.

'I don't want to talk about it,' he states, staring down at me firmly.

'Okay,' I nod, deciding to give up. He's going to be a hard nut to crack. I push my head into his chest. But then I realise he's being a hypocrite. He'd be the first one to pull me up on it. 'No.'

'No?' he grins, pulling back, his eyes crinkled with confusion. He's so stubborn.

'You can't be a hypocrite, Will. That's just not you and you know it.'

'Fine!' he snaps, his eyes blazing. I stand off his feet, suddenly feeling exposed and vulnerable. Why did I have to push him? 'If you must know,' he says, his voice like acid, 'we rode Mitsy together just before she died. It's my last proper memory of her.' His eyes shine with unshed tears. He's too stubborn to let them fall.

Oh God, what have I done? I've forced him to share this with me and now I feel awful. You can't just force these soul exposing confessions from people. They're supposed to *want* to confide in you.

'I'm so sorry.' I grimace, wanting more than anything to take his pain away.

I step forward and push my head back into his chest, my body's way of apologising. I don't think he'd appreciate my boobs being pushed at him right now. He surprises me when he wraps his arms around my back, keeping me in place. I feel his heart beat begin to slow down. I'd like to think it's because I calm him, only I know that's not true.

'She must have known she didn't have long,' he says, still keeping me in place. 'She was supposed to be in bed, hooked up to morphine, but she told me we were going on an adventure. She ripped out her IV and we sneaked out the back door. At the time I thought it was fun.' He laughs, only it's clear it's a laugh to cover his pain.

'We walked to the stables, but we had to keep stopping for her to sit down. I was used to it by then. The cancer had spread to her bones.' I squeeze him tighter.

'We took Mitsy out and I helped her up. We rode around the village while everyone was sleeping and she told me stories about me as a baby. She said I was born stubborn and sulked for a week when James was born.' He laughs at the memory.

'I remember feeling proper special and loved, with the moonlight above us illuminating her fragile features. She made me promise to look after James, and I knew by the way she spoke she knew she didn't have long. When we got back dad went mad. It didn't matter anyway. She had passed by the morning.'

If it's possible my heart is actually breaking for him. I feel physical pain for his loss. He was so young; just an eight year old boy who should have been carefree and silly. Instead he was trying to hold his family together. How could anyone ever get over that?

'I'm sorry, Will,' I say into his chest, still feeling too upset to look at him. I'm sure to burst into tears if I look at him too quickly. 'I didn't mean to push you.'

'Yes you did,' he laughs, the sound strained. 'But it's okay. I just…I don't know if I can ride her again. It would bring it all back, you know?'

I nod, pulling back slightly to look at his broken face. 'But have you ever thought about making new memories? Don't you think your mum would want to look down and see you enjoying her memory?'

Not that I've ever believed in an afterlife, but after something like this I'm sure you'd cling on to the idea.

'I don't know. I'll think about it,' he shrugs, noncommittally.

My poor hunky damaged Will.

'Why don't we go to ride her this Sunday?' I press. I have a feeling that if he rode her he'd start healing.

He looks unsure. 'I'll think about it.' In other words, no.

The next track, Rock Around the Clock, comes blaring through the speakers and the mood immediately electrifies in the room. Every single resident perks up. If we were in a nightclub they'd be shouting 'I love this song!'

Ethel and Harry start full on jiving in the middle of the floor. It *is* slow jiving. There's no cool moves like Grease in there, but it's still fun. People start joining in around them. Peter even lugs his zimmer frame to the dance floor and starts shaking his hips. He sees me watching him and decides to throw his zimmer frame into the corner. I nearly pass out from shock. He's throwing some shapes now, clapping his hands together and lifting his feet off the floor, as if he were jumping. Will beams at me. I don't see him happier than when I bring happiness to others.

Everyone starts to turn round and look at us. It makes me realise we're still slow dancing. I look up at Will, blushing, and its then I realise they're not looking at us at all. They're looking beyond us. I turn around, still in Will's arms to see two policemen. Will follows my gaze and his body stiffens as he appears just as stunned as me.

'Excuse me,' the tall one says. His moustache is so long it seems to be growing into his mouth. 'But we have a few questions for you. You are William Buckley, the general manager here?'

Will releases me from his arms. 'Err, yes. That's me. Follow me to somewhere quieter.' He walks towards the hallway, glancing back to give me a quizzical look and shrug.

What the hell are they doing here?

I suppose I'll have to wait. I can be patient. Right? Oh God, who am I kidding?

***

'More shots?' Riley sings, already half way to the bar.

We've gone to a bar in the next village. Riley took matters into her own hands and organised it with Elsie. She was a bit unsure about coming here though. Something about a long running feud between villages. Not that I have any loyalty. It's actually fun in here. It's got dim lighting with small rickety miss-matched tables and chairs. If I squint I can imagine I'm in a vodka bar back home. Only the drinks would be five times the price.

Elsie's still laughing from her joke about the panda. Who knew Elsie could be so much fun? Just ply her with red wine and watch her go. I can't believe she's giving this all up to join Saint Ville. I *have* to save her. She's got so much potential.

While Riley's at the bar I figure it's my best opportunity to quiz her.

'Els, this Riley…' I say carefully, 'is she for real?'

I mean, she seems really friendly and genuine tonight. Maybe I've completely misjudged her.

'What do you mean?' she asks, her innocent little face squished up in confusion.

'Just that. Is she real? Can I trust her?'

'Oh yeah,' she smiles reassuringly. 'Riley's the nicest girl I know. Her dad's the vicar. I've known her forever.'

I forgot about the vicar being her dad. That's got to make Elsie biased. And I *am* asking possibly the nicest girl in the village. I doubt she'd say a bad word about anyone.

'So she's trustworthy?' I press.

'Yes, Rose!' she giggles, her lips starting to turn purple from the wine. 'You need to start trusting people more.'

I roll my eyes. She needs to start being a bit more cautious.

Riley walks back to the table with more tequila shots. I knew I liked her deep down. We grab one each.

'To trusting people,' I toast, before slamming mine down my throat.

***

I can't believe I've had such a brilliant night. Who knew the other village was happening. I may, *may* have gotten slightly shit faced. The truth is that I kind of passed out at our booth and Elsie had to wake me by throwing a glass of water over my face. But whatever, I had fun! I feel giggly, a bit spaced out, but most of all I feel pure unfiltered love for Elsie. Who knew she could be so much fun? Not me for sure!

We shower Riley, my new good friend, in kisses and drop her off at hers, before pulling into our road.

'That'll be forty five ladies,' the cabbie says, not even bothering to look back at us.

'What?' I shriek. Forty five for a bloody fifteen minute journey? 'That's a bloody joke,' I snort.

He turns to look at us. 'That's the fair I'm afraid, pet.' He doesn't look sorry at all. 'I don't like coming into this village anyway.' He looks around distastefully as if he might catch something.

So that's what this was about. He's a bloody village racist. What is it between these villages? What the hell happened to make them all so bitter? Either way, I'm not going to pay for it.

'We're not putting up with this!' I scream, opening the door and dragging Elsie out with me. She's like a rag doll, she's so wasted. Apparently she doesn't normally do shots. And tequila can take down the best of us.

I can barely see straight. It's so dark, the only light coming from a faraway street lamp. Nothing to do with the shots. I'm almost sure of it.

'Hey!' he shouts aggressively.

Oh crap. He's getting out of the car. I should run, only I'm too busy trying to keep both my feet on the ground. I feel a bit wobbly if I'm honest. His cold eyes meet mine, sending a bolt of fear to the pit of my stomach.

'Rose, its fwine,' Elsie slurs, barely able to stand. 'Let's just pay him.'

'Now listen here girls,' he starts, reaching into his back pocket. Suddenly the alcohol dulls, replacing it with adrenaline pounding round my body.

Oh my God. He's got a knife! A fucking *knife!*

'Elsie, RUN!' I scream, lunging forward and kicking him hard in the balls. His mouth drops open to form a silent O. He starts to collapse onto me, but I manage to push him off, frantically running after her.

It's clear she's pissed because she's running in zig zags and not actually going anywhere. I grab her arm and drag her down an alleyway. I pull her around a corner and push us against a bramble bush. It cuts into my arm, but I can't feel any pain. Not yet. I'm too scared thinking of how we're about to get murdered by a taxi driver. And in Belmont bloody Village! I thought we were safe here!

'What are we going to do?' she shrieks, her blurry eyes wide.

I can practically feel bubbles of panic riding through me. I clasp my hand around her mouth. It's the only quick way I can get her to shut up. Something tells me she won't be reasoned with. Her frantic breathing pushes out of her nose, onto my hand. I try desperately to listen, but I can't hear him chasing after us. Just the whistle of the wind in the trees. Phew. I take a deep breath and start to relax. I think we're in the clear.

I pull Elsie closer. 'Don't worry, Els. We'll be home soon.'

I feel completely sober. What a waste of alcohol.

I wait until I'm pretty sure he would have given up and gone home. I release my hand from her mouth, but signal with it to keep quiet. I point at her shoes and she follows my lead and removes them. We creep slowly out onto the road, sticks prickling our heels, and turn the corner into our street. His car's still there. Shit.

Where the hell is he? And what is it he wants? Blood?

'We can't go home,' Elsie declares, her shaky hands rising to cover her face. 'What if he's already in our house? Waiting for us?'

I roll my eyes, faking confidence. 'Don't be stupid, Elsie! He doesn't know where we live.'

I grab her arm and start walking towards our house when I see him. He's walking out of our next door neighbour's front door. I grab Elsie and duck down behind the wall.

'Shit.'

'Don't swear, Rose,' she berates.

'Now is NOT the time,' I snap, my jaw tense.

What the hell are we going to do?

'Quickly,' Elsie says, nodding towards Lauren's house. She runs out of my grasp before I have a chance to slap some sense into her. How stupid is she? She's going to be seen and murdered.

I begrudgingly follow her, crawling on my hands and knees. He's still talking to our neighbour. All he'd have to do is glance over and he'd see us. Elsie crawls commando style to the flower pot and retrieves a key from underneath it. She snakes her body up against the door, letting us in. I'm sweating now. We crawl in as quickly as we can, my heart beating so hard I fear it'll actually jump out of my chest and run over to him screaming.

We shut the door quietly and both collapse onto the carpet in relief.

'Who's there?' Lauren shouts down the stairs.

We both look up to see her running down the stairs, crazy eyed, holding a baseball bat. Does *everyone* in this village have a baseball bat? She trips on a step and tumbles down the stairs, landing just a centimetre before us, her t-shirt up over her head, exposing her boobs.

'Jesus!' I shriek, pulling my head to the left to avoid taking a nipple into my mouth.

'Don't use his name in vain!' Elsie snaps, already starting to try and get her rosemary beads out from her bag.

'I think this bloody calls for it, don't you?' God, she can be annoying with all of her God bothering! Especially when she's trashed.

Lauren pulls herself onto her elbows and quickly pulls her t-shirt down. 'What the hell are you guys doing here?'

'Long story,' I sigh, snatching the rosemary beads away from Elsie. 'Put the kettle on and we'll tell you.'

***

We watch out the window as we sip our tea and eat our bacon sandwiches. Did I mention I love Lauren? He eventually drives away, after what feels like an eternity. We thank Lauren and go back home. We're just shutting the door when a lady in her sixties comes barrelling through it. I recognise her as our neighbour that was talking to him. Oh my God, this must be Mavis.

'There you are, my lovelies! I've been worried sick.'

She's got a small, sweet face. Not the kind of face you imagine screaming about milk in her coco puffs. Ugh, just thinking about it makes me shiver.

'There's been an attack on a taxi driver,' she shrieks, her jet black hair still in her rollers.

Elsie and I exchange looks before bursting out laughing. She looks at us, confused.

'Actually…he said it was two lasses…was it…' She lowers her voice to a whisper. 'you two?' she asks, unbelieving.

'He pulled a knife on us!' I shout in our defence, pulling Elsie behind me. If anyone's getting in trouble here it's going to be me.

'A knife?' she shrieks, her hands up to her chest. 'Oh my goodness! And I gave him some Vaseline for his balls. The *bastard* took my Vaseline!'

Elsie looks at me and we both spontaneously collapse into hysterical giggles. This place gets weirder by the second.

***

Chapter 11

Friday 17th October

'I'm telling you, Phil, I haven't stolen any bloody chocolate!' I shriek the next night at work.

He's been tip toeing around asking me all night.

'I'm not accusing you, pet,' he says, leaning his belly on the bar. 'I'm just asking you. Since you've started, the chocolate stock take has been down.'

Who fucking cares? God, this dude needs to get a life.

'Well then, maybe you need to learn how to count again,' I snarl. 'I don't even eat that much chocolate.'

Okay, maybe more since I've moved here. Just from boredom. But not *stolen* chocolate. I have some self-respect. I just take Elsie's when she's out.

'Okay, I'm sorry,' he says regretfully.

He doesn't look sorry. He looks like he believes I'm the chocolate thief. What an arsehole. I'm guessing this will be a bad time to ask if he'd donate some booze for the outdoor cinema screening.

'It's just I heard about the stolen polo's.'

Oh for goodness sakes!

'That was an emergency!' I roar.

Damn it, you steal a few packets of polo's and you're branded a thief for life.

I walk over to the other end of the bar, pretending to be busy. Hopefully he'll leave me alone now. Violet and Riley walk in looking angry. Well, at least Violet does. My stomach lurches with fear. Oh shit. This is all I bloody need. Them coming in here to accuse me of things...well, of things that I've actually done. I discreetly try to duck behind the bar, but they spot me. They stomp towards me, steam practically coming out of Violet's ears.

'Rose,' she hisses, as if it disgusts her to just say my name. 'Why the hell did you lie and call me a liar?' she screams, leaning over the bar.

I stand as far away from her as possible, but with the bar I can't help but feel pinned in. Riley stands behind her, mouthing sorry. The few regulars at the bar turn around to watch the unfolding scene.

My stomach begins churning. It's as if my insides are playing the accordion. I try to stare back confidently. 'I…I don't know what you mean,' I stutter. Why couldn't my voice be smooth? I even *sound* like a liar.

I clean down the bar, hoping she'll drop it and leave. It's not looking likely. I can practically feel the venom dripping from her.

'Yes you do! You said I lied about the poo you showed me. Why would you say that?' She narrows her blue eyes at me accusingly.

Everyone's staring now. I suppose when you throw the word *poo* in there, you're going to get some funny looks. I can feel their eyes on me. And most of all I can feel Riley watching behind her. I wipe my sweaty hand through my hair, trying to appear unfazed. What the hell am I going to do? Admit it was my poo? I don't *think* so.

I try to maintain what dignity I have left. 'Because…you clearly couldn't be arsed to volunteer there and…and….you just came up with an excuse.' I lean on one hip, hoping I look confident. It's the only way. She's going down.

'That's not true. I'm *not* a liar,' she whines weakly, stomping her foot.

I smile. Did she actually just stomp like a toddler? I've got her now.

'Listen, just because you're the vicar's daughter does not mean you don't lie. Maybe you have a problem or something. Maybe you're a compulsive liar.' I inspect a fingernail, feigning boredom.

'More like you!' she screams, pointing her shaking finger at me.

'Come on, Rose,' Riley tries to reason. 'This has gotten out of control.' She looks so awkward, bless her. Elsie must be right about her. If she wanted to ruin me she could have joined in by now. 'Come on, Violet.' She starts leading her away, which seems harder than you'd imagine. That little bitch looks strong.

I wait until they're almost out of the door.

'Yeah, you go spread your lies somewhere else!' I shout after them. I'm such a coward.

The door slams behind them. I look around at the customers, shrugging as if I have no idea why she's so crazy, praying the silenced pub can't hear my accelerated heartbeat.

God, what is wrong with me? This is *so* mortifying. Talking about poo in public. I've hit a new low. I turn and pretend to busy myself in one of the fridges, while I attempt to slow my breathing. Whoever stocked this is an idiot. None of the labels are turned towards the front. I start re-organising, glad to have something to take my mind off the whole situation.

'Rose, can I speak with you?' a smooth honey voice asks. I know it's him from the way my body tingles all over in excitement.

I swivel round to see Will leaning over the bar, dressed in jeans and a white shirt. Does he *always* wear a shirt? Shit, how long has he been here? How much did he see? Was my arse hanging out of my jeans?

'Sure,' I squeak, sweat immediately forming on the back of my neck. God, what now? 'Phil, I'm just taking a quick break.'

I walk out to the front, not waiting for his approval. I hear Will following behind. The cold night air attacks my skin, sending goose bumps all over. I cross my hands across my chest, sure my nipples will be the next to react.

I refuse to look back at him, knowing he'll look smug. He's obviously heard from Riley about Violet's showdown. I glance up at the starry sky instead.

'So…you're still going with the whole Violet is a liar thing?' he asks, with a smile in his voice.

I sigh dramatically and turn round to face him, suddenly feeling bone tired. How can one village carry so much drama? That's right, because *I'm* living here now.

'Why are you so intent on trying to catch me out all of the time?' I ask pleadingly. I just want to be left alone. I didn't ask for any of this.

‘I’m not,’ he says, his eyes squinting with hurt. ‘But I’ve known Violet since she was a baby. She wouldn’t lie, especially about something as random as this.’ He raises his eyebrows expectantly.

‘But I would, right? You’ll take Riley’s word over mine any day.’ I’m still just a newbie outcast when it boils down to it.

He steps closer to me. So close I could almost reach out and touch him.

‘Rose, whose poo was it?’ He scrunches his face up in disgust at having to say it.

Oh God, how the hell am I going to get out of this one? I cannot, repeat *cannot* tell him it was my poo. I’ll not only look like a psycho, but he’ll think of me as gross. Girls aren’t supposed to poo. They’re supposed to shoot unicorn glitter. At least that’s what guys are supposed to think.

But I have to be honest. It's pretty clear he’s not going to drop this. And how long can I go on insisting it was Violet lying?

‘It…it was….’ He already looks disgusted, his face braced in preparation. Oh God, just say it. Just say it was mine. I take an unsteady deep breath. ‘It was…Peggy’s.’

‘Huh?’ His mouth gapes open.

What the hell is wrong with me? I mentally hit myself on the forehead. I just don’t have the energy to tell him the truth right now. Looking after Mitsy every day is exhausting me.

‘You mean…Peggy…had an accident?’ I can see him trying to figure it all out in his head.

Sorry, Peggy.

‘Yes,’ I nod frantically. ‘I didn’t want to say anything for her sake. She made me promise. She’d…even probably deny it.’

‘I had no idea.’ He puts his hand to his forehead. ‘Poor Peggy.’

Yeah, poor Peggy, getting blamed for my poo fiasco. But hey, mess with my Betty and expect to get taken down.

‘Why are you so irritable tonight anyway?’ he asks with a smirk.

I’m so stressed I feel like I want to crack every bone in my body, in the hope that it would relieve some tension.

'Ugh! Because everyone's always bloody picking on me! You're on at me about your car and Mitsy, Elsie's on at me to stop swearing, Phil's accusing me of stealing chocolate and no one believes that Mavis and Bernie are dirty sex freaks!'

They kept me up *again* last night. It seems that the rush of hearing about that taxi driver made Mavis horny. I had rushed in to tell Elsie, but I couldn't wake her up for the life of me. I even sat on her face at one point. She just snored louder. No wonder she can't hear them.

'Mavis and Bernie?' he repeats, his face bemused.

'See!' I shriek in defeat. 'Everyone thinks I'm a bloody compulsive liar!'

'Okay.' He puts his hand up, as if to try and calm me down.

I take a steady breath, trying to regain *some* of my composure.

'I'm sorry, but I can't believe your story on Mavis and Bernie.'

'But-'

'No, Rose,' he interrupts. 'I'm sorry.' This is clearly not open for discussion. He stares at me for a few seconds, creasing his chin in thought. 'But you being accused of stealing chocolate?' He smiles. 'Tell me more.'

I sigh loudly, no fight left in me. 'I agree it sounds stupid when you say it out loud, but yes.'

He pauses for a moment, presumably thinking. 'So what are we going to do about it?' he eventually asks.

'We?' I ask narrowing my eyes on him. He wants to help me?

'Yes, we.' He seems determined. 'I don't trust you to prove your innocence on your own. You'll probably be caught with chocolate smeared all over your face.' He chuckles at the thought.

A smile spreads on my face, but I bite my lip, trying to hide it.

'I didn't fucking take it! I don't steal!' I shout, laughing. I can't help it.

I should be worried about why everyone in this village is against me, but as I look at his eyes, warm with humour, I can't help but grin.

'I believe you, dickhead,' he smirks. 'Which is why I'm going to help you prove your innocence. Just shut up and listen t' plan.'

***

Saturday 18th October

So by the following evening Will's plan is in place. My nerves are on tender hooks. Now that we're actually putting the plan into action I feel like it's stupid. So much could go wrong. And I mean, why do I even care so much? *Because I want to prove my innocence, that's why.*

Phil's left me to lock up as usual on a Saturday night, only I've locked me and Will in. We're hiding in the alcove, where the dart board is based. According to Will, we'll be able to sneak out back and look at the security tapes. Apparently he knows Phil keeps tapes after being broken into a couple of years back. I still can't imagine any crime in this place. Look at the drama over a packet of polo's.

Loud echoing footsteps sound from the bar.

'Sssh!' I hiss, 'I swear I just heard someone.'

Oh my God, what if it's an animal? We are in the country. It could be a bear. Or a moose. Or a badger. Shit, I haven't thought this danger through. I automatically stand closer to him, my hand finding his strong, broad chest. My fingers tingle at the touch.

'You're imagining it,' Will whispers. 'They've gone to bed. I heard them.'

I shake my head, my hand now clutching onto his shirt in terror. I'm not an idiot. I know what I heard. Unless…what if it's not an animal? What if someone's breaking in again? What if we're stuck hiding here while they rob the place and then they find us? And hold us hostage? Oh shit! I'm panicking now.

A sound makes me jump again, this time so close that I practically jump into Will's arms. I look up at him, realising that I'm pressed against his firm chest, absentmindedly stroking the muscles beneath. I try to calm down my breathing, which is suddenly so erratic I'm sure it can be heard in Watford. I'm sure it's more to do with the thought of a possible intruder and not the close proximity to his lips.

He's breathing pretty hard too. Oh, how I'd love to be the one making him pant.

A weird scuffing sound starts, coming closer. I grip onto Will's shirt in alarm. This is it. We're dead.

He raises his hand and for a second I think it's to push me away. Instead he wraps it round my head and pulls me further into his chest, comforting me. I relish the feeling of his warm ripped chest and inhale his sexy scent. He smells of mint and soap.

'I can hear it too,' he whispers into my ear, his lip brushing my ear lobe. I shiver from the intimacy.

I close my eyes and pray to God that I'll live. If only to feel him up some more.

'Wait…Megan?' he blurts out.

'What?' I spin around to see her in her pyjamas, her mouth full of chocolate.

'Aaaagghhh!' she screams, a cube of chocolate falling out onto the floor.

'What the fuck?' I shout, running over to her and throwing the chocolate from her hands. '*You're* the chocolate thief?'

Her sweet face scrunches up in fright. 'Please don't tell dad! I just need chocolate sometimes, okay!'

'It's not okay when your dad's accusing me of stealing it!' I shout. I'm ridiculously hurt that she was willing to let me take the fall.

'Shit. Really?' she asks, her eyes wide with worry.

At least she wasn't *deliberately* dropping me in it.

'Yeah!'

She turns to Will, her eyes like a deer caught in the headlights. 'I'm sorry.'

'Don't apologise to *him*!' I shriek, slapping her arm. 'Apologise to *me!*'

'I'm not worried about you,' she snorts. 'We're soul sisters. I know you won't tell on me, but Will…'

'What?' he says, seeming offended. 'I look like a tattle tale?'

I bite my lip to stop from laughing.

'Well…' she looks down at the floor.

I can't help it. I burst out laughing, clutching my sides from the ache.

'Well thanks!' he huffs over my chuckles, crossing his arms over his chest.

What a little drama queen.

'I keep telling you, Will,' I giggle, putting my hand on his arm, 'you have to take that stick out of your arse.'

He throws off my hand, his eyes clouding with anger and hurt. 'Whatever, I'm out of here.' He stomps over to the door, unlocking it and storming out.

I roll my eyes at Megan and tell her to go back up to bed. She explains that her dad doesn't get that she gets cravings when she's due on. Her mum's not around to explain. I don't know what happened with her, but I decide not to ask. She'll tell me when she's ready.

I lock up and put the keys through the letter box. The village seems almost creepy this time of night. Only one street light and the stars are out to guide me. I really wish the church grave yard wasn't across the road from the pub. Visions of a zombie Michael Jackson emerging from it and forcing me to dance clouds my head. I push the collar of my jacket up around my neck and cross my arms, my nipples already turning to ice. I don't often see stars at all in Watford. Probably all the pollution. Or maybe I'm normally too wasted.

'Rose,' someone whispers close by.

I jump out of my skin, my heart trying to jump out of my throat, and instantly jump into a karate move. Who would have thought all of my martial art training would come in handy in this twee little village? I channel all the Jackie Chan movies I've seen. Well… I've seen Rush Hour one and two. I focus in on the hooded figure, preparing myself to either kill him or run for my life. I'm not sure yet. My shins still ache from chasing the horses. I could really do without it.

He takes a step towards me, out of the shadows and into the shine of the street light. It's only then that I can see the smug smile of Will.

'Will! For fucks sakes, I could have killed you!' I shriek, putting my hand to my chest, realising my heart still not calmed down.

'Yep,' he grins rolling his eyes. 'I was proper scared there for a minute,' he deadpans.

'What are you still doing here?'

He left ages ago. Well, he stomped off ages ago.

'I'm a gentlemen,' he says, as if in way of explanation. 'I couldn't leave you to walk home alone in the dark. Especially when it was my idea to stay up late,' he says it as if this excuses him of hiding in the shadows and nearly scaring me to death.

'I'd have been fine on my own,' I snap, already turning and walking away quickly. I hate how he makes me feel like I'm an inadequate little girl that can't look after herself. I'm normally the one in control with guys. I make it that way.

'Yeah, well, at the time I didn't realise you had these killer karate moves.' He chuckles as if it's hilarious.

'Shut up,' I snap, slowing down slightly so he can keep up.

We walk together in silence for a little while. I can't help but feel awkward about the whole thing. I still can't shift the unsettling feeling that he doesn't trust me and thinks I'm some trouble making slut from Watford. Which, you know, I am. For some reason I want him to trust me. It's nothing to do with his warm chest that I can't stop remembering being snuggled up to. It was just so warm. It's like the dark is giving things an exciting, erotic under tone.

Luckily his house is before mine so it's not long lived.

'Well, thanks for walking me home,' he says with a grin, a cheeky twinkle in his eyes.

'Wait, was I *your* protection?' I laugh.

'Maybe,' he grins. 'It's not safe for pretty boys like me to be walking around unguarded. And well, the minute I saw your karate moves, I just knew you were the one for the job.' He's so sarcastic.

I giggle despite myself. 'Well, I'm glad I could have been some help.'

I decide to walk him to his door in a desperate attempt to stay with him longer. I hear some music as I get closer to his door. I wrinkle my forehead in confusion. It's probably the first time I've heard modern music since I moved here. It feels strangely unnatural.

'Oh, shit.' He puts his hand up to his forehead, as if remembering something. 'My housemate must have invited some people back.'

No way. Someone in this village having a party? I'm immediately itching to get in there. It's like a magnet pulling me in. Could I…

'Do you wanna come in for a drink?'

I stare at him in complete shock. He smiles mischievously, a sexy glint in his eye. Does he want to party with me?

'Read my mind,' I grin.

I'm suddenly up for a party. And the tingling sensation in my Lulu has nothing to do with it.

Chapter 12

He leads me into a dimly lit living room filled with people. I'm surprised to see that it's bigger than Elsie's, but obviously not as nice. The flowery curtains look like they should have been thrown out years ago and the carpet feels worn under my boots. He leads me into the small wooden clad kitchen and introduces me to everyone. I wave politely, but forget their names as soon as I hear them. He pours me a vodka and coke and hands it over. When he's not looking I pour some more vodka in. I need to catch up with everyone. I feel stupidly self-conscious being the outsider.

By 3am I'm *slightly* tipsy and I've got the major horn. Will hasn't been sitting with me and it's really pissing me off. My eyes have followed him around the room while he's chatted to bloody everyone except me. His eyes have sought me out almost every time I stared, as if he sensed I was looking at him. I've watched as he laughed heartily, dribbling a bit of beer out of his mouth and catching it with the back of his hand. I've watched while he stuck the tip of his tongue to the corner of his mouth when he was interested in something someone was saying. It's too much. I've waited enough.

It's like I can feel it building in me and I need the release of his touch. Desperately. Before I combust. I excuse myself to go to the toilet, just wanting to see his room. Maybe sit on his bed. That's all.

I let myself into his room like the stalker I am. I recognise his hoody on the floor and I pick it up to smell it like the loser I am. Before I know what I'm doing I'm stripping down to my bra and knickers and jumping under the covers, a thrill of excitement buzzing through me.

Only…well, now I'm here I'm not so sure this is a good idea. I mean…he might just tell me to piss off. I could have completely misread the signs. But then, he's not going to refuse a drunk girl in his bed, right?

I hear footsteps on the stairs and hide under the duvet, realising it's too late to run. I brace myself for his shocked face. A tingle of excitement runs through me, though. I can't wait.

The door opens and someone stumbles in. That's weird; I didn't think Will was drunk. Maybe he's one of those drunks that always appear sober. Then I hear a giggle. What the fuck? Will doesn't giggle. And it weirdly almost sounded like…I hear them lip smacking aggressively against each other. Oh my God. I peer out from the duvet to see him kissing some brunette girl passionately, about to fall on the bed. My heart plummets. Shit. What the fuck am I going to do now?

I feel the bed dip as they collapse down next to me. I look at them in horror. I *have* to get out of here, while I can contain some dignity. AWKWARD! I roll and drop myself onto the floor. THUD. It leaves a silence. That and an aching hip! Ouch! I bite my lip so I don't cry out.

'Did you hear that?' she asks. God, she sounds girly. I hate her.

I hold my breath over the giant pause. She doesn't get a response. Just a grunt and then the gross lip smacking noises again. Ugh! Just the thought of someone else's lips on his is like a dagger to my heart. I need to get out of here before I let this humiliation take hold of me.

I crawl around the bed, grabbing my strewn clothes. Why did I have to strip so dramatically? Maybe my mother was right and I should fold them neatly in one place. I start commando style crawling out of the room when I hear a gasp.

'Oh, Jay!' she coos in ecstasy.

Jay? I sit up and look closely. It's Jay, not Will. Thank God. I must be in the wrong room. Relief washes over me. It's not Will. He's still mine for tonight. Well, unless he's already in there with someone else.

I crawl out of the room and stand up, running into the next one. Now that I'm in here it does seem more Will. He has proper curtains and blinds for one. The place is just generally cosier. As I crawl under the red covers I also notice that his sheets are far cleaner. I push my face into his pillow and smell the Ylang fragrance, mixed in with his own mint and soapy smell. God, I could eat the pillow.

I push myself up by my elbows and take a look around. It's all so perfectly organised. I wouldn't even be surprised if this was a woman's room, it's so clean. Just a small desk next to a wardrobe. I pick up the photo frame on his bedside table. It's a little boy with a woman in her thirties with long auburn hair. They're both on a horse and when I look closer I realise its Mitsy. That must be his mum. I can see where he gets his looks from. She's breathtakingly beautiful.

Footsteps begin to bound up the stairs, so I quickly place it back and slide under the covers, my hair pooling above my head. I hear him enter, the door creaking on its hinges, but I'm suddenly scared that this isn't a good idea. I should have run when I had the chance. Why do I let vodka make my decisions?

I'm expecting a gasp or something, but instead I hear him unbuckle his belt and get undressed. My scalp prickles with nerves. Doesn't he notice a big lump in his duvet? I'm hardly invisible.

The bed cover is pulled back and he squeezes into bed next to me. I can feel his body heat warming my skin, even though we're not touching. The anticipation is killing me. This is quickly becoming humiliating. He's not saying or doing anything. I turn round to face him, smiling shyly.

'Hi,' he smiles, completely unshocked. 'Do you make a habit of sleeping in strange men's beds uninvited?' he asks, scrutinising me.

'You think you're strange?' I smirk, ignoring the question. I seriously need to get the upper hand back here.

'Maybe,' he grins. God, that *dimple.* 'But I can't be that bad, or you wouldn't be sleeping in my bed right now.' He puts his arm under the pillow, propping his head up.

'Who said I want to sleep?' I purr seductively, pushing my boobs out with a wink. Thank God I only wear lacy matching underwear. Tonight I'm wearing my neon pink one with black polka dots.

His eyes become hooded, hunger flooding them. His chest rises and falls faster than normal, but he looks unsure. God, I want him. All the more for being shy. He's bloody adorable. Maybe I need to *show him* how eager I am.

I lean into him and let the vodka buzz consume me. I cup his cheek in my small palm, relishing the feel of his soft skin, the softest hint of stubble beginning. I pull his lips to meet mine, and God, they feel incredible. Soft and sweet, but also powerful and in charge. He runs his hands through my hair, sending every nerve ending in my head into over drive and then rests them at the back of my neck. Oh God, I want him to touch me that delicately all over.

He presses me down against the mattress and hovers over me, smiling mischievously. He slowly draws his fingertips down my body, starting with my collarbone, past my nipple and navel, pausing just before getting to my Lulu. I smile against his mouth in anticipation. I cannot wait for this. I'm already panting, my heart in my mouth as if I might sneeze it out.

Just when I feel I'm about to combust with longing, he takes his hand away from me and pulls back, leaving me feeling cold and bereft. He lies down next to me with his hand behind his head again, as if nothing ever happened. What the hell? He smiles arrogantly, making me feel crazy angry.

'What's wrong?' I sound slightly more desperate than I was going for.

'Nothing.' He smiles broadly. 'But I'm not having sex with you.'

My mouth drops open. Did he *seriously* just say that? Did he really just refuse me? My jaw juts out as I start to sulk like a toddler.

'Why the hell not?' I whine. I don't mean for it to come out as pathetic and needy as it does, but I can't help it. How can he tease me like this and then just stop? He must have the willpower of an ox.

Then it hits me. He's too much of a gentleman. Of course; he thinks I've had too much to drink and obviously doesn't want to take advantage. Sweet, sweet Will. It only makes me want him more.

'I'm not drunk, you know.' I smile mischievously. 'I've only had a few drinks. Don't feel bad about that.' I stroke my finger down his chest. He's got just the right amount of light brown chest hair on his perfectly sculpted chest. He's bloody ripped, but not in a weird muscle man kind of way. That beautiful line of hair down from his belly button is leading to what I want. God, he's sexy.

He smiles devilishly and climbs over me again. My breath accelerates. His smell is incredible; mint and soap invading my nostrils. I wish I could bottle it. Or at least steal his pillow to sleep with. This is it. Me and him. It's gonna happen.

He looks at me seriously. 'Rose, no matter what you might think, I'm not being a perfect gentleman here. I *will* fuck you.'

My mouth gapes open.

'But when I do, you will be completely sober, you'll be officially mine, and there won't be anyone else in the house to hear us, because, believe me; you'll make a lot of noise.'

I'm stunned into silence, my mouth gaping open so wide he can probably see my tonsils. I try to discreetly shut it and compose myself, but my head is spinning. Just hearing him speak like that makes me want to chain him to the bed and take him against his will. Officially *his?* What does he mean by that?

'Good luck,' I snort. 'No one has managed it yet.'

He narrows his eyes on me questionably.

'O...kay,' I stammer, swallowing down the lump in my throat. I look at the bed, unable to talk. Well, this is awkward. 'I...suppose I'll go then.' I sit up and swing my legs over the side of the bed, resigned to going home alone and unsatisfied.

No matter what he's said I still feel rejected and humiliated. I've never been refused sex before. Ever. It stings like he's hit me in the chest. Probably my pride dying.

Will's arm is around my waist, pulling me back into bed in an instant. I look up to him as he leans over me with an affectionate smile.

'Why would I want you to go?' His face turns serious, as if he's worked it out. 'Do you think sex is all you're worth or something?'

Do I? I think back to every relationship I've had. If I could call them that. I don't think I've ever just hung out with a guy without it ending in sex. Is that weird? It's never *felt* weird. I've only ever done what I wanted to do at that moment. Even if I do regret it in the morning.

I look away from him, unsure of what to say. I'm embarrassed and half naked. It's a bad combination. He grabs my chin, forcing me to look back into his probing eyes.

'I'll answer the question for you.' He locks his pale green eyes with mine so intensely that if he wasn't holding my face I'd probably pass out. 'You're worth far more than that.'

I feel myself physically swoon, melting into his touch. Where the hell has this even come from? I was up for a quick shag, but I had no idea he really liked me like that. Hell, liked me at all.

I feel so exposed, up close and unable to look away from him. Not that I'd really want to. I could look into his eyes forever. But why is he being so nice to me if he doesn't want sex right now? I don't get it.

'So…what do you want to do instead?' I ask awkwardly, clasping my hands together in my lap.

'I'm tired,' he yawns. 'I want to sleep and I think you should too. So roll over and let me spoon you.'

Is he for real? Or have I fallen asleep downstairs and this is all a dream?

I grin, giggle, and follow his orders happily. He presses his warm body against me, and it's then I realise that he has a raging erection. He *does* want me.

'Are you *sure* you don't want to play? Your body is telling me different,' I tease, reaching my hand back to grasp it.

He grabs my hand and places it back in front. 'Don't listen to Big Willy. He's always hard.'

I laugh at the nickname, my shuddering giggles vibrating off his strong chest. He pulls my hair away from my face, tucks it behind my ear and then kisses the back of my neck. It's so tender and sweet that it makes me tingle.

'Goodnight, Rose.'

As if I'm going to be able to sleep with that thing tempting me. I think Big Willy and Lulu are going to be great friends.

***

Sunday 19th October

'Rose!' Elsie calls up the stairs. 'You have a visitor!'

Ugh. My head rattles. I got next to no sleep last night while Will seemed to snore happily away. I got up at six and snuck away, retreating back under my own warm duvet. The thought of having to face him was too much. I drag myself out of bed and stomp down the stairs, not bothering to look in the mirror. Whoever it is can fuck off anyway.

Elsie's grinning like a Cheshire chat. What does she look so happy about? I squint at her questionably as I swing the door open to find Will.

'Are you ready?' he asks, smiling casually as if I didn't spend the night in his bed. He's wearing a navy beanie hat, which only seems to make him more utterly gorgeous. I have to physically stop myself from drooling.

Ready? What is he talking about? Then I remember. Shit. I completely forgot we'd arranged to go to the stables today to attempt to ride Mitsy. But then, I thought he said he'd only think about it? I was sure that was a no. Nothing was properly arranged. I can tell he's nervous. He's biting his thumb nail, which I've noticed he seems to do when he's unsure.

'Uh…yeah.' I put my hand to my hair, realising it must be standing up in all directions. I must have panda eyes too. He grins roguishly, as if reading my mind. 'Let me just get ready.'

I close the door and run upstairs, ignoring Elsie's grin. I have to make myself look half decent.

Five minutes later I'm bounding down the stairs apprehensively. I mean, is he going to mention last night at *all?*

We walk the long stretch to the stables in awkward silence. We change Mitsy out of her pyjamas, let her out, and lead her towards the field.

'So where shall we go?' I ask, avoiding his gaze. I wonder if there are any pretty paths along here that he knows of. I've only just started looking after her so I've just cantered around the field.

His face drops, fear evident in his eyes. 'What? I thought we were just gonna ride around the stables?'

'What's the point in that?' I grin, loving the shock on his face. 'No, I'm taking you for a ride.'

I only wish that were true. I can still remember the feel of his erection pressing into my back.

'You know I can hear your dirty mind at work,' he says, wiggling his eyebrows. 'Stop being such a pervert and follow me up.'

How does he do that? He puts his leg into the stirrup and swings his leg over Mitsy. He sits back in the saddle and reaches out his hand. It's only when I look closely I realise he's shaking. Bless him. Trying to be all Tarzan-like in front of me. I ignore his hand and climb up, sitting myself in front of him.

'Why do I have to be up front? Can't I be behind you, like on a motorcycle?'

'Because you're smaller than me,' he says, his voice strained. He's really scared, bless him.

He kicks his legs and Mitsy starts walking along. His arms find their way around my waist, sending electronic currents of desire through me. Every now and again his chin drops down to rest on my shoulder. I roll my eyes, but it's bloody adorable. What is happening to me?

He leads me out of the stables field and along a deserted dirt track. He seems to know where we're going so I let him lead.

'Do you think I'm a bastard?' he blurts out from nowhere.

I try to turn and look at him, but Mitsy starts to freak out.

'What?' I ask.

Is he talking about last night? Because he refused sex?

'For letting my mum down.' He drops his head onto my shoulder again. I think it's sweet until I realise it's so I can't turn and look at him. He's so manipulative.

'Letting your mum down? What are you talking about? How the hell have you let her down? By not riding Mitsy? That's stupid,' I snort. Whoops. Try not to sound like a pig, Rose. Men don't normally find them attractive, and if they do they're not the type of men you want to know.

'Nice snort, porky pig,' he laughs. Damn. 'No. By not looking after James.'

I'm confused. James seems fine.

'He might seem okay,' he says, reading my mind again. 'But I basically abandoned him to look after dad all by himself when I went to uni. Then I got the job in Leeds. I never looked back. I just wanted to forget all about it. This place had too many memories. I only came back because of my grandad dying. It made me realise that life was still continuing here, regardless of where I was.'

I'm not really sure what to say to that. Deep and meaningful does not mesh well with me. The deepest conversation I've had with Janey was what we'd do if a guy asked to be exclusive with her.

'What did you do at uni?' I ask, trying to change the subject.

'I studied accountancy.' I hear the smile in his voice.

I roll my eyes, knowing he can't see me. God, even his course was boring.

'And you didn't die from boredom? Honestly, Will, only the biggest bores become accountants.'

I feel him smile into my shoulder. 'Well then you've clearly never been to a firms Christmas party. They get freaky!' He chuckles.

Freaky? Images of drunk accountants in grey getting spanked in the stationary cupboard flashes through my mind. Possibly because I lost a job that way. Oh, but Billy Ruthers was *so* worth it. I shake my head to get rid of the delicious image.

'So, what, you're telling me you honestly get excited over numbers?'

He sighs heavily. 'Numbers are straight forward. They can't be interpreted. It's just right or wrong in any language. I like that.'

I suppose that makes sense to some extent.

'Loser,' I giggle. I lean back, secretly revelling in the feeling of being in his arms. A calming feeling settles over me. I realise it's me feeling content. I look straight ahead, revelling in it. I spot an old dilapidated building with old grey stones. 'What's that?'

He follows my pointed finger. 'Oh, it's the old castle. It's been in ruins forever. No one ever comes this far.'

I feel him tense his arms up and I realise it's because he's noticed how far we've come.

'Can we look at it closer?' Maybe if I take his mind off riding again he might start to relax.

He guides Mitsy towards it and helps me down into his strong arms. It's strangely romantic and reminds me of how Betty said girls used to be courted in her day. I walk to the wall and start to stroke the cold stone. I wonder what kind of shit went down in an old place like this. I bet a lot of debauchery.

'You like old buildings?' he muses. 'I wouldn't have had you down as the sort.'

'To what? Appreciate beauty? Thanks, Will,' I snort. He must think I'm just a sex mad bimbo.

'Hey,' he protests, turning my chin so that I face him. 'You know I didn't mean that.'

He plants a quick feather light kiss on my lips. My legs almost go weak with the hunger for him. He's treating me too nicely and not following through with sex.

That's it. I can't wait any longer. I need to know what the hell is going on between us.

I pull away so there's some distance between us. 'What is this?'

He starts chewing his lip, his eyes puzzled. 'An old castle. I told you.'

'You know what I mean,' I say while hitting him on the chest, trying to hide my smile. God, it's perfect. 'What's going on between us?'

'Easy. You're mine,' he answers with a cool smile. 'You just don't realise it yet.'

I'm his? He's so fucking cryptic. It's really starting to piss me off.

'If I'm yours then take me! Why can't we have sex?' I demand, my hand on my hip. I sound *slightly* more hysterical than I planned.

He scrunches his forehead. 'I've told you, Rose, not yet.' He seems annoyed. He has no bloody right to be. 'And we shouldn't be public yet.'

Wow. That stings more than it should. He's ashamed of me. Ashamed of the village whore.

'Fuck you, Will!' I spit, turning and stomping away. To where I have no idea. I didn't pay attention on the way here. I was too busy relishing in the feel of Will pressed up against me. Bloody idiot.

He grabs my arm roughly and swings me round to face him.

'I'm not ashamed of you, if that's what you think,' he snaps, his eyes pissed. 'I think we just need to get this incentive programme over with first. I don't want people to think you're getting preferential treatment at the home. I'd hate to ruin your chance of winning.'

Oh…yeah. That makes sense. I need to win to get to Mexico. Only…well, now the thought of leaving this village makes a sadness burn heavily in my heart, which is weird. I'm not going to change all my plans for a bloody man. Especially one who is refusing sex.

I need to change the subject. I should never have asked. Wow, he's going to think I'm in love with him or something. 'Oh, and what did the police want the other day?' I ask as casually as possible.

'Proper bizarre.' He crinkles his forehead. 'They wanted to check what our policy was on residents dying.'

'Huh?' How random.

'I know,' he nods. 'They wanted me to know that any deaths need to be registered, regardless of whether there are any living relatives. It was so strange.'

That really is strange. Uh-oh. It hits me like a bullet. Oh my God. Eric. It's Eric. It's that stupid bullshit story I told him about residents dying of the plague. Only he's gone and had a hissy fit, crying to the police. I need to find him before this gets out of hand.

'Hmm, very strange.' I nod vaguely, hoping he'll change the subject.

***

‘So how did you leave it?’ Megan asks me, leaning over the bar as she sips her lemonade. I’ve obviously filled her in on my romantic afternoon with Will.

‘He seemed quite sad and quiet for a bit so we just said bye.’

‘No kiss?’ She sounds so disappointed.

‘Sssshhh!’ I hiss. ‘Keep your voice down. This could cause me to lose my job.’

‘Oh, because I’m sure you always wanted to be a care worker when you were growing up,’ she snorts.

Chapter 13

Tuesday 21st October

I hid all day yesterday at the care home. I was petrified of bumping into Will before I work out what's going on between us. It's Tuesday morning and I still have no bloody idea. I still don't even understand when I even really started to like him. *Since I realised he was sexy as fuck.* No, shut up.

And what about his brother that I was previously shagging? This could all get awkward. Well, awkward for me anyway.

Today, everywhere I turn Will's there, winking at me with a sly grin on his face. And I can't help but smile like a big bloody girl! Since when did I get this gooey over men? It's this bloody village turning me crazy. Although at least this weekend opened my eyes to see that people still manage to have fun here. There does seem to be a secret night life, only it runs in the form of house parties.

I've just broken up another bitch fest between Betty and Peggy when I see Will welcome an official looking woman into the building. Who the hell is she? She's wearing a navy suit and has harsh looking spectacles resting on her nose. Definitely not one to fit in here.

He starts leading her upstairs as a bad feeling makes itself home in my tummy.

I run over to Beth and pull on her arm. 'Who's the suit?' I nod towards them disappearing up the stairs.

'No idea.'

'Crap.'

Is she here to assess us or something? Did he tell on me for trying it on with him? He wouldn't do that after Sunday, right? Unless he's a two-faced evil bastard.

'Let's look at the sign in book,' she offers.

I practically run over to the reception desk and run my finger down the people log.

Felicity Meller, Yorkshire Social Services.

What the fuck?

My stomach hits my toes as it comes to me. Peggy. Could this really be about Peggy? Because I said she shit herself? I run back into the lounge and look around for her, but I can't see her anywhere. Double crap.

'Has anyone seen Peggy?' I shout frantically, quickly losing my mind. Way to play it cool, Rose.

'Someone told her to go to her room. Has a visitor.' Archie explains as he puts his teeth back into his mouth.

Oh God, I'm going to vomit. This is bad. *Seriously* bad. Why the hell did I ever think pooing in a bucket was a good idea? And why is Will such a bloody jobs worth! He should have just left it.

I run up the stairs, taking them two at a time and then along the narrow corridor to her room. The door is ajar slightly so I peer in. Peggy is sitting up in her bed, while the suit leans over her with a clipboard.

Think, Rose. You have to do something to sort this out. This is *your* shit storm. Literally.

'Peggy! I sing, swinging the door open. 'Here you are!'

Will looks at me, bewildered.

'She's always running away from me, this one,' I explain to the woman. 'Has the energy of a twenty year old!'

Mrs Meller lowers her glasses and inspects me. 'And you *are?*'

'I'm Rose.' I raise my hand and do an awkward wave.

Will shoots me a look which I think says 'what the hell are you doing here?' I ignore him.

'Rose, we're in the middle of something,' he says nicely enough, but only I can tell he wants to drag me out of here and ask what the hell I'm doing.

'Of course, William,' I smile sweetly, excusing myself. 'A quick word outside?'

He takes my arm to guide me out, more forcibly than needed. As soon as the door is shut behind us he narrows his eyes on me.

'What?' he asks bluntly.

'Why is that woman here? What's going on?' I ask in a hushed whisper.

He rolls his eyes. 'You know its policy not to discuss our patients. Patient confidentiality.'

God, he's infuriating.

'Cut the bullshit, Will,' I snap impatiently. 'Why the fuck is she here?'

He glares furiously at me long and hard before giving in. 'She's here to assess Peggy.'

'Assess what?' I shriek. I realise I'm on my tiptoes leaning dangerously up into his personal space.

He lowers his voice to a whisper, looking around to check if anyone is near before speaking. 'Whether she can continue to live here.'

'Why the fuck wouldn't she?' I demand, my stomach feeling sicker by the second.

'Mind your language,' he hisses, furrowing his brows. 'You told me yourself she's having problems controlling her bowels. This home can't cater for that type of care. She needs proper care.'

'She doesn't! I'm sure it was just a one-time thing!' I whine. I'm starting to sweat.

'I don't have time to argue with you, Rose. I have to do what's best for Peggy.' He opens the door and walks back in, leaving the door to slam in my face.

Fuck. I've just fucked over Peggy. I should really just walk away. Just let them find out for themselves that she's fine and she can stay here. Only…what if they make the wrong decision and she's transferred all because of me? I couldn't live with myself. I'm walking back into the room before I change my mind.

They all turn to look at me again, Will's face maddened. I'm seriously pissed off.

I try to blend in and busy myself folding some of her clothes. They watch me until it's clear to them I'm not going away.

'Peggy, do you often have incontinence problems?' Mrs Meller asks her.

'Incontinence?' Peggy blurts out in revulsion. 'Isn't that when a man can't get himself…to stand to attention?' she whispers.

I burst out laughing, unable to stop myself. Will shoots me an irritated look.

'No, Peggy,' he smiles. 'It means having problems where you can't make it to the toilet in time,' he explains.

Her face slowly registers what he's saying and she's immediately appalled. 'William! How could you ask me such an awful question?'

'It's okay, Peggy,' he says in a soft, encouraging voice. He perches on her bed. 'It's nothing to be ashamed of.'

'I'm not ashamed about anything, William,' she snaps, her face like thunder. 'Because I don't have a problem.'

'Are you having any problems with your memory?' Mrs Meller asks, scrawling something on her clipboard.

'My memory? Of course not!' she shrieks, sounding highly offended.

'Look, Peggy,' Will tries to reason. 'We know about the…incident. We're just trying to establish if it was a one-time thing or if you've been struggling for a while.'

'The only thing I'm struggling with is you rambling on about nonsense!' She's getting red in the face now. 'I still remember you being potty trained and, let me tell you, it took you a good few years to get out of those training pants!'

I bite my lip to stop it from breaking into a grin. Will looks back at me, his face resigned. 'Maybe you can reason with her?'

All eyes turn to me. Me? I'm the one who's got us in this bloody mess! But he's not to know that. He obviously thinks I'm here because I care.

'I'm not sure what I can do,' I say quietly, wondering if I can run from the room without them suspecting anything is wrong.

'You were there, Rose,' he encourages. He smiles, his eyes wrinkling, pleading for help.

'There?' Peggy asks, confused. 'Rose, what on earth is he talking about?' She looks at me, pleading for my help.

'Um...' They're all staring at me now. There's no way out of this. 'They know about...the incident,' I mumble, tripping over my words.

Please let her think this is about something else.

'Oh,' she nods, seeming to understand. 'Yes, that. If you're thinking I'm sorry then I'm not. I'd do it again!'

She must think I'm talking about her fight with Betty.

'You'd do it again?' Will repeats, scratching his head in confusion.

'You bet I would!' she shrieks, crossing her arms stubbornly over her chest.

Oh for God's sakes. This doesn't look good. She'd hardly be bragging about pooing!

Will looks between me and Peggy. 'Are we talking about the same thing? About the...poo?' he whispers.

Peggy's face scrunches up in disgust. 'Poo? What bloody poo?' She looks at me demandingly.

All of their eyes are on me now. I feel a flush of embarrassment flurry in my chest, spreading upwards to my cheeks. I look down at the floor, so they can't stare at me any longer, but I can still *feel* their eyes on me. What the hell am I going to say?

'You know, Peggy,' I smile sweetly, deciding on a whim to brash it out. 'The poo. I'm afraid I had to tell Will.'

I'm afraid she's going to have to go down after all. I *cannot* be known as the girl who pooed in the cardboard bucket. It's just not an option.

'Tell Will what?' she scrunches her eyes up, narrowing them on me. 'Rose, I have no idea what you're talking about.'

Will's brows furrow, as if he might be doubting me for a second. I'm tempted to flash a boob to distract him.

'She's got a terrible memory,' I say to Mrs Meller. 'Mind like a sieve!' I laugh, unnaturally high pitched.

'Do you often forget things, Peggy?' She turns back to us. 'This could be early signs of dementia. Then she'd be looking at going into a special dementia home.'

Oh my God. I'm sending her off to a loony bin.

'No, she's not senile!' I yell. Keep it cool, Rose. Don't lose it.

'Of course I'm not!' she squeals, her cheeks red with panic. 'I just didn't have an incident involving poo!'

This is going to end badly. I start backing out of the room. Maybe if there's so much confusion they won't even notice me run for the hills.

'Rose,' Will says turning round to me, just as my hand is on the door handle. 'If it wasn't Peggy's poo…what could it have been?' He studies me, his green eyes growing suspicious.

'Um…'

Shit, shit, shit.

'Rose?' Will says again, staring at me, his eyes almost penetrating my soul. 'Was it…Peggy's poo?'

I can't believe were having such a stressful conversation around poo.

'Umm…' My hands are clammy and my legs are turning to jelly. Think, Rose! For fuck sakes, THINK!

'Well?' Mrs Meller demands, glaring at me.

The room is starting to spin around me. I hang my head in shame. Trying to remain a shred of dignity.

'No.'

'Well if it wasn't Peggy's poo, then whose was it?' he asks, looking between us all.

'It was…' think of someone, Rose! But I can't think. All I can do is feel; feel the sweat forming on my lower back. Feel their eyes on me. Feel their suspicion.

'And before you answer, remember that this is going to be taken extremely seriously,' Mrs Meller reminds me, glaring at me behind her spectacles.

'It was…' I swallow the lump in my throat and clamp my eyes shut. 'It was…mine.'

I drop my head, listening to their disgusted gasps. Oh dear bloody God. Please God, take pity on me and strike me down dead.

'Shit,' they all mutter at the same time.

You're telling me.

***

'So, wait,' Elsie says, gasping for air as she wets herself giggling. 'You admitted to pooing in that thing yourself?'

I stare down at the carpet ashamed, but also feeling the intense urge to giggle. It's just too ridiculous. Plus, I've never seen Elsie laugh so much, especially about something so stupid. I just assumed she'd tell me off.

'Don't laugh!' I throw myself back onto the sofa and cover my face in my hands. 'I'm mortified!'

Just thinking of their faces again brings back a fresh dose of helplessness.

'Well, I'm proud of you!' She pours herself another glass of red wine and fills up my glass.

She really drinks a lot of red wine for someone claiming to be a wannabe nun.

'Why the hell would you be proud of me?' I laugh. 'Yeah, I can poo with the best of them! Hardly one to brag about.'

Oh God. Will word get around? Will I get a cruel nickname? I *cannot* be called *Winnie the Pooh*, or worse…something like *shit bag*. Or *hers don't smell like Roses*. I shudder at the thought.

'But you told the truth,' she grins, her lips already turning purple from the wine. 'You *could* have lied and you told the truth to save Peggy.' Marbles the cat jumps on her lap, meowing loudly.

'Only when I was backed into a corner! I lied until I *couldn't* anymore.'

Oh God, why did I ever think it would be a good idea to poo in a bucket? I wasn't even drunk. This is going to haunt me until the day I die.

'I'm still proud of you,' she smiles, leaning over and patting my hand like a dog. Marbles gives me a dirty look. She's clearly not proud. She barely tolerates me.

'Thanks,' I snarl sarcastically, secretly loving her affection. I can think of only a handful of times in my life someone told me they were proud of me. And one time it was after a blow job, followed by a high five. 'I doubt Will is though.'

I can't get the look on his face out of my mind. Every time I see his fallen confusion my stomach flips over and I feel queasy. The worst thing was that he didn't say anything. Mrs Meller just told him she was leaving. I heard her go. I didn't look up. I was too mortified.

When I eventually did look up he just stared at me, complete disappointment in his eyes. Then he left the room without uttering a single word. I wish he'd shouted or something. The silence was far worse. And knowing I've let him down makes me feel so evil. But I have a plan to take my mind off it.

'Which is why you need to help me plan this outdoor cinema thing. It's the only way I can redeem myself,' I declare, nodding with determination.

If Will sees me selflessly doing something for the community he'll have to see I've got a heart after all.

'I thought you didn't care what he thought?' Her eyes light up, as if she's just realised something. 'You fancy him! I knew it!' she shrieks with undeniable glee.

'No, I don't!'

She grins knowingly. 'So where did you stay out to on Saturday then?' she asks with a sly smile.

How does she know this? I thought I'd snuck in without her noticing. She can't be a nun; she's got the natural reflexes found in a mother.

'They were having a party,' I shrug. 'I passed out on the sofa.' I pretend to inspect a finger nail.

'Oh, purlease!' she sneers. 'Next you'll be saying boys are yucky.' She chuckles, spilling some wine onto her pink fleece pyjamas.

'Oh, coming from you, desperate to join the nunnery. You can't love dick if that's how you feel.'

Her face contorts in disgust. Oops. Why did I have to be so mean?

'Don't be crass, Rose,' she snaps, her eyes filling with some heavy emotion.

'I'm right though.' I can't help but press her. Something in her face tells me there's a story somewhere. Anything to get her off the Will subject. I'm confused enough as it is, although I'm sure the poo thing means he never wants to see me again, let alone kiss me.

She ignores me, choosing to stroke Marbles instead. I can't help let curiosity taking hold.

'What happened, Elsie? How did you suddenly decide to give it all up?'

She looks away, but I can tell she's deciding whether to tell me or not. Please, Elsie, I beg inside. Confide in me.

'There was a guy…'

'I knew it!' I laugh triumphantly. 'It's *always* over a guy. But don't you think that's a stupid reason to join a-'

'Let me finish,' she interrupts, suddenly looking upset. She's breathing heavier and not looking me in the eye.

What a drama queen. 'Sorry, go on.'

'Well…it was quite simple really.' She takes a large gulp of wine. 'He was the one.'

The *one?* How bloody dramatic. Someone's seen The Notebook one too many times. No wonder she wants to join the nunnery if she's expecting guys to act like Ryan Gosling.

'And how did you know that?' I ask sarcastically.

Her eyes become moist, making me realise what a heartless bitch I am.

'Well…it's a little embarrassing.' Her cheeks start to flush red.

I roll my eyes. Is she serious? 'Els, I just told you I pooed in a bucket. I'm pretty sure there are no boundaries between us anymore.'

She giggles loudly with a snort escaping at the end. It must run in the family.

'Well…' she begins. I make myself comfortable on the sofa, wishing I had popcorn. 'He's the only man to have ever…given me an…an orgasm.'

My mouth drops open. I don't know if it's because Elsie just said the *word* orgasm or because she's had the same problem as me. Only she cured it. How the hell did she cure it?

'No way?!' I shout, a bit pissed off. 'I can't get an orgasm no matter how hard I try.'

And I've been trying, let me tell you.

'That's how I knew,' she nods, staring ahead into the fire. 'I fell in love,' she whispers with a sigh. 'My mum used to say the women in our family were cursed by a witch. We can only orgasm when we're in love.'

No way! It sounds stupid and far-fetched, but it would make sense.

'Anyway, he didn't want to be serious and go public, so we ended it. I knew if I couldn't have him I didn't want any other man for as long as I live.'

Wow. That's some bloody declaration.

'Jesus Christ, Elsie. He must be shit hot in bed!' I gush, chuckling hard. I can still remember Will's warm hands on me.

'Lord's name in vain!' she abolishes, as if I'd just said *he* was shit hot in bed. 'It wasn't just that. We connected. I'm sure he felt it too, but he was scared.'

'Scared of what?'

Was she a really full on girlfriend? I could imagine her clingy. Or is part of the curse that when we do orgasm we try to kill the guy afterwards? Like one of those weird insects.

'Who knows?' She smiles weakly, a delicate tear falling down her face.

'Who was he?' I have an overwhelming urge to pummel him in the face. Anyone around here must know what Elsie's like. They clearly took advantage of her sweet nature.

'No one.' She wipes the tear away quickly and straightens up. 'He's no one to me anymore.' Marbles shoots me an evil look, as if to say 'see how you've upset her?' 'But maybe Will is your one. It's worth a try, right?' She looks hopeful.

I smile, trying to work out if I heard her right.

'Sorry, Elsie, nun-to-be, but are you telling me to have sex with Will?' I ask incredulously.

She locks her wide eyes with mine. 'If it's for love, Rose, I'd tell you to walk over fire.'

Whoever he is, he sure broke her heart. And when I find him I'm going to break his arm.

***

Chapter 14

Wednesday 22nd October

Betty has not been to the lounge today so I head towards her room for a visit. She'll make me feel better. Beth comes bounding round the corner just as I open the door.

'Rose, Will wants to see you,' she says.

My stomach sinks. 'Okay,' I squeak.

Oh God, he's going to fire me. It took all of my courage to come in today, but it's been a waste of time. Goodbye orgasm. Goodbye Mexico. I suppose you can't miss the things you never had.

I walk into Betty's room anyway. I may as well get cheered up by her before, especially if I'm not allowed to see her again. The thought leaves me sadder than I would have thought. I've grown to love her like a Grandma I never had. We're alike in so many ways.

She's in bed again and looks like she's just woken up, her hair knotted and her face free of make-up.

'Hello, lazy bones,' I grin, forcing myself to sound cheery.

I wish I could get under those covers and never resurface.

'When you get to my age there's not much to be awake for,' she says, smiling weakly.

The smile drops from my face. God, what a terrible way to think. Someone's having a down day. I suppose I'm not the only one with problems.

'You look troubled, love,' she says, narrowing her brown eyes on me. 'What's on your mind?'

Bless her; worrying about me. I sigh and throw my head down on the bed. 'I've fucked it all up, Betty,' I whinge.

'Language, sweet heart,' she berates calmly.

I raise my head to look at her sweet, compassionate face.

'Sorry,' I sulk, biting down on my lower lip.

'Now tell me what you've done to make yourself so pale. Get my blusher. It's in my bag.' Bossy as ever, I see.

I grab her bag and let her apply so much blusher to my cheeks that I look like I've run a marathon and am about to keel over from a heart attack. I tell her everything, the whole shebang. When I'm finished I realise she started caressing my hair, as if I were a cat.

God, I love her. I don't think I've ever really felt looked after like this. My grandparents are dead and my mum never really liked me. She and my dad are GP's, so they work all hours, and at the end of the day I almost seemed like an inconvenience for them. They just wanted to crash on the sofa and I was there asking what's for dinner.

'Oh, Rose. You do make me giggle, my love.' She smiles compassionately at me. 'But it's hardly the end of the world.'

'That's easy for you to say. I'm about to get fired,' I say sadly.

Her face turns mischievous. 'I thought you and Will had a cheeky kiss?' She winks with a cheeky grin.

'Yeah. So?' I shrug. 'That doesn't mean he's in love with me. He's hardly going to just let this go.'

I shit in a bucket for God's sakes.

'You never know. Life's too short for grudges,' she smiles. I can always count on her to take my side. But I doubt she'd be saying this if we were talking about Peggy. She must be delirious with exhaustion, bless her. I overheard Ethel telling Billy that they snuck down to watch a film last night. Little rebels.

I look toward the door and think of the wrath waiting for me. Goodbye Mexico. I haven't wanted to admit it to myself, but I guess while Will and I were doing…well, whatever it was we've been doing, the possibility of not getting to Mexico didn't seem all that bad. Something about being promised an earth shattering orgasm. But now I'll have no Will, no Mexico, and soon no Betty. Great.

Oh well, no point delaying the agony.

'Anyways, I better go face the music.' I kiss her goodbye on her powdery soft cheek, inhaling her sweet talcum powdery smell, and close the door quietly behind me.

I take a steady deep breath. Come on, Rose. You can do this. You can face him. So what if he looks at you with more disgust than someone looking at a crocodile that's eating a hippo? So what? Why do I even care what he thinks? *Because he's gorgeous and you fancy the pants off him.* I wish that inside voice would shut up. She's such a slut.

I walk down the corridor, desperately trying to get a hold of myself. I feel like I'm about to meet the headmaster. *We think your black lipstick is breaking the uniform rules, Rose.* God forbid I go through a Goth phase. The truth is black lipstick suits me. I have no idea why. It just does. And I liked not conforming. I didn't grow my boobs until I was eighteen, so I had to be noticed some way.

I take another steadying breath and knock gently on the door. I know better than to storm in. I don't want to piss him off the minute he sees me.

'Come in,' his calm voice calls.

My legs tremble with fear. Shit, I'm nervous.

I force myself in and find him sitting at his desk, paperwork stacked up on either side of him. He's writing something down or maybe he's just pretending to write something down to look busy. I stand up against the wall, the furthest away I can get from him. I feel chilly, but it's more to do with his reception than the temperature. My nipples are completely unaffected.

He finally looks up, a blank expression on his face. I swallow, my mouth dry. It could really go either way right now. Then the edges of his lips start twitching. I'm not sure what's happening at first. Is he having a stroke? Should I call someone? Then, before I have time to question it, he's laughing. His eyes are creased and he's laughing his arse off, clutching at his sides, as if it's causing him physical pain.

I stand back, my mouth gaping open. I'm massively offended. How dare he laugh at me?! Am I really that bloody comical? But then I realise he's not pointing a finger and calling me a dickhead. He's laughing about the whole situation. This awful, humiliating situation. He's laughing *with* me.

A smile tugs on my lips, but I try to fight it. This isn't funny. Only the more I look at him, laughing with that adorable dimple on his left cheek popping up, the more I can't help it. I laugh, exploding into it suddenly, unable to control my body any longer. That only makes him laugh more, his chuckles getting deeper, as his eyes start to water.

I'm laughing so hard now I can't look at him. Every time I do he creases me over in a fresh dose of the giggles. My eyes are watering now too and I feel like I could pee. Muscles I didn't even know existed in my stomach are aching like I've done a million sit ups.

I fight against the hysteria, concentrating on slowing my breathing down long enough so I can talk.

'Why are you even laughing?' I force out.

'I'm sorry, Rose,' he says in between laughs, still clutching his sides and trying to wipe the tears from his eyes. 'It's just so outrageous. I mean, how do you even get yourself in this shit?' He smiles at me with affection.

'In this *shit*?' I giggle, smiling playfully.

He collapses over again. 'Honestly, you kill me!'

Well this is going better than expected.

'So…you aren't going to fire me?' I ask tentatively.

'Fire you?' he repeats, his face turning sober, before breaking into another beautiful smile. 'I don't think so. You're volunteering, for starters. That, and I'm pretty sure you've learned your lesson.'

My cheeks pink up at the reminder. I'll never get over this humiliation. I look down, avoiding his face. Anything but that dimple. I want to bite it. *So hard.*

'I have.' I nod, feeling utterly pitiable.

'Then you can get back to work. Unless…' I look up to see his eyes light up in excitement, but he seems unsure about whether he should finish the sentence.

'Unless what?' My voice shows how eager I am. Damn. I was going for unbothered.

'Unless you want to blow…no, don't worry.' He looks down, his cheeks blushing. Will blushes?

Blow? Is he…asking for a *blow job?* What's going on here? I thought he didn't want me to touch Big Willy?

'You're asking me for…a *blow job?'* I blurt out before I can stop myself. 'Is that why you've let me off with this? You think I'm going to blow you?' I ask, outraged.

What a bloody arsehole! Not that I'm not a little turned on at the thought. Quiet down, Lulu. It's just that if he thinks he can do me favours here in exchange for sexual favours, he has another thing coming. I have some standards. And there he was with that whole speech about keeping it professional at work. What a joker.

He looks back at me, his forehead creased and his mouth agape. That silenced him.

'Well, maybe if we were in a social situation and maybe if I wanted to, it'd be different,' I blabber, his silence unnerving me. 'Or if you'd have asked nicer. But, I mean, that's just rude.' I laugh to show how offended I am.

'Rose!' he shouts, putting his hands up to his ears. 'I wasn't asking for a blow job! Jesus!' He seems genuinely mortified.

'Well then, what were you asking?' I'm so confused. What else would he want me to blow?

'I was asking if you wanted to blow off the rest of the day and go for a drink? But don't worry.' He folds his arms over his chest and leans back in his chair, clearly having changed his mind about being anywhere near me.

'No! I mean…a drink? I could do with a drink.'

***

Three hours later I'm drunk. And I think I'm in love with Will. Well, not real Will. Fantasy fun Will that I've met today and over the weekend. He is so funny and adorable. And sexy and stubborn. I can't stop looking at his chest, knowing I was lucky enough to be pressed against it only a few days ago. It's so broad and muscular. I just want to drag my nails all over it and then soothe his pink skin with my tongue.

I'm not even *that* drunk! But Will seems to be keeping up with me, even though he's only on bottles of beer and I'm on vodka, lime and soda.

'You're cute when you pout,' I blurt out before I can stop myself.

He straightens up in is chair and pouts dramatically. 'Don't you think I'm cute all of the time?' He grins, showing off his perfect teeth. He must have worn braces. It'd be unfair to think they were naturally that straight.

'No, actually,' I say as I lean in close to him. We're sitting on the same side of the pub table so there's nothing between us. I can smell his aftershave. I'm not sure if I'm happy with him covering up his natural scent of soap and mint. 'Most of the time you're a pompous arse.' I smile, pleased at his stunned face.

'Gee, thanks,' he smiles, the hint of a blush on his cheeks. He takes another swig of beer.

A flash of red hair catches my eye and I realise Riley has arrived and is sitting next to him. Too fucking close. She's almost on his lap, her hands resting on his thigh. Little whore. I know we're supposed to be friends now, but if Will is going to be mine I have a feeling I'm going to be quite possessive. It's him filling me with all of this romantic nonsense.

'Rose, I'm so sorry,' she says, distressed. She runs her hand through her hair, her eyes sympathetic. 'I assume by the drinks that you've seen the posters?'

'Huh?' I slur.

What the hell is she talking about? I look to Will, but he looks just as confused as me.

I try to think through the vodka. Wait, did Elsie go ahead and get the posters of the outdoor cinema printed without me? It sounds like something she'd do. Damn busy body.

I open my mouth to respond, but she puts down an A4 poster to silence me. I know straight away it's not the pink themed template we chose over red wine. It's me. With my tits out.

Oh. My. God.

I slam my hand down to cover my nipples, sickened that Will's seen them. My head starts spinning and I know it's nothing to do with the vodka. Will's mouth gapes open in horror. Above my picture is written '*Would you trust this girl with your elderly care?*'

‘Oh my God,’ I mumble, my voice barely audible. I start hyperventilating, my breath unable to fill my lungs in time. I feel light headed and woozy.

‘Where the hell did you get this?’ Will demands, slamming his own hand down to cover the rest of my dignity.

I’m still reeling in shock. He’s going to hate me. Everyone’s seen my tits before him! He was trying to make me special, but I out-slutted myself yet again.

‘They’re all over the village,’ Riley says, scrunching her face up apologetically. She genuinely looks sorry for me.

I look closer at the picture, trying to work out if it’s old or new. I see that I’m wearing the same clothes as the other night when I went out with Elsie and Riley.

‘I’m so sorry, Rose. I thought when you walked off with Gerry you were just getting lucky.’ She cringes for me.

‘Huh?’

I don’t remember any of this. It must have been when I blacked out. Who the hell is Gerry? Surely I’d remember a guy photographing my tits? But then I do look pretty wasted. And why is she bringing up that I willingly went off with this guy in front of Will? I look so slutty.

‘That bastard Gerry’s gonna pay for this!’ Will shouts, banging his fist down hard again on the table.

‘You know him?’ I ask, still trying to take this all in.

Will’s reaction has attracted stares from the locals. I can't help but wonder if they’ve seen it. If they’re judging me. Silly little slut from London.

‘Aye,’ he nods. ‘Riley used to go out with him. He reckons I stole her off him. We’ve hated each other since. Then there was the whole feud between villages. But this is too far. Even for him.’

I can feel everyone’s eyes on me.

‘The whole village has seen my boobs?’ I hiss out in a distressed whisper.

It doesn’t matter how much I try to make a fresh start, I’m still going to let myself down.

'I have to get out of here.' I stand up onto wobbly legs, with Will following close behind.

'Don't worry, Rose,' he says determined. 'He'll pay.'

Thursday 23rd October

I cried all night. Well, in between trying to block out the filthy sounds coming from next door. They really don't seem to tire like normal people. It would be impressive, if it wasn't so gross.

Never before has something upset me so much. And I've had some pretty bad shit happen to me. Once I jumped on stage at a local gig and managed to fall off, exposing my arse to everyone. They called me Rose Bum for years.

I think it's because I had the chance of a fresh start here and now it's ruined. God, everyone has seen me naked! Not that I don't have great tits. I do. I really do. Well, apart from that badly placed freckle that could pass as a third nipple, but that's not my point.

Elsie storms through the door, making me jump. She stomps to the kitchen, throwing her keys on the side. Marbles suddenly appears from nowhere, meowing and pressing herself against Elsie's legs.

'What's wrong?' I ask, my mouth full of chocolate. 'Don't tell me they got you too?' I laugh. Even my laugh sounds fake.

'Don't be stupid,' she snaps, her face like thunder. 'I manage to keep my breasts *inside* my bra.'

Ouch. She might as well have thrown a knife at me.

'Who shit on your parade?' I whimper, my voice breaking. Do NOT burst into tears.

'No one.' She sits down and starts stroking Marbles. 'I just...' She takes a deep breath, obviously trying to calm herself down. 'I found out I can't watch television when I become a nun.'

Is she for real? My life is in ruins and she's talking about TV?

'Seriously?' I fume. 'This is why you're so upset? The whole village has seen my tits!'

I can't believe her! She's normally so selfless.

'I know, I'm sorry.' She sits down and pats my head. 'I just...I knew I was giving up my life, but...' She looks into the fire sadly.

‘But what?’ How can she be so bloody naïve?

‘Well, I suppose I didn’t think that would include Netflix. I mean, missing Orange is the New Black? I’m not sure I can do it.’ Her eyes well up, as if she’s going to cry.

‘THIS is what’s making you reconsider becoming a nun? A television programme?’ I ask in disbelief. She’s unbelievable.

‘Not just one, Rose,’ she snarls, her eyes shut. ‘I’ll miss *every* show.’

God, she’s ridiculous, but hey, whatever makes her change her mind has to be a good thing.

A knock at the door startles me, but I’m glad for the distraction. I swing the door open to find Will still looking as pissed off as when I saw him yesterday. Clearly time has not calmed him down. He pushes past me, his face determined.

‘Err…hi?’ I mumble.

‘I’ve figured it out,’ he announces, making himself comfortable on our sofa. He’s so big against it. I have to stop myself curling up in his lap and demanding he stroke me like Marbles. ‘I’ve figured out how we’re going to retaliate.’

This sounds interesting.

‘Retaliate?’ Elsie shrieks. ‘There will be *no* such thing!’

God, she’s such a goody two shoes.

‘You *are* joking, right?’ Will asks, his face disgusted and furious. ‘The bastard flashed her tits all over the village! He deserves to pay.’

I’ve never seen him so angry. He’s trying to protect my honour. It feels kind of awesome. And Lulu throbs, telling me she’s also impressed.

‘Well, I’m having no part of it!’ she shrieks, rushing upstairs.

Don’t pee yourself, Els. God, she's a baby.

I grin at him, rolling my eyes. ‘So, what’s the plan?’ I ask, an excited grin on my face.

I’m stupidly pleased at the idea of spending more time with him. I didn’t think he’d want to know me at all. I assumed he’d be completely ashamed to be seen anywhere near me.

'Easy. We give him a taste of his own medicine.' He smiles devilishly, his eyes lighting up with malice.

'And…that means?'

'Jay used to play rugby with them and says he has a tiny dick.'

I burst out laughing. Is he serious?

'We're going to get him drunk and take a picture of it.'

My eyes widen in shock. Wow, I'm impressed. Who knew Will had it in him?

'William, you're so cunning,' I joke. 'Who knew you had it in you?'

'But…' he shifts uncomfortably in his chair. 'Well, you'll need to get him drunk and flirt first.' He looks uneasy at having to ask me.

'You're whoring me out?' I giggle, raising one eyebrow in question. The thought of that prick's hands on my body repulses me.

'It's for a good cause,' he grins. 'So, I'll pick you up after work?'

'Okay,' I nod, a stupid dreamy smile spreading on my face.

Whatever you say, Big Willy.

***

I force myself into work at the pub that evening. Will says it will give me a bit of an alibi. He's thought this through so much its almost scary. Remind me never to piss him off. I'd really just like to be left alone with my thoughts of self-loathing, but I can't seem to get rid of Megan. She's dismissed the whole thing, explaining there was a girl in her year that it happened to.

'So it's my birthday next week and I'm not allowed a party. How stupid is that?' she moans, pouting her lips. 'It's only my sweet sixteenth!'

God, teenagers and their dramas.

'Why can't you have a party? You live in a pub.' I point around at all of the booze. 'Surely you'll have it here.'

'Not according to my dad,' she whinges, throwing her head down onto the bar. 'He said he doesn't want young people here drinking, risking his liquor licence.'

'I suppose I get that,' I reason. God, when did I grow up?

'Don't take his side!' she snaps. 'I'm only going to turn sixteen once. Plus everyone at school will think I'm some sad loser.' She looks at me, dead serious. 'Help me plan a secret party?'

'What? Where?' I pretend to wipe down the bar, feigning being busy. I really don't have time for this.

'Err…I was hoping you'd help with that too.'

I look up into her pleading face, her pout prominent, her brown eyes drooped.

I'm now planning children's birthday parties. My life gets more obscure by the second.

Chapter 15

'Are you sure you want to do this?' he asks as we wait in the car outside Gerry's house.

The plan changed slightly. Will picked me up after work and we headed to the bar Gerry works at. Only we found out he'd got shit faced drunk and gone home. We watched him stumble in half an hour ago, and I would bet anything he's completely passed out by now. We plan to break in and take the picture while he's asleep. Only this is better. I don't have to pretend I like him for more than a second. I wasn't sure if I could do it without squeezing my hands around his neck.

I nod my head. He grips my hand, squeezing it reassuringly as we get out of the car. I take a deep breath as we creep towards his back door. Just as Will thought, his spare key is under the mat. How bloody predictable. He opens the door, it making an enormous creaking noise. I nearly pee my pants.

'Ssssh!' Will whispers accusingly.

'I didn't say anything!' I hiss back.

He places his hand at the small of my back, sending tingles down to my toes.

'Upstairs,' he nods, pointing the way.

I let him lead me up the stairs, every step seeming to creak more than the last. I can feel adrenaline coursing through my veins. What if we walk in and he's murdered or something? What if we end up getting fingered as the murderers? I mean framed. Why am I thinking about being fingered? I need to get some. Lulu is lonely and Will continuing to touch me at every opportunity isn't helping.

Will points to a bedroom door and ushers me in. How he knows so much about his house I don't know. I'll have to ask him later. I walk in and find him asleep under a spider man duvet. His arms are hanging over his head, dribble on his pillow. Gross, but at least I know he's out for the count.

Will takes his camera phone out and I slowly, ever so slowly, pull the covers back. He's in Simpsons boxers. I swallow the disgusted feeling in my gut and quickly pull them down before Will has to ask me. I burst out laughing. He's got the smallest dick I've ever seen! It's actually comical. It's almost a vagina.

'Sssh!' Will snaps, covering my mouth with his hand.

He stirs, a low moan echoing through the room. I freeze in place, my own hand over his on my mouth. If he wakes up now we're in big trouble. He stills again and I nod for Will to take the photo. The room brightens up for a second with the flash.

'Got it,' he mouths.

I sigh in relief. Thank God for that. I slowly lower the bed spread back to cover him not wanting him to notice any foul play. Will takes my elbow and guides me out. I'm glad for the help. My legs feel like jelly. This is *so* illegal. It's basically breaking and entering. We walk down the stairs and out the door, placing the key back in its place under the matt.

'Thank God that's over,' I say, panting from my held breath. My body starts to de-clench itself.

'You can say that again,' he smiles, leaning back against the brick wall.

'Thank God that's over,' I say again, smiling from my little joke.

He grins, popping his adorable dimple.

'I mean it,' he says, his face turning serious and upset. 'Watching you touch him made me feel sick.'

He looks so possessive, his eyes blazing with some furious emotion.

'Wow, you must really hate him.'

I wonder what he did to him to get this reaction. Could it really be over Riley? If he still feels anger, does he still have feelings for her?

He stops to look at me earnestly, his green eyes staring intently at my lips. 'Or I just really like you.'

My breath leaves my body all at once. I stare back at his jealous face. He's jealous, over me.

Before I know what's happened, I'm being pushed against the wall by his sexy hips and my arms are placed around his neck. He pushes his lips on to mine roughly, as if he couldn't breathe without them. He lets go of my arms, my fingers intertwining in his glossy hair. I feel him smile against my lips before applying more pressure with his. He presses his chest harder against me until I'm almost being crushed. I like it though. Then I feel his erection.

Wowzas. I wasn't over playing the memory. Big Willy really is big.

He suddenly pulls away. My lips follow him until its clear he's not going to kiss me back. I open my eyes. He looks apologetic, running his hand through his already dishevelled hair.

'Sorry. We should stop. I'm sorry,' he says regretfully, his forehead creased in worry.

'Why?' I ask, dumbfounded and pissed off. I grab the collar of his shirt and pull him back to me, his lips meeting mine again. God they're sweet and warm. I never want them to leave mine.

He pushes me back, his arms on my shoulders. I glare at him as he puts his hands in his pockets.

'Because you're my employee. This is totally inappropriate. We need to wait.'

I almost burst out laughing, until I realise he's serious.

'*Wait?* Why the hell should we wait? What are we waiting for?' I sound so pathetic and needy. I don't care. I'm already trying to push back into his arms.

'Besides, I don't know you properly yet.' He smiles and tucks a bit of hair behind my ear. 'I can feel you holding yourself back still.'

'Holding myself back?' I shout, suddenly enraged. 'I'm offering myself to you on a plate. You've seen my tits, as have half the village. What the fuck am I not giving you?'

'And what beautiful tits they are,' he smiles. He strokes my face with his thumb. 'Good things come to those who wait.'

'Yeah, well, curiosity killed the cat and right now my pussy is dying a slow, painful death.' I turn on my heel and start to storm off. Fuck this; I'll walk home if I have to.

He laughs and grabs me around the waist, pulling me into him for a hug. A measly hug. How boring. Although it is nice being in his arms, smelling his scent and feeling warm and secure. God, I sound like a girl. See what he's doing to me?

'Come on,' he smiles. 'Let's get these posters made.' He grabs my hand and starts leading me back towards the car. I hesitate, suddenly not so sure if this is a good idea. 'What's wrong?' he asks, clearly noticing my trepidation.

'I'm not sure if we should retaliate,' I blurt out, without fully thinking it through myself.

'What?' he shouts, his mood swinging back to irritated in a second. 'Rose, the guy took advantage of you and spread pictures of it all over the village. He's lucky I didn't cut it off.'

Wow. This dark Will is different. And sexy as fuck.

'You're being dramatic,' I shrug.

'I'm being dramatic? That creep had his hands on you. God, just the thought of him touching you makes me want to kill the guy. You're mine, remember?'

He's so possessive. God, it's hot.

'Wow. I didn't realise you were so possessive. I kind of like it.'

'And you should,' he smiles. 'Think about it seriously before you decide.'

I just think Elsie might be right. What good can come of this? And what if he has more photos? He could post more and this could continue for months. Perhaps I should just be the bigger person for once.

'Why do you hate this guy so much anyway? There's clearly more to this than just me.'

He stares at me silently, chewing on his lip, obviously assessing whether he should tell me.

'He was one of the people who created this village rift.'

This village rift thing is ridiculous.

'What actually happened? It must be serious if you hate him this much.'

He sighs loudly, as if to portray how annoying I am. 'It's a long story,' he shrugs, as if to dismiss me.

'Fucking spill, Will!' I shout, drawing the attention of a neighbour who turns their lights on. 'Please,' I whisper, knowing he'll be upset with me. He grabs my hand and begins to walk us back to the car.

'We used to have a village rugby team. We played their village team and there was some argument about a tackle. The story goes that we blamed Damon Trevy for cheating. Only their village said we were lying and being racist. We were disgusted they'd dare call us racist and it kind of went on from there. We heard stories back and forth about them all talking about us and it sort of blew up.'

Rugby? They fell out over rugby? A leather ball?

'So wait, this whole feud is over a bloody rugby match? Are you serious? You have to see how dumb that is, right?'

He nods, but looks away. 'A lot of cruel things were said, Rose. The people of this village have their pride, if nothing else.'

'Okay,' I nod, having no intention of leaving this alone.

I don't know how, but I'm going to try everything in my power to fix this pathetic feud. It just sounds like a huge misunderstanding.

***

Friday 24th October

So tonight's the outdoor cinema event and I should be excited, but instead I'm worried about Eric. Having the whole poo fiasco and then my tits on parade distracted me, but now I can't stop thinking about it. I still can't believe he went to the police. What if he turns up at the home and starts mouthing off in front of everyone?

I've tracked him down to Lye Lane. Apparently he lives in the small farm at the edge of the village. I know I'm close when the pavement disappears and turns into mud. Damn it, these boots are going to be ruined soon. I follow the sound of sheep and finally come across a small brick house with smoke coming out of the chimney. I knock on the front door and wait, shuffling impatiently from foot to foot.

'Around the back!' someone shouts. It doesn't sound like Eric.

How the hell does he live here with his OCD? The mud and mess must drive him insane.

I walk around the back of the house and find a man in his early sixties shearing a sheep. God, it's weird to think my jumpers are made of that.

'Hi.' I wave awkwardly. He ignores me.

The sheep shoots me an evil look. I suppose if a man with a razor was sheering me I wouldn't want someone stealing his attention either.

'I'm looking for Eric,' I shout over the razor buzz.

'He left this morning,' he says gruffly, still not giving me any eye contact.

'Oh, right. So…what time will he be back?' God, it's like pulling teeth.

'Nay idea. He's moved to London. Something about pursuing a singing career.' He rolls his eyes.

'You're joking?' I laugh.

He turns to look at me and I realise I may have offended his son. Oops.

'Afraid not, love. He cleared the pub at the last karaoke, but he's got it set in his head that they're just jealous of his talent.'

'Wow,' I breathe. This is amazing. If he's not around he won't be able to cause any trouble for me.

'Plus he reckons he can live cleaner down there. Good luck, I told him. He'll be in a studio flat with six other people, full of rats, for the crazy prices down there.'

I nod along, already throwing a celebration party in my head. Thank God tonight's the outdoor cinema. I can celebrate in style.

***

I look around at the amazing turnout. Almost the whole village is here. I suppose not much happens here, so this must be exciting for them. The way Elsie's been leafleting I'm surprised there isn't everyone here. She threw herself into doing it after she felt bad for shouting at me the other day.

I've got the care home residents sitting on fold up chairs, as I doubt I'd be able to get them back up from the grass otherwise. Everyone else is sat on the picnic blankets I laid out. I've told the oldies it's because they're VIPs. They seemed to like that idea.

As the sun sets the cool autumn air brings with it a chill. Jumpers are put on and couples snuggle up closer together. I turn on the twinkle lights that I've hung above us. It's going to look amazing when it gets dark. I watch as the light leaves the projection screen.

I take a deep breath and walk to the front as soon as I think it's dark enough. Expectant faces look back at me. I'd try to imagine them naked in order to calm myself down, but it's hard when I know they've all seen *me* half naked.

'Erm…hi, I'm Rose,' I mumble nervously.

'We know!' Violet jeers. Her friends laugh cruelly.

I make a mental note to trip her later.

'Thanks so much for joining us today,' I say, reading from my speech. 'We're here to raise money for the care home. It might feel like a lifetime away for most of us, but we're all going to get old one day. So any extra contributions would be welcomed. Thanks.'

A few people clap as I run over to the laptop and press play on the film. I sit down on my blanket as quickly as possible, still reeling from the embarrassment of public speaking. I take a deep breath, trying to centre myself. Or whatever it is those yogis say.

I feel someone sit down next to me and from the close body heat I know it's him.

'Nice speech,' Will says. I turn to see him stuffing a handful of popcorn into his mouth.

I shift in my seat, instantly feeling awkward around him. I've barely seen him since the other night, so yet again I feel lost and confused. Why does he always make me feel like a kid?

'Want some?'

I stare at him open mouthed, my heart speeding up. Oh, I want some alright. I stare at his plump lips, remembering how they softly caressed mine. He shakes his popcorn bag at me again with a bemused expression on his face.

'No thanks.' I shake my head. I couldn't eat. I feel too jittery around him. 'Have you heard any more from the police?'

'No,' he says through a mouthful of popcorn. 'I'm pretty sure that's all over now.'

Thank God. I can start sleeping again. Well, I can if Mavis and Bernie were to give it a rest one night. They've got the stamina of people half their age. It's weirdly impressive.

He leans in closely. 'Do you girls actually like this film?' he whispers into my ear, his lip brushing my ear lobe again.

'Duh,' I laugh. 'I always wanted to go out with Danny Zuko.' I smile at the memory of me and Elsie learning all the routines when we were seven. I always made her put her hair in a ponytail and be Danny.

'Why?' he laughs. 'The guy is a tool who tries to grope Sandy at a drive-in.'

Such a clueless man. Danny's hot.

'He gives her a ring,' I try to reason.

'Yeah, off his hand,' he snorts. 'Hardly well thought out and romantic.'

It's hard to take him seriously while he shovels popcorn into his mouth like that.

'Well, what would be your idea of romance, oh font of all things romantic?' I ask sarcastically.

He thinks for a minute. 'I don't know…exactly.'

God, he's full of it. I roll my eyes.

'I just know that Danny's not in the kind of love that I want to be in when I fly off into the sky in a car.' He smiles at me so sexily I feel Lulu wake up, beginning to throb in excitement.

I giggle despite myself. 'Explain,' I demand, discreetly trying to sit in closer to him. His body heat is so inviting.

'I want the kind of love that takes over you. The type that my mum and dad had.'

I frown. His dad hardly seems happy.

'Dad's a broken man now,' he says, yet again reading my mind. 'But that's what I want. I want her to be my everything. To have the potential to break me.'

God, he's fit when he's talking all this romantic shit.

'That sounds horrible,' I reason. I've never been one to be all lovey-dovey.

'It's really not,' he shrugs. 'What's horrible is the thought of not finding that person, or worse, finding them, but missing out on your chance.'

I think of Betty and Will's Grandfather. She knows better than anyone how that can be true.

'Take my grandad, for example.' I sit up straighter. He knows about Betty? Why didn't he say anything when they had the fight? 'He once told me that he met the love of his life, but it wasn't my Nan.'

No way. His grandad still felt the same for Betty?

'That must have shocked you,' I say, trying to act natural.

'To say the least,' he grins. 'He told me that he met her before my Nan. Apparently she lived in the village and they were madly in love. Only he proposed too quickly and she got scared off. She left and then he met my Nan. Don't get me wrong, he was more than happy with Nan, but he never forgot about her. And he never stopped wondering 'what if?''

Oh my God, I cannot wait to tell Betty this. She'll be so happy. But then, will she? Knowing he felt the same and yet they still were never together again. It might break her heart.

'Love doesn't last anyways,' I muse, suddenly feeling depressed by the hopelessness of it all.

He stares back at me perplexed, his green eyes practically penetrating me. God, how I wish he'd penetrate me. He looks around before spotting Mavis and Bernie, my sex mad next door neighbours. They're sat next to each other holding hands. It is rather sweet, only all I can think about is their loud grunting sex. Last night they sang *Where is the Love.*

'Look at Mavis and Bernie,' he offers, pointing at them. 'They're a perfect example. Old couples make you realise that someone can love you forever.'

God, he's basically a girl. It doesn't stop my heart flapping pathetically though.

'Who knew you were such a big softie,' I joke, digging him in the ribs with my elbow. 'But I know these two are a little too in love. One night off the sex would be nice for my eye bags.'

He rolls his eyes, obviously dismissing my comment.

'You're the softie,' he grins. 'Organising all this for the home.' He gestures around. Now that it's fully dark the fairy lights do look amazing. 'It's proper thoughtful.'

I love the praise from him. Too much. I'm basing too much approval on a man's opinion of me. It's pathetic.

'It was nothing.' I shrug indifferently.

He covers his warm hand with mine, sending tingles up my arm.

'No, Rose. It was something. Thank you.' He smiles and it's so beautiful that I think I could look at it every day for the rest of my life and die happy.

Could I really be…no. Could I…be falling in love with Will? No. I laugh at the thought of it. I'm not the kind of girl that falls in love.

***

Saturday 25th October

I've decided to tell Will I'm definitely not going to retaliate with Gerry. I've spoken to Elsie about it and I know that no good will come from it. The truth is everyone's seen my tits by now regardless. I've come through the stares and whispers. I just have to move on and try to be a better person from it.

I suppose I could have told Will today at the home, but then that wouldn't have allowed me to turn up at his house unannounced wearing my black lacy thong. I've got a sneaking suspicion that he might not be able to refuse me if I catch him off guard. Okay, I'm hopeful at least. He always seems so controlled.

I take a deep breath and knock on the door. After a bit of shuffling inside the door opens, only it's Riley. What the hell is she doing here? I can practically feel my cat claws being released.

'Oh, hi Rose,' she smiles. 'I was just leaving.' She passes me. 'Give me a call and we'll go for coffee,' she shouts back with a wide grin.

I walk into the hallway, unsure whether to go into the living room. I mean, what, he's too lazy to open the door now? I tentatively walk in, feeling far more insecure than I planned. I was supposed to feel empowered and sexy. But it seems Riley's given him his fill of sexy for one night.

'Hey,' he smiles, looking up from the sofa.

Oh, don't rush over or anything. What a gentleman. Not. The man's a walking contradiction.

'What was Riley doing here?' I blurt out pathetically. God, for once I wish I could engage my mouth and brain at the same time.

He reaches out for my hand and pulls me down to sit in between his legs on the couch. At least he still wants me close.

'We were just talking,' he whispers in my ear. 'Don't be jealous.' He kisses me behind my ear and I shiver from the contact. Damn him and his smooth moves.

Jay walks in and it suddenly feels strangely intimate to be sitting like this in front of him. I don't even know if Will's told him about us. Whatever we are. I go to move, but Will holds me in place. Maybe he *has* told him about us?

'I'm gonna have a brew. You guys want one?' he offers, smiling knowingly. Oh, he knows all right.

'Yeah, ta,' Will nods.

I shake my head politely. I don't know what it is, but I'm a bundle of nerves. It's probably the proximity of Will's dick to my arse. I swear I can almost feel it, he's so huge. I wipe the drool discreetly from my face.

Will's hands move to the side of my stomach the minute Jay leaves the room. I take a sharp intake of breath. He slowly uses his fingers to pry my top up slightly, slipping his hands under, the heat of his fingers making my skin burn. I close my eyes, trying to ingrain the feeling to my memory. He starts tracing patterns into my skin with his thumbs. It's beyond erotic, which I realise is ridiculous. He's barely touched me and I'm a ball of hormones. Keep it together, Rose. Calm down, Lulu.

He moves his hands slowly down my sides to my hips and starts caressing them, his fingers so close to the place that is throbbing. He's totally teasing me, the bastard. I wonder if I should say something, but the silence between us is almost adding to the electricity.

Instead I throw my head back onto his shoulder when I can't stay still any longer. I don't meet his eyes, still feeling too shy. His tongue touches my throat, licking down it, the tip of it barely making contact with my skin. I shudder against him. God, this guy's good.

His hands quickly move to my boobs making me gasp out loud. He palms them over my top, but my nipples are already as hard as ice. He pushes them together, clearly glad I haven't got a bra on. I smile to myself. I knew that would drive him crazy.

I feel his laboured breath at my ear as he nibbles the lobe. I've never really been into the whole ear thing, but my God, with him I could just explode. I push myself back against him, desperate to encourage him. That's when I feel his erection. Fuck yeah!

'It's a bit dark,' his roommate says, re-entering the room. Will's hands drop from me as if I were on fire. 'But we've run out of milk.'

What the fuck? How can he just drop me like that? Way to leave a bitch hanging.

'Nah worries,' Will smiles, taking his tea from him. 'I'm actually shattered. I'm gonna bring it up to bed.'

My heart quivers as I realise this is it. We're finally going to have sex! I'm still out of breath as I stand up. I watch as he gets up, re-arranging his jeans so it's not obvious he has a boner. It's still pretty obvious. And soon that's going to be inside me. I lick my lips in anticipation.

'Bye, Jay,' I smile, not even looking at him.

I follow him into the hallway, almost skipping with glee. Finally!

He opens the front door, letting the cold night air in. I stare back at him, my forehead creased in confusion. What?

'Huh?'

'Goodnight,' he smiles, kissing me tenderly on the cheek.

'Are you fucking joking?' I shriek, far too dramatically. I'm actually shaking with fury. 'You can't get me all hot back there and then send me home!' Way to sound desperate, Rose.

'Anticipation, Rose,' he smirks, putting his arms around me, squeezing my bum cheeks. I press my breasts against his chest, desperate for him to change his mind. I could burst into tears with longing.

'Are you going to the Halloween party at the pub next week?' I ask desperately. I overheard Phil talking about it. He's getting a DJ and everything. It's probably the biggest social event this village has ever seen.

'Probably,' he shrugs. 'Anyway, I'm proper tired. Dream of me?' he smiles with a mischievous glint in his eyes.

'You'll be lucky,' I smirk. I really want to get the upper hand back.

He leans in and kisses me, his lips hot and welcoming. He quickly and confidently parts my mouth, our eager tongues meeting and playing until we're almost tangled. I wrap my hands around his neck, frantic for it to go further. I *need* it to.

I jump when he swats me on the bum. He pulls back, effectively dismissing me.

'Goodnight, Rose.'

He turns and saunters up the stairs, his arse reminding me what I'm missing out on.

What an *absolute* bastard. And I didn't even get to find out why Riley was here. Or mention what I came here about. Damn that beautiful dickhead.

Chapter 16

Friday 31st October – HALLOWEEN

I always look forward to Halloween. They do the best club nights and there's always such an air of mischief about. I even lost my virginity on Halloween night. People always assume I must have been young when I lost it and I just let them believe whatever they want. The truth is that I was nineteen and I didn't even wait that long because I wanted to be in a serious, loving relationship. I couldn't have lost it if I wanted to.

I had a completely flat as a pancake chest until I hit eighteen, then they appeared almost overnight. There were even rumours I'd had a boob job. Up until then, although never a shrinking violet, I kept myself away from boy situations. I was far too self-conscious to even entertain a boy trying to grope through my extremely padded chest, let alone get naked in front of them. So I busied myself by being a Goth and making myself as scary and unapproachable as possible. And like I said, I rock the black lipstick and eyeliner. That's just another reason I love Halloween.

Anyway, I met Janey at some shitty temp job and she encouraged me to come out of myself. With my new boobs, and therefore confidence, it was easy. I lost it to Dave Benton in the back seat of his Fiat Punto while dressed like a slutty angel. How ironic.

I've decided that today I'm going to have a bit of fun and dress up. I'd already packed my costume, thinking I'd be in Mexico. I'm not sure how Elsie's going to react to me being a slutty nun. The habit over my head only covers a small bit of my hair, so you can still see my curled hair underneath. My dress is low in the bust and short on the leg. I've teamed it with some black fishnets and my biker boots. I think the boots dress it down enough.

I skip downstairs, excited to see Elsie's reaction, but she's not there. I find a note.

Didn't want to wake you. Gone into the home early. Beth wanted me to cover. Wants to celebrate the devil worshipping day that is Halloween. How stupid. Catch ya later x

Devil worshiping? Is she *serious?* God, she's a spoil sport. I walk up to the home relatively unseen. The cashier from the shop gave me a filthy look, but she's obviously going to hate me now. Hobbling about in those crutches feeling sorry for herself.

I rush into the hallway, eager to escape the bitter cold. I see that the few decorations I put in the hallway have been taken down. How weird.

I walk into the lounge to find Elsie ripping decorations down all over the place. Her face is flushed and angry. She looks down like she's having a breakdown.

'Elsie, what the fuck are you doing?' I demand as I throw my coat off.

Everyone turns to look at me at once. The old men's eyeballs nearly pop out. Some of the women look at me judging, although Betty's not one of them. She's clapping and wolf whistling. Bless her.

'Rose,' Elsie fumes, her face the colour of beetroot, 'What the *hell* are you wearing?'

I decide to brash it out. I do a little twirl, to the men's delight.

'I thought you'd like it,' I say innocently batting my eyelashes. 'I hope you don't mind me borrowing your new outfit,' I grin. Betty pisses herself laughing.

She looks like she might have a coronary. Oops. She clearly hasn't gotten the joke. She seriously needs to lighten up.

'Rose, how could you do this?' she asks, already welling up.

God, she's dramatic. There's no need to cry about it.

'Jesus, calm down, Els,' I snort.

'Don't take the Lord's name in vain!' she berates, her eyes almost bursting out of their sockets with rage.

I roll my eyes.

'And don't roll your eyes! I knew you wanted to celebrate this ludicrous devil worshiping holiday, but to bring it into this home? To put decorations up and dress like a…' She swallows, as if she can't even say the word.

'A slut?' I offer, enjoying the way she squirms at the word. 'I don't see what the big deal is. It's just a bit of fun.'

‘A bit of fun?’ she spits. ‘Devil worshipping is not just a bit of fun. It’s the work of the devil!’

She’s seriously lost it. I ignore her and start tidying up. Ronnie pinches my arse, but instead of finding it funny and flattering like I normally would, I instead feel cheap. Damn Elsie for ruining my fun!

I’m just about to challenge her when the door opens and in walks the vicar. Dressed like a Dalmatian dog. He’s even painted his face. No fucking way!

‘Happy Halloween everyone!’ he smiles. ‘I’ve come to give you communion.’

Elsie’s face is a picture. Several emotions cross over it in a matter of seconds. Shock, confusion, hurt, horror.

‘Vicar! You can't tell me you condone this devil worshipping?’ she squawks.

He looks back at her oddly. ‘There’s no devil worshipping about it, Elsie. It’s to celebrate All Hallows Eve, where we pay respect t’ dead.’

She balks, clearly not knowing what to say.

‘And besides,’ he smiles, ‘it’s just a bit of fun, isn’t it.’

Elsie looks at me as if I’ve forced the vicar to dress up before storming out of the building.

***

Elsie had calmed down slightly by the time I got home from my shift. I didn’t understand why until I tried to log onto Facebook to see if Janey had replied. The google page was already open and in the search box was *All Hallows Eve*. It seems she clicked on all the links. Bless her.

As I apply more black lipstick before my shift at the pub I feel her shifting around me.

‘So…I’m sorry about earlier,’ she says sheepishly.

Marbles shoots me an evil look. She’s not sorry about anything.

‘Don’t worry about it,’ I smile. ‘I did kind of rile you up with this outfit.’ And I can't pretend I didn’t enjoy it. She’s so easy to rile.

‘Yeah,’ she nods, deep in thought. ‘Do you really think so little of me that you don’t mind humiliating me like that?’ she asks, her voice barely a whisper.

‘Elsie…’

Well, now I feel shit. I hadn’t thought she’d take it so personally.

‘It’s okay, Rose,’ she interrupts, her hand up in defeat. ‘I know you’re sorry and I know you didn’t realise how much you’d hurt me. Which is why I forgive you.’

She forgives me? Just like that? So easily?

‘Seriously?’

‘I forgive you, Rose,’ she nods. ‘But you have to start thinking. Thinking about how your actions can hurt others. If you’d learned that six months ago maybe you wouldn’t even be living here.’

Her words smack me around the face. Does she not want me here anymore? And is she right? Of course she is. Only I’ve never really been bothered about pissing off my parents. With her it feels different. I have an ache in my chest that I know won't go away for a long time, regardless of whether she says she forgives me. She’s done so much selflessly for me and how have I thanked her? By taking the piss out of her.

‘I’m so sorry Elsie.’ I reach out to her, but she moves out of my grip.

‘You’ll be late for work,’ she says with a weak smile before walking into the kitchen.

Well, I feel shit. Happy fucking Halloween.

***

Megan greets me at the pub dressed as a sexy kitten. Well, she is until Phil makes her put on a more *appropriate* outfit. He doesn’t like the look of mine either, but I’m not his daughter.

The party’s a major success with most people in the village turning up. James is here, and although a little awkward, he explained that Will has got a stomach bug. I wondered why I didn’t see him earlier. It made me realise that I don’t even have his mobile number.

Megan goes off to the dance floor so she can dance to the Macarena with her friends.

Riley turns up dressed as a nurse. She's sexy with her red lips and heels, but her dress hem is just above the knee, a respective length. She says hi briefly as I get her a glass of rose wine, but then she's off to get lost on the dance floor.

I work flat out all night, it only starting to empty out in the last half hour. I'm just collecting empties at the quiet end of the bar when I feel the need to wee. Must be those peach schnapps shots I helped myself to earlier.

I walk through the double doors into the hallway, strolling towards the handicapped toilets. I have no idea why there is one. There's no one in a wheelchair in the village and they don't seem to have any passing trade, but I suppose it's still a good thing.

I open the door, already hitching my dress up, but stop dead in my tracks when I let my eyes focus on what's in front of me. My stomach drops and recoils.

The baby change unit is pulled down and sitting on it is Riley. Her legs are open and pressed up between them is James. He's kissing her neck and groping her breasts, which are bursting out of her exposed bra.

I swallow down the vomit. What the actual fuck?

They both turn their heads and spot me at the same time. Riley looks horrified, quickly covering her breasts with her hands. James looks almost sorry. He opens his mouth, his forehead creased in regret.

'Rose…' he starts.

'Wow! Sorry!' I blurt out, my entire body flushing from embarrassment. 'I didn't realise someone was in here.'

Ever heard of locking the frigging door?

I turn and run out, frantic for some fresh air. I need it. Now. I feel like there's someone's hands around my throat, trying to break off my breathing.

I burst through the back door and try desperately to take some air into my lungs. It's hard when I feel so shaky and hysterical.

Why do I even feel so weird? I'm sort of with Will now. I shouldn't give a shit who James sticks it to. But Riley? I've never seen the two of them even talk before. And now they're shagging? Since when? Not while we were, right? God, if he was shagging her at the same time I'll just die. Thank God I always insist on a condom. Betty was right. He's bad news.

And her? Doesn't she have any shame? God, if Will ever found out about them he'd be devastated. His ex and his brother. Surely that's too close for comfort. At least she doesn't know me and James ever hooked up. I hope. I assume she doesn't. But then, imagine if he ever found out about *me* and James. We haven't even had sex yet. If he found this out he'd never want me.

Has James told Riley about us? What if she tells Will? But then, now I could tell on her. I may have just gotten myself some leverage. I need it. If I don't have Will I'm going to combust.

I turn to head back inside, but jump when I see James walking out towards me.

'Rose, please,' he begs, 'let me explain.'

'There's nothing to explain,' I blush. 'It's none of my business.' I walk past him, hoping this humiliation doesn't last any longer than it needs to.

'I haven't told Riley about us,' he blurts out.

I stop, silently thanking God that he can *sometimes* be discreet. I turn round to face him.

'Thank you,' I smile.

'And I want you to know,' he continues, 'that I'm not some heartless bastard that is shagging the whole village.'

'I believe you,' I nod sarcastically.

'No, I mean it.' He looks earnest. 'My last relationship was seriously fucked up. She really did a number on me, and I suppose since then I've been trying to forget about her.'

'By sticking it in every vagina possible?' I laugh. I don't mean to sound cruel, but it sounds it.

'Well…yes. Riley and I have a mutual understanding. Every now and then we use each other, but we know the score. You didn't, and for that, I'm sorry.'

He looks genuinely sorry.

'You're forgiven,' I smile, before walking away.

I'm not sure Will would be so forgiving,

Saturday 1st November

Are you around for that coffee?

It's way too early to be receiving a text from an unknown number. I throw myself back down onto the bed and cover my eyes with my arm. Too bright. The birds are loud, as if their sole purpose is to make me hate them. Then it starts; the moaning. Oh dear God, not this early! The bed starts hitting against my wall and I know it's happening again. What the hell is wrong with them?

Okay! I'm awake. I jump out of bed and run downstairs, now knowing that anything would be better than enduring that again.

I look at the text again. It must be Riley. Probably shitting herself that I'll tell Will about her getting off with his brother. I should text her back really. It's not like I'm doing anything this morning. I don't have my shift at the home until this afternoon and I only planned on sleeping in, which now seems impossible.

We arrange to meet at the one café in the village, as if they'd be anywhere else. I walk in and spot her already at a table, two coffees sitting in front of her. Her hair is as glossy and smooth as ever and she's wearing a sundress over black tights and a denim jacket. She waves over to me, as if I could miss her in between Mrs Whitmore and Mr Baker. She's far too glamourous for this village.

'Morning,' I smile to Mavis behind the counter. It's slowly getting easier to look her in the eye. I can see why everyone thinks I'm lying about her. She really does seem like the sweetest lady.

'A brew, love?' she asks, her usual smiley face looking a bit forlorn. The bags around her eyes are puffier than usual. Shagging your husband at all hours will do that to you. Dirty scally wag.

I nod even though I see Riley's got me a coffee.

‘Are you okay, Mavis?’ I follow her to the counter so that the others can't hear.

‘Yes, love, just a bit stressed out. Got a few unsuspected bills today.’ Was that before or after rogering your husband? The dirty mare. She looks far more stressed than she’s letting on.

‘But…you’ll be okay though, right?’

A look of panic flashes over her face, before she plasters on a fake smile.

‘Of course. We’ll…we’ll get through it. Just…struggling without the regular contracts from the other villages. But we’re fine.’ She hands over my tea and walks back over to Mrs Elerry.

How can this village feud be affecting their trade and *still* people are insisting on keeping it up? It’s dumb. They’ll all be bankrupt and living on the streets before they admit they need their help.

‘Hey,’ I smile at Riley, sitting down and taking a few large gulps of the tea. I need the caffeine. She looks at the coffee she got me, seeming embarrassed by the snub. I didn’t mean to be vicious.

‘You look great, Rose,’ she smiles, her eyes scanning me excitedly.

I look down at my skinny jeans and Elsie’s baggy pink jumper. Now I *know* she's lying.

‘Yeah, right,’ I snort. ‘Just tell me the real reason I’m here today. I already said I won't tell Will about you and James.’

‘I know and I’m so grateful,’ she gushes. ‘This might sound weird, but James and I don’t even like each other. We use each other sometimes when we’re missing affection, but there’s no real love there. I’m pretty sure we’re both in love with other people.’

In love with someone else? Will? She *is* after him. I just know it.

‘Is it Will? Is something going on between you?’ I ask before I can stop myself from sounding less pathetic.

‘Oh my God, no!’ she shrieks, blushing and fanning her face. ‘We’ve been just friends for ages now. It’s just…okay, I’m worried about you.’ She folds her hands over each other on the table.

'About me? Why?' I take a sip of my tea, trying to think over her intentions. Why the hell should she be worried about me? Surely this whole thing was to persuade me not to tell?

'I just want you to be careful of Will,' she warns, her voice grave. Her eyes are sympathetic.

'Careful? What do you mean, careful?' I sound far more intrigued than I should, my voice high pitched and needy, but damn it, I want to know what she's going on about. Is it because she's fucking him too?

She looks down into her coffee. 'It's just…I know you really like him and I don't want you hurting yourself.'

'Why would I get hurt?' I scrutinise her body language. She seems awkward, but her hands are open while she talks. Isn't that supposed to mean honesty? Or is she just trying to upset me?

'Err…no reason.' She avoids my eye line.

I narrow my eyes on her. 'Tell me, Riley,' I demand, hitting my hand hard on the table.

The ladies stop to stare at the drama.

'Nothing to tell,' she laughs, seeming as if she wishes she hadn't said anything. She starts to signal Mavis. 'Can we get two muffins over here please?'

'Stop changing the subject.' Although I could do with the muffin. 'What has Will done?' I demand, getting angrier by the second.

'Nothing,' she says, waving her hands dismissively. 'I'm sure it's just me being stupid. I really wish I hadn't said anything. So how's the volunteering going?'

Is she seriously trying to change the subject?

I pick up my butter knife and shove it in her face.

'Tell me now or, I swear to God, shit's about to get real!'

Possibly a little dramatic. She looks back at me, her eyes wide and stunned.

'Shall I call the police, love?' Mr Baker asks her, looking over his newspaper as if I've lost my mind. Maybe I have.

'No, it's fine,' she smiles at him, swallowing hard. She hunches over the table, lowering her voice to a whisper. 'He…he kind of said that he was going to nail the new girl when he heard you were moving to the village.'

My mouth drops open as I stare at her aghast. This doesn't sound like Will. She must be making this up. I mean, we haven't even had sex yet. The guy's a perfect gentleman. She's just jealous. But then, he said not to tell anyone. How does she even know about us? He wouldn't have told her, right?

'He said he was going to play with you for a while; wait for every other guy to have a go first and then lure you in. He planned to refuse sex for a while, so you were eager and willing to do absolutely anything in bed.' She twists her hands in her lap, looking apologetic.

I sit there, my body still, as my mind reels. Play with me for a while? Refuse sex…willing to do *anything* in bed? How can this be happening? How could he have said all of that? Riley wouldn't know this unless he'd actually said it. She'd never guess that we hadn't slept together yet. The whole village thinks I'm a slut. If she had any suspicion of us she'd just assume we were shagging.

'I'm so sorry,' she says, showing pain I know I should be feeling.

All I feel is numb.

'No, thanks for telling me,' I whisper, my voice hoarse.

I stand up and walk out without saying goodbye. I don't think I could speak if I wanted to. I'm barely out of the door before the tears start trickling down my face. I'm surprised I feel them. I can't feel anything else. I won't allow myself to truly digest this until I'm home.

I jog the few streets to the cottage, collapsing over with a stitch once I reach the door. Lauren's coming out of her house, so I quickly turn away, fumbling for my keys.

'Hey, Rose!' she calls.

I turn and wave at her, still avoiding eye contact. I open the door, slamming it behind me. I rest back against the door and let the emotions surface.

I'm nothing but a joke to Will. Some silly little slut from Watford who is too thick to realise when someone's being fake with her. I'm nothing to him. *Nothing.*

A sob escapes my chest, so loud I'm shocked it even belongs to me. I feel physically wounded, the hurt twisting inside me. I startle when the door bangs behind me. I stand up, wipe my tears away with the back of my hand and plaster on a smile. I pull the door open to find Lauren. God, she's persistent.

'I'm coming in,' she says, pushing past me. She turns to me, her face questioning. 'What the hell is wrong?'

I burst into tears, them falling thick and fast. Hardly the kind of actions of someone trying to compose herself.

She pulls me to the couch and cradles me into a hug. You can tell she's a mum. She just knows what to do in situations like this.

I tell her everything, off-loading all of my worst fears and worries. She nods encouragingly, grimacing in the right places. She opens a bottle of wine and makes us some cheese on toast. Maybe she really is an angel.

'That's so shit, babe,' she sighs. 'What can I say, but all men are bastards.'

I snort out a laugh, unwittingly blowing a snot bubble out of my nostril.

'You can say that again,' I sniff, placing my head in her lap. I need to be treated like a cat right now. Marbles never seems to have problems. 'Is Noah's dad a bastard?'

She sighs. 'He's not even a bastard. Just…someone who made a mistake.'

She doesn't hate him for abandoning her while pregnant? How can she be so forgiving when he ruined her life?

'So…who is Noah's dad?' I ask, twirling a piece of hair in my hand. My attempts at flicking it around in her lap, hoping she'll be encouraged to play with it, doesn't seem to be working.

'No one,' she says quickly, jumping up and pushing me off her lap. She collects our plates and starts putting them in the dishwasher. 'Why? What have you heard?' Her voice is clearly panicked.

'Nothing! I just…I guess I just wondered is all. Were you already pregnant when you moved to the village?'

She walks back into the siting room and sits down on the sofa.

'Yeah. Eight months.'

'So why move here? Didn't you live in Leeds? Doesn't it make more sense for you to live there, so you could be closer to work?' I can't help but blurt them all out. I'm so curious.

'Aren't you Miss Questions this evening?' she grins.

I blush, but then realise she's avoiding the question. 'So really, why?' I push.

She looks away and sighs heavily. It's as if she's considering whether she should tell me or not. I hope she does.

'The father wanted me to move here,' she admits reluctantly, twiddling a thread on her jeans.

My mouth drops open, dribbling wine onto my lap. 'No fucking way! The father lives here?'

'I didn't say that!' she retorts flicking her curls back. But her cheeks are uncharacteristically red.

'But it's true!' I can tell by the way she's avoiding eye contact.

Oh my God. How awkward must that be! Imagine your baby daddy being round the corner, but you're sworn to secrecy.

'Okay, it's true. He wanted me to move here so he could be closer to Noah.'

'I can't believe he moved his mistress here! The dirty bastard,' I laugh.

'I'm not his mistress!' she exclaims, suddenly rattled. 'We broke it off as soon as I found out I was pregnant.'

'How lovely of him,' I snort. Sounds like a right charmer.

'Don't blame him. He's got a lot to lose.' She looks out of the window, her eyes clouded with grief. I realise how heartless I'm being.

Oh my God, what if it's Will? No…right?

'Like what?'

She looks down at the floor. 'Like a family of his own.'

She had an affair with a married man!

'WHAT? Who is it?' I shout, jumping up and down in my seat.

I'm already going through the options in my head. Who the hell could it be? I didn't think there were any good looking guys here. Especially married ones.

'I'm not telling you,' she says defensively. She drains her wine glass in one go.

'Why not?' I whine, putting on my best sad eyes.

'Because he's a pillar of the community. This coming out would ruin his life, and I don't intend to be the one to do it.''

'So let me do it!' I joke.

'Ha-ha,' she deadpans, not at all seeing the funny side. 'Let's change the subject. Did something happen between you and James?'

Oops. I'd tried to keep that out of the story, but I'm obviously a little transparent.

'Err…it's complicated.'

'Exactly,' she smiles cunningly. 'Drop it, Rose. I'll never tell you, so just stop.'

***

She left and didn't tell me, but I can't stop thinking about it. Noah's dad is living here in the village. I think I'm probably clinging onto it, so I don't have to concentrate on my own problems.

Elsie comes in, slamming the door. She heads straight for the kitchen. God, she's a drama queen.

'What's up, Els?' I shout in after her.

'Nothing,' she shouts, slamming the fridge door loudly. 'Only that the vicar's wife, Jeanette, is such a bitch.'

I giggle to myself. I love when she swears. It shows there's a natural, honest person in there who would rather eat shit than be a nun. She won't last two minutes.

'I swear,' she continues, walking in with a large glass of red wine, 'I have no idea how he's managed to stay married to her for so long. She's such a witch.'

I look down at my hands, thinking of Will's betrayal.

'People in love do stupid things,' I reason. Not that I'm in love. Of course not.

'I really don't see love in his eyes, though.' She moves Marbles from the sofa so she can sit down. She hisses in protest. 'I think he feels he has to just hang in there because of his status and the girls.'

'Poor guy,' I scoff, hardly feeling sorry for him. He could walk away at any time.

He must have his reasons though, I suppose. His status. Hang on a minute…pillar of the community? Lauren's son is called Noah. As in Noah's Ark. He lives in the village and has a family of his own and a squeaky clean reputation to up hold.

Holy shit. The vicar is Noah's dad.

Chapter 17

Monday 3rd November

'I am so excited, Rose!' Megan beams at me. 'I've told everyone we'll text them on the evening so they can't blab the location. I'm literally all the school is talking about right now!'

Bless Megan and her enthusiasm. I've told her we can have the party at the old abandoned castle I found with Will. It's far out enough that no one should see. *Will.* Just thinking of him makes me want to wallow in my disaster life. I hate how he just thinks of me as the new slut in the village. The village bike. I'm used to people having opinions about me at home, but this feels different. I can't believe I actually bought that he was different. What a joke. He's just an evil knob head. Far worse than anyone I've ever gone home with.

'You don't seem very excited!' Megan whines, poking me in the ribs.

I shake my head, trying to get out of my own thoughts.

'Sorry, Megs. Don't worry, it'll be amazing,' I say as upbeat as I can muster. I still sound hollow. I am.

I was up all night telling Elsie and I think I've exhausted myself from all of the heavy emotion. I've never cried so much in my life.

The pub door swings open dramatically, hitting the wall with a hard thump. I jump out of my skin before turning round, my heart in my throat. Standing before me is Will and he looks furious. His face is red and blotchy and it looks like he didn't sleep very well last night. What the hell has *he* got to be upset about? The pig.

I have to get out of here. I can't see him yet. Just a quick glance at his beautiful face and I'm already trying to talk myself into forgiving him.

I turn to Megan, sat at her usual spot at the bar. 'I'm taking my break.'

I haven't had the heart to tell her what happened. She's so excited about the party. She doesn't need to worry about my drama.

Being a teenager is hard enough. She looks back at me strangely, obviously thinking I'm a weirdo.

I duck out of the bar and run to the back room to grab my bag and coat. I escape out of the back door and am almost out of their garden when I feel an arm on my shoulder, roughly pulling me around. I face Will, his green eyes boring angrily into mine. Crap.

'Rose! Slow the fuck down!' he shouts, his voice hoarse.

I sigh heavily. I don't have the energy for this. I *cannot* have this conversation right now. Please God, let something happen so I can get away. Some earthquake, some thunderstorm, something!

Suddenly something drops onto my shoulder. I swivel my head to find what it is, but an intense pain in my neck stops me. It feels like…teeth, clamping down on me. I look at Will, and he's staring in open repulsion.

'What is it? Get it off me!' I scream, breaking into a sprint, running back and forth the length of their garden. I desperately try to bat it away, but at the same time I'm scared to touch it. Whatever it is has locked its bloody jaw around my neck. What if it's a fox?

'Calm down, Rose,' he says slowly, his eyes showing his barely concealed panic.

'AAAAGGGGHHHH!!! Please get off me, you bastard!!!' I start ramming my neck into the fence. I nearly collapse from the force. Why won't this fucking animal get off me?! I can feel its teeth biting into me. And what the hell is it? It's too small for a fox. A bird? A cat?

'Rose, it's a squirrel!' he shouts over my screaming, his hands through his hair in desperation.

'A squirrel?' I shriek. A bloody squirrel? What is a squirrel doing attacking me? 'Throw it a fucking nut or something!'

He bursts out laughing, spitting all over me. I glare at him. He quickly recovers himself, seeing I'm in no joking mood. Well, with his help I'm done for.

I'm feeling weaker now. The original adrenaline slowing down in my veins. I'm going to die. This fucking squirrel is going to kill me. How pathetic. I can go home drunk with bloody randoms and somehow end up not raped and murdered, but oh no, a squirrel will get me. I knew I wasn't made for the countryside.

'Err…stay there,' he says, backing out of the room before turning and running off.

Is he fucking *serious?* As if I could go anywhere! Where the hell does he think I'd go?

Right, think Rose, think. How do you bargain with a squirrel that wants to kill you? With all of the self-help books out there you'd think they'd be a *living in the country survival guide* or something. God, if I survive this I'm googling it. I need to know what other risks are out there.

I take a deep breath, summoning up the last bit of courage I can muster and clench my hand around its tiny, hairy body. God, it feels creepy. I can feel its bones. And not soft like I thought it would be, but covered in coarse fur. I start pulling it away, but it's got such a latch on my neck that it's just going to rip my throat out. Breathe Rose, breathe. Will's gone to get help.

BANG!

A gunshot makes me jump so high I have time to wonder if I've wet myself with fear on the way down. I look around, my body trembling, to see Phil and his shot gun. I look behind me to see a hole in the fence. The squirrel scuttles off, clearly shitting itself.

'I told you about those fucking squirrels!'

***

'You didn't have to come with me,' I moan bitchily, as I slump down onto a plastic chair in the A & E waiting room.

That's not really true; Phil insisted Will drive me. Not that I made the journey easy on him. I basically blanked him the whole time, only answering with a 'FINE!' every time he asked me how I was feeling. Everyone knows fine in girl code means go fuck yourself.

'I could hardly leave you to drive yourself.' He sighs and sits down next to me.

I humph. He's so bloody logical. It's infuriating.

His scent invades my nostrils. He's too close to me. I can feel my body already reacting to him, wanting to curl into him. I try to remind myself that he's a two faced bastard. Not a delicious, beautiful hunk of a man.

'Well, I'm here now. You can go,' I snap, folding one arm over my chest. The other is still holding a tea towel to my wound.

'Just shut up, will you,' he berates, his voice frustrated. 'Let me see it.' He leans in closer to my neck.

I sigh wearily, tired of arguing. I lower the tea towel to give him a look. I hear, rather than see his sharp intake of breath.

'Is it really that bad?' I ask, my eyes wide and scared.

Now I'm worried. Maybe that squirrel bit a vein and I'm close to death. I could be bleeding out right now and I'd have no idea. And I'm really hungry. I didn't ever imagine dying hungry. If I had a snickers bar I'd go happily right now. Just a bloody snickers, universe! But of course I forgot to bring my bag. There's something about bleeding from your neck that makes you forget anything logical.

'No, I was joking,' he says forcing a smile, unable to hide the repulsion.

'Jesus, Will. At least lie well!' I shout, my voice wobbly. I shoot him a look of utter contempt.

'So…are we going to talk about why you were running away from me in the first place?'

I turn to face him fully, my face like thunder. 'What do you want from me, Will?' I ask acidly, narrowing my eyes at him.

The worst thing is that he looks hurt at my tone of voice and that actually makes me want to burst into tears and rush to him. He's made me feel so much affection towards him without me even realising it. The sneaky bastard. No, he's an arsehole. Remember that.

'Do you mind telling me why you've been ignoring me?' he demands, his face contorting in rage.

Why the hell is *he* angry? He has no right.

'Ha!' I snort, not so delicately. 'I'm afraid your little secrets out, Will.' Sudden tears prick my eyes. I blink them away. Do NOT cry. Don't give him the satisfaction.

His face crunches up in confusion. He rubs his forehead, as if trying to gather jumbled thoughts. Lies more like.

'Little secret? What the hell are you talking about?'

I study his face, trying to read it.

'Miss Chapman?' I look up to see an Indian lady doctor. Saved by the bell.

She assesses me and then a nice nurse gives me some butterfly stitches, covering it with a large white plaster. I walk back into the waiting room thirty minutes later to find he's still waiting for me. I was kind of hoping he'd leave me alone to get a taxi. Not that I can afford one.

'You stay here. I'll bring the car round.' Bossy as ever.

I nod, having no energy to smile and be gracious. I slump down onto a chair and put my head into my hands. Why is life so bloody hard?

I look up, right into the face of a young teenage girl in black clothes, sitting across from me. She's got red spiky hair cut close to her head. She's looking at me really intensely. She must know I'm a former teenage Goth. It's the only explanation.

I lean back and cross my arms, feeling self-conscious. I look out of the window, hoping Will will appear in a minute. I glance back and now I'm sure she's staring at me. What the hell is her problem? She stands up and walks to sit next to me. Great. I turn to look at her questionably, now unable to ignore her.

'Your neck,' she points with a black painted fingernail. 'What happened?'

No hello, how are you? How bloody rude are teenagers these days?

'A squirrel bit me,' I say, no emotion in my voice. I'm too exhausted.

'Oh, aye,' she smiles suspiciously. 'Animal attack, eh?' She raises her eyebrow questionably. Why is she being so weird?

'Err…yeah…a squirrel. Like I said.' I nod, trying to turn away from her. Why do I always attract the nutters?

'It's okay,' she whispers, leaning in close. 'I *know.*'

‘Know what?’ This bird is seriously freaking me out. Is she psychic? Did she see the squirrel attacking in a dream or something?

‘That you’ve been bitten. It’s okay. I know you need to feed to fully turn.’ She looks around us. ‘If we find somewhere quiet I don’t mind letting you do it. But only if you turn me afterwards.’

‘What?’

Did we wander into a mental ward by mistake? What the hell is she going on about?

‘You can cut the bullshit,’ she snaps, quickly turning on me. ‘I know you’re a vampire. So are you going to turn me or what?’

‘A VAMPIRE?’ I shriek, my mouth gaping open.

‘Shush!’ she snaps. ‘We can’t have people hearing. They’ll have you locked up straight away.’

‘I’m not surprised. Anyone who believes in vampires is insane.’ She narrows her eyes at me. ‘Look, I don’t know what you want, but I am not a fucking vampire!’ I hiss low so no one can hear me. I can hardly believe I’m having to clarify this.

Will’s car horn beeps and I stand up, seeing his car out of the window. I look back to her. ‘I suggest you forget about this stupid conversation.’

‘Oh, no,’ she smiles, ‘I’m not on Vervain. That’s why I offered you my blood. I’m sure the whole of Yorkshire’s on it, so good luck,’ she snorts, folding her arms and leaning back.

What the hell is Vervain? And why is she picking on me?

I basically run out to the car and jump in, still feeling her eyes on me. What a creepy bitch.

‘You okay?’ he asks with a bemused smirk.

‘Yeah fine, just…yeah, I’m fine.’

Somehow I don’t think he’ll appreciate the vampire story. I lean back into the chair, ready to sleep this nightmare away.

‘So…are we going to talk about why you’ve been ignoring me?’ he asks, keeping his eyes on the road. I suppose we’re doing this now.

I breathe out a heavy sigh in exasperation.

‘I know what you really think of me, Will. I know that you went around bragging that you were going to screw the new slutty girl.’ I want to spit out the words, but my voice carries no emotion. I really wish I was looking gorgeous when I confronted him, not pale from blood loss.

‘Huh?’ he mutters, his eyes off the road, narrowing on mine.

‘But what I really don’t get,’ I’m on a mission now, anger and humiliating spurring me on, ‘is why bother with the whole nicey nicey thing? Why not just fuck me and get it over with? Why all this fucking with my head?’ My voice is finally carrying some conviction.

His eyes dart helplessly from side to side.

‘Rose, you’re being crazy. I have no fucking idea what you’re talking about.’ He sounds sincere, but I should know by now what a great actor he is.

‘Of course you don’t,’ I snarl sarcastically.

My chest crushes with the need to cry. Why the hell do I want to cry when I’m so bloody angry? He hurt me and he won’t be allowed to do that again. I’ll kill him first.

He notices I’m about to bawl and leans over to me, his hand going to dry my tears.

‘No!’ I snap, throwing his hand away in disgust. Even though I want nothing more than for him to comfort me. ‘Don’t you dare try to be nice to me, Will! Don’t you dare. Just drive me home.’

I’m silent for the rest of the ride home. Silent apart from the tears that escaped and refused to go away.

***

Tuesday 4th November

I’m still fuming by the next day that I feel I need to do something. I have all of this nervous energy from the confrontation and I have a feeling if I don’t act on it now I’m likely to burst into tears and crush my face into the sofa for the rest of the year. Elsie tried to console me, but no amount of wine would do it.

Gerry. That's who I can go after. That little bastard. He's the one that spread my nakedness around the village. I smile to myself, glad to have another target for my fury.

I get the bus to the next village and go straight to the bar. It's still early so they're just cleaning the tables and getting it ready. Gerry looks his usual smug, arrogant little prick of a man self. I should have let Will print that photo.

I take a deep breath to steady my nerves and storm over to him, adrenaline running through my veins.

'Rose?' he says, seeming shocked to see me. More like scared. He should be.

'Surprise! You're a fuck-wit!' I shout, punching him in the stomach.

He doubles over, winded. What a pussy. I take the opportunity to grab hold of his nipples through his thin white t-shirt and twist them. His face scrunches in agony and he lets out a low, pained growl. Almost like a wounded animal.

'Don't like that?' I smile sarcastically. 'How does it feel to have someone take advantage of your tits without your permission, huh? How. DOES. IT. FEEL?'

God, I'm mad with power. But it feels good to let all of my frustration out on someone.

'I'm sorry! I'm sorry, I'm sorry, I'm sorry,' he whimpers, while his colleagues look on in amusement. Clearly this guy doesn't have any friends. He probably pulls shit like this all the time.

'Why the hell did you do it? What did I ever do to you?' I ask, more upset than angry.

'Nothing!' he shrieks, his face scrunched up in pain. I release his nipples slightly. 'She made me do it. I'm sorry.'

'She? Who the hell is she?' I blurt out confused. Blaming it on someone else. Typical coward.

'Riley!' he whimpers, a tear falling down his face.

Riley? My Riley? Why the fuck would she do that? She's supposed to be my friend. She's never done anything for me to think otherwise.

'She gave me the picture and forced me to spread the posters around, or she'd tell everyone I had a small dick.'

His colleagues laugh at his admission.

I search his face for the truth. Oh my God. He's telling the truth. He *does* have a tiny penis. Riley took advantage of that.

'You didn't even take the picture?' I ask, my head spinning. How could she have taken it?

'No! Jesus, I could get done for rape doing something like that.'

I look at him bewildered. 'You mean we didn't hook up?' I'm so confused. Elsie and Riley said I went off with him briefly. It *sounds* like me.

'No. You were too smashed to be up for anyone,' he admits, grimacing.

How mortifying. But I'm glad I never got off with this tosser.

'But Riley? Why the hell would Riley want to do that to me?' I release the full grip of his nipples. I just don't get it. She's supposed to be my friend.

He places his hands over them, his face beginning to get some colour back.

'Do you by any chance have anything to do with Will?'

He clutches his chest rubbing his nipples.

'Will? Yeah, why?'

This can't be about Will, right? She says he's just a friend.

'You do know she's *obsessed* with getting back with him, right?'

I stare back, motionless. 'WHAT? I thought they were just friends now.'

I knew I should have gone with my first instinct. Damn Elsie, making me all forgiving and naïve.

He smiles regretfully. 'Look a little closer. You'll see the real Riley.'

I *cannot* believe this. What a two-faced fucking bitch. I need to bitch slap her. But then what would that achieve? No, I need to use this for a bigger purpose. I have a chance to make a change here. To bring down an evil bitch.

'Okay, you need to do something for me,' I demand. 'I need you to gather the village. I have to speak to everyone.'

This village feud is going to be fixed. Too many people are suffering because of it.

He rolls his eyes. 'Oh, that's it, is it? Just get the whole village together?' he asks sarcastically. 'That's hardly going to be easy.'

I lean in closer to him so no one can over hear me. 'What won't be easy is the entire village and internet seeing your tiny dick!' I shriek, punching him again in the stomach.

'You wouldn't!' he pleads, bent over in pain. 'Rose, you promised.' He looks terrified.

'Yeah, well now I have a condition. Friday night, your village hall, 8pm.'

***

Chapter 18

The bus ride home gives me time to process everything. Riley is after Will. Of course she is. I can't believe I ignored my gut and let myself be swayed by some nice words. She must have lied about what Will said about me too, right? She must have. It seemed so out of character for him, yet I chose to believe that poisonous wench over him. The one person who's actually wanted to get to know me and I easily believed so badly of him. I'm such a douche.

My mind wanders to every time she's spoken to me. How her words must have been hiding disdain towards me. I remember her being nice as pie to me at the stables that day. Making out that we could be friends and inviting me out.

Hang on a minute. Was that the same day the horses escaped? I can't remember. I could have sworn I closed that gate, but just assumed I'd done it wrong. What if *she* was the one who opened it? What if she set me up? Oh, this bitch is *unreal.* I swallow down the fury.

I have to find Will and apologise. I just hope he forgives me for doubting him so easily. I'm not sure I'd be so forgiving if the tables were turned.

As soon as I'm off the bus I run to his house. I say run, but I stop every now and again to double over from a stitch. I really need to do some more cardio.

I knock on the cottage door and Jay opens it almost immediately.

'Hey,' he smiles, taking in my sweaty appearance with disgust. 'Whatever you've done to that guy, you better fix it. He's been an absolute nightmare to live with since yesterday.'

I smile, secretly glad I've affected him so much.

He grabs his coat and goes to leave. 'He's upstairs.'

I bound up the stairs, desperate to see my man. That's what I feel he is now. My man.

I stop outside of his room and take a deep breath, before walking in. It's empty, but I hear the shower running, so decide to wait for him. I perch on his bed and tap my fingers impatiently.

Having this time to think is making me anxious. Maybe I'll just go through his drawers to keep me entertained. He's bound to have some dodgy porn to cheer me up. I open the second drawer and to my absolute surprise I find posters of me topless. The same posters that were all over the village. He had something to do with it? Could Riley and he have been in on it together?

I take them out and notice the Sellotape around them. These have been ripped down from places. He did this to save me from embarrassment. My body sags with relief. I rifle through them and there must be at least fifty. How could I think he was bad again so easily? I have some serious trust issues.

The door swings open and he walks into the room dripping wet, smelling of soap and aftershave. He's wearing only a towel wrapped around his waist. He's towel drying his hair with a hand towel, as droplets of water cascade down his lean muscles. He stops in the door way when he sees me. I can't tell whether he's pleased to see me or pissed off. Damn that beautiful, impassive face.

'What are you doing here, Rose?' he asks harshly, walking over to his chest of drawers and taking out some boxer shorts. Completely avoiding eye contact.

Shit. He's pissed with me. Not that I blame him. He must think I'm some sort of psychotic bitch. No, that's your ex.

I'm shocked to see that he has a large tattoo over his broad back. How did I not notice before? But then I suppose the last time he was topless around me I was a *little* bit drunk. I only get a quick look at it, but I see a mix of images meshed together under a starry sky. He turns back to me, still looking pissed. You could cut the heavy tension with a knife.

'I'm sorry,' I blurt out, my voice small with fear. 'I mean…I came here to apologise. I shouldn't have believed those things about you.'

He glares at me, now wearing his black boxer shorts. Jesus, his body! I'm getting a lady boner just looking at him. How could I have doubted this God of a man? *Because I don't deserve him,* my inner voice tells me.

'That's right. You shouldn't have.' He looks away again and I see the hurt I've caused him. I feel bloody awful.

'It was Riley!' I whine pathetically.

'What?' he asks, scrunching his face in confusion.

I stand up. 'She was the one who told me you were saying all that shit. And she's the one who made these posters and she let the horses out.' I'm out of breath from my rambling and I worry I haven't made any sense.

He walks over to me, still keeping his distance, leaning one shoulder against his wardrobe.

'Riley? Nah, she wouldn't do that.' He shakes his head.

He believes *her?* Not me?

'What? So you'll believe her before me? Isn't that just what you were shouting at me for not doing?'

'I'm not shouting.' He sighs heavily.

He's right. He's not. His quietness is worse. Maybe he's stopped caring.

'But you're right,' he admits. 'I'm sorry.' There's a big pause while I wait for him to continue. 'Tell me who it was.'

'I just told you! Riley!' God, he's so infuriating!

'Not her.' He rolls his eyes. 'The guy that broke your heart and made you so hard to crack.'

God, he's a bloody drama queen.

I roll my eyes and sigh loudly. 'Sorry to disappoint you, Willy, but no one has ever broken my heart. I don't have some sad little love affair to tell you about. And I'm not hard to crack. You're just hard to shag.' I smile at my own joke.

'That's because I want your trust first.' He stands closer, towering over me. I sit down on the bed, his dick now close to my face.

'I trust you,' I smile cheekily.

I reach my arms around his waist and press my face into his stomach in a weird kind of a hug. He hugs me back, stroking my head like a dog, while his abs ripple beneath me. God, I feel so safe and protected in his arms.

I slip my hands down the back of his boxers, my thumbs tugging them down.

'Woah!' he says, backing away, as if I'm on fire. 'What are you doing?'

Rejection again.

'I thought that much was obvious,' I grumble. Colour spreads over my cheeks. Why the hell does he always make me feel so unwanted and needy?

He sits down next to me and takes my small hand in his large ones. 'Rose, why the hell do you always want to use sex to cover your feelings?'

Why is he so emotional all the time? I'm all for being sensitive, but this is getting stupid.

I snort. 'You know, I'm starting to think you're gay.'

He looks at me intensely, shaking his head.

'So, what's with the tattoos?' I ask, trying to change the subject.

He looks down at the floor bashfully, rubbing my hand affectionately. Is he seriously embarrassed?

'Just a reminder, I suppose,' he says quietly. Sadly.

I snort. 'How can it be a reminder if it's on your back?'

He sighs heavily, before sitting down next to me on his bed. 'My grandad always told me to keep the past behind me.'

I peer over his shoulder. 'So what does it mean?' I ask. God, it's like pulling teeth.

'It's just something I had done. Kind of in honour of my mum and grandad.

'Let me see,' I beg, putting on my best puppy dog eyes.

He begrudgingly turns so that I can study it. Wow, it's incredible. It's all done in varying shades of black. There's a night sky filled with delicate stars. In the middle of it is an angel, her back turned away from me. Her wings are spread wide. On either side of the wings I notice eyes coming from the sky. The bottom of it is completed with the most beautiful roses. It's almost haunting.

I trace the angel's wings, feeling his muscles react underneath. 'The angel's your mum?' I guess.

He doesn't answer, but I feel him nod.

'And the eyes are hers?'

'One set,' he nods. 'The others are my grandad's. The sky is an exact copy of how I remember the sky looking the night I lost her.'

He must mean when she took him riding. My chest tugs with emotion for him.

'Whenever I see a similar night sky it reminds me that they're looking down on me.'

My heart physically aches. He's such a beautiful human being. And he's *mine*.

He wouldn't want my pity though.

'And the roses…have they been added since I got here?' I chuckle, trying to lighten the mood.

He turns round to face me, his eyes incredibly vulnerable. 'They were my mum's favourite flower.'

My poor damaged baby. Seeing the pain in his eyes, as if it were fresh, makes me want to burst into my own tears.

I look away and pick up one of the posters.

'You really took all of these down?' I ask, sure he'd want me to change the subject.

'Of course.' He leans in, pushes my hair to one side, tracing his finger down my neck. 'For you, Rose, I'd poke everyone in the village's eyeballs out, if it meant saving your dignity.' He leans in and kisses me, reminding me why I'm falling head over heels in love with this man.

***

Thursday 6th November

I can't stop smiling the next day. Everything's sorted now. He's promised to speak to Riley and assured me that I don't need to personally hunt her down, although I still want to. He finds me the next day and asks if I fancy pizza and a movie tonight at his place. Of course I said yes. The idea of snuggling up to him on a sofa is heavenly. What is happening to me?

As I knock on the door that night sudden nerves start to bounce around in my stomach. I know it's dumb, but I still get stupidly excited and tingly right before I see him.

'It's open,' I hear him call from inside.

Bloody charming. Now he can't even answer the door to me. I push the door open, realising it must be on the latch. Is nobody in this village concerned with security?

I walk into the sitting room, my skin prickling with fear when I find it in darkness. My scalp prickles. Oh my God. What if he's been broken into and they've got him tied up in the dark?

When the door fully opens I see that there's candles lit around the room, emitting a warm glow. What the fuck? Is he having a séance? Halloween was last week.

'Surprise!' Will says, appearing out of the shadows, holding a glass of champagne. He's wearing a three piece black suit complete with a dickie bow. He's ridiculously handsome. He hands me the glass, a smug smile on his face.

'What? What the hell is going on?' I ask with a nervous giggle.

'I thought we'd celebrate.' He smiles as he clinks glasses with me.

I crease my face in confusion. 'Celebrate what?'

Did I miss his birthday?

'Tonight,' he grins, his eyes dancing with humour. 'I'm giving you my flower.'

I burst out laughing, spraying wine onto the floor. I try to regain my senses.

'Are you serious?'

'Yep,' he grins, popping the P. 'Well, apart from it being my flower. You know what I prefer to call him.'

'You're…' I take a deep, steadying breath, 'giving me Big Willy?'

He locks his eyes with mine. 'Tonight he's yours.'

A thrill of excitement runs through me. Oh my giddy aunt. I'm going to have sex with Will. I'm allowed!

Although now that it's been announced like that, in this room full of candles, with him dressed all romantic-like, I'm nervous. And underdressed. Am I even wearing matching underwear underneath this hoodie and leggings? Normally I'm good at those things, but without our cleaner constantly washing my clothes it's hard to keep it together. Dear God, I'm wearing pink fluffy socks. I didn't floss. Did I take my pill? DID I?!?

'Don't be nervous,' he says, pushing my hair back from my face, making me tingle all the way down to my already throbbing Lulu. 'It's going to be amazing.'

He presses his mouth against mine; his warm lips making me melt around him. He pulls me into him, half having to support my weight as I'm basically floppy with want.

'Let's go upstairs,' he whispers seductively.

He takes my hand and guides me slowly up the stairs. I can't believe this is finally happening. What if my legs aren't smooth enough? When did I last shave them? This morning? Or was it yesterday? Dear God, what if I have stubble? What if he takes one look at my legs and refuses to have sex with Chewbacca?

He stops abruptly in front of his bedroom door and begins untying his dickie bow. God, he's hot. My breathing is laboured already and he hasn't even touched me.

'Now, I knew you'd be nervous.' He takes my hand and kisses my fingertips. 'Which is why I thought I'd try to make you more comfortable.' He opens the door and ushers me in.

I walk in to find that his normally neat and tidy bedroom is an absolute mess. His duvet is creased up at the bottom of his bed, there's clothes strewn everywhere and there's an open pizza box on the floor by the bed, half of it missing. I turn to face him and see his jacket is off and he's undoing his shirt.

'You…you messed up your room for me?'

He smiles. That's the only affirmation I need. He knows I'm used to sleeping with scuzzy guys who couldn't give a shit about my feelings. He knows that's what I'm used to. He's tried to recreate it, only this time it's with someone who actually cares about me. I could tear up. It's strangely more romantic to me than the candles and the suit.

'This is so sweet,' I gush, a lump forming in my throat.

He walks forward, his shirt open; showing off his delicious bronzed six pack. How did he get that living in Yorkshire? I wonder if he fake tans. He starts kissing me, his lips like a piece of heaven. God, I'm melting and he's barely touched me yet.

'I'm going to make love to you now, Rose. And you're going to have your first orgasm.' He smiles arrogantly, shrugging out of his shirt and letting it fall to the floor.

Wait, I didn't tell him I'd never had an orgasm before. Did I? He's so full of himself. But with a body like that I would be too.

I scoff. 'I've had sex loads of times, you know. What makes you so sure of yourself?'

He steps towards me and I already know the answer. I'm mad about him.

'No, Rose. You've been *fucked* lots of times in the past. You've never been made love to. You'll see the difference.'

I hope he's not going to start crying and confessing his undying love for me. That would be awkward.

He pulls my hoodie over my head, then my top. He grins, marvelling at my boobs which are pushed up by my red lacy bra. Thank God it's a good one.

I'm not sure if I'm happy with this 'making love' business. What does it even mean anyway? He hasn't told me he loves me, so how on earth would he '*make love*' to me? It probably just means it'll be slow. Slow and boring. I hope he doesn't light anymore candles.

I'm pushed back onto the bed before I have time to change my mind. He drops to his knees, removing my converse and socks. He grins when he notices the fluffy socks. He starts kissing my ankle bone, making me squirm. Goose bumps appear all over my body as I contemplate my jumbled feelings for this man. The truth is that I know I'm falling hard and fast for him and that scares me more than anything.

He unbuttons my jeans and yanks them down roughly. I look down to see that I'm wearing an old thong which used to be white but is now grey. I cringe. Why oh why didn't I see this coming? He doesn't seem to notice or care though. Thankfully my legs are smooth. Phew.

He licks up my left inner thigh, his hot breath setting my skin on fire. He comes so close to Lulu that I can practically hear her whimpering. Instead he begins again on my right inner thigh. I shut my eyes and drink it in.

Then his breath is on Lulu. I gasp and try to muffle the desperate groan escaping my lips. I'm bursting for him. He pulls on the sides of my thong, tugging it down. I lift my bum to help him. I feel so exposed under his gaze, spread open for him.

He strokes Lulu with his nose before planting feather soft kisses all over her. He's teasing me. I shamelessly grind against his face, my desire for more consuming me. He delves his tongue in, devouring me as if I'm his last meal. Something inside me fires, setting my heart racing. The blood pumping around my body is so loud I fear he'll hear it.

It's not enough though. I need him inside me. Now.

I grasp his hair in my fingers and tug hard. He looks up at me, his lips glistening with my arousal. It should be gross, but it's fucking hot. I smile shyly. Since when am I shy? He gets the hint and starts travelling up my body, his hands removing my bra and squeezing my raised nipples roughly. The sweet pain zings through my body, every nerve ending on high alert.

He sucks one into his mouth, alternating between nipping and sucking. My whole body is on fire. My brain feels like it might over heat from all of the sensations. Every time he touches me somewhere new my breath hitches in my throat, becoming thick and impossible to breathe out from my lungs.

I grab his belt and tug impatiently. He smiles against my lips before taking over. He quickly undoes his trousers, pushing them and his boxers down his legs and kicking off his shoes.

He confidently kicks my legs further apart with his knees before reaching into his drawer and getting a condom. I part my thighs further, allowing him as near as possible. I swallow the lump in my throat when I hear the rip of the foil packet. This is really happening. The one thing I've wanted more than anything. Let's hope after all this waiting I'm not a big disappointment to him.

A moment later he's resting against Lulu. She's only too happy to oblige. He looks intently into my eyes, his pale greens gazing with probing intensity.

'Please,' I whimper pathetically. I'm not too proud to beg.

He kisses me slowly and deeply, his hand on my face, touching me, cherishing me. My hands delve into his hair, grasping and pulling urgently. With one quick movement he's inside me, balls deep. Fuck! He's huge! I've never felt so full in all of my life. It's overwhelming.

A tear springs to my eyes from the shock. I take a deep breath, trying to collect myself. It's almost painful. He stills, letting me get used to him, planting a kiss on the end of my nose. I smile up at him, overcome with feelings; relishing being as close as two people can physically be.

He begins moving slowly, his thrusts gentle, his hands roaming through my hair. As I get used to it I start pushing my hips up to meet him, desperate for more friction. My hands travel down his back, urging him closer. He notices and quickens his pace, his hands now gripping my hair roughly, exposing my throat to him. He nips and kisses at my chin and nibbles my ear lobe. Something I never even knew I liked.

Heat floods my body so quickly I feel a sheen of sweat cover me. He's hitting somewhere inside me that feels like electricity sparking up, travelling up my spine and hitting my brain with a rush. Butterflies flutter in my stomach, spreading out to my toes. They curl, the butterflies quickly turning into shivers. My breath hitches in my throat. I can't breathe. It's a sensation overload. What the fuck is happening? Should I ask him to stop? Will I survive this?

He changes position slightly and quickens up some more. *Right there.* Dear God, its heaven. Euphoria explodes in my brain. Spots dance in front of me and I can't focus on anything. Nothing but the sexy sound of his skin slapping against mine.

Someone is screaming 'Oh my fucking God,' over and over again. I try to force myself out of the other planet I'm floating on to see who it is. Has Jay come home? Has he found us shagging? It's only then that I realise it's coming from me. Will wraps his arms around me, kissing my face as I ride it out. I've never taken ecstasy, but from what Janey describes, this sounds pretty similar.

A serene calm enters my veins, drunk on the love we've just made. Oh. My. *God.*

He tenses above me as he finds his release before collapsing on top of me, panting breathlessly.

He flips me over so he's on his back and I'm lying on his chest, equally out of breath, my chest rising and falling dramatically. Well fuck me, if that's making love then all I ever want to do is make love again. I had an orgasm. An earth shattering fucking orgasm. I can't believe it, but it happened. How I'd ever previously thought I might have had one, I don't know.

It was....well it was so fucking unbelievably all-consuming that at first I wanted to ask him to stop. I didn't know what was happening. I just knew that something was and it was incredible and scary. At one point I actually thought I was going to die. I'm not even joking. My body experiencing so much at once was like a sensation overload.

'I told you,' Will says in between breaths.

I put my arms on his chest and raise my head to look at him with a grin on my face. He can't resist telling me he's right, even in moments like this. I mean, he's still got his dick inside me for Gods sakes.

'You were right,' I grin. 'I know how you love to hear that.'

'I do,' he smirks, swatting my bum.

I yelp, but snuggle in closer to him. Is this what I've been missing out on? I've never felt the need to snuggle before, but my God, I suppose that's what an unbelievable orgasm does to you. I feel like I should worship him. In fact, I intend to do just that for the rest of the night.

He kisses me on the forehead before pushing us onto our sides and pulling out of me. I lean into him so he's got his arms around me, when suddenly it happens.

SQUEEEEEELCH!

Oh my God. The earth stops revolving as I look down at Lulu in absolute horror. Did that sound really just come from her?

'What was that?' he asks, seeming completely lost. He looks around the room.

I move to face away from him, but it only makes it happen again.

SQUEEEEEEELCH!

I'm sure now. I've fanny farted. Fanny farted in front of the man I'm falling in love with. I cover my face with my hands, as pure unfiltered humiliation courses through my veins. Why God, why?!

'Did you just…' He narrows his eyes, before the corners of his mouth twitch. He bursts out laughing and tries to take my hands away from my face. 'Did you just fanny fart?' he barely manages to ask, his chuckles booming around the room.

I throw his hand away and plant my face into the mattress. It's the only way to avoid looking at him. How the hell could this have happened to me? I have the most amazing bodily experience of my life, only to be followed by the worst bodily function to exist to mankind.

'Look at me,' he chuckles, trying to pry my shoulders from the bed.

'No!' I grumble, my voice muffling into the mattress. 'I want to die!'

He wraps his arms around me and rests most of his body weight on top of me. I know he's holding some back because I can still breathe. He nuzzles into my neck, spreading sweet kisses.

'I'll be here when you get over it.'

He shifts his weight and moves so that I'm on my side, his body spooned against me. I listen to his breathing slow, getting more comfortable, until I hear his soft snores. I may have just fanny farted, but right now, in the arms of the man I'm falling for, I don't feel half bad.

Friday 7th November

By the time I wake up the next morning I'm facing him completely. He groans softly before his eyes flutter open, his pert mouth falling into a lazy smile. I smile back, happy in the knowledge we'll never speak of fanny fart gate again.

'So,' he smiles slowly, 'I take it last night was your first orgasm.'

How the hell would he know that? I never confirmed that to him.

'What?' I blush. 'How did you…'

'You kept shouting that you were scared as you were coming close to it,' he grins widely. 'Not the normal reaction of someone used to how their body orgasms.'

I cover my face in my hands. If possible this is more embarrassing than the fanny fart. No. Dear God, I'm definitely wrong. Both are mortifying.

'I'm your first,' he grins confidently, stroking my hip, 'and I'll be your last.'

***

As the bodies start shuffling in, removing their coats and scarfs, I start to feel my nerves play havoc. Why did I think this was a good idea again? I should have at least watched a motivational YouTube video on public speaking. The last time I did this was in English class when I couldn't pronounce Ophelia and everyone laughed and said it sounded like I was saying 'Oh feel me now!' I shake my head to try and get rid of the sound of laughter. Kids are so cruel.

When the last person's sat in place and I have the attention of the crowd, I take a last deep breath and begin. Here goes nothing.

'Hi, everyone,' I call out feebly. 'My name's Rose Chapman, and I'm from Belmont Leaf village.'

'We all know who you are,' a teenage boy at the back laughs.

'Aye, nice tits!' another one chuckles.

I forget people have seen my breasts. Well, not just people; *everyone.* I shake my head, trying to gather myself.

'Anyway, I'm here to talk about the village feud.'

Angry faces stare back at me. Wow, tough crowd.

'What would you know about it?' a fat man in his forties shouts. 'You're a bloody Southerner.'

They are such Southerner racists up here.

I smirk. 'I may be a Southerner, but I'm living here now.' I turn to the rest of the crowd. 'Anyway, can someone tell me how this feud started?'

I already know our version, but I want to hear it from them.

A thin lady shoots her hand up. I nod for her to talk. 'They called us cheaters at the rugby match.'

I nod contemplating. 'Okay and what was your response to that?'

'Well, it's obvious isn't it?' the fat man shouts. 'They're a village full of bloody racists!'

Jump to conclusions much?

'Why would you come to that conclusion?' I counter. 'Do you realise that we have our own black residents, Lauren and Noah? They've received nothing but love and support from the village. Why on earth would they only pick on one man from your village?'

Confused faces stare back at me.

'Well, that's what we heard,' the thin lady says. 'And the next thing we know they're all slagging us off. Mrs Bluebell said my pies were disgusting!'

I put my hand up to stop her. 'I've heard first hand from Mrs Bluebell that your pies are the best in Leeds, so that's rubbish. She also told me how you called her a fat weable. Is that true?' It's hard to keep a straight face.

'Well…' she looks down sheepishly, 'only after she said that about me pies.'

'You mean after you heard the Chinese whisper that she had?' I challenge.

This is all so like high school.

'Um…' She looks down discomfited.

'Look,' I say loudly, grabbing the attention of even the chatting teenagers in the back, 'a lot of stuff has happened, but it's mostly hearsay and misheard gossip. Now, I don't know about you, but our village economy has suffered because of this. And I'm betting yours has too?'

'They all buy their pies at the super centre in Leeds now!' thin lady shrieks. 'My takings have gone down forty percent.'

'Only because you insist on buying all of your stuff from there too,' her teenage daughter says.

'So what are you suggesting?' the fat guy asks, scratching his head.

'I'm suggesting we call a truce. Have a party on the village borders. Anyone who shows up is willing to put this whole stupid thing behind us and start again.'

Any excuse for a party!

'No one will show up!' a teenager shouts, sipping from his can of coke.

'I think you'll be surprised.' I smile confidently. Of course, I'd have to actually talk to them first, but they don't have to know that.

'Why should we?' another one shouts. 'We have our pride!'

I sigh loudly. 'God, enough of the pride!' I shout. 'With the way things are going people are going to have to sell up and move on. Then you'll be stuck with a loud of Southerners looking for a weekend home and you know what dicks we are.' They all look terrified at the thought. 'OR we can support each other and continue to live here in harmony. It's up to you guys. Saturday, 5pm at the borders. Think about it.'

I grab my coat and flee out of there before I can burst into tears from the confrontation. Well that was fucking horrible. I'm not built for this shit. I can only hope they'll consider it.

I'm not holding my breath.

***

Chapter 19

Saturday 8th November

Now that the whole talking to the village fiasco is behind me, I can finally sit back and revel in my happiness. I still can't remove the smile from my face. I just can't. Is this really what I've been missing out on all these years? I had no idea!

It's such a beautiful day that I've decided to hang some washing out in the garden. I'm also hoping it'll distract Elsie from realising I've shrunk her whites. These washing machines are tricky bastards.

I swear the world even seems brighter. I look up at the blue sky and absorb the warm sun's rays on my face, as I listen to the birds singing merrily along. Now, thinking about how Elsie used to sing to the birds, it doesn't actually seem that strange. They're kind of cute. As long as they don't poo on my head.

'Someone's happy.' I turn around with a peg in my mouth to see Lauren grinning across the low fence. 'Can I assume something happened?'

'Yes!' I shriek excitedly, jumping up and down on the spot. 'We only went and did it!'

'Had sex?' she whispers, hunching her shoulders over as if to protect some privacy.

'Nope,' I shake my head, trying to play serious. 'We *made love.*'

We burst out laughing, happily cackling like a couple of school girls.

'You lucky cow,' she laughs. 'I take it he rocked your world?' She cocks one eyebrow playfully.

'Rocked it and threw it into orbit,' I gush, throwing my hands to my chest dramatically. Just talking about it brings a fresh wave of euphoria.

'Oh God, I remember the days,' she says sadly, clutching onto the fence. 'Actually it was so long ago I kind of don't.' She laughs, but I can tell she's sad about it.

'It can't be *that* long ago?' How bloody long could she have possibly gone without it?

She looks to the ground, her cheeks reddening. 'Try nearly eight years. I haven't had sex since the night I conceived Noah.'

WHAT? Eight frigging years? She hasn't had sex since I was…fifteen?

'No fucking way!' I screech in surprise. 'Your vibrator must be battered to pieces.'

'I don't have one!' She shudders at the idea. 'I just live from my memories. 12th September 2005 in a Leeds hotel.' She looks off into the distance as if recalling the memory.

12th September 2005. Poor Lauren. Everyone has needs, right? There I was whinging about not having had an orgasm and poor Lauren's had nothing. At least it was some sex. Some kind of emotion. 12th September. I try to commit the date to memory. This could actually help me find out who daddio is.

***

I look at my phone and consider it one last time. Is this a good idea? I already know it's not, but that doesn't stop me wanting to still do it. Megan deserves a kick ass party. And by holding back the location until tonight I've reduced the risk of getting found out. I type it out.

Old barn castle, Manor Lane, Lang raw fields

My finger hovers over the send button. Should I really do this? I think back to my sixteenth. I didn't have a party. It was just me and one friend watching Muriel's Wedding. I've never felt sorrier for myself. Fuck it, you only live once. I press send and down another vodka and coke. She deserves this.

Three hours later and the party is in full swing. It's amazing what a good quality boom box and some portable disco lights can do to excite people round here. Everywhere I turn teenagers are telling me what an awesome party it is. I just have to keep warning them not to tell their parents. People hate me enough already.

I go on a search for Megan. I haven't seen her properly since the start and I want to check that she's alright. We should probably sing *happy birthday* soon. I'm so pleased I've made her happy. Without a mum to look out for her she deserves someone on her side.

I round the corner, towards the front of the building, and see her.

She's on the floor, passed out. Her little friends are around her panicking, hitting her in the face and flapping their hands hysterically. Shit. This doesn't look good. I rush over and push them aside.

'Megan? Megan?' I wail over the loud music, my stomach in knots.

No response. I feel her skin and it's cold. She's so bloody cold. Oh my fucking God. I lift her arm, but it falls back down, completely floppy. Goose pimples spread over my own body, as the situation dawns on me. She's completely un-conscious. I feel her neck and thank God, she's got a pulse.

I turn to her friends. 'Call a fucking ambulance!' I scream, my voice strangled.

They freeze, obviously uneasy. 'But…we'll get in trouble,' one of them wails.

Are they *serious*? Their friend is lying here unconscious and they're worried about themselves?

'Not as much trouble as you'll get in if your friend dies,' I growl.

I grab the phone out of her hand and call it in. The operator tells me they'll be here in around ten minutes. That's the problem with living in the middle of bloody nowhere. I just hope to God she can last another ten minutes. I take off my coat and wrap it round her. Trust her to wear a skimpy gold dress.

'We're out of here!' her friend yells. I turn to seem them running across the field.

Some fucking friends.

I lean over her, pressing my body against hers, hoping to transfer some heat. I wish Will were here. He's always so warm bodied.

'Don't worry, Megs. Help is on the way,' I say, my chest heavy with unshed tears. 'Just stop playing silly beggar and you can stop me from having a heart attack, okay? Just wake up!'

I grab hold of her hand and press it against my cheek. Maybe it'll warm her. It's so limp. Too limp. Please don't say she's dying because I'm a fucking idiot who should have been watching her. I should have been more concerned, but here I was planning the party of the year and not giving a shit about her. About my friend. The person that looked to me for guidance. She's so mature it's easy to forget she's only fifteen. Has she even drank before? I should have bloody asked her all of this before, but she's just so confident. I suppose I just assumed.

I look up to see hordes of people running past us and across the field. Someone must have spread what's happened. They're clearly all shitting themselves, concerned that their parents will find out. I have bigger problems on my hands.

'Don't worry, Megs. I won't leave you,' I whisper in her ear. I feel a tear slide down my cheek. Please, *please* be okay.

Ambulance sirens sound in the distance, but it's too far away. It's taking too long. Please God let it arrive quicker.

'Nearly there, Megs. Stay with me, okay?'

The sirens are getting closer now. I mutter a few swear words under my breath. What's taking so long? I suddenly worry they won't be able to find the place. It *is* in the middle of nowhere.

'I'm just going to leave you for a second, Megan. Don't go anywhere or I'll kill you myself!' I joke, kissing her on the cheek and making sure my coat is covering her as best it can.

I jump up and run towards the ambulance sirens, waving them over. They park to the side of the road and get out, hurriedly carrying their kits with them.

'What's happened?' one of them asked.

'I think she's had too much to drink. She's passed out. I can't wake her up!' I wail, immensely relieved to have someone here to help.

'Name?'

'Megan.'

The paramedic hovers over her. He takes a torch out of his pocket, droops her eye down and shines it into her pupil. She's not even flinching. Her eyes look dead. Please God, no. Guilt is growing inside me like a spreading disease.

'Megan? Megan, this is a paramedic,' he says in a deep voice. 'Can you hear me? What have you had to drink tonight?'

Didn't he fucking hear me? She's passed out!

The other female paramedic gets an oxygen mask out and places it over her face. I can't even watch anymore. This is horrendous. Like a bad episode of Casualty, only it's all my fault.

Before I know it they've transferred her onto a stretcher and are wheeling her to the ambulance doors.

'I'm coming too. I'm…her sister!' I jump into the back, clutching onto her hand which now has a drip in it.

'Okay, fine,' the woman smiles reassuringly.

She slams the door behind us and the siren starts sounding as we begin to move. Fuck, it's horrible in here. With windows on either side its making me feel travel sick. She cuts off her dress with scissors and I think about how mental she's going to go when she finds out. She saved up three week's pocket money for that dress. Plastic things on wires are plugged onto her chest, a loud beeping beginning on the screen. It must be monitoring her heart.

Thank God, it seems steady.

'Will you be able to ring your parents?'

My parents? Why on earth would I tell my parents about this? Oh yeah, she thinks we're sisters. Shit. How the hell am I going to tell Phil that his baby daughter is in the hospital with alcohol poisoning? And it's all because of me.

A dull long beep breaks my thoughts. I look up to see the paramedic leaning over Megan.

'She's flat lining!' she shouts to her colleague. 'Step on it.'

Oh my God! Her heart stopped! Chills run down my spine. I swallow convulsively, my stomach heaving.

She gets out those electric shock things I've seen on TV and starts rubbing them together.

'Get back,' she shouts at me. She places them on Megan's chest.

Megan convulses, her whole body rising to the shock paddles, as if they were a magnet. The monitor starts beeping normal again. Thank God for that. I've never been more relieved in all my life. Thank you God.

'We've got her back,' she says, out of breath. She turns to face me, her eyes grave. 'Time to call your parents.'

***

I take a deep breath and try to stop my stomach from quaking. Just press call. This is all of your stupid fault. You need to own up to it.

I press call and hold it towards my ear, my hand shaking.

'Hello, Dog and Pond?' Phil answers after four rings.

'Hi…um, it's Rose.' My voice is no more than a squeak. Get it together, Rose. 'There's been an accident. You…you need to come to the hospital. It's Megan.'

'Megan?' he asks, bewildered. 'But she's staying at Rachel's. And what do you mean accident? Has she burnt herself with her straighteners again?'

I wish it were that simple.

'I mean…look, it's a long story. Just get here quick, okay.'

I hang up the phone and throw it to the floor. I have to hide and it has to be quick. I run back up to try and speak to someone in intensive care.

I grab a nurse. 'Megan Cartwell? Any news?'

She looks sad and for a moment I fear the worst. Please God, no.

'Her heart stopped again and we've had to pump her stomach, but we've managed to stabilise her. All going well, she should be transferred to a ward later tonight.'

Thank God! At least there's *some* good news.

'Her dad's on his way, but I have to go.' I turn and jog away, realising I need to pick up my phone from the floor. I must stop being so dramatic. It's really not helping the situation.

'But…Miss!' she shouts after me.

I'm not stopping for anyone.

I run down the stairs and jump into a taxi. It's okay Rose, I try to reason with myself. She's alive. She's fine.

Yeah, she just had to have her stomach pumped! My God, her heart stopped twice; that's not normal! What if she's affected by it for the rest of her life? What if her face droops down on one side like she's had a stroke? I could have ruined her life. Like it's not enough with all her mates talking about her.

It's all my fault. No one else but mine.

The taxi pulls up at home. I run in to beg Elsie for some money. She hands it over no problem, but asks for an explanation when I get back in. All I can do is vomit on the cat. Well, that's not going to make her like me anymore.

***

Sunday 9th November

I wake up determined. Not that I slept at all. I tossed and turned the whole time, thinking about poor Megan all alone in her hospital bed. I can't believe I left her. I'm such a heartless bitch. I need to see her. I know she might not want to see me right now, and I'm hell as sure her Dad doesn't want to see me, but I have to try. I have to try and apologise.

'I'm really not sure this is a good idea,' Elsie warns as we walk towards the ward she's apparently been transferred to.

'I have to try, Els.'

She nods. She was so supportive when I told her. Focused on me calling the ambulance instead of being irresponsible to hold the party in the first place. She really is a saint.

I walk into the room and spot them immediately. Thank God they haven't got one of those stupid blue curtains pulled around the bed. Phil's got his head in his hands, resting his forehead against the bed. As I walk closer I see Megan. Oh my God.

She looks terrible. So pale, her skin almost grey. A drip is still in her arm and her hairs a bloody mess. She must be asleep. I hope to God it's not a comma.

I walk to the end of her bed and clear my throat. Phil looks up and Megan's eyes fly open. She smiles weakly.

'Are you fucking joking, pet?' he shouts jumping up and getting in my face. I'm suddenly scared he's going to hit me. Why didn't I consider this?

'You get my daughter so wasted that she almost dies and you think you can just stroll back in to visit her like nothing happened?'

'No…I…I…wanted to apologise,' I stutter, swallowing down the lump in my throat. 'I'm so sorry, Megan.' My voice breaks as tears start falling down my face.

'Sorry?' he roars, his jaw tense in disgust. 'That's all you've got to say for yourself!'

'Dad, it wasn't her fault!' Megan says weakly. It seems like it's taking all of her effort to talk.

'Yes it was, Megan! She's supposed to be a grown up. But she couldn't be responsible for a house plant,' he spits.

That hurts. My house plant *did* actually die.

'I only begged her to have the party because you wouldn't let me have one!' she tries to shout, her voice still barely a whisper.

'Oh, so this is my fault is it?' he demands, his eyes crazy wide. 'Because I wouldn't let a group of teenagers get drunk? There's reason for this. Look at yourself; that's my reason.' His voice breaks and I realise he's on the verge of tears.

The enormity of it hits me like a freight train. I almost took his daughter away from him. I deserve every harsh word.

'Your dad's right, Megan. I'm an idiot. I'm so sorry.'

'You're not to see each other again,' Phil says, standing up to block my view of her. 'And consider yourself sacked.'

It's no more than I deserve. I nod my head, resigned to my punishment, and walk out of the room into Elsie's arms. I'm such a fucking moron.

***

By the time I get home I decide I have to tell Will. Although I really, *really* don't want to. He's going to realise what a skittish, dipshit bitch I really am and dump me. But I know news is going to spread fast in this village and I'd rather he heard it from me.

I decide to be a coward and text him.

I fucked up.

I press send and wait anxiously for a reply. After a while of me pacing my room the phone beeps. I nearly drop it to the floor in fear.

Are you pregnant?

Oh my God, he's a dick. We literally only did it a few days ago. As if I could be pregnant already. Unless…unless he thinks I'm pregnant by someone else? Ew.

No. Far worse.

Build it up, I say. Make it sound worse than it is. As if that's possible. I almost killed a teenager.

Nothing could be worse. I'm on my way.

He's coming here? Shit. I didn't consider that. I run to the mirror and remove the smudged mascara from my eyes. I look like crap. My eyes are all puffy and red, my chin looking like it's about to break out in acne at any minute.

The door knocks. He's here already? I'm not even wearing a low cut top. I can't even distract with my boobs.

'It's Will!' I shout, as I run frantically down the stairs. 'I'll get it.'

I swing open the door and jump when I see the vicar.

'Oh…hi,' I say, trying unsuccessfully to hide the disappointment in my voice.

'Rose,' he smiles sadly, his eyes sympathetic. 'I heard the news. I'm here to offer you some solace.'

'Huh?'

Elsie comes into the room sheepishly. 'Sorry, Rose. I called him. I didn't know what else to do.'

I turn back to her, furious.

'So you told on me? To the village bloody vicar?!' I shriek. How the hell could she do this to me? Does she not think I'm suffering enough?

'Please, Rose,' he smiles, 'I'm not here for judgement. I'm here for you to talk to.'

Trying to pull the whole nice vicar act. He just wants to find out the gossip.

'Hey.'

I spin round to see Will standing behind him, out of breath as if he's run here.

He looks between the vicar, Elsie and me. Well, this obviously looks odd.

'What's going on?'

'Nothing!' I laugh loudly, sounding insane. 'Just...come through to the kitchen.' I grab his hand and lead him through. I lean against the sink, my hands in my back pockets. It helps that it pushes my boobs out.

'So...do you want to tell me what's going on?' he asks, his eyes narrowing with curiosity.

'Err...'

Oh God, once he hears this everything's going to change again. He won't want me anymore. He'll realise what an irresponsible twat I am and dump me for good. The thought terrifies me.

Before I have time to change my mind I crush myself against his chest, pressing the side of my head into him. I breathe in his scent and revel in the feeling of warmness. I feel so safe when I'm with him. I'm not going to have this anymore. I can't believe I'm so stupid.

'Rose,' he says pushing me away to arm's length, his eyes concerned. 'You're scaring me. What is it?'

'I...well, I fucked up,' I admit, looking down at the tiled floor.

'Aye, you said,' he nods. 'But how?'

Not knowing must be killing him.

‘I…kind of organised a birthday party for Megan, only it got out of control and she drank too much and now she’s in hospital because of it…and…and…’ I let the tears fall out freely, a strangled sound escaping from my throat.

‘Come here, you doughnut.’

I’m pulled back into his chest, only this time he’s pressing me against him. He’s rubbing my back soothingly. I pull away, covering my face with my hands.

‘Don’t you hate me?’ I ask, shocked by his reaction. ‘Don’t you realise what an idiot I am?’

How can he be taking this so well? Doesn’t he understand?

‘I always knew you were an idiot,’ he smiles, tucking a bit of hair behind my ear. ‘But that doesn’t mean that you’re not sweet.’ He pecks a kiss on my lips. ‘And sexy.’ Another kiss, curling my lips into a smile. ‘And mine.’ He pulls me fully into him and takes my mouth completely.

Woah. God. How the hell am I getting rewarded for being such a dummy?

‘But…’ I try to pull back.

‘No, Rose, listen,’ he insists sternly. ‘You set out to do a nice thing for Megan, right?

I nod.

‘Well, then. Could you have been more responsible? Of course. Do I wish you’d told me? Yeah. But it’s done now and there’s no point beating yourself up about it.’

God, he’d make an amazing father one day. Woah! Where the hell did that come from?!

The vicar knocks on the kitchen door. We both look up, quickly jumping apart. I keep forgetting we’re a secret. He walks in smiling compassionately.

‘Ah, I see you also have Will to comfort you.’ He smiles warmly at him. ‘But I still wanted to offer a shoulder to cry on. Phil was furious when I tried to reason with him. Understandably of course.’

Understandably? Who does this arsehole think he is? Some up his own arse hypocrite who has an illegal love child?

'Don't you DARE judge me!' I shout, pointing my shaky finger at him.

Elsie walks into the room, obviously hearing the drama. She looks at Will confused. He seems just as bewildered.

'I beg your pardon?' he asks, completely taken aback.

I know I should stop talking and apologise. I know I should. But I can't.

'How dare you judge *me!* You're such a hypocrite! As if you haven't done stupid things in your life. I know a thing or two about you that I'm sure you wouldn't want to get out.' It sounds like a threat. Oh God, what am I doing?

'I really don't know what you're talking about, Rose.' He raises his eyebrows questionably. 'But I have no secrets from my congregation.'

'Bullshit!' I shout, now furious.

I've seen red. All of this weekend's drama forces itself to the front of my brain. I'm angry at my own stupidity. How I've hurt Megan, how Phil's never going to forgive me. I'm furious and I *need* to take it out on someone.

Elsie jumps in front of me, her face full of concerned horror. I feel Will's hand on my hip, clearly trying to restrain me. Ten policemen couldn't hold me back.

'You don't call a love child a secret?' I spit, looking at him with as much revulsion as I can muster.

'Love child?' he whispers, his eyes wide with disbelief.

'I know Noah's yours!' I scream.

I hear Elsie and Will gasp in horror, looking back to the vicar for his denial.

'Noah? Lauren's boy?' He scratches his head in confusion. 'Rose, I don't know why you think that, but you're wrong.'

'Oh, *really*!' I snarl. 'Where were you the weekend of 12th September 2005, then?'

I've got him now. The hypocritical bastard.

'2005? That's a long time ago to remember, Rose,' he tries to reason.

'You don't remember cheating on your wife?' I raise an eyebrow accusingly.

Elsie and Will are watching him now, obviously wondering what the hell I'm going on about.

'I have *never* cheated on my wife,' he states firmly. 'Why on earth would you think I had?' He seems genuinely upset. Obviously used to lying.

'Hello! His name is Noah. Like Noah's Ark. You're a pillar of the community. It doesn't take a rocket scientist.'

He must think I'm a fool, just like everyone else in this village, but a dog collar doesn't guarantee an honest person in my book.

'Well, it clearly takes someone smarter than you,' Elsie snaps. 'He can't have been doing that. I was being confirmed by him that weekend.'

She remembers the weekend she was confirmed? What a weirdo.

'Oh yes,' he nods. 'I do remember,' he smiles fondly. 'I'm sorry to disappoint you, Rose, but the only children I have are my two girls.'

I look deep into his eyes, but all I see is truth. I'm wrong?

'Oh.' Silence fills the room. Well, this is awkward.

'I think you should apologise, Rose,' Elsie snaps. 'You just accused the man of cheating on his wife.'

God, I'm a monster. I'm really on a roll.

'Sorry,' I mutter, looking at the floor. 'I…guess I was wrong.'

***

I peek around the hospital curtain; my body trembling at the possibility of bumping into Phil. Megan's sat up in her bed, flicking through her copy of Heat magazine.

'Hey, trouble,' I whisper, sneaking up to her bed.

'Rose!' she beams, her voice still scratchy. 'Thank God, someone to entertain me!'

It's so good to see her smile again.

'I think you've had enough entertaining for a while, don't you?' I tease, raising my eyebrows in warning.

'Okay, so maybe I had a *teeny tiny* bit too much to drink,' she smiles.

'It's all my fault.' I throw my head down onto the bed dramatically. She's a teenager, so I know she'll appreciate the dramatics.

She pats me on the head. 'You never forced me to drink like an idiot,' she says reassuringly. 'If anyone, blame Scott Blank. He's the one who brought the jelly shots.'

I raise my head to pout at her. 'I'm such a bad adult.'

She laughs. It's such a nice sound. Young and jovial. I can't believe we were so close to never hearing that again. 'You're a great adult. I want to be just as cool as you when I'm older.'

'No you don't.' I adamantly shake my head. 'If you end up like me I've failed you.'

She laughs. 'But seriously,' she warns, her voice serious, 'you should get out of here before my Dad gets back.'

He's literally going to kill me. I'm actually genuinely scared for my life.

'Exactly how mad is he still?' I ask, already knowing the answer.

'Well…he's kind of the maddest I've ever seen him.'

I drop my head in shame.

'In fact, I haven't seen my Dad this mad since I was eight and he found the note my mum had left him, saying she'd left us.' She looks off sadly into the distance, twiddling her fingers nervously.

She's never told me what happened to her mum before. I just assumed she didn't want to talk about it. She left her? How could she do that to her?

'He was so cut up he sent me to stay with my Auntie for a while. Apparently he went to stay with a friend in Leeds and spent a few weeks getting absolutely bladdered.' She chuckles at the irony.

'I'm so sorry, Megan. You were so young for it to happen to you.' I take her hand in mine.

I've had such an easy life compared to her, yet she never allows herself to wallow.

She nods sadly, squeezing my hand back. 'I remember the date. 12th September 2005. It's like it's engraved into my brain. The day I lost my mum.'

I frown. Why does that date ring a bell? How old was I then? My stomach drops as realisation comes jolting through my veins. That's the night Noah was conceived. In Leeds. By a man well thought after in the village. Oh my fucking God.

Phil's the daddy.

***

Chapter 20

Wednesday 12th November

I don't know why, but I can't face Lauren. I just can't. Knowing that Phil is the daddy has brought so many new dilemmas up. Noah is Megan's half-brother. I've avoided her too, which is easy considering I don't work at the pub anymore and half the village is talking about what a terrible example I am. I've heard that she's back home and back at school. She's even texted me a few times asking for me to visit, but I've said her Dad needs to cool down first.

Instead I've thrown myself into planning a village fête. Another way to raise money for the home. And hey, if it redeems my reputation with some of the locals, all the better. Luckily Elsie's dived into it full pelt. I think she's using it as a distraction. She still seems so confused about the whole nun thing. Plus she seems desperate to save my reputation, bless her.

I'm putting up posters advertising the fête in the village, when I spot her. She's walking home from school with Noah. Lauren. Crap. I try to hide behind the lamppost, but with these boobs it's hard not to be noticed.

'Rose? Hey, stranger,' she calls smiling widely. 'It feels like I haven't seen you in ages.'

Has it been that obvious that I've been avoiding her?

I smile as naturally as I can. 'Yeah…I've just been so busy,' I explain hurriedly. I point at the poster as it to explain.

'And I bet Will's been keeping you busy,' she winks, laughing cheekily.

I smile, but avoid eye contact. All I can think about is Phil naked. His big fat belly crushing Lauren. Sweating all over her. It's so gross beyond belief.

'Noah, why don't you go play on the swings?' she says with a mum smile, warning him to do as he's told. She turns back to me, stern faced, her dark eyes inquisitive. 'Okay, cut the shit. What's up?'

Oh God, she's got me now. How can she know? I thought I'd gotten better at these things. God knows I've done nothing but lie since I've got here. It's that damn mum intuition. I might as well just come out and say it.

'I *know*,' I whisper, raising my eyebrows suggestively, hoping her imagination will fill in the blanks.

'Know what?' she asks, her face bemused.

I look at the ground, shifting awkwardly from one foot to another. God, please don't make me say it. I wish I'd never forced information from her. This is all my own fault for being a nosy bitch.

'I know who the daddy is,' I blurt out. I take a strand of hair and start twiddling with it, trying to gauge her reaction.

Her face drops as realisation settles over her. She grabs me roughly by the arm and pulls me further away from Noah.

'What the hell are you talking about?' she whispers angrily. I've never seen her so pissed off. She's normally so laid back.

'I know it's Phil,' I hiss.

She scrutinises me, trying to work out if I'm trying to trick her into confessing. 'How the hell did you find out?' she asks, her jaw tight and her brown eyes intense.

'I'm not dumb.' I roll my eyes and place my hand on my hip. 'I worked it out.'

'Buggar.' She shakes her head. 'Please don't tell anyone. It would ruin *everything*.' Her eyes plead helplessly with me.

She's so dramatic.

'What exactly would it ruin, Lauren? Noah doesn't know his father now. He might be living close and contributing financially, but how can he carry on as if nothing's happened? He has a son.'

It makes me sick to think he'll grow up never knowing his Dad lives round the corner.

'Keep your voice down,' she snaps, looking back at Noah. He's oblivious luckily, too busy playing on the roundabout. 'It's…complicated.'

'Well, lucky for you I wouldn't be able to tell anyone even if I wanted to. Megan's just back from hospital and it would kill her to know her dad did this. That she has a brother she never knew about. And that he was conceived the weekend that her mum left her. I mean, you could write an ITV drama around it.'

She looks at me sharply. 'Look, don't act like I don't already feel terrible every time I talk to her. I've managed to avoid her until you came storming into my life, bringing her with you.'

I hadn't thought about that. Had she been awkward? I never noticed, but then I never knew what I was looking for.

'I won't say anything. I promise.' I smile, to let her know this doesn't change our friendship. 'For now.'

But I suppose it does. How the hell can I choose a loyalty between two women that have become like best friends to me? I suppose it's weird that one of them is a woman in her early forties and one is a sixteen year old girl. But that's neither here nor there.

***

As soon as Will opens the front door I crush myself against his chest. He obligingly wraps his warm arms around me. I need this right now. I need his comfort and his love. Plus his constant warmth is so nice after the chills of outside. I'm really starting to wish I packed more practical clothing.

'Woah. What's up?' he asks, kicking the front door closed behind me.

I slump in his arms. How long has he got?

‘Can you keep a secret?’ I ask, pulling away and looking into his pale green eyes. God, he’s hot. How did I get this lucky again? I really have no idea.

He raises his eyebrows at me. Then I remember we ourselves are a secret. I keep forgetting. It’s annoying me too. Why can't we be together publicly? I don’t want to have to pretend outside of his house.

‘I want to talk about that anyway,’ he says, releasing me and shoving his hands in his jeans back pockets. He looks uncomfortable. What’s up with him?

‘Why? What?’ I ask, my voice shaky.

What the hell could he want to talk about? Is he dumping me? Is it this whole Megan thing? Am I an embarrassment to him? How the hell will I carry on without him? He’s become my rock, my total constant.

‘You first,’ he insists.

Oh God. I might as well off load before he chucks.

‘Well…Phil is Noah’s dad. And now I’m just supposed to forget about it and not tell Megan. And so I’m torn between my two friends and I don’t know what to do.’ I blurt it all, not even pausing for a breath.

‘Shit,’ he says stiffly, his eyes wide with shock.

‘Well, that was helpful,’ I deadpan.

‘Sorry,’ he smiles, running his hand through his hair. ‘It’s just a lot to take in.’

‘Tell me about it. I *hate* being this stressed.’ I start stroking his biceps. ‘I think I need some distracting.’ I wiggle my eyebrows suggestively.

He smiles, his eyes twinkling with mischief. He pushes my hair out of my eyes. I love how he makes me feel so looked after. ‘I’m sure I can think of something.’

***

An hour later I’m lying in his arms in his bed, my troubles are a distant memory. I rest the back of my head against his chest and look at the ceiling. His words ring through my head again. *I want to talk about that anyway.* Is he really dumping me? I can't bear the thought of not being with him. He's made himself irreplaceable and it's not even the orgasms. Although they do help.

'So…you said you wanted to talk?' I try to sound vague, but I know I sound how I feel. Desperate and scared.

What if it's the fanny fart? Of course it's the fanny fart. I just know it. Of course it freaked him out. It bloody freaked me out!

He adjusts himself beneath me, so that both his arms are wrapped around me. I try to memorise the feeling of being in his arms. Of being cherished. It's probably the last time. God, just the thought of it leaves me feeling cold and bereft.

'Aye, I did.' He clears his throat. 'I've been thinking…'

Oh God. This is it. It's over. I brace myself, but at the last minute decide I can't look him in the eyes while he says the usual trite. *It's not you, it's me.*

I roll over onto my side and sit up, facing away from him.

'It's okay, Will. You don't have to say it out loud. It's fine.' I want to be mature about this. Not make it any harder on him.

I go to stand up, but he grabs my arm and pulls me back into his arms. I look at him, trying to remember his perfect features. His jawline. His crooked nose. Those beautiful clear eyes. I already miss him, an ache in my chest feeling as if my heart's turning to stone.

'What the hell do you think I'm saying?' He studies me with curious eyes. 'Do you think I'm breaking up with you?' He looks appalled.

'Aren't you?' I ask quietly, still not able to meet his eyes.

'No, you dickhead,' he laughs, pulling me closer. I rest my head on his chest, relishing the feel of his strong muscles. 'I'm asking you what you think of going public. You and me.'

I pull away, completely flabbergasted. I look into his sincere face. Is he for real?

'What? Like…telling everyone we're together?' I utter in disbelief.

He nods. My eyes skim over his features. I realise for the first time that he seems nervous. His usual cocky demeanour is nowhere in sight.

'But…I thought you didn't want people to think you were giving me preferential treatment at the home?' This is confusing.

'That's why I thought I'd ask you. I understand if you want to wait until after the programme's finished. But…' he looks down at the floor, 'I just can't bear the thought of you going another night not in my arms. It kills me knowing you always have to get up and leave. I want you here. In my bed. In my arms when I wake up in the morning.'

I stare at him aghast, my heart singing. Is he serious? Can he seriously be this into me? Have I actually died and gone to heaven? This is all too surreal. Too good to be true. I don't deserve him.

'You…you really want to be with me?' I stammer, looking into his eyes, searching for the truth

At his expression I feel the blood draining from my face. Oops. He's mad.

'Rose, why is that so hard for you to believe?' He sighs as if I'm a massive inconvenience and runs his hand through his hair in exasperation. 'I've fallen hard for you.'

My stomach drops as if I'm on a roller coaster. Oh my God. He's fallen for me? He's…in love with me? This is crazy. Beyond crazy. It doesn't stop my chest beaming with pride. This boys fallen for me. He's mine. He wants no one else but me.

'I…I like you too.' I sound completely underwhelmed, but it's only because I'm still reeling from shock.

His mouth droops in disappointment, his forehead creased in sadness. 'I was hoping for something a bit more poetic than that.' He smiles bashfully.

Oh God, now I feel awful. My poor Will. I do love him, right? Only…I've never been in love before. How can I know, when I have nothing to compare it to? I don't want to say it unless I'm one hundred percent sure. Will deserves that.

‘I’m sorry,’ I shake my head, as if it’ll help me to pull myself together. ‘You know I’m not good with this girl stuff. But…I mean, I accept. I want to be with you too. Can't you just imagine all of those slushy words you were expecting? The main thing is that I feel it, right?’

He looks at me seriously, his eyebrows narrowed, before relenting. ‘Right.’ He leans in and kisses me. ‘This weekend then. At the fête,’ he nods. ‘We’ll tell everyone.’

‘Okay,’ I nod, beaming back at him. I have a boyfriend! Wait, do I? ‘So…does this mean you’re my boyfriend?’ I know I sound like a teenage girl but I just want to clarify. I feel like I can ask him stupid questions like this and he won't think less of me.

He looks at me with amused eyes. ‘I was always your boyfriend, Rose. We just hadn’t told people.’

Wow. When did this happen? Am I seriously that dumb that I didn’t see how crazy about me he is?

‘Hey, as long as I’m getting Will sex on tap, I’m happy,’ I grin, trying to lighten the mood.

***

Saturday 15th November

‘Fuck it!’

It’s not the sound I’m expecting first thing in the morning, let alone from Elsie. I run down the stairs and into the kitchen, expecting to find something serious, like a fire. Instead Elsie is sat on the floor, her knees pulled up into her chest, crying into her hands. What the hell’s happened?

I look around to grab a tea towel for her tears, but it’s then I notice the state of the kitchen. There’s flour everywhere, including her hair. The oven has remnants of black smoke billowing out of it and there’s a tray of cupcakes on the counter, so burnt they’re actually black.

‘Els?’ I find a tea towel half covered in cupcake mix and crouch down next to her, attempting to dab at her eyes.

'I can't do it,' she states, grabbing the tea towel and blowing her nose into it. Gross.

Oh God, Elsie's chosen today, of all days, to have a nervous breakdown. How inconsiderate. I'm already crapping my pants about the fête today. I mean, why on earth did I think it would be a good idea to try and meddle between villages? I'll probably just get everyone from this village hating me too. Not that I'm miss popularity anyway.

'So what?' I laugh. 'So you aren't good at baking. It's hardly the end of the world,' I try to reason.

'It is for me', she sniffs, her eyes red and puffy. 'It's just another thing Jeanette's going to remind me I can't do.' She looks so broken. Over cupcakes.

'Who's Jeanette?' I want to punch her in the face.

'Riley's mum. The vicar's wife.' I remember her bitching about her before.

'She's always insinuating I'm not good enough for the church,' she wails, her chin wobbling.

It kills me that this woman can reduce Elsie to tears.

'Hello? The woman's daughters are monsters,' I shriek, making a monster face. 'You should pity her.'

'I suppose,' she says sadly, smiling at my monster impression. 'But, I promised I'd make cupcakes for the stand.'

I look around at the devastation surrounding us. I've never seen British Bake Off, but I'm pretty sure this isn't how it's supposed to look. There's no salvaging those cupcakes.

'Why don't I give it a go?' I offer, wanting nothing more than to bring a smile to her face.

Because apparently I don't have enough going on, what with worrying about whether the other village will show up and trying to make sure everything else runs smoothly. I really need to learn when to shut my mouth.

***

Two hours later and who would have thought it? I'm good at baking! Unfortunately, I'm *not* so good at icing them, so between me and Elsie we've bodge jobbed it. They don't look too bad, but at least they'll taste nice.

We've only got about five to go when there's a knock at the door. Elsie runs to get it, while I desperately try to make them look more appetising. Maybe more icing? I hear him talking and then Will walks into the kitchen with an amused grin.

'Honey, I'm home,' he says in a silly Fred Flintstone voice. 'And you baked me my favourite.' He grabs a cupcake and raises it to his mouth.

I slap it away. It falls on the counter, icing squishing against the worktop. 'No eating,' I warn, my face stern.

He grins, his eyes changing. They become hooded, hungry for something other than cupcakes. He pushes me back against the oven with his hips until our bodies are completely pressed together, his erection now obvious. This reaction over a cupcake? I should bake more often. I look at his plump lush lips and realise I'm panting.

He leans back, picking up the cupcake again. He moves my hair behind my shoulder and plants a bit of the cold icing on my neck. I shiver in anticipation. God, he drives me crazy.

'I can't eat *anything*?' he teases, his eyebrows raised, as he leans down to my neck. He looks up at me through his dark lashes, as if daring me to say no.

I roll my eyes in response. It's hard to act unaffected.

He licks and sucks the icing from my neck, inch by tortuously slow inch. My whole body trembles involuntarily, as I put my hands through his hair, begging him to continue. When every last drop of the icing is gone and I'm sure Lulu's made a puddle on the floor, he leans up and takes my mouth.

He ploughs his tongue into my mouth, letting me taste the sweet vanilla icing. They might look like crap, but they taste amazing. He tastes amazing. I pull him closer, leaning over the oven so I can feel his erection press up against Lulu. I want him to push me up on the worktop and take me now, but I'm sure Elsie would protest. Plus, it probably wouldn't be very hygienic.

I'm vaguely aware of the door knocking, but I couldn't care less right now. Elsie can do one for all I care at this exact moment.

A forced cough forces us to stop abruptly and look up through our hazy with lust eyes. Elsie is standing at the door of the kitchen next to an astounded looking Janey. Janey? What the fuck is she doing here?

'Janey?!' I scream, pushing Will away and bouncing over to her, so high I almost touch the ceiling.

'Freckle Tits!' she exclaims, throwing her arms around me, embracing me with her boobs and her bergamot scent. She feels like home.

'What the hell are you doing here?' I gush, pushing her back so I can take in her tanned limbs. They look amazing set against her dark hair and turquoise eyes. Mexico clearly agrees with her.

'I *had* to see it for myself,' she says, her deep husky voice filling the room. She eyes up Will slowly, from head to toe. 'It seems you've made friends.' She winks.

He crosses his arms awkwardly over his chest, leaning back against the oven. Luckily his boner isn't obvious. He releases a hand to do an awkward little wave. God, he's adorable.

'Yeah, sorry.' I bush, remembering my manners. 'This is Will and this is Elsie.' I'm so proud to show them off.

She completely ignores Elsie and instead grabs Will's hand.

'Charmed, I'm sure,' she flirts, batting her eyelashes and flicking her hair.

It gets my back up immediately. *He's mine, bitch,* I want to shout as I slap her slutty hands out of his. I suppose I've never had a serious relationship around Janey before. This is weirdly unsettling. Can I trust her? What am I *saying*? She's my bestie. Of course I can.

'Well…I should get back,' Will says, smiling at me, seeming amused. He obviously finds it funny that my mate's as nutty as me. 'I'll see you at the fête.'

He goes without giving me a kiss goodbye. It makes me feel sad and needy. What's happened to me? Janey won't recognise me.

She claps her hands in front of my face, breaking me from my day dreams. 'Okay, you need to tell me what the hell is going on,' she shrieks, jumping up and down on the spot.

I have my friend back!

Chapter 21

We took so long catching up that it means we arrive late at the fête. She knows about Will and that we're still a secret, although I held back my more embarrassing gushy feelings for him. I don't think she'd get it. We've never talked like typical girls. More like *'you tap it? Nice.'*

'So you seriously think you can win this incentive thing?' she pries as soon as Elsie is out of ear shot.

I look over to her setting up the cupcake stand while a lady scrutinises them. That must be Jeanette. Can I win? Sure, but I don't even know if that's what I want anymore. Mexico has taken such a back seat lately. I've been too busy enjoying myself. I nod vaguely, avoiding eye contact.

'Don't let a penis hold you back, Rose.'

I flip my head round to face her. She knows me too well.

'There's plenty of dick in Mexico and they taste of tequila.' She raises her eyebrows and flashes me a dirty smile.

'Gross,' I mutter under my breath, smiling despite myself.

'But seriously, you are coming, right?' She looks at me, her gaze accusing.

An uneasiness creeps into my stomach.

'Of course,' I smile, more to get her off my back than anything. 'But, Janey, how come you didn't answer any of my emails?' I try not to sound pathetic, but I realise it still sounds it.

She rolls her eyes. 'Oh, babe, I was busy!' she dismissed, waving her hand around. 'You must have seen my pics. It's been non-stop.' I've forgotten how her hand gestures are so big. 'Plus, I found a man.' She raises her eyebrows up and down comically.

'Really?'

No way? Janey settling down? What is the world coming to? Maybe we're all just growing up.

'Yeah,' she grins, her face nearly splitting in half. 'The owner of the club. He's the reason I'm here. He paid for my flight.'

Owner of the club? How old is he? And paid for her flights? Is he her sugar daddy? She'd always joked about finding a rich man, but I thought she was kidding.

'Is he rich or something?'

'He's…got his fingers in a few pies,' she smiles, her lips pursed together. 'And me most nights,' she cackles loudly. A few people turn around to stare at the loud stranger.

'Don't be crass, Janey,' I snap, smiling politely at people as we pass.

'When did you become such a prude?' she snaps back, looking at me as if I'm an alien.

She's right. I sound like Elsie. I cross my hands over my chest defensively.

'I'm not,' I say sulkily. 'I just…' I look over at Will helping the residents get comfortable and can't help the smile breaking across my face. Betty waves at me.

'Don't tell me you've gone all gooey over him?' she accuses, her mouth open in disgust. 'Don't get me wrong, he's hot, but hoes before bros remember?'

'Yeah,' I shrug dismissively. 'Anyway, you picked the right day to visit. You'll see the village in all its glory.'

I feel stupidly proud to show it all off. I just bloody hope it goes without a hitch. With Janey here it could really go either way.

***

A few hours later the fête is in full swing. The Morris dancers have been on, as have the line dancers. It was hard to concentrate on them when Janey was taking the piss the whole time. I pretended to laugh along, but I was terrified someone would hear her. They'd done their best to perform and they'd offered their entertainment for free, so that we could raise money for the home.

It makes me realise how much I've changed since I got here. Wasn't I the same as Janey when I arrived? Sarcastic and selfish. Only now the people in this village managed to worm their way into my heart. I've formed real relationships here. Not that those relationships have been formed with anyone in the other village. *None* of them showed up. Not one. The unforgiving bastards. I'm starting to agree that they can go fuck themselves.

The tapping of a microphone pulls my attention away. I look up to the stage to see Megan's friend's band, Beauts, starting their set. Its two guys and a girl singing some happy, dance tune. They're actually pretty good.

Janey grabs me and we run to the front of the stage to dance with Megan and her friends. The same friends that abandoned her in her time of need. They seem to be glad with the attention. We hardly had to push people out of the way. But slowly a crowd of teenagers form around us, the girls swooning to the lead guys love lyrics.

The band kicks out some more tunes and soon everyone is dancing, holding their plastic cups in the air. Even Mavis! A dark threatening cloud begins to loom above us and soon rain drops onto my shoulder. I try to ignore it but as it gets heavier people start shrieking and running to take cover under the small marquee.

'What a shame,' Megan says, sad for her friends.

The disappointed look on the bands faces makes me stop from following them. Poor little guys getting their moment ruined. I grab Megan and Janey's hands and carry on dancing, this time pulling the hood of my coat up. The look on the bands faces is enough for me to see its worth getting wet for.

Everyone soon joins us and Will shuffles up beside me, smiling. I know he's pleased with me.

'Rose,' Elsie calls, pointing behind me.

I turn to see a mob of people walking over the bridge towards us. The other village. They came! Everyone stops dancing and turns to stare towards them. The band seems to notice the weird atmosphere and stops playing. Crap. Maybe this wasn't a good idea.

They all come to a halt in front of me, with the fat man from the meeting walking to the front, looking like he means business. I hold my breath as everyone stares at me with questions on their faces. What the hell have I brought on myself? Have they come for a fight? Oh God, what have I done?

'You call this a party?' he asks, a small smile spreading on his face.

I sag with relief. Thank God, he comes in peace!

'What the hell are they doing here?' Will spits, stepping forward, his face red with fury.

Fat man looks at me, puzzled. 'We came to accept your apology,' he says, nodding with a gracious smile.

'Apology?' Will laughs cruelly. 'No one ever said we were sorry.'

Damn it, why is Will being such an arse?

'Hey, hang on now,' fat man says, shaking his head, clearly outraged.

'STOP!' I shout, jumping between them both.

Everyone is looking at me.

'Can't you see how this has gotten completely out of hand? You've all fallen out over pure hearsay and most of it is wrong.' I take a deep breath.

'Now you have two choices. One, you can keep up this grudge and slowly ruin your own villages. Businesses will be lost and enemies made once more. Or option two. You make up, forget whatever's happened, and work together to become the community you once were. When you helped each other. I come from a place where that is very rare, and let me tell you, once its lost its fucking hard to get back.'

There's silence as everyone seems to contemplate this. Oh God, what the hell have I done? I should have just kept my nose out of it. Why did I ever think meddling would be a good idea?

'I'm game if you are,' fat man says, offering his hand out to Will.

Will looks down at his hand, his face impassive. I hold my breath. Please, *please* be the bigger person. Silence covers the crowd as everyone waits for his reaction.

'Okay,' Will says, shaking it firmly, his face unreadable. 'Forgotten.'

Cheers erupt around us with people beginning to chat as if nothing's happened. I suppose I've forgotten that there were a lot of true friendships ripped apart over this. Not that it stopped them from their own stubbornness.

Within an hour everyone's a little shit faced. As the alcohol flowed so did the talk. Most people found out what they heard wasn't true. Riley was mentioned a few times. Nobody seemed to put two and two together, realising she was shit stirring the whole time. I haven't even seen her today, thank God. Although I'd have loved to have seen her face when Will announces we're a couple.

The school head masters pledged to give the bread contract to Mavis and everyone's agreed that they'll help each other.

Mavis and the thin lady are holding each other extremely close, while they dance to Lady in Red, courtesy of Lauren's boom box. The fat man is passed out in the grass, with the teenagers drawing a moustache on his face. Friendships are being re-made everywhere you look. It's heart-warming.

'That was a nice thing that you did,' Will whispers in my ear, making me jump.

I wink back at him, a warm fuzzy feeling going through me at the idea of making him proud. All I ever want to do is make him happy. Lulu wants to make him happy too. She's got an evening planned.

'I'm going to get a drink. Want one?' he asks, his hand on the small of my back. It's a friendly enough gesture to everyone else. Only I know the heat and want behind it.

'Vodka, lime and soda,' I grin.

He knows Phil still doesn't want to see me since the whole Megan thing. She barely got away with dancing with me before Phil called her back. He still set up a beer tent though. He seems to be doing a roaring trade, judging by the way everyone's stupidly drunk.

He makes a point of slipping his hand to my waist as he walks away, sending electricity to bolt through my spine. God, I want him.

I go over and chat with the band, telling them how good they are. They should audition for the X Factor or something. Maybe I could be their manager. When I've inflated their egos enough I decide to go look for Megan, as Janey seems to have gone missing too. Maybe she can get away from her Dad again.

I walk round the oak tree and head towards the beer tent. Maybe she's helping out with glasses or something. It's hard to get through with all of the people buzzing around, trying to thank me for such a great day.

I'm almost at the tent when I see them. It's dark enough so that the twinkle lights round the tent are the only illumination. Will's standing at the make shift bar holding our drinks while chatting to Janey. Only I *know* Janey; I know when she's throwing herself at someone. I feel queasy.

She's leaning into him, her hand stroking the collar of his shirt. Get off him, bitch. She keeps throwing her head back laughing, as if whatever he's saying is the funniest thing in the world. It works to get her tits thrust in his face too.

Worst of all is that he's laughing along, as if he finds her endearing. She calls over Phil who pours them two shots of tequila and hands over some salt and lemon slices. They both line up the salt on their hands and down them. Will dribbles a bit down his chin, which Janey catches with her thumb.

Get. Off. Him.

They quickly lick the salt and stuff the lemon in their mouths to suck. They both grimace, with Janey jumping dramatically up and down on the spot, bouncing her boobs in his face. She puts her hand to her mouth and pushes her face into Will's chest, as if to help comfort her from the pain.

I can't watch anymore. I need to turn away. I *must* turn away. But I can't.

Will pats her on her back playfully. Why is he encouraging her at all? She looks up at him with a cute smile and then it happens. She leans up and kisses him.

I turn away and close my eyes, my stomach seizing and contracting. I try to fight the nausea with all my strength, but I still fear I'll vomit.

How? *How* could they do that to me? How could *Will* do that to me? I thought he loved me? Was that just a load of bullshit? Was Riley right all along and he is playing me for a dickhead. My head whirls with unanswered questions.

I turn and run, ready to run, but instead bump into Lauren.

'Rose,' she says sternly, like she's been looking for me. 'Tell me you haven't told Megan?'

I can't deal with this right now. I'm barely keeping it together.

'About Phil? No, of course not.'

'She was just telling me how she'd have loved to have a younger brother or sister. I thought maybe she knew.'

'No, but she should. It's not fair on Noah either. Not knowing his own dad runs the local pub.'

'What?' We both swivel our heads to face Megan, two glasses in her hands. 'Wha…what did you just say?'

Oh holy fuck. I open and close my mouth several times, desperately trying to think of something to say, but I've got nothing. I'm too busy dealing with my own heartbreak. I need to be alone.

They both look at me furiously. 'I'm sorry,' I mumble.

I turn and run, not sure where I'm headed, just wanting to sprint away from it all. The ache in my shins is nothing compared to the crushing pain in my heart. Will's fucked me over. The one guy that I trusted. He lured me into a false sense of security and now he's making out with Janey. My Janey. My best friend.

I stop when I reach the stables. I hadn't realised I was heading here, but my mind must have subconsciously wanted to see Mitsy. A friendly face. I haven't got many of those left now. I go to her stable and stroke her mane affectionately.

'Fancy a ride, Mitsy?'

She neighs, which I take to be a yes. I lead her out into the darkness and jump on, leaning down to cuddle her. Why couldn't I be a horse? Life would be so much simpler.

I take her out into the open field. It's only when I've been riding a while I allow myself the pain. To think and feel.

A sound escapes my throat and I realise I'm sobbing, my throat closing in. How could Will do that to me? It was obvious she was hitting on him. A fool could have seen that. And he wasn't stopping her. If anything he was encouraging her. Doing shots and letting her touch him. It still makes me sick to think of her hands on him. What if they've taken it further and they're currently shagging in the field? The thought of it makes me heave.

And that's before even considering the fall out caused with Megan and Lauren. I should have tried talking in code. What was I thinking talking about it like that, just casually in an open field? I'm a moron.

I start encouraging Mitsy to go a bit faster. She's bound to want to stretch her legs. I only managed to give her a quick walk this morning and I want to feel the wind in my hair. I can't believe we've bonded so well. I actually like Mitsy more than I like some humans. Maybe even my parents. That's slightly worrying.

'Come on, girl. Let's go a bit faster.' I lightly kick her with my thighs, encouraging her to let go.

She's cautious at first, but the more I encourage her the more confident she gets and before we know it, we're flying through the field. It actually feels like I'm flying. The wind in my face, the trees rushing past me. I feel free. Free from all of the bullshit in real life. Untouchable. Alive.

Chapter 22

Sunday 16th November

I wake up and go to stretch, my bones aching like I've run a marathon. Only something pulls on my arm, restraining me. I open my eyes and look down to see a drip in my arm. What the hell? I bolt upright, looking around, desperate to get my bearings. The place stinks of disinfectant. Will is asleep in the chair next to me, his hair even more ruffled than normal. I'm wearing an ugly hospital gown. Ew. I'm in a hospital bed. What the hell happened?

My pulse starts to quicken, as I desperately try to remember something. What happened to me? The last thing I remember is going on Mitsy for a ride. Did I fall off? Did I have a heart attack? Was I attacked?

Will starts stirring in his chair, as my breathing gets louder from distress. God, the thought of the drip being in my arm is making my stomach flip with disgust. I swallow down the bile. Try not to think about it. I scrunch my eyes shut and try to concentrate on happy things. Unicorns, rainbows, Mitsy, Betty.

'You're awake.'

I open my eyes to find my happiest thing. My Will. He's leaning over me, touching my face tenderly, as if to check I'm real. I look into his light green eyes and reach out to touch his chiselled jaw. Thank God he's here looking after me. I've never been so happy to see anyone.

But then I remember him and Janey. Him and my best friend flirting and kissing and God only knows what else. The betrayal burns in my chest.

'What happened?' I croak, my throat dry.

He moves his chair so he's sitting closer. 'You fell off Mitsy and knocked yourself out. You've sprained your ankle and got a few bruises, but you should be fine.'

I did WHAT?

'They sedated you, so we've just been waiting for you to wake up. What were you even doing there anyway? Why'd you leave the fête?' He studies my face for an answer.

'I'm surprised you noticed,' I snap bitchily, staring at the ceiling. I must look like a monster which is not how I wanted to look when I'm confronting him about this.

'Huh?'

I look at him and he honestly seems clueless. What a good liar. He must be a professional. I choose to ignore him.

'What do you mean?' he asks, his voice showing hurt. Oh, he's *good.* 'I went to get us a drink and then found you'd disappeared. Is there something you want to tell me?' He has the cheek to look accusing.

'More like is there something you want to tell *me*!' I shout, almost breaking my voice from the effort. 'I saw you.'

Perhaps I'm choosing the wrong time to pick a fight. My whole body aches like a mother fucker and my eyes are heavy, begging to go back to sleep.

'Saw me doing what?' he demands, leaning back into the chair, his arms crossed defensively.

I take a deep breath to stop myself from getting choked up.

'I saw you kiss Janey.' I try to convey how furious I am, but my hoarse, tired voice doesn't seem to portray my anger. 'I thought you were different, Will, but no, wheel in Janey and her big tits and available clunge and you're a sucker for it. Just like *everyone* else.'

Did I really just say *clunge?* Ew. I really must stop watching The Inbetweeners re-runs.

'Woah, you've got this all wrong!' he says, his hands up in defence. 'Yeah, she was flirting with me, but I was just trying to be friendly back. I know how close you two are and I wanted her to like me. But then she caught me off guard by kissing me. I threw her off. Then I came to find you. I had to hear from Elsie what had happened. I was going out of my fucking mind.'

He seems pissed and I know it's because he was scared he'd lose me. Just like he lost his mum.

‘Really?’ I ask a tear escaping down my cheek.

‘Really,’ he nods sincerely. ‘Look, we’ll talk about this properly later, but I should call Elsie. She’ll want to know you’re awake.’

‘She’s awake!’ I turn to see Elsie at the door, her wide eyes nearly popping out of her head. ‘Thank the Lord! She’s awake!’ she screams, running into the room and throwing herself on top of me, her full body weight suffocating me.

‘Jesus, Elsie!’ Will snaps, delicately lifting her off me and placing her down on the chair. ‘Don’t suffocate her.’

I smile. Typical bossy Will. My Will. Please still let him be my Will.

‘Freckle Tits!’

I look up to see Janey at the door, jumping up and down with joy, her own breasts about to give her a black eye. She runs over to me.

‘You’re alive! She’s ALIVE!’ she chuckles, sounding like Frankenstein. She squeezes both my boobs while bellowing ‘HONK, HONK!’

I push her off and fold my hands over my chest, but quickly realise it’s kind of impossible with the gross drip.

‘Why do you even care, Janey?’ I ask shortly. ‘You didn’t give a shit about me when you were snogging Will last night.’

Elsie gasps and stands back. She hates confrontation.

Janey rolls her eyes. ‘You’re welcome,’ she smiles. ‘Had to test out if he was trustworthy for my freckle tits, didn’t I?’ She smiles back at me, completely oblivious to the red hot fury growing inside of me.

‘Janey, that’s not how friends act!’

Elsie and Will stand by awkwardly. I can tell they’re trying to decide whether to leave. I give them a warning look. They leave and then I’ll *really* go mental.

‘You don’t kiss your friend’s boyfriend to see if he’s a nice guy. You just trust me to make my own decisions.’

‘Okay,’ she snorts, ‘don’t have a heart attack.’

I look at Will. He shrugs, as if to say I told you so.

I can feel a string of words forming at my lips. Pent up words which I've carried around with me for the last couple of years.

'No Janey! You need to hear this.' I realise I'm speaking so loud I'm almost screaming, but I don't care. I need to get this out now while I'm drugged up on morphine or whatever. 'You didn't reply to one of my Facebook messages.'

'I told you I was busy,' she retorts, eye rolling to the heavens.

'Oh, fuck off. You had time to upload the photos of you getting shit faced and having the time of your life. A real friend would care that I was abandoned in a strange Northern village, where I knew no one.'

'You said yourself, you had the nun.' She points to Elsie, who looks to the floor sheepishly.

'She has a name!' I shriek. 'Her name is Elsie and she's been a better friend to me in the last few months then you have our whole friendship.'

I'm out of breath from the effort. Why am I picking a fight when I'm so shattered?

'Whatever,' she snorts. 'I'm done. If you stop being such a drama whore let me know.' She turns to walk out of the door.

'Yeah,' I spit. 'I'll send you a Facebook message. Oh wait, you never fucking reply!'

She's already walking down the corridor.

'That was intense,' Elsie says, letting go of a breath she seems to have been holding. She perches herself on the bed timidly.

Will takes my hand and strokes it with his thumb. 'I'm sorry you fell out over me,' he says with a grimace.

I click my tongue, my body wrung from frustration. Or maybe the accident. Who knows.

'That was coming for a long time. Besides,' I look between them both, 'I have you guys and I'm more than happy with that.'

Elsie smiles before diving on me, hugging me so tightly I'm fighting for breath.

'Hey.' I look up, over her shoulder, to follow the voice and see James standing awkwardly at the door, holding a coffee.

'James,' I say startled. 'What are you doing here?' My voice is high and squeaky. I really need a drink of water. Or a shot of Prozac.

Panic courses through me, as I become aware that this is a dangerous situation. I've never been around Will and James together in the same room. I know it was forever ago, but I really don't think Will would be happy if he knew we hooked up. He's possessive as it is.

'I wanted to check you were okay.' He walks in and perches on the end of the bed.

'She's fine,' Will nods confidently, looking at him bewildered. Obviously wondering why he's here.

'And I wanted to apologise,' he continues. 'I was such a dick to you and I didn't mean it. I just didn't want anything serious.'

Fuck, James! Why are you talking about this in front of them? I glare at him, trying to communicate to shut up!

I nod frantically, desperate for him to be knocked out by a passing nurse. I try to shoot warning looks at him while behaving confused in front of Will. It's hard when I possibly have a concussion. He looks seriously baffled. So does Elsie.

Shit, shit, shit.

How the hell am I going to handle this? Deny everything? Call James crazy? Or admit to it and quickly apologise, hoping for the best?

I decide I'm not going to say anything. If I stay mute I can't be dragged into this dangerous territory we're teetering on. I shall neither confirm nor deny.

Will looks back and forth between James and me, his forehead creasing as awkward silence fills the room. I press my lips together, essentially gluing them shut. I close my eyes trying to block it out.

Please move on, *please* move on.

'What do you mean?' he asks James, quickly realising that I'm refusing to talk. 'Didn't want anything serious?'

Oh God. It's happening. It's like a car crash right in front of me.

James looks back between us confused, obviously wondering why Will even cares. He doesn't even know we're together. So many secrets and lies.

'Nothing,' he shrugs. 'We just had a thing. I treated her badly. You know,' he smiles, 'same old story.'

For God's sakes James, shut the fuck up! Why can't he read my mind? I'm thinking it so hard I'm surprised he hasn't become telepathic.

Will's eyes narrow as he places his hand up to his temple. I notice it's shaking. I haven't worked out yet if it's from stress or fury. Although I'd put money on the latter.

'I didn't know,' he says bluntly, avoiding my gaze. I feel bile start to rise in my throat, my stomach curdling.

James smiles, looking between us both. I feel like I'm about to implode with humiliation. He has *no idea* the bombshell he's just dropped. The bloody idiot.

'Wait, are you two…' he looks between Will and I, 'are you guys sleeping together?' he asks Will with an oblivious smile.

I look to Will, my eyes trying to plead with him to listen to me.

He nods, deliberately going out of his way not to meet my eyes. He's furious. I can tell. That vein in his neck is raised. Oh fuck.

We're not just sleeping together, you fucking idiot! We're going out with each other! I'm in bloody love- err I mean…it's serious, just secret. How the hell do I communicate to him that James meant nothing to me?

James laughs, as if it's no big deal.

'You little sneaks,' he chuckles. 'Hey, Will, what about that weird freckle that looks like a third nipple? Isn't it funny?' He doubles over in hysterics, clearly having no idea of the disaster zone around him.

Will finally meets my eyes, but when I see the pure disgust in them I wish he hadn't. He's looking at me as if I'm a cheap slut. As if I just sleep with anyone regardless of my feelings for him. Which I suppose I am. I *am* a cheap little slut. At least I was until Will changed me and made me feel special. Worthy of being looked after. Now it's ruined.

I suppose it doesn't help that I was only just accusing him of getting off with Janey. I can see it there, in the same eyes that creased with affection when they looked at me. Now there's nothing but revulsion and pain.

'We did have something,' Will spits, his nostrils flaring with rage. He looks away, hurt pouring from his face. 'But it's over now.' He stands up, the chair squeaking loudly against the tiled floors, before storming out.

I feel the loss hit my chest like a sledge hammer. I've lost him. I've fucked it all up. It's completely my own doing. Tears sting at my eyes, my throat clogging with emotion. I try to swallow down the grief and instead take in some air, but it's useless. I scowl at James, wishing he'd never been born.

He grimaces before running out after him. I finally force down the lump in my throat and look to Elsie for support. I've never needed her more. I'm not sure if I'll survive this.

Only her normal smiling, supportive face isn't there. In its place is a face similar to mine. One of loss and hurt.

'Elsie?' I whimper, a loud sob escaping.

'Don't,' she snaps, holding her hands up defensively. 'Just don't.'

Why the hell is she so mad? What the hell have I done to her? It's *my* own life that I've ruined.

'Don't what? Why are you mad?' I don't understand why she's so pissed off. A tear escapes down my cheek.

'You couldn't leave him alone could you?' she spits, jumping up to standing. Her jaw is tense. She actually looks so mad she could kill me.

Leave who alone? What the *hell* is she talking about?' This is definitely too much with a concussion

'James,' she hisses, her face red and furious. Her eyes are glassy, as if she's storing tears. 'I told you he was trouble.'

I've never seen her so livid. And I've stolen her chocolate.

'Why are you so pissed off?' I ask, my voice high pitched and wobbly. I'm not doing well at holding it together.

'Because you've ruined things *again*, Rose. Why couldn't you just try and have a normal life without shagging *everyone* in sight!'

My mouth hangs open in shock. She grabs her handbag and storms out, banging the door behind her. Leaving me completely alone.

I welcome the crushing devastation taking over me, burning my chest, closing my throat and stinging at my eyes. Tears stream down my face, making a small puddle on my chest. I've brought this all on myself by being a dirty little slut. Maybe Elsie's got the right idea. Nun-ville here I come.

***

Monday 17th November

The next morning I put the keys into the cottage door, pausing to see if I can hear anything. I'm still shocked Elsie didn't pick me up from the hospital. I mean, I know she was mad, but I thought she'd have gotten over it by now. I mean, how does this even affect her? I'm an idiot, sure, but surely she knew that anyway.

I didn't have any money for a cab, so I had to get two buses. With crutches. That's harder than you'd think. I'm shattered, my bones screaming in agony, but more than that, let-down.

I swing the door open and find her sat on the sofa, her pink duvet wrapped completely around her, barely leaving her head exposed. She's watching what looks like The OC box set and her eyes are all puffy, as if she's been crying. This can't just be about me messing things up with Will. There has to be more to it than that.

'Elsie, what's wrong?' I throw the crutches against the wall and wobble over to her, throwing my hospital bag on the floor.

She raises her head, as if she's just realised I'm here. Didn't she hear the door? Why is she so spaced out?

'Oh, hi,' she croaks, forcing herself to give me a half smile which doesn't meet her eyes. It's so unlike her. It's almost scary. Definitely unsettling.

'What the hell is wrong? Why have I pissed you off so much?' I perch awkwardly on the edge of the sofa. I'm not sure she'd appreciate me trying to hug her.

'You just had to ruin things,' she says quietly. She's still looking ahead into space. Has she had a breakdown?

I'm so confused. 'Ruin what? My relationship with Will?' I swallow down the tears barely kept under the surface. Yeah, I already know I fucked up there, but why the hell does that affect you so much?'

I really don't get it. I'm devastated enough without her turning on me too.

'I warned you off James.' Still no emotion in her voice.

I smile to myself. 'Don't you see how appealing that made him?' I force a laugh, despite feeling more alone and gloomy than ever. 'And what's the big deal, it was just sex,' I shrug. 'And it was before Will. I didn't cheat.'

She snaps her head towards me, her eyes filled with contempt.

'That's all it ever is to you, isn't it, Rose? Sex.' Well, her voice has emotion now. A tone of bitter resentment. 'That's what your whole life revolves around. Don't worry about anyone else.'

My mouth drops open. This new Elsie shocks me so much. I just want a cuddle and to be told everything's going to be okay. Instead she's being bitchy. This isn't like her. Maybe I *will* have to get her committed. I'll need to google the symptoms of a breakdown.

I try to open my mouth to say something, but close it quickly. I don't know if anything will help. It has the potential to make it worse.

'You want to hear something funny?' she snarls, her eyes ablaze with abhorrence. 'I was supposed to save you. The vicar told me to help someone I know. To save them from their ways. It was my very first test. Well, I've blooming failed now, haven't I? Because you can't keep your knickers on.'

Ouch. It's like she's hit me square in the nose.

A tear escapes down my cheek, but I don't feel it. I can't feel anything. A numbness is taking over. I think it's my body's way of trying to protect itself.

The one person who I thought would always be on my side, who would love me unconditionally, has turned their back on me. Why am I even surprised? My own parents have, but this one really burns.

'I...I'm sorry,' I blub.

I turn away, not wanting her to see me cry. I force my tired limbs up the stairs, having to revert to crawling because of the shooting pain in my ankle. I slam the door behind me and climb under the covers, still fully clothed. I bury my head in my pillow like a wounded animal. I hear a rustle and realise a note from Janey has been left on the pillow. I assume, as I haven't heard from her, that she's gone back to Mexico. Some friend she is.

Hun,

I've got to go. I still want you to come join me in Mexico, but I get it that Will's keeping you here. I tried it on with him last night and he just blatantly refused me. He's a keeper!

Love ya! xxx

I pull my knees up into my chest reverting to a foetal position, as I start to contemplate it all. How could she really think trying it on with Will was a good friend thing to do? Where could she have thought she was looking out for me? It doesn't matter. She's gone now.

I've got no one left. Will hates me. The one almost traditional relationship I've had and I've fucked it up by sleeping with his brother. It's like some horrible Jeremy Kyle show. But I mean it was before I even knew I liked him. Not that it matters, him and Elsie hate me now. I've probably stopped her from fulfilling her dream as a nun. Maybe I *should* keep Janey sweet. She's my only friend in the world right now. Lauren and Megan are bound to turn on me when they find out how much of a horrible person I am.

The front door slams, shaking the door frames. I spring from bed and hop into Elsie's room to watch out the window. She walks down the road, her arms crossed over her chest and her head down. She looks devastated. I'm so upset I've disappointed her. The truth is that I couldn't give a crap about her becoming a nun; I think it's a big mistake, but to hurt her like this is unforgiveable. In my old life I never really cared enough to worry when other people were upset, but this feels different. She's always had so much time for me and I've failed her.

I turn to leave, deciding to spend the day crying in bed, but I trip over her ridiculously long curtains. I land flat on the floor, my hands just breaking my fall. The pain in my foot shoots up my leg. She really needs to get someone to hem them.

I lift my head and look beneath her bed, trying to get my bearings. The doctor told me to take it easy, not go falling about like a clumsy bitch. God, for a Christian woman she's got a lot of shit under here. Doesn't Godliness mean cleanliness or some crap like that? Maybe I should clean it for her. Try to earn some brownie points.

I move a dusty box out when I see it. A shoe box marked with a black pen SAVINGS. Savings? Why would she hide money under the bed? Is she a secret bank robber? Is that why she feels she needs to repent?

I grab the box lid before I can reason with myself and rip it off, sitting back on my heels to examine it. Shit, there's loads of notes in here; fifties, twenties, tens, all scrunched up messily. I start counting it and see there must be at least two grand in here. What the fuck? Hasn't she ever heard of a bank?

I feel the creased notes between my fingers as my mind wanders. This could solve everything. I'd get to Mexico, and Elsie and Will wouldn't have to look at my pathetic face every day with hatred in their eyes. I'd be doing her a favour. She's obviously too polite to ask me to leave and I can hardly go back to my parents with my tail between my legs. Janey's obviously already forgotten about our fight. I could make up with her properly and live the life we'd always planned on.

Before I've thought too much about it, I've staggered into my room, emptied the money into my handbag and am stuffing clothes into my hospital bag. It's the only way.

***

Chapter 23

Monday 17th November continued

The heels of my boots slam against the tiled airport floor as I struggle to get to the flight desk with my crutches. It's drawing more attention to me than wanted. I carry my bag over to the First in Flights desk and start queuing up. I must be the only British person that hates queuing. It's so annoying having to wait. It's giving me too much time to think about this, and the more I think the more I'm considering if this is the right thing to do.

I mean, why am I even considering staying? Sunny Mexico over the Yorkshire boring countryside? Sand and tequila over grass and tea bags. Of course I know which one is more appealing. All I can think about is Will's face the moment he realised I'd slept with James. He was sickened by me. There's no way he'll ever be able to look at me the same again after that, let alone want to be with me. Then there's Elsie and how I've messed up her whole churchy assignment. What if she can't become a nun because of me? She'll never forgive me. But then, isn't the whole church thing supposed to be based on forgiveness? I doubt she'll ever get over it. I'm so confused.

I try to shake the thoughts of them from my mind and concentrate on Janey. My hilarious, spunky friend Janey. Only…well, she's hardly been a good friend to me since I've moved here. She didn't reply to *one* message I sent her. I suppose I could blame it on her being busy in Mexico, but I mean she must have some time off, right? She had enough time to find a rich sugar daddy. Her pictures on Facebook show a lot of lazing on the beach. That doesn't look too busy to me.

And then just turning up here and trying to steal Will away from me. I know she says she was trying to look out for me, but that isn't how normal friends act, right? I can't imagine Elsie, Megan or Lauren behaving that badly.

Thinking about it now, it's almost hard to believe we're friends. I suppose if I were to really dissect it we could just be compared to acquaintances who live similar lives. We both like to live life the same way; party hard, fuck everyone else. But when I truly think of what a friend should be, I'm not sure if she fits the description. I've never confided a secret to her and we've never really even talked about anything more superficial than who we currently fancied, or how to get out of Watford. The girls have been more than a friend to me in the seven weeks that I've been here.

An impatient tapping foot brings me back to reality. The queues moves forward, but I'm still standing here, staring into space. I smile an apology at the frustrated woman behind me and quickly move along. I'm suddenly feeling nervous now that I'm this close to the desk. This close to leaving the only place that's ever felt like home to me.

I allow myself the pain of thinking about leaving Mitsy and Betty. I've been trying not to think about them at all, as if to ignore they ever existed, but how could I? Both have changed my life in so many profound ways and I didn't even get a chance to say goodbye. I wonder if Will will think to go to the stables and feed her? And what if Betty hears about me leaving and is upset she didn't wave me off? The woman's like a grandmother to me and this is how I treat her? What is wrong with me? Oh, that's right, I'm a selfish slut. That's without even thinking about Lauren and her straight talking sass and Megan's sweet sense of mischief.

The lady in front of me finishes and walks away. I swallow down the lump in my throat and hop up to it. My head feels like a whirlwind, my chest right, as every emotion I've been supressing decides to resurface at once.

'Your…next flight to Mexico please.'

***

As the taxi passes the sign for Belmont Leaf Village I smile to myself. I've made the right decision. This place is home now. I know it. It doesn't matter how much apologising I have to do. I *have* to try. It pulls into Elsie's road and I spot Will and Elsie stood outside talking. My heart melts when I see him. I can't wait to run over to him and apologise for that whole James misunderstanding. I've thought about it and I know I can explain it to him, so that he understands. I know I can claw back what we had. I just have to be willing to beg. When he understands that it was before us he'll forgive me.

I throw a twenty at the taxi driver, making a mental note that I will still owe Elsie twenty quid, and jump out as quickly as possible with my holdall and crutches. They both turn and stare at me in disbelief.

'Hi guys!' I beam.

Why are they looking so weird? I've only been gone two hours.

I can't believe how euphorically happy I feel. I hadn't realised how making the decision to stay would make me feel so good. It's like I've been subconsciously stressing about it without even realising.

Will narrows his eyes at me so harshly I shiver, as if he's turning my bones to ice. He's still this angry? I look at Elsie, my own brow furrowed. She looks pissed too. Uh-oh. My hopes that they'd have calmed down a bit evaporate.

'What's up?' I ask quietly, my precious confidence quickly dwindling.

'You're back?' she asks, muddled. She scratches her head. 'I thought you'd left?'

'Left?' I force a fake awkward laugh, urging myself not to turn red. 'Why would I have left?'

I didn't leave a note. How could they have guessed that?

Elsie crosses her arms over her chest and looks sulky. 'I just thought you'd gone,' she mutters quietly.

'It's not rocket science,' Will interrupts scornfully. 'You arrive back in a taxi after stealing all of her money.' His voice carries such disdain.

My eyes widen as the gruesome realisation settles over me. She knows. She knows I took her money and she's told Will. Now I look at her closer I can see that the rims of her eyes are red. She must have been crying. Guilt swallows me up as I look at her, already trying to forgive me. I feel sick to my stomach.

'It's okay,' she smiles bravely, shrugging. 'It's fine.'

'No, it's not, Elsie!' Will barks, making us both jump. 'Will you stop being so fucking reasonable?'

He hates me. I can see it now. There's going to be a *lot* of begging.

'Will, I'm sorry,' I whisper, my eyes dropping to the floor.

I feel so ashamed. Could this really be the man that was confessing his love only a few days ago? I've made him despise me.

'Sorry for what?' he roars with a smirk. 'For sleeping with James? Or for stealing Elsie's money and deciding to run off without even a goodbye?' His words burn my face like he's thrown acid.

Is he hurt? Could this be coming from hurt?

'I came back,' I whisper, my chest feeling as heavy as lead. It sounds so pathetic compared to everything else I've done.

'Well, congratulations,' he snarls sarcastically. 'You decided to come back. Only no one wants you here anymore.'

'Will, that's enough,' Elsie interrupts. I have so much love for this woman. Fighting in my corner even after I've stolen her money. 'She came back. Let's all go in and have a brew.'

I feel the unshed tears thickening my throat. Is it possible I can feel worse with Elsie standing up for me? I truly don't deserve her. But I want Will's forgiveness too.

'No! Fuck the tea!' he roars, his face becoming red and blotchy.

Uh-oh. He's refusing tea. This is bad. *Seriously* bad. I can actually see how wounded he feels.

'Leave her,' Elsie snaps, pushing him away and grabbing my arm. 'Come in, Rose.'

I smile warmly at her as a tear escapes. I'm grateful, but I need to face up to him.

'Go in, Elsie. I need to talk to Will.'

She begrudgingly walks in, but not before shooting a warning look at him. I turn to him, head hung in shame.

'There's nothing to talk about,' he snaps, shaking his head. 'I don't know why I bothered,' he says quietly, as if to himself. He turns and starts walking away. Potentially forever.

My heart strings pull, begging me to fight for him.

'Will, stop!' I beg, stumbling over and pulling on his arm. 'You don't understand.' My voice is starting to break. I can't hold it in much longer.

He whips round to me, his face like thunder. 'Don't understand?' he scoffs. 'Don't understand what? How you *fucked* my brother?'

It's like he's hit me with a hammer.

'How you were just working at the home so you could escape to Mexico? How you started a relationship with me, when you had *no fucking intention* of sticking around? Go on, explain! Explain your way out of that!'

I look into his hurt eyes, desperately searching for some way to explain myself. Some way of telling him how I feel. I search my mind for the right words, but nothing comes. It's blocked by the pathetic tears streaming down my face. He hates me. It's all over his face. Maybe there's no coming back from this.

'I thought so,' he says, his eyes resigned, nodding his head slowly. He turns and walks away. This time I don't stop him.

I walk into the house, forcing my legs to move. I can't feel the pain in my ankle anymore. Compared to the fresh pain in my heart it's nothing.

As soon as the door closes behind me I slump down onto the floor, letting the tears flow freely. I've fucked up everything. I'm such a giant loser.

Elsie prises my hands away from my face and plants a hot cup of tea in them. God, just looking at the tea makes me think of him. Before him I didn't even drink it. Much like him, I had no idea what I was missing out on.

'I'm sorry.'

I look up to see that it's not me that's spoken. It's Elsie. I scrunch up my forehead in bewilderment. Why the hell should *she* be apologising?

'Elsie, why the fuck should *you* be sorry? I'm the bitch. I'm the one that stole your money.' God, just saying it out loud makes me collapse into fresh sobs. I'm a horrible, *horrible* person.

'But I drove you to it,' she says, her eyes clearly pained. 'When I came back from my walk and you weren't here, I just knew. I was so horrible to you.' She looks ashamed, bless her.

'You had every right to be, babe. I'm the monster. I ruined your chances of saving me. What if you can't become a nun?'

It's not enough that I've ruined my life, I've gone and ruined hers too. I take a sip of my tea and cry some more.

'Oh, don't worry about that,' she shrugs airily. 'Wait…do you think that was why I was upset?' She seems puzzled.

'Yeah… Wasn't it?'

I'm so mixed up right now. My head feels like a washing machine. Am I now losing track of how I'm pissing people off? I should get a notebook.

She takes a big deep breath. 'I was upset because of James,' she says quickly as she releases it.

James? What the hell has he got to do with it? I stare at her, too baffled to talk.

'We used to go out,' she shrugs, as if this news is no big deal whatsoever.

WHAT?

Elsie and James? The trainee nun and the village bad boy? Only the biggest fucking deal EVER! No fucking way.

'But you warned me off him?' I blurt out, still not understanding or trusting this to be real. I'd probably believe the breakdown theory before I'd believe this.

'Yeah, because I know first-hand.' She looks away, her eyes wounded, as if reliving some memory.

What did that bastard do to her? He might have fucked me around, but I'm used to it. Poor little naïve Elsie must have been destroyed by him.

'How long were you going out for?' I blurt out, trying to work out the depth of her hurt.

She sighs, pushing her hair away from her face. 'Three months. Long enough for me to fall in love with him.' She looks down as if ashamed.

Love? How could she ever think he was capable of love?

'And he didn't feel the same?' I guess.

How could anyone not fall in love with Elsie? Only James could be such a prick.

'Worse. I'm sure he did, but he refused to admit it to himself.' She takes her tea off the side and takes a sip. 'He told me I was wrong and that he didn't like me anymore, but I know he was just scared to admit it to himself. Oh, I don't even know anymore.' She throws her hands up in the air in distress and throws herself onto the sofa, spilling half her tea. 'Aah! Hot! Hot!' she shrieks, pulling her t-shirt away from her skin.

'So that's why you warned me off him?' It all makes sense now. She wasn't trying to protect me. She was trying to protect herself from jealousy. 'Wait, is this why you decided to be a nun?'

Did that bastard damage her so much she'd turn to God, rather than try to find love again?

'It might have had something to do with it,' she admits reluctantly, as she dabs herself down with a tea towel. 'I might as well dedicate my life to God. It's not like I can ever have sex with anyone else ever again. He *ruined* me.'

'Ruined you?' I laugh, physically unable to stop the hysterics.

This is *too* hilarious.

She glares at me knowingly. 'Remember how you told me about Will giving you your first orgasm?'

God just the memory of him touching me sends a fresh sting of pain to my heart. I'll never feel him again. I really don't know how I'm going to break it to Lulu.

'Well, let's just say that the brothers were made for us.' She winks cheekily.

'He made you come!' I can't help myself shouting. '*He's* the guy!'

No *way!*

'Yes,' she nods, her cheeks flushed. Just saying the word come is making her blush. How did she go out with James? 'And I know I won't *ever* again. Not with anyone else, so what's the point? And it's like my mum always said, be with a man that ruins your lipstick, not your mascara.'

'Don't be stupid, Els!' I shout. 'Will has clearly dumped my arse, but I'm not going to give up sex and join a convent!'

'It's complicated,' she shrugs, dismissing me completely.

Yeah. I'm a slut and she's not. God, I hate myself.

'All I'm saying is that you should really think it through. It's giving up your whole life for the church. It's a *big* deal. It's your *life*.' I really can't stress this enough.

'I know,' she nods, her forehead creased in thought. 'But you need to do the same.'

'Huh?'

I *really* hope she's not planning on giving me a lecture right now. I'm too emotionally drained.

'You need to work out what you want from life.'

'Understatement of the year,' I snort.

***

Two hours later, Elsie's tucked me in her duvet with popcorn and a chick flick. The door knocks and I get up quickly, hopping to it, in the desperate hope that it might be Will. He might have changed his mind. I swing it back to reveal…my mum and dad. What the hell are they doing here?

They look just as shocked to see me. 'Rose? You're home?'

Oh crap. Elsie must have phoned them when I did a runner. Great, they're here to lecture me. Couldn't this have been done in a phone call?

I look back to Elsie. 'I'm so sorry! I forgot to call you,' she explains. 'It's all sorted now.'

'Is it really?' dad asks dubiously, pushing his glasses up his nose. 'Because Elsie sounded pretty frantic on the phone.'

Elsie grimaces apologetically. 'How about I make us all a brew to apologise?'

Dad follows her into the kitchen, no doubt to talk about me while I flop myself back down on the sofa. Well this is all I need. Mum and dad here to join the *beat Rose down* party.

'So…' I should attempt some small talk, 'how've you been?'

This is far more awkward than a normal mother/daughter reunion.

'I'm sorry, Rose,' mum says, looking off into the distance. It's so quiet that I wonder whether I might have imagined it. Or she's sleepwalking. 'I'm sorry for being a bad mother.'

Where the hell did this come from? Apologising to me? Well this is awkward. What the hell am I supposed to say to this?

'Err…you weren't…'

Should I lie? She looks so sad and pathetic sitting there twiddling her hair nervously. I don't relish the thought of kicking someone while they're down. I should know. I can't get much lower right now.

She sighs and takes my hand. It feels so foreign for us to be holding hands. They're so cold.

'I just…I don't think I was made to be a mother.' She rubs her face wearily. 'I thought it would come easy to me, but…it never happened.'

Wow, that was honest. How can she admit this? How can she admit that she looked into her new-born daughter's eyes and felt no love? I've always known she was fairly indifferent towards me, but to hear it out loud, to hear her omission, it hurts more than I thought it would.

'The thing is,' she looks at me, catching my eyes, 'I do…you know.' She nods, like she's sure I know what she's talking about. The truth is that I don't. 'I'm proud of you.'

Proud of me? What a joke.

'You just never loved me,' I snap, throwing her hand away, as the bitterness rises in my throat.

‘Of course I did,’ she protests, wiping at her dry eyes with a tissue.

How *dare* she act annoyed. Next thing she’ll be telling me she has one of her headaches.

‘You can't even say it, Mum,’ I scoff, seething internally.

I don’t know why she’s wasting her time saying all this, if she still can't tell me she loves me. It’s such a simple, basic requirement for a mother to love her daughter.

‘I know and I’m sorry,’ she nods. ‘I worry every day that my actions led you to behave how you have.’

Behave how I have?

‘What?’

God, she’s so annoying. Where the hell is all of this coming from? Her mothering skills had nothing to do with how I am as a person. She was always at work. And I’m not a bad person. I refuse to apologise for who I am.

‘Sleeping around. Looking for love everywhere. Looking for acceptance.’

My mouth drops open in shock. Jesus, just say it like you see it, Mother. This is *so* cringe worthy. My own mother talking about me being a slut. It’s not like I ever brought anyone home.

‘I should have tried harder, but I was selfish,’ she continues. ‘I threw myself into work. It’s the only thing I’ve ever done that comes naturally to me.’

That’s enough for me to see red. Fucking bright, vibrant, angry as fuck red.

‘You’re a GP! Your job is caring for people!’ I scream, my heart beat quickening. I’m in the mood for a confrontation.

How can she not care for her own daughter?

‘You say that like I don’t care for you,’ she answers calmly. ‘I do, Rose. I love you.’ She seems sincere, but embarrassed.

She *does* love me? An unnamed emotion brews in my throat. I suppose on some level I know it’s true. Though it wouldn’t hurt her to tell me every now and again.

'Do you know that's the first time you've ever told me?' I ask, my voice breaking slightly.

She takes my hand again, smiling tiredly. 'Like I said, I'm sorry. I know I have no right to be, but I'm proud of you.'

'Proud of what?'

'You've made a life for yourself here. Elsie says you're very well thought of by everyone.'

'Thanks,' I guffaw. She obviously spoke to her a few days ago. Today no one thinks highly of me.

But it does actually mean a lot. But then, how can she say she's proud of me when Elsie's told them I stole her money and planned on going to Mexico? It makes no sense.

Dad and Elsie walk in, holding mugs of tea and bourbons, which they share around.

'So,' dad begins, shifting uncomfortably in his chair. 'Elsie rang and told us you were considering returning home. Do you still want that?'

I look at Elsie questionably. She never told them I stole her money? She covered for me? She winks, which could mean anything.

'Um…' My head is imploding right now.

'Because me and your mother have decided that we'd be okay with that.' He dunks a bourbon in his tea as if to avoid eye contact.

Huh? They want me back? What the hell has Elsie told them?

He smiles at me tenderly. 'Elsie's told us about how far you've come since coming here. The charity work, the making new friends. To be honest, I found it hard to believe. But being here, seeing you; I realise it's true. You even look different.'

That's what a sprained ankle and twenty four hours of crying will do to a person.

'Really?'

'Your skins glowing,' he smiles. 'I can see you're happy here.'

It feels so weird making them happy for once. It's even…dare I say it…nice.

'Thanks. And thanks for the offer.' I look over at Elsie, who looks a bit afraid. I smile warmly at her. 'But I'm more than happy here.'

She smiles back and I know I'm still wanted. My heart warms. I might not have friends, but I'll always have family.

Chapter 24

Wednesday 19th November

Dear Betty,

Sorry I haven't been in to see you for a while, but a lot of ~~shit went down~~ stuff has happened. I don't know if Will's told you, but he's dumped me. Not just dumped me, but I'm pretty sure he despises me now. I've done so much stupid ~~shit~~ stuff, it's honestly no wonder. I hate myself. He's not answering my calls and he ignores me if I'm walking down the street. He's made it pretty clear that he doesn't want to see me. It breaks my heart.

I'm still seeing Mitsy every day. She's keeping me busy, but I've begged Clare to tell Will someone else is looking after her. If he knew I still was he'd probably stop me. That would really break me.

The only person who seems on my side is Elsie and I have no idea why. Maybe she should be a nun; she's so bloody selfless. She's told me not to tell anyone, but I stole her money and almost used it to go to Mexico. I came back, but it was too late. I've hurt Will, and now I don't even get to see you. Its ~~shit crap~~ rubbish. I should have gotten on that plane while I had the chance.

Anyway, I hope you write back. I miss you.

Rose xxx

Thursday 20th November

'You need some fresh air,' Elsie says as she forces my coat onto my shoulders. 'It'll be good for you.'

'Where the hell am I gonna go?' I plead. The whole bloody village hates me and I know Lauren's working today.

'Don't care,' she shrugs, smiling. 'Here, take my iPod. This will be good for you, I promise.'

I've barely opened my mouth to protest again before I'm shoved outside, with the front door slammed in my face. Well, this is mean. What the hell am I going to do with myself?

I start walking, thankfully no longer needing the crutches, zipping my coat up as I go. The temperatures really dropped today. I swear the countryside is colder. Probably all that pollution back home keeping me warm. I crunch the brown autumn leaves under my boots, deciding to go to the park. I can sit on a swing or something, like a *real* loser.

I finally reach it, but find Noah and a friend on them. Lauren's not there, thank God, but the other kid's mum recognises me and waves over. I wave back, but carry on walking. I'm in no mood for small talk.

Where the hell am I going to go now? Next to the park is the graveyard. I might as well take a walk through it. It occurs to me that Will's mum must be buried here. I'd never considered that before.

I walk slowly along the grave stones, discretely trying to read them. I don't want to look like some weirdo reading everyone's graves. I'm just about to give up when I spot it. She's buried in the back corner of the plot under a willow tree. I bend down to read it properly.

Here lays Cynthia Diane Buckley
Proud Wife, Mother and Daughter
Loved by all who knew her
RIP Angel

I don't doubt that she was loved by everyone. Most of these graves are covered with moss and overgrowing grass. This one has been smartened up and there's a bunch of orange roses laid next to it. They're beginning to die, but it's still lovely. I take a quick look at the note attached to it.

Love you Mum. Will x

My throat thickens with emotion. He must still bring her flowers.

A tear falls down my cheek for Will, the broken little boy who's mum died. I wonder if he talks to her. He must do. About me? I dread to think what she's heard. Maybe I should clear some things up.

I clear my throat. 'Er, hi, Cynthia. I'm Rose. You've probably been hearing a lot of bad things about me. I'd love to say it's all lies, but unfortunately they're not.' I laugh, my voice strained. 'But the one thing that is true is that I need Will in my life. He just…he makes things better. He even makes me better. Do you think you could talk to him about forgiving me?' I wait patiently.

Nothing. Not so much as a cold breeze or leaf falling onto her headstone. Well how on earth am I supposed to tell if she heard me? Oh God, I'm talking to a headstone. I'm not even sure I believe in this stuff.

'Morning, Rose.'

I jump round into karate stance, my body on high alert, to find the vicar smiling kindly at me.

Well this must look strange. He caught me chatting to Will's mum's headstone. And now I'm trying to karate chop him. But then, I suppose he does pray to a man in the sky. Hardly one to judge me.

'Er…hi.' I lower my arms and put them behind my back.

'Elsie said you might be at a loose end this morning,' he smiles, sipping a mug of tea that says 'Jesus is my homeboy'.

Of *course* she did. Annoying little meddler. I wouldn't be surprised if she set this whole thing up.

'I was wondering if you fancied mowing the lawn?'

I look around at the high grass and unmanageable weeds. Is he *serious?*

'Don't you have a gardener or something?' I ask in barely hidden disbelief.

He locks eyes with me, sending a chill down my spine.

'Afraid not,' he grimaces, shaking his head. 'But if you're feeling lost sometimes doing a selfless act can help to heal the soul.'

Oh Jesus, he's going to get the bible out in a minute and start preaching.

Step away from the devil, child. THE BODY OF CHRIST COMPELS YOU!

'Okay,' I nod, completely unenthused. At least this way he'll leave me alone.

'Marvellous news,' he beams. Probably can't wait to report back to Elsie. 'You'll find the mower in the shed.'

***

After wrestling the mower out of the shed and finding an extension lead long enough, I'm finally mowing. It's strangely satisfying to do such a simple job. Seeing the grass come out fresher and cleaner looking is soothing. Plus I've got Elsie's iPod on, blasting out some Missy Elliot. I'm surprised she's got her on here.

I'm bopping away, sashaying my hips in time to the music, when I feel a hand on my shoulder. I jump, throw the hand off and try to turn around to face my attacker. Only the lead gets twisted round my foot and before I know it, I'm losing my balance and falling to my right. A hard, intense black pain takes over my head before it goes dark.

I open my heavy eyes, my head banging so bad I can barely focus on the person hovering over me.

'Rose? Rose, speak to me.'

I focus in on his features and realise its James. James? What happened?

'Are you okay?' he asks, concert etched into his voice.

Just embarrassed that I'm such a clumsy bitch.

'Yeah, I'm fine.' I roll onto my side, attempting to sit myself up when a roll of nausea hits me. I vomit weakly into the grass, my stomach making sure to retch up my entire breakfast.

'Shit, Rose,' I hear, feeling cold hands on my shoulders. 'That's it; I'm taking you to hospital.'

The stream of vomit stops enough for me to catch my breath.

'I'm fine.' I wipe my mouth with the back of my hand. I feel anything but.

He grins, his eyebrows raised sarcastically. 'Humour me.'

***

It turned out I'd gashed my head open quite badly, but luckily not badly enough to need stitches. My hair seems to cover it, which will be good once I can rinse out the dried blood. Right now I look like a zombie. I'm under strict orders to rest up and take it easy. See, Elsie, this is what happens when you force someone outside.

We pull into the village, the sky now dark even though its only 7pm.

'I'll walk you in,' James says, as he pulls over the car.

Bless him. He's been an angel. Holding my hand, even when I insisted I didn't need it. Apparently he and Will take it in turns to bring roses to their mum's grave. How sweet is that? She might have only been able to raise them for a short time, but what she did, she did right. Maybe this is her weird way of sending me a sign not to give up on Will. She must have a sick sense of humour.

I let him lead me from his car, treating me as if I'm made of glass.

'So,' he says when we reach the door. 'When are you going to talk to Will?'

I roll my eyes. 'When are you going to talk to Elsie?'

He grins. 'Touché. But seriously, I'm sorry if I fucked things up for you. For what it's worth, I can tell he's mad about you. He's got the same look on his face as when he used to watch Fun House.'

'Fun House?' I snort.

'The twins,' he grins. 'The very sexy twins.'

I laugh, glad he's broken the tension. 'Well anyway, thank you.'

'For what? Causing the accident?' he grimaces.

'No, for looking after me.'

'No worries,' he smiles genuinely. 'But I meant what I said. Speak to Will.'

'Thanks. I will.'

I lean in to give him a quick hug. I feel like I need it after the shitter of a day. He hugs me back, rubbing my back reassuringly. It's nothing but friendship and it feels nice. I could really do with a friend right now. Really, when you look at it, James and I are very similar.

I lean back, ready to get my keys, when I spot him. Will. He's stood in the middle of the road, his face venomous. Why is he so angry?

I think to what he must have seen. Me and James hugging. Could he have mistaken friendliness for passion?

'Will…' What the hell can I say so that he sees this for the innocence it is?

He locks his eyes with mine, a glare so cold it turns my heart to ice.

He shakes his head. 'Screw you both.'

Friday 21st November

The next morning I wake up determined to try and win Will back, regardless of how long it takes me. I mean, this whole thing is based on a stupid miss-understanding. Well, the whole stealing Elsie's money thing was probably straight forward, but…well, I'll cross that bridge when I come to it. He did tell me he loved me. Unless that was a lie, why wouldn't he at least try to forgive me?

I pull the hood of my jacket up and brace myself for the rain. I walk through the drizzly village at lunch time. I'm sure everyone's eyes are already on me anyway. Judging me. I've felt like this since the accident, although Elsie assures me it's my imagination.

I knock on his front door and jump impatiently from foot to foot, while I wait for an answer. The door opens and I see my poor dishevelled Will. He's got more stubble than normal and his green eyes seem smaller, like he hasn't slept in days.

'Will,' I breathe. It almost sounds like a prayer.

I've barely got his name out, before his face contorts in rage and he slams the door in my face. Well, that was mean.

I swallow down the bile and knock again, this time a bit more frantically. He swings the door back open, leaning on it arrogantly.

'What do you want, Rose?' He sounds so despondent.

'I want to talk. Want to explain,' I plead, putting my hands up in prayer. I'll get down on my knees if I have to.

'There's nothing to explain. I understand fully,' he says curtly. Coldly.

I look into the house. The house I felt so comfortable in only a week ago. 'Can I come in?'

'No.' He stands still, as if he has no shame in denying me entry. I thought his politeness would have taken over by now. 'But we can talk out here.' He grabs his coat and walks out into the street.

I follow after him like a lost puppy.

'Please, Will. You have to understand that I was never with James while we were together! It was way before that. It was before I even knew you. What you saw last night was just a friendly hug.'

He whips his head back in annoyance. 'You don't get it, do you?' he spits, his jaw tight. 'He had his dick inside you,' he hisses.

I retract as if he's hit me.

'He caressed your skin; *my* skin. It sickens me.' He runs his hand through his hair. 'Don't you get that? I can't get the idea of you two out of my head.'

Wow. He's *never* going to forgive me. The realisation hits me like a fat woman in a hurry.

'I'm…I'm sorry,' I blub, tears running freely down my face. I've ruined everything.

'But that's not even the worst of it,' he continues with disdain. 'To think that everything we had was fake. Just a fucking rouse to get more shifts at the home. So you could fuck off and go to Mexico. No wonder you wanted to shag so quick. All the talking too much, was it? Did I bore you?'

'No! Will, you never bore me. I want you back,' I beg, my voice weak and pathetic.

'Oh *really*?' he mocks. 'Is that your decision *this* week? How long until you change your little fickle mind again?'

His words are like acid. I thought he loved me. No one who loved me could treat you like this.

'Please, Will. Don't be so horrible.'

'Then tell me it's not true,' he challenges.

I look down at the pavement. 'Will…'

'No, not that,' he snaps. 'I had the police at the home this morning with a warrant. They spent all morning digging up the garden, looking for bodies. Apparently someone had told a volunteer we'd illegally buried residents back there. Tell me Rose, tell me how that wasn't you.' His face is hard and unforgiving.

Oh my holy fuck. The police took it that far? I just assumed they'd have forgotten about it. I'm going to murder Eric.

'Please, Will, let me explain.' I try to touch his arm.

'I'm not interested,' he snaps, throwing his hand off, an angry vein on his neck popping out.

I look down at the floor, wishing it would swallow me up.

He stands still and takes a deep breath. He must be trying to collect himself.

'I'm sorry,' he says, a smidgen calmer. He runs his hand roughly through his hair. 'I just…I told you a lot of shit and you betrayed me. You're not who I thought you were.'

I've never felt so bad in my life.

He gives me one last look of hurt before turning and walking back towards the house. I watch him go, unable to move. Unable to do anything but hurt. He's almost there when Riley pokes her head out.

'Oh, there you are,' she smiles, locking eyes with me with a smirk.

He just left me and already he's shagging Riley?

He looks back at me for my reaction. I don't even have one. He talks about me betraying him, but now he's sleeping with the enemy? He looks almost apologetic. He should.

'Fuck you, Will.'

I turn and run back home as best I can on my fragile ankle, my life falling apart a little further with each step I take.

***

Saturday 21st November

Well, it's only been a day, but it's already obvious I'll never recover. Everything just seems grey, half as good as before. I found a jumper he left last time he was here and I've clung onto it. It still smells like him and while I've got it close to me I can close my eyes and pretend that he's holding me. That I'm safe and loved. When I'm really scared and alone. I look outside at the autumn leaves starting to fall, replaced by bare trees. It's how I feel right now. Bare.

It hasn't helped that I haven't had a response from Betty. I feel like she's the only one who could cheer me up. The only conclusion I can come to is that Will's told everyone what I've done and made it sound a million times worse. Maybe they all think the only reason I was there was to get to Mexico. Which I suppose is how it started, but it turned into so much more than that. I ended up falling in love with them all.

I'm missing them all so much. Even Ernie and his disappearing dentures. But most of all Will. Every time I even think of him my chest aches so bad that I fear I'll actually collapse and die from a broken heart. I'm sure it's possible.

The front door slams, throwing me out of my self-destructive thoughts. I know its Elsie from her flowery perfume. Even her perfume is wholesome and girlie. I don't bother turning around. I'm too depressed to move.

'You're home early?' I look at my watch. 'I thought you said you were volunteering there till 6pm?'

I muster my last bit of energy and turn to look at her. The minute I see her face I know something's happened. She's paler than normal and she's fidgeting. She takes a breath and tries to speak, only a small sob escapes first.

Fuck, what is it? What has someone done to her? Is it James? I pant harshly, my breath coming out in erratic spurts.

'Tell me! Who upset you?' Rage fills me as I take in her vulnerable eyes, afraid to tell me. 'I'll fucking kill them!' I mean it too. Especially if it's James.

'No one's upset me,' she weeps, wiping away a tear. 'It's…its Betty.'

A cold chill spreads over my face and a shiver travels down my spine. Betty? Not *my* Betty?

'What about Betty?' I ask, my breathing faster by the second. My stomach is doing somersaults.

She slowly walks towards me, perching on the edge of the sofa, her eyes intense. They almost look fearful. I hope to God she's just being dramatic. 'She's ill. You need to go see her. She hasn't got long.'

I'm out of the door and running up the hill in my slippers before I can even form a coherent thought in my head. I'm vaguely aware of Elsie shouting after me, but I don't care. The only thing I know is that I *need* to keep running. I need to see her.

I stop when a stitch attacks my side halfway up the hill. I push through it and force myself to keep moving, if not a little bit slower.

She's ill? Ill with bloody what? And since when? I only haven't seen her in two weeks. Could she have caught a cold and it turned into pneumonia? And does 'not have long' really mean what I think it may mean? Bile rises in my throat. I can't even think about that right now. I shake the thought out of my head.

I get to the top of the hill and run into the home, not pausing to speak to anyone, as I barrel up the stairs and along the corridor towards her room. Will is stood outside talking with the vicar. If he tries to stop me being here I'll punch him into next week.

'Rose…' he says on a breath. The vicar smiles feebly at me and walks into the room.

I don't have time for Will's bullshit.

'No, Will! Don't you fucking *dare* tell me I can't be here right now! If Betty is ill I need to be here and you'll have to physically remove me from this building, because I won't go without a fight.'

I push past him, only for him to grab me by my arm. I look down at it in disgust. How dare he grab me and stop me from going in there. I glare back at him, ready to rip his throat out, only to see him looking apologetic.

'I never said you couldn't be here. It was you that decided to stop visiting. Who do you think sent Elsie to come get you? You need to be here.'

I nearly fall over from shock. The adrenaline coursing through my veins slows down and I come out of fight mode. I'm strangely disappointed. I ignore his kind face, creasing my eyes shut. I can't deal with it right now.

I take a calming deep breath, before pushing the door open. The vicar is standing over her with rosemary beads. He's reading her last rights, or whatever it is religious people do.

I look at her lying limp in the bed. She looks awful; her face is grey and her cheeks gaunt. Her hair is a mess, which I know she'd be furious at. She's attached to a drip that a nurse seems to be checking.

As if realising my presence, she looks away from the vicar and slowly turns her head towards me, as if the movement is taking all of her energy.

'Rose,' she breathes, her voice raspy. She smiles weakly.

It breaks my heart, one piece at a time.

I run over to her bedside and pull up a chair. 'Betty,' I all but sob.

Keep it together, Rose. You *cannot* lose it yet. You have to be strong for her.

'Sorry I didn't reply to your letter,' she rasps, 'but I'm dying.' She smiles as if her joke is hilarious.

A tear escapes down my cheek but I hastily brush it away with my sleeve.

The nurse turns to me with a sympathetic smile. 'The morphine can make her a bit confused,' she explains.

I know better. I know Betty's dark humour. I'm sure if she was feeling better she'd be rolling her eyes at the nurse right now.

'Don't worry,' I say, forcing a laugh out of my clogged up throat. 'Thank God I'm here. Your hair's a bloody mess.'

The vicar shoots me a quick look of disdain. Whoops, I suppose I shouldn't be taking the Lords name in vain. Not that I could give a shit right now.

I walk over to her dresser and pick up her silver enamel hairbrush. It's the only thing I can think to do right now. I softly brush her hair, trying to hide the horror when some of it falls out onto the nylon bristles. My chest aches as I look down at her, her eyes closed, truly relaxed. She's almost like a little baby. God, how the roles have reversed. I take a pearl hair clip and pin the hair out of her face.

'There,' I smile fondly. 'Now you look like a million dollars.' I just about get it out before my voice breaks fully.

She sighs, as if she knows I'm placating her. I grab hold of her hand and pull it up to my face. I turn it so her silky soft palm cups my cheek. I can't believe this is happening. Why Betty? Why now? I thought she had so many more years in her.

She looks as if she's gone to sleep when she bolts slightly, pressing her hand into my face.

'Rose, you must promise me,' she croaks, her eyes desperate and pleading.

'Promise you what?' I try my best to smile and look positive. When all I want to do is sob uncontrollably.

'Promise me you won't make the same mistakes I've made.' Her chest is rising and falling rapidly as if she's fighting for breath.

I look at her, puzzled. What mistakes?

'Don't be scared of following your heart.' She squeezes my cheek affectionately. Shivers run down my body. I squeeze her hand back.

'What do you mean?' I ask, knowing full well what she means.

She gestures towards Will, who's talking to the nurse in the corner of the room.

'Don't play dumb with me, Rose,' she smiles. 'It doesn't have to be Will, but just promise to follow your heart and not ignore it like I did.' Her breath is raspy and she stops to catch her breath. I wait patiently. 'Look at me, Rose. I'm on my death bed and I have no family surrounding me. I'd take back all the trips and adventures to just have someone here that cared.'

'I care,' I sob, no longer able to keep it in.

I care so fucking much and yet she's being taken away from me. How can I ever believe in Elsie's God when he pulls shit like this?

'I know darling, and I love you for it.' She caresses my hand with her thumb, filling me with complete love and admiration for this brave woman. How could she have been dealing with this without me?

She closes her eyes again, as if just talking has completely exhausted her. I pull her hand closer to my face again.

'I love you too.' The ache in my chest brings fresh tears to my eyes and I let them fall freely this time.

I lean onto the bed, pushing her hand against my cheek again as if to comfort me.

***

I don't know how much time has passed, but it's dark outside now. The nurse leans over the other side of the bed and lowers her ear to Betty's mouth. She takes out a stethoscope to check her heartbeat. I see it in her sympathetic eyes.

'I'm afraid she's passed,' she explains kindly.

I look down at her hand in mine and realise it feels colder than when I was first in here. She's gone? Gone forever.

The full gravity of it hits me. I'm never going to see her again. Ever. My chest starts tightening as I gasp for breath. I place her hand gently down on the bed and use my hands to pull at my t-shirt. It feels tight around my neck.

'No!' I sob, only it comes out more as a whisper.

I feel a hand on my shoulder and I jump from the contact. I don't look up though. I don't have the energy. I already know its Will. I can feel his body heat behind me and smell his unique scent. He squats down in front of me and pulls my crying body into his warm chest. I fight it at first. I'm so angry with him, but he holds firm, until I give in and eventually let my body sag against his.

I push my face into his neck and inhale him. It only makes me sadder. I can't relax in his embrace anymore. The guy doesn't even like me. I sob even harder, feeling my snot drip onto his shirt. I've got no one.

I'm manoeuvred so that I'm transferred into Elsie's arms. When did she even get here?

'It's okay, Rose,' she soothes, patting my back. 'She's in a better place now. She's not in pain anymore.'

The words should comfort me, but they have the opposite effect. I wouldn't know how much agony she's been in, because I haven't been here. No one told me. I'm suddenly overwhelmed with fury and resentment. Anger towards Will. I turn to him, my face contorting with rage.

'How could you have kept this from me?!' I scream, pointing my finger accusingly at his chest. 'I knew you hated me, but to keep this from me is a new low!'

His forehead creases in obvious pain. 'Rose, she made me promise not to tell you. I had a duty to her to keep her wishes.'

'Keep her wishes!' I screech, almost launching myself on him. Elsie holds me back. 'You knew how much she meant to me and you kept it from me anyways.'

'Rose,' he says weakly, pulling his hand through his hair in distress.

'No!' I shout. 'Don't *Rose* me! I'll NEVER forgive you for this.'

***

Chapter 25

Monday 24th November

I blow my nose into Elsie's handkerchief, hoping she won't want me to give it back to her. I mean, what do people with handkerchiefs do with them? Wash the snot with their own clothes? It's beyond gross.

I look down at my black dress and wonder if it's been washed with Elsie's bogies. It's a bit short for a funeral, but I thought I'd only be wearing this in Coco Bongo's in Mexico. Not to bury a surrogate grandmother. Elsie lent me her tights and a little jacket, so it doesn't look too slutty. Not that Betty would have cared. She'd probably have wanted me to flash my boobs and dance on the coffin to YMCA.

I can't though. I can't even speak today. I've barely said two words to anyone. I'm going to fight it though. I have to. Betty deserves an amazing speech. She might not have been surrounded by family and friends before she died, but I'm going to show her that we all loved her. The impressive turnout shows just that.

I still can't believe how she went. She was so helpless, so weak. I guess I always imagined she'd die like she lived; with a glass of wine in hand screaming 'I had the best time!' Now when I look at that wooden coffin it's hard to imagine she's in there. Gone.

The service has already started, but I can't seem to listen to the vicar's words. I'm so nervous about my speech that I can't stop myself shaking. Elsie insisted I write something down as she was sure I'd forget what I wanted to say. The only thing I managed to write was *'Betty was loved by so many people and...* I just know it'll come to me when I'm up there. I've always been better at these things when I'm in the moment.

Far too soon the vicar is gesturing for me to come up to the alter. He must have introduced me, but I was too busy staring into space.

Elsie smiles at me encouragingly. I stand onto my shaky legs and force them to walk towards the stand. I hunch my shoulders so that my hair acts as a cover against the pitying stares. I can't bear them. Everyone telling me how sorry they are to hear. Not as sorry as me.

I step onto the carpeted alter, the floor underneath creaking like it's made of cardboard. I lean against the pillar, take a deep breath and look up into the crowd of expectant faces.

This is it, Rose. Time to make Betty proud.

'Betty…' my voice waivers with emotion, but I desperately try to push it back down.

Think of happy things. Smiles, rainbows, unicorns. Betty's smile was the warmest I've ever seen. And she used to give it to me. My heart squeezes with the raw pain. I'll never see that smile again.

I clear my throat, forcing myself on. 'Betty was lov…loved…' My breath comes out in short sharp bursts, making it almost impossible to talk.

Fresh bouts of tears erupt from my eyes, while my throat clogs up to the point of suffocation. I can't do this. I can't even make her proud be doing a kick arse speech. A heavy sob escapes my throat, echoing through the church microphone.

I break down completely, the tears falling one after the other. An arm snakes around my waist and I look up to see Elsie holding me. I whimper into her chest, needing to smell Betty's talcum powdery scent, not her flowery one.

'You want me to read it?' a male soothing voice asks me.

Just hearing his voice sends fresh bolts of pain to my heart. I look up into Will's eyes, their clear pale green soothing my rising panic. I don't answer. I couldn't if I tried. I just pass him my speech, or should I say lack of speech.

He clears his throat, clutching onto the sides of the pillar.

'Betty was loved by so many people…' He turns to look at me with a puzzled expression.

Well, I suppose that was all I had written down. I've really left him hanging. I'm glad. Let him feel half as angry as me.

'And she loved many others too. She never got to get married or have children, but what she didn't realise was that she touched so many people's lives. Whether it was her being sassy to me, fighting with other residents or just giving a compliment to one of the cooking staff, demanding to know their secret ingredient in the chili or she'd have them killed. She always made an impression.'

Everyone smiles and there are even a few chuckles. How can he be making this up on the spot?

'Although Betty was upset that she never found true love, she managed to travel the world, learn four languages and at one point she even ran The Dog and Pond.'

My mouth gapes open. How can I feel like I know her better than everyone and not know some of this? But then I suppose Will doesn't know she *did* find true love, but it escaped her. She only told me real things. How she felt, not a factual biography of her life. That's worth far more.

Will looks towards the coffin. 'Goodbye, Betty. You will be truly missed.'

Any anger I had for him evaporates. What a beautiful speech.

I walk back to the bench and listen to the rest of the service feeling numb. Completely numb to the loss. I suppose I'm in denial about the whole thing. I keep half expecting her to run in here shouting GOT YA!

It isn't until I'm walking out of the church, while the last waltz plays, that I realise she's truly gone forever. The ache in my chest rises to unbearable again. I spot Will in the crowd and a fresh dose of grief takes over. I've got no one. Now on closer inspection I notice that he's got bags under his eyes, as if he hasn't slept for a while. Good. I hope his secret has played heavily on his mind.

'Excuse me, Miss Chapman?'

I look around to see a small balding man in a black suit.

'Yes?' I say hesitantly.

'I'm Mr Harrogate. I'm the executer of Miss Ballantine's will. I'd like you to accompany me to the reading.'

I crease my forehead in confusion. 'Reading? Me?' That's weird. 'Okay, whatever. When?'

'Now. If you could accompany me t' care home with a…' he looks at his note pad, 'A William Buckley.'

I roll my eyes, but nod my head. He goes off in search of him.

I decide to give myself a minute before I have to face him again. I walk against the traffic of people, avoiding their pitying stares, to the front of the church and to the left towards the confessional box. I know the vicar's outside, so I won't actually have to confess anything. Plus, it's hidden away enough so that no one will see me duck inside.

I open the door, my mouth dropping onto the floor. In front of me is Mavis, her American tan stockings on show, her skirt pulled up around her waist. Bernie is shagging her; his hairy pale arse confronting my poor, *poor* eyes.

They're so hard at it, their eyes scrunched closed in ecstasy, that they don't even notice me. I should really shut the door and run away, but I can't move. I'm too dazed.

A loud sigh behind me shocks me into turning. The vicar is stood behind me, shaking his head disapprovingly.

'Mavis! Bernie!' he shouts. It's the loudest I've ever heard him speak.

They both spring their eyes open, staring in horror, between us both.

'You promised me this would never happen again!' he berates. 'You gave me your word. This is a place of worship!'

They both look down, clearly ashamed.

'Sorry, vicar,' Mavis says, her husband still clearly inside her.

'Rose…I,' she looks so humiliated.

I put my hands up to stop her. 'Trust me, nobody would even believe me if I tried.'

***

Will's already waiting in his office when we get there. I follow in Mr Harrogate, glad for the small shield he provides. Will's taken his suit jacket off and pulled his black tie down, opening the top button of his shirt. He looks yummy. Yummy and not mine anymore. My chest aches from the reminder.

He looks up. 'Mr Harrogate, Miss Chapman,' he nods politely. He gestures towards the chairs, as if this is my first time here.

We both sit down with Mr Harrogate immediately opening a folder and shuffling papers.

'I want you both to know that it's extremely unusual for me to read out someone's will like this. We normally just write to you, but as I feel these circumstances are unusual, I've decided to talk to you myself.'

I nod, although I'm still not sure why I'm here.

'Miss Chapman, you have been listed as the beneficiary of Miss Ballantine's estate.'

My stomach drops out of my knickers with shock.

'Sorry?' I ask, my voice quivering. What the hell is he talking about?

'I could read it all out, but the general idea is that Miss Ballantine has left you her home in the village. A number 28 Leaf Tree Drive.'

'You're joking?' Will blurts out, his eyes wide and confused. I turn to look at him, his mouth gaping open. 'I'm sorry, but what? She's only known Rose a few months.'

I'm hurt by the accusation in his voice. He clearly has no idea what we meant to each other and that hurts more than it should. I thought he knew me.

'Aye, but it seems she made quite the impression.' He smiles, leaning back in his chair.

I'm so bloody confused right now.

'Sorry? So…are you sure there hasn't been a mistake?' There must be.

He nods. 'I wrote the will myself. She was quite insistent. Add to that the fact that she has no living family to contest it and I'm telling you the house is yours.'

I stare at Will, then back at him. I…I own a house? What the fuck is happening?

'She asked that I give you this letter to explain.' He hands over a cream envelope.

I open it and pull out the thick cream card. It's scrawled with Betty's chaotic writing. Just seeing it makes my eyes tear up again.

How can her writing be here, but she be gone? My chest aches for her. I wish I could speak to her one last time. Ask her what the hell she was thinking.

My dearest Rose,

Follow your heart. If that's Mexico then sell the house and have an amazing adventure. But if you've found something bigger than yourself, stay here and put down some roots.

B xxx

A tear slides down my cheek and I hastily wipe it away. That's it? That's the last letter from her. I know it sounds strange, but I really wanted her to have told me she loved me. I could have treasured it. Kept it under my pillow and known that someone is always rooting from me. Even if it's from another side. But this? Sell the house and go to Mexico?

'Have fun in Mexico, Rose,' Will says in a low bitter voice. He grabs his jacket and storms out, the door slamming hard behind him.

***

I wander around the house, still wearing my funeral dress, lifting dust sheets as I go. It's really the cutest little cottage. It's older than Elsie's with its sash windows that aren't double glazed. If you stand close enough you can actually feel the breeze coming through. I'm guessing the wooden floors are original as they're rough underneath my socked feet. But through all of that I can see the potential. The real brick fireplace. The small basic kitchen which you could easily squeeze a table and chairs into.

It will be a perfect family home for someone. Just not me.

I dial the number and look around, just in case Betty's ghost is stalking me.

'Arnold Estate Agents,' a dull bored voice greets me.

'H-Hi,' I stammer. 'I'd like to put a property up for sale.'

***

<u>Wednesday 26th November</u>

I feel like everyone's watching me in the village. They've definitely turned on me the moment that For Sale sign went up outside Betty's house. I don't see why they should care. I've never really fit in here anyway. You'd think they'd be happy for me to go.

I'm just going back to the original plan. I should have gotten on that flight while I had the chance. Instead I chose to come back and get my heart broken further. I could be in Mexico right now, sunning myself on the beach, oblivious. I wouldn't even know that Betty died. But the thought of not having seen her just before she died fills me with a dreadful sickness. I'm lucky I got to speak to her. I suppose I can see now how affected Will was after not making it back in time to say goodbye to his grandad. And all because of work. But maybe that was Will's dream. Maybe he was living it and that's where he belongs. Maybe we were never meant to meet at all. The love God's fucked up somewhere.

But then I know that's wrong. I'd have never had an orgasm. I believe Elsie one hundred percent when she says we can only orgasm with our one true love. He was it for me and I messed it up. I've got no one to blame but myself. And I deserve the misery. In a strange way it's actually comforting. A weird sort of self-harm.

Add to that the fact that Lauren is still avoiding me and Megan's sent me several texts saying how she can't believe I kept this from her. She feels betrayed and I can't blame her. I don't dare go anywhere near the pub. If Phil didn't hate me after poisoning his daughter, he definitely will now.

I walk into the stables, but stop at the notice board. There's a picture of Mitsy. What the hell? Please don't say she's gone missing again. I lean in to read it.

FOR SALE

Mitsy – Liver Chesnut with Flaxen mane and tail, 16hh

5 home only for this special horse, home more important than price.*

Mitsy the horse. Born and bred in the village. Needs an owner with the time to look after.

It's like someone's taken a brick to my heart. I gasp for a breath, but it's like my lungs are being squeezed. He's getting rid of Mitsy? *My* Mitsy? Why the fuck would he do that? He made a promise to his mum. How could he do that? To her and to me? I suppose he doesn't know I'm still looking after her, but still. Without her I'll have nothing left to stay here for. Well, apart from Elsie.

I go into her stables, undress her from her pyjamas, and lead her out into the field. I look at her brown coat and her beautiful blonde hair. I've already lost Betty. I'm not about to lose her too. I know in that instant that I can't leave her. I'm not going to Mexico. I'll sell the house and buy Mitsy. It's a sign. I belong to her. I'm meant to stay. I think I've known that all along, deep down.

A strange sense of peace and satisfaction comes over me the minute I realise it. This is where I'm supposed to be. This is my home.

'Can you believe he's selling you, Mitsy?' I say to her. 'What an arsehole. And after his mum begged him not to sell you. I can't believe he's just gone and done it.'

Footsteps crunch the leaves behind me. I know it's him before I turn around.

'Actually, I haven't just gone and done it.'

I whip round to face him, looking ferocious and sexy, dressed in black jeans and a navy quilted coat. Whoops.

'Will!' I shrill. 'What are you doing here?' My voice is as jumpy and uneven as I feel.

He raises his eyebrows. 'Me? What are *you* doing here?' he demands, a hand on his hip like a diva.

'I'm just looking after Mitsy.' I look away, embarrassed at being caught.

'You don't have to worry,' he snarls at me. 'Mrs Fenham's been looking after her for me since your accident.' I can feel the venom in his voice.

I keep my eyes downwards, so he can't tell I forced her to say that. I can already feel my cheeks reddening, betraying me.

'Unless…' He steps closer, invading my space. He grabs my chin and forces me to look at him. God, I miss him. His touch is like electricity through me. 'Have you…no….' He narrows his eyes at me. 'Have you been looking after her too?'

He keeps hold of my chin so I can't look away. Looking into his eyes I know I can't lie.

'Try instead of,' I mumble.

He takes a sharp intake of breath. 'But then, why would she say that?' He nods, as if he now understands, his hand going to cup my cheek. 'You told her to tell me that.' I nod. 'What, were you worried I'd stop you?' he asks, his green eyes boring into my soul.

I scoff, pulling his warm hand away. 'The last time we spoke we were hardly friendly.'

There's a long awkward silence. I stroke Mitsy, trying to pretend he isn't here. Trying to ignore my heart being crushed as if it was the very first time.

'I thought long and hard about keeping her.' He strokes her mane affectionately, our fingers touching for a second. It sends tingles up my arm. 'But there's going to be no one left to care for her after I'm gone. It's not fair on her.'

I give him a hard look. 'What's not *fair* on Mitsy is palming her off on someone you know nothing about,' I practically spit.

His green eyes flash a quick look of hatred. 'Actually, I fully intend to find out about her new owner,' he snarls back.

When did he start to truly hate me? When he found out about James? When he realised I was using the care home for a holiday? Or when I put Betty's house up for sale. So many unforgiveable things, but I still crave his forgiveness. I'm selfish like that.

I suddenly replay his last statement in my head. *When he's gone?* He said *he*, right? Not when *I'm* gone.

'Wait. Did you just say when you're gone? Where are you going?'

He looks down at the floor, kicking some dirt, unable to meet my eyes.

'I'm leaving, Rose. I'm moving back to Leeds.'

'You're what?' I ask, the breath leaving my body. I stand motionless, blinking rapidly, my brain spinning.

'I've got a new job.' He looks at me briefly, before going back down to the floor. 'I'm starting Monday. I leave this weekend.'

He's leaving? He won't be here anymore? What the hell is the village going to be like without him? I swallow, trying to force the lump in my throat down. It only makes me feel more suffocated.

How can he leave me? And how can this be how I found out? Didn't I at least deserve to be told rather than find out like this? A surge of red hot hatred courses through my veins.

'And *THIS* is how I find out?' I stare at him, my eyes hard, my heart turned to ice.

He shrugs, glancing up at me. 'You weren't talking to me, Rose. I hardly thought you cared.'

'You weren't talking to me first!' I retort, like a pathetic child. He looks remorseful and it's enough for me to soften slightly. 'What job is it?'

'An accountant.'

WHAT? He's leaving me behind to go and be a bloody accountant?

'Accountant?' I shout. I take a deep breath, trying to calm myself. 'Why on earth would you go back to that boring job?' I ask in a calmer voice.

'Because it's time I grew up, Rose,' he barks sharply. 'What am I going to do? Work at the care home forever?'

'Yeah, if it makes you happy!' I shout frankly.

He sighs heavily. 'I have to grow up, Rose. We all do. It's time to move on.'

He groans, running his hands down his face. I realise he looks bone tired, like he hasn't slept in days. Not that he doesn't look good. He does, of course he still does.

But wait? Did he *ever* plan on telling me?

'So… If I hadn't been with Mitsy right now, would you have even told me you were leaving?' I feel the sudden prick of tears behind my eyes. Do not cry. Do NOT cry.

He digs his hands in his pockets and looks at the floor. I glare at him until he feels my eyes on him. He looks up at me, his eyes blazing with so much unsaid.

'What, Rose?' he sighs, defeated. He locks his pale green eyes with me in question. 'Are you going to say something that's going to stop me from leaving?'

Shit, now he has me. I look into his eyes, now cloudy with some emotion I can't read. What the hell could I say that would make him stay? I can't think of anything that wouldn't freak him the fuck out.

'That's what I thought,' he nods, his green eyes burning. 'So this is our goodbye.'

A bolt of fear goes through me. He's going. I'm really losing him for good.

I fling myself against his chest before I have a chance to talk myself out of it. I wrap my arms around his waist, trying to ingrain the memory into my mind. How he smells, how he feels. He wraps one arm around my waist and the other cradles the back of my head, as if confirming this is okay.

I feel the emotion brewing in my throat. I'm going to cry. Wail like a proper pathetic girl. It's bringing it all back; what it's like to be with him. The tingling sensation on my skins as he caresses me, the sweet taste of his kisses, his smell. I push away before I can make it any more painful for me. It's just delaying the inevitable.

'I should go,' he says regretfully. He runs his hand through his hair. 'Riley will be waiting for me.'

WHAT?!

'Riley? Why? Why would…?' I can barely get the words out. It's as if I'm being strangled. Strangled by his betrayal. His constant fucking betrayal with Riley.

'She's helping me pack. I'm staying with her aunt while I look for a place.' He avoids my pained eyes the entire time.

A raged frenzy fills my body. I give him the hardest look I can muster, so hard he's forced to look up, but I can't show it in a look. I want to wrap my arms round his neck and strangle him.

'Riley? You're going to live with Riley!' I'm shouting, but it's hard to hide the hurt from my voice. I sound like a scared, vulnerable little girl.

He sighs heavily, the sigh that tries to tell me I'm overreacting. 'Not live with her. Just staying with her aunt while I find a place. Why do you care anyway?'

Is he that fucking stupid? Can he seriously not see how Riley wants him? How he's playing right into her greedy, evil little hands. How this hurts me so deeply I'm surprised I'm not actually bleeding from my chest. But I can't say that. I've already let myself look too weak in front of him.

'I just don't want her changing you,' I say defensively, crossing my arms over my chest, hoping the pain lessons.

He grabs hold of my arms and tips my chin up, so I'm forced to look at him again. I hold my breath. He gazes at me, his eyes probing with intensity. There's no chance of me looking away. My body starts to tremble.

'One more chance.' He unleashes the full devastating power of his eyes on me, as if trying to communicate something crucial. 'Is there something you need to say to keep me here?' he asks earnestly.

He's suffered so much pain in his life. His mum dying at such a young age and now me coming into his life and fucking everything up. I can't promise him anything. Hell, I can barely look after myself, let alone him. The last thing I want to do is promise him something and then hurt him beyond all repair. Again. That I could never forgive myself for.

I shake my head. 'No.'

'That's what I thought.' He picks up his bag and walks away from me forever.

Chapter 26

Saturday 29th November

He's leaving today. I've managed to avoid him since we last talked. What I haven't managed to avoid is the whole village mourning him going. Anyone would think he was a war hero the way everyone goes on about him. Everywhere I go there are people talking about how much they're going to miss him. How much of a great guy he is. How great he smells. Okay, so maybe that last bit was just me.

'So when's he leaving?' Elsie asks, as she hands me over a tea.

Who knew I'd learn to love tea so much? I'm drinking it so much lately. It's the only thing I can seem to keep down. But it's just another thing to remind me of him.

'I don't know,' I shrug, trying to act unbothered, when it's obvious she can now read me like a book, or a bible in her case.

I still can't believe how close we've grown over this short time of knowing each other. She feels more like a sister than a cousin.

A knock at the door shakes me out of my daydream. It was a nice place there. Happy and innocent, back to when Will thought I was a decent person.

I look over to Elsie who takes a gulp of tea and opens a magazine, clearly pretending she hasn't heard it. She keeps telling me I need to try and carry on as usual. Like that's even an option.

I drag myself up off the sofa and swing the door open. I jolt when I see its James. What on earth is he doing here? He looks as gorgeous as ever, dressed in a red and black flannel shirt, with black jeans and converse.

'Oh…hey,' I smile, hopping from one foot to the other awkwardly. I haven't seen him since my head injury.

I should be mad at him. This guy is the reason Will and I broke up. He's the reason he turned back that night, getting the wrong idea about us. And he broke Elsie's heart. But I just can't hate him. He's too loveable and he looked after me when I was in pain.

'Hey, Rose,' he says quietly, not his usual confident self. He leans into the door, slightly looking at Elsie. 'Hey, Els.'

Ah, so that's why he's here! She looks up long enough to give him a false cutting smile before looking back at her magazine, although I have no doubt she's not actually reading it.

'So, anyway,' he shakes his head, as if trying to gather his thoughts. 'I just wanted to come and check you were okay after the whole head thing.'

'It's fine,' I shrug. 'It was just an accident. You really didn't do anything wrong.'

'HA!' Elsie shouts cruelly from behind me.

I look over but she's back to pretending to read a magazine. Subtle Elsie, *real* subtle.

'Still,' he shrugs, leaning against the door frame casually and crossing his arms. 'I'm sorry.'

'Apology accepted.'

He smiles, but doesn't go to leave. I grab the edge of the door not so subtly. Why is he still here?

'And I just wanted to invite you both to my birthday party tonight. It's at the pub. Seven thirty.'

I look to Elsie who just stands up and walks into the kitchen, slamming the door behind her. I imagine Phil's reaction to me turning up. Angry, bald tomato man doesn't look good on anyone.

'Thanks, but I seriously doubt Phil would want to see me.'

I've just ruined his life.

He grins. 'He would. I've already asked his permission.'

'Really?' I ask hopefully.

He must have this wrong.

'Yep. Says since you stopped the village feud he's decided you're not pure evil.'

I don't understand. Surely there was a massive fallout after Megan found out. She *must* have confronted him, right?

'Gee, thanks.' I roll my eyes for good measure. 'But will your brother be there?'

'So what?'

I shrug non-committedly.

He leans further into the house. 'Can I…can I talk to Elsie?' he asks nervously, as if I'm going to attack him.

'If she'll listen,' I laugh, rolling my eyes again. 'Good luck with that.'

'She's always been stubborn,' he smiles fondly. It gives me an insight into what their relationship must have been like.

'But,' I warn sternly, 'you upset her and I'll put your balls through a mincer.'

His eyes widen in horror. 'Understood,' he nods with a cheeky grin.

He walks past the sofa and into the kitchen, shutting the door behind him.

I sit down on the sofa, straining my neck, desperate to hear some of their conversation.

'What the HELL are you doing here?' Elsie shrieks. I've never heard her so pissed off. It's actually scary.

'I already told you,' he says calmly. 'I'm inviting you both…'

'Don't bullshit, James,' she interrupts. 'Why are you here, in this kitchen, trying to talk to me?'

God, she's harsh, but I suppose he deserves it. I can't imagine how broken she must have been to consider becoming a nun.

'I'm sorry, babe.' I hear his feet scuffle closer, the floor board creaking underneath him.

'Don't *BABE* me!' she roars. 'I'm not fucking interested, James. I know we broke up and you can do whatever the fuck you want, but my cousin? Sleeping with my cousin? Was it just to hurt me, or was that just a bonus?' The hurt is obvious in her voice.

I still can't believe I unwittingly did that to her.

'I wasn't trying to hurt you, okay!' he shouts back. 'I was just trying to forget you.'

There's a pause and I wonder what their facial expressions look like.

'Fuck, since we've split all I've been trying to do is forget you, but it doesn't matter how many people I sleep with I *STILL* can't forget.'

There's an eerie silence and I know Elsie must be shocked by his admission. I bloody am.

'Well, soon I'll be off to a ministry so you can forget me for good.' She doesn't even sound like she's convinced herself.

'Don't go, Els,' he says softly. 'It's bullshit!'

'I need to!' she shrieks, a small sob escaping. 'I can't bear being in the same village as you anymore.'

'You're acting like I broke things off. It was you, Els. You broke my heart.'

Huh? Broke *his* heart? I thought he didn't want to commit to her? Did she overreact?

'I thought you didn't *have* a heart,' she snaps. 'That's what you said, wasn't it? You weren't sure if you had a heart left to love anyone. Well, I can't just wait around with my legs open until you decide I'm worth your time.'

Wowzas.

'You were always worth my time!' he shouts aggressively. 'All I was asking for was some fucking time! And you just upped and left me, proving to me that all women leave me in the end.'

He must be talking about his mum. It's clearly fucked him up.

There's silence and I know it's because Elsie has no idea what to say. That's some fucking speech James. I'm impressed.

'You know what, fuck this,' he says quietly.

The door swings open and I try to sit normally and act as if I wasn't eaves dropping. He strides through the sitting room, his hand through his curls, before slamming the cottage door behind him. It rattles the whole house.

I look towards the kitchen, not knowing what to do. Should I leave her be? Or will she want comforting? I eventually walk slowly over and peer through the door. She's slumped down on the floor, crying silently.

'Oh, Els!' I cry, rushing over and pulling her into my arms, so I can soothe her.

'Did you hear that?' she sobs, her breath coming out in harsh spurts. 'He just needed time…and…and I just messed everything up.

And now I'm becoming a nun…and…and I can't even watch TV!' She wails the last bit, before hitting her head hard against my chest. It hurts like a mother fucker, but I swallow down my swear word and instead rub her hair.

'What are you going to do?' I ask, when her sobs decrease down to whimpers.

She leans back onto her ankles. 'I don't know, but I know that we're going to that party and we're going to look lush.'

I back away from her, my skin covering in goose bumps at the thought of seeing Will.

'Els, I'm not going. You have to be joking. Will is going to be there. It's probably a joint party.'

'Which is why you're gonna look banging. Come on.'

***

Elsie takes my hand and guides me into the pub, my hand trembling uncontrollably.

'Calm down, Rose,' she snaps, more edgy than I've ever seen her. 'You look amazing.'

I take a deep breath to calm myself. She's right. I'm wearing my wet look leggings with my gold embellished short dress that shows just the right amount of boob. I look good, if I do say so myself.

With a dart of apprehension I let her lead me up to the bar. I look at the floor, not yet feeling confident to face people. I need vodka.

When I get enough courage I look up, expecting everyone to be staring at me. They're not; just chatting and enjoying the party atmosphere. When people catch my eye they smile. I glance up above the bar to read James' Happy Birthday banner. Next to it's another banner. 'Good Luck.' I know it's for Will.

'Can I have a word, pet?' Phil asks, appearing behind the bar.

My stomach curls up in fear and runs out the door. I nod, following him to a quiet corner. He's going to kill me. In front of all these people.

He turns to look at me when he feels we're far away enough from everyone.

'I'm sorry,' I blurt out before he can speak.

He shakes his head. 'Listen, Rose, luckily Lauren calmed me down and explained what happened. I realise you didn't intend to hurt Megan. That's not saying you didn't. But, well, it got me and Lauren talking. I didn't realise how unhappy she was with the current arrangement. Anyway, now that Megan knows there's nothing stopping me from being a real dad to him.'

'Really?' I ask in disbelief.

Noah's going to have a dad? That's amazing!

'Aye,' he nods. 'Megan will come around eventually.'

I nod, even though I'm pretty sure she won't be so forgiving with me.

'You could have a word with her, mind.'

I shrug non-committedly and join Elsie back at the bar.

'When's Will leaving?' Elsie asks Phil as soon as he's back behind the bar.

'Tonight, pet. He's setting off about nine thirty.'

Tonight? I assumed, with the party, he'd wait until the morning. I thought I had more time. For what I don't know. I'm never going to see him again, starting from tonight? The pain crushes against my chest, far harder than Elsie's skull did earlier.

I can't breathe. The one man I truly love…I mean, I really like him. Why is breathing so difficult? It's like the realisation has punctured a lung.

'Rose, are you okay?' Elsie asks, looking alarmed.

I have to get out of here. Everything's too loud, too overwhelming. I need a minute.

I turn and run towards the toilets, only I slam into a hard chest. I know it's him before I've even looked up. His smell, the curves of his muscles, the way my body reacts. It all screams Will.

'Rose,' he whispers softly.

I look up at him apologetically and slowly untangle myself from his body. He looks amazing. He's wearing a black shirt, the sleeves rolled up to his elbows like always. He is showing off those forearms I love. His hair is its usual dishevelled mess and his face is impassive as usual. He's so hard to read. Not that I'll need to after tonight. My heart squeezes a bit tighter at the thought.

'Sorry,' I mumble, ducking out of the way and walking around him. I can't deal with this.

He grabs my arm and pulls me back towards him, so close our bodies are almost touching again. The heat from his chest warms me and the urge to collapse into it is almost uncontrollable. He grabs my chin and lifts it up so that I'm looking into those beautiful green eyes. God, how I've missed them. It's painful to think it'll be the last time.

'Aren't you here to say goodbye to me? Don't you think you should?' He looks so deadly serious. He takes my breath away.

'I was…James invited me,' I blab out, my voice shaky and uneven.

As soon as he hears his name his shoulders sag and his jaw tightens. Why did I say his name?! Am I *trying* to remind him of the horrible situation?

Idiot. *Idiot.*

'*He* invited you. Of course he did,' he nods, looking away, as if too disgusted to even look at me. 'Tell me, did you even know it was my leaving do as well?'

I drop my eyes to the floor, ashamed. I guessed, but I was hoping I wouldn't have to face him.

'I see,' he answers for me. 'Well, I'll make this proper easy for you, Rose.'

I look up to him expectantly, into his cold, steely gaze.

'Goodbye,' he breathes frostily, giving me his iciest look, before turning and stomping away.

The hurt twists inside me like a knife. Tears are pouring thick and fast, ruining my smoky eyes. I have to get out of here. And now.

I push past people, as I all but run out of the pub and into the street. When I'm free of bodies I double over, trying to catch my breath.

How can my life feel like it's falling apart all over again? It's like I can't breathe without him. He's my oxygen. God, what a stupid girl thing to think.

I force myself to stand straight and walk back to the cottage, all the while wailing like an injured seal.

I let myself in and fill the kettle, flicking it to boil. God, I'd never drink tea if it wasn't for him! He's made me who I am today in so many ways. No, stop this.

I slap myself in the face. Fuck, that hurt. I've got quite a right hander. That's good to know.

I drag myself up stairs, my chest rattling as if I've run all the way home. It's just my grief trying to crush me. I won't let it though; I'm determined.

Instead I take my make up off, change into my pyjamas and settle down in front of Elsie's The OC box set. God, life would be so much easier if I was living in Orange County and looked like Marissa. *Sigh.*

The only problem is that now I'm alone in the house, all I can think about is him. Times we were together. The winking. The way he rolls his sleeves up to expose those perfect bronzed forearms. How gentle he was with me, treating me like I deserved it. Which I didn't.

Even though I completely understand his reasoning's for going, I still selfishly don't want him to. I don't get how he can just run off and leave without pursuing the possibility of us. I mean, even if I had slept with James while we were together, wouldn't I still deserve to have a second chance? Doesn't everybody?

I should be stronger. I should be more of a feminist. The fact that he's just running away should prove to me that he's not worth the heartache, but… Oh, but who am I kidding? I'm bloody mad about him. Head over heels in…lust? Love? I really don't know. Just head over crazy arse. And knowing he's going with Riley is just salt in the wound. Maybe they're already back together.

I might as well just turn in for an early night. I'm not even concentrating on the TV. Cry myself to sleep.

I'm just about to lift my sad arse off the sofa, when I hear a key in the door. Crap, that must be Elsie. She must have come after me. I'm *so* not in the mood to talk right now. I quickly turn off the lamp and TV, so I'm in total darkness. Hopefully she'll just assume I'm asleep and go back to the party.

I watch Elsie's body stumble in, but I quickly realise from the smooching sounds, that she's not alone. Oh crap. Is it James?

I sink down onto the sofa, praying to God not to be seen. I hear them coming closer and I pray it's to the stairs. They're coming to the sofa. Crap.

They fall on top of me and I yelp out a scream, Elsie's elbow hitting me in the stomach.

'AAAAGGGGHHH!!!' Elsie screams, jumping off me.

'FUCK!' James shouts at the same time. 'What is it?'

The light flicks on, as I attempt to catch my breath. The bitch winded me in their moment of passion.

'Rose?' James says, staring at me in disbelief.

'What the fuck are you doing sitting in the dark?' Elsie demands, her face red and her pink lipstick smudged.

I love how *they're* the ones shouting accusations.

'What the hell are you two doing anyway?' I giggle, clutching my tummy. Like it's not obvious.

'Nothing!' Elsie shrills, turning beetroot. James stands behind her and wraps his arms around her waist, grinning knowingly at me. 'Nothing at all!'

'Okay, kids,' I smile, rolling my eyes. 'Just use protection.'

'We will,' James sings, pulling her towards the stairs.

'We're not even doing anything,' she insists as he pulls her away.

He rolls his eyes.

'This is weird,' she muses, clearly trying to pull herself together. 'I should stay here. Let Rose talk some sense into me. I mean, I'm supposed to be a nun soon.'

James continues to drag her up the stairs, ignoring her.

It's only when they're at the top that I hear him say, 'Trust me, the things you were saying to me earlier should not be coming out of a nun's mouth.'

Ugh, gross. I wonder if Elsie's a dirty bitch in the bedroom? The whole librarian in the day, freak in the bedroom kind of thing. Go Elsie!

The door knocks, someone banging urgently. For a second I'm scared to open it, in case it's someone else trying to join the party banging around upstairs. I shake my head. Don't be ridiculous, Rose.

But then hope springs into my heart. What if it's Will to confess he can't leave without me? I pinch my cheeks in the pathetic attempt to look a bit more attractive and a little less like a blob fish.

I open the door and jolt when I see a man in his late fifties. It takes me a minute to focus on his face and realise its Will's dad. What the hell is he doing here?

'Oh…hi.' I grimace, having no idea why the hell he's here.

He doesn't say anything. I shift my weight from one foot to another, nerves travelling up my legs and into my stomach. Why isn't he speaking?

'Hi, Rose, is it?' he asks, seeming shy and unsure.

I don't know what I'm more stunned about. The fact that he's here, or the fact that he's speaking. I've never heard him speak before. Ever. I almost thought he was a mute.

'Yeah, that's me.'

The vixen that's had sex with both your sons, I want to add.

Oh God. A horrific thought crosses my mind. What if he's here thinking I'll sleep with him? What if he's heard I'm easy and just thinks he can knock at my door and I'll spread my legs? Am I the village bike? I look at his beer belly and shudder. Could he *really* think that?

'Look, I know I have no right to be here, and you probably don't want to hear this, but you need to tell Will how you feel,' he announces calmly.

I gawk at him, my mouth hanging onto the floor. What the hell does he know?

'What? How I feel?' I laugh, to show how ludicrous the idea of feelings for him is. 'I don't know what you're talking about.'

This is *so* humiliating. I really wish I wasn't wearing Elsie's care bear pyjamas right now.

He gives me a knowing look. 'I'm not stupid, Rose. It's obvious how much he loves you.'

His words floor me. He still loves me?

'He's different leaving this time. I know he doesn't really want to go.'

He creases his face in grief. The poor man's already lost his wife. Now I've driven his son away. I can understand why he'd cling onto any reason for him to stay, but I'm not it. Will's made his feelings clear.

'Well then why on earth would he be going?' I challenge, placing my hand on my hip.

It makes no sense. Love makes you fight for someone. I only wish it were true.

He sighs, shoving his hands into his pockets. It reminds me of Will.

'Because he's very stubborn and because you clearly haven't told him how *you* feel. Will's had enough heartache in his life.'

A flush of sadness crosses his face at the mention of his wife's death.

'Just please promise me you'll tell him? He's leaving now. You have to go now if you want to catch him.'

Leaving now? I thought he wasn't going until later. It's only nine fifteen. Not that I've been checking the clock every two minutes.

I bite my lip, as I start to comprehend that he might actually still be hoping I beg him to stay. Could it be possible? He did ask me to give him a reason to stay, but I didn't think it was fair of me to ask him to stay.

I mean, maybe his Dad has it all wrong and I'll make an absolute fool of myself. I couldn't bear for my heart to be broken further. It's already in jagged pieces. But then I think of his face, smiling down at me in bed. His dimple. His broad chest. Him holding me. God I've turned into such a soppy bitch.

Sudden adrenaline goes coursing through my veins. Fuck it. I don't care what I said or did before, I have to tell him. I can't let him go without knowing all of the choices he has.

'Thanks…Will's dad,' I shout, as I slam the door after me and run towards the pub.

Chapter 27

I don't care that I'm in my slippers and pyjamas. I'm sure he won't mind. Well, he won't mind if he loves me. If he doesn't I'll just get rejected in my pyjamas. At least I can crawl straight into bed to cry.

I round the corner of the road to the pub, just in time to see Riley's car pulling away with him in it. I race down the road, waving my arms frantically and yelling for them to stop. I just get exhaust fumes in my mouth and confused faces from everyone waving him off. I must look extra nutty right now.

What the fuck am I going to do? I need to tell him now. If he gets settled in Leeds first he might not ever want to come home. He might be together with Riley by then, if not already. She'll get her whorey claws into him as soon as she can.

I spot Mr Allington getting into his car and rush over, noting my opportunity. I grab the keys from his hand, push him to the floor and get into the car.

'What the on earth are you doing?' he screeches, clutching his sides as if I've winded him. What a drama queen.

'I'm sorry. It's an emergency!' I don't have time to explain. I slam the door and start the engine.

He tries to open the door, but I've already locked it. I suppose they aren't used to car jacking's here. But I mean, I'll bring it back. He's *totally* over reacting.

Lauren and Megan bang on the opposite window.

'We'll follow you,' Lauren shouts.

I nearly burst into tears at realising they still want me as a friend and are willing to go out of their way to help me. I nod and smile back at them.

I put the car in gear and race after Will, heading for the main road that joins the two villages to the motorway. I have to over-take a few cars, but I'm finally behind Riley's red Ford Fiesta.

I start flashing my head lights frantically, but all I get is her giving the finger in her rear mirror. She mustn't know it's me. Or she knows it is me, but isn't stopping. She knows she's going to have Will all to herself. The little bitch.

I start honking the horn.

HONK. HOOOOOOOOOOOOONK!

She's still not slowing down. I'm just getting some weird looks from other drivers. It doesn't help that I'm in pyjamas. I must look crazy. Or at least crazier than normal. And I'm bloody freezing. I have no time to mess around with heating dials right now.

Right, that's it. I'm clearly going to have to take drastic action. I go to overtake them and slow down when we're side by side. I start hooting again. They start looking and I smile, relieved. Thank God! Will looks baffled. Riley looks violent.

I glance back at the road and realise a car is coming towards me in my lane. I'm in the wrong lane! SHIT!

Floor it! I put my foot down and manage to swerve in front of Riley, but I must clip it as my car spins round, throwing me to my right side, before stopping right in front of their approaching car. I see the fear in their horrified faces. I scrunch my eyes shut and cover my head with my hands, knowing they won't be able to brake in time. I'm going to die. Head on collision. Goodbye cruel world. This is going to hurt.

I hear a crunch of metal, as every muscle in my body tenses in anticipation. The air bag hits me in the face, but the pain I'm expecting doesn't come. I don't know if it's because I'm in shock or because I died instantly and I'm in heaven. I tentatively remove my hands and slowly unscrunch my eyes. I wrestle the air bag and look to the car in front of me. It's smashed into my car, but my legs aren't crushed. I'm alive!

No one's in the seats though. Fuck, I've killed them! They mustn't have been wearing seatbelts and they've been thrown from the sun roof. Oh my God, I'm a murderer! What the hell have I done?

A bang on my door makes me jump out of my skin. I turn to see Will trying the door handle. He's alive! Thank you baby Jesus!

I unlock the door and start to fight the air bag, letting myself out onto unsteady jelly legs. I throw myself at him. Luckily he catches me in his arms.

'Will, you're alive! Thank God! Or are you an angel? Am I dead?' I'm crying now, hysterically sobbing, snot dripping from my nose. This was too close to death.

He hugs me back fiercely, wrapping his arms around my waist, as if he never wants to let go. Then he pulls back, leaving me feeling bereft. I need more.

'What the fuck are you doing, Rose? You could have killed yourself!' he berates loudly. He looks furious, his eyes mad.

I look back at the tangled cars and burst into heavier sobs. I see Lauren and Megan pull over and go to stop Riley from coming over here to confront me.

'I could have killed *you*! I'm so sorry. Are you okay?' I start checking him all over. Any excuse to touch his perfect biceps.

'I'm fine,' he says, shooing me away with a cute smile.

'My car's not!' I turn round to see Riley screeching at me, her face almost purple from what looks like pure rage. Lauren and Megan are physically trying to hold her back. 'What the fuck is your problem, you bloody idiot!!'

I now notice that the car behind her has gone into the back of her car. Whoops. I've caused quite a pile up. Luckily they seem fine too. Well, you know, apart from their car.

'It's not her fault, Riley,' Will protests, standing protectively in front of me. I cling onto his back. 'Well…it is, but…oh, just shut up. We'll sort it.'

I can't believe he told Riley to shut up. He turns back to me.

'What are you doing here? Why were you trying to get our attention? And why on earth are you in Mr Allington's car?'

I pull a face. 'Um…it's kind of a long story.'

'Right,' he nods, seeming amused.

I grab hold of his biceps, almost fainting from the feel of his muscles under my hands. Must get a grip, Rose. Focus on the task at hand.

'Don't go,' I whisper pathetically. It's all I can think to say right now. I hadn't factored in a car crash.

'What?' he asks, his face soft and vulnerable.

'Don't go,' I repeat, louder this time. 'Stay here. Stay with me. Stay with Mitsy.' My vocabulary really isn't impressing anyone here.

His face clouds with regret. 'Rose, if this is about Mitsy… I'm sure you can make some kind of arrangement with the new owner to still see her.'

He thinks this is about a horse?

'That's not what this is about! *I* own Mitsy. *I'm* her owner.'

He scrunches his forehead in confusion. 'No', he says slowly, as if speaking to a child. 'You're not.'

He must think I've had some sort of nervous breakdown.

'Yes, Will,' I say just as slowly. 'I am.' I let go of his arms, so I can explain. 'I got Mrs Fenham to put the offer in for me. I knew you wouldn't want to sell her to me.'

'Why would I have stopped you?' He seems genuinely puzzled.

'Because…you know…you hate me now.' I line my foot against the ground, not feeling a smidgen of the confidence I felt while chasing him.

'What?' I look up to see a smirk starting on his face. 'Rose, why on earth do you think I hate you?'

I sigh, another sob escaping. 'Because you found out about James, *WHICH,* may I add, was way before I even knew I liked you. And then you found out I stole money from Elsie, because I'm a horrible fucking human being. So of course you hate me.'

He looks at me intently. 'Rose, I thought you didn't care. I assumed we'd talk about it when I'd cooled down, but then I heard from Mrs Fenham that you weren't looking after Mitsy anymore. Then when Betty died you told me you hated me. What was I to think, but what your words and actions had told me?'

God, men are thickos. Can't they read women? What's so bloody difficult?

I look down at my wobbly legs. 'Well I don't hate you. I might even…' I stop myself before I make a complete dick out of myself.

'You might even…what?' he asks, leaning forward in interest.

My eyes widen, caught in the headlights of his probing eyes.

'Nothing.' I look to the floor, nervous.

'Look, Rose, last chance,' he warns with a heavy, weary sigh. 'If you have a reason for me to stay say it now. I'm not going to stick around for you to play games with me.'

'I don't know what I feel!' I admit, throwing my hands in the air. 'I just know that I hate you being anywhere near Riley when she wants you back. I know that the thought of you leaving and not seeing you again fills me with so much fear, I could vomit right here in the street. But I also know that if this is what you really want to do, then I'll let you go. I know I stole Mr Allington's car so I could stop you in Elsie's care bear pyjamas. I know that I don't want to be your Betty. That's all I know.'

'Huh?' he asks bewildered.

'Betty was your grandad's great love. Only they lived their life with the regrets of their lost love. I don't want to be like them. I want to be like Mavis and Bernie; so ridiculously in love that we have to shag each other's brains out in a church confessional.'

'Rose,' he tries to interrupt, clearly baffled.

'Anything beyond that…I guess I'm just a feeling moron or something.' I shrug apologetically. What a bloody word vomit. I've definitely lost him now.

He takes my hands, a smirk on his face.

'Well…I'm not a feeling moron and…I think you just told me you loved me.' He seems to find me hilarious.

'No, I don't!' I shout, hitting him on the chest.

'You *so* do,' he smiles, crinkling his beautiful eyes shyly. 'You just described being in love.'

I cringe from the word. 'Stop saying it! It sounds gay.' Why couldn't I be a normal girl and be able to talk all this crap?

'Okay…shall we just say that you kinda like me?' he asks, amused.

'Yes,' I nod, feeling far more confident with that assessment. 'I kinda like you.'

He pulls me into his chest, wrapping his arms tightly around me. 'Well lucky for you, I kinda like you too.'

He pulls back slightly and grabs my chin with his forefinger and thumb, tilting my head so I'm looking into his eyes. God, I could look into them forever. He's far too beautiful for his own good.

'You know this means you're mine, right? Completely and utterly mine and nobody else's?' he says smugly, but I also sense it's a bit of a question.

'Yes,' I breathe, willing him to kiss me. Our lips are so close I can feel his breath.

'Good.' He lowers his sweet lips to mine and pulls his hand round my neck, sending tingles down my spine. My heart swells with appreciation. *You did good,* it tells me.

'Err, hello?!'

We both jump and turn to look at Riley. She looks ready to commit murder. He smiles apologetically. I smirk arrogantly, making sure not to leave his embrace. I've got him now, bitch.

'Sorry, Riley, but I'm not going to Leeds,' he says, looking affectionately down at me as if to explain.

'But what about the job? Don't tell me you're turning it down?' She practically has steam coming out of her ears. She can see her perfect plan coming apart at the seams.

'I am,' he nods, turning me around and pulling my back into his front so I can fully face her as he wraps his arms tightly around my waist.

'You're crazy! You're turning down a real job and a real life just so you can stay and be with that slut?' she spits.

'Hey!' he barks. 'Don't talk about her like that.'

God he's so dreamy. Especially when he's sticking up for me.

'That's enough,' Lauren shouts.

'Let me punch her,' Megan begs. 'Just one punch.' Lauren rolls her eyes and restrains her.

'Whatever. You have to get real, Will, and realise you need to grow up.'

'I think he's grown up mighty fine,' I grin, tracing the muscles on his arms. 'And if you cared about him half as much as you pretend you do, you'd be telling him to do what makes him happy. Not take a job he feels he should.'

'Yeah, good luck with that,' she scoffs back, getting into her badly battered car and attempting to drive off.

'Come on,' he says, pecking me on the cheek. 'But this time I'm driving. I think we have some explaining to do to Mr Allington.'

I dig him in the ribs and happily follow him to the car. To start my life with him.

Best day ever.

THE END

Three Years Later

'Betty!' I call, watching her take another tumble dangerously close to horse poo. 'I've told you to be careful, babe.'

She gets herself up, dusts down her pink dress and laughs at herself.

'Sorry, Mumma,' she giggles. 'Horsey did it.'

I smile, shaking my head at my adorable two year old. How the hell did I get so lucky? Oh, that's right, I moved here. Will and I decided, after all that drama, we'd save up and take a holiday to Mexico. He said I needed to get it out of my system, before settling down and I guess he was right.

We partied every night; dancing on bars, chugging on tequila, having sex, forgetting to wear a condom. That's right, I got pregnant on our first ever holiday together, only a couple of months after we got together. It was *so* me!

I didn't actually find out until we got home, but Will proposed to me on our last day on the hotel's private beach, with a photographer capturing the moment. We decided that we didn't want a lot of fuss, so we changed our flights so that we could swing by Vegas on the way home.

We got married by a Chinese Elvis, relaxed in our jeans and t-shirts. Well, Will was wearing a shirt. When isn't he? Although it was hilarious and spontaneous and okay, maybe a bit crazy, it was still the most romantic moment of my life. Will declaring his love to me forever.

Soon after we got back we found out I was pregnant. I was beyond shocked, while Will was ecstatic, immediately planning the nursery in Betty's old house. That's right, I never sold it. Will gave back Elsie the money she'd lent me to buy Mitsy, so I took it off the market and now it's our family home.

Everyone in the village obviously assumes that we had a shotgun wedding because of the pregnancy, but we don't care. Let them think what they want to think.

We had two names. Betty for a girl, after my Betty, and Thomas for a boy, after Will's grandad. I won!

Will scoops Betty up in his arms and holds her high above his head. She chuckles in glee.

'Are you ready to go see Nanna and Grandad?' he laughs.

My mum and dad moved here soon after she was born. They decided to retire early, downsize, and live in the countryside. Now that I don't actually live with them we have a fantastic relationship. Especially since Betty's birth. It's made me realise how hard being a mother is. I can understand how my mum struggled with it.

He turns to kiss me on the lips, Betty now perched on his hip. 'Are you okay to close up here?'

'Of course,' I grin, giving him another cheeky kiss.

I started up my own horse mucking out company. What started as me just doing a few little jobs for people for a bit of extra cash has now turned into me hiring two girls.

Will's a freelance accountant. He's managed to somehow become the whole village's accountant and he loves it. What a snore! But hey, whatever gets me out of paying taxes!

I wave to Lauren and Phil, taking Noah out for his first horse ride. It's great that they can now co-parent, although no one is under any illusion that they'll get together as a couple. I have someone I met at a horse fair lined up for her anyway, not that she claims she's interested.

Megan really took Noah under her wing as her little brother. She's just gone off to UCL to study Law, little brain box that she is. Turns out all it took was for her to watch Legally Blonde, and after that she was a girl on a mission. It helps that she found out she can extend her degree by a year and study abroad in America, Australia or Singapore. I miss her already.

Elsie decided against nun-ville, thank God. She's now the manager at the care home. It's the perfect way for her to still feel like she's making a difference, but be allowed to have sex. She and James are getting married next month in the most over the top ceremony I've ever heard of. There's going to be swans, harps, the lot. But she deserves it, she deserves the world.

She's asked my dad to walk her down the aisle, which made him blub hysterically. It must run in the family. I'm maid of honour, Will is the best man, Lauren and Megan are bridesmaids and Betty is their little flower girl. Although with the way she's behaving lately, I'll be lucky if she doesn't cartwheel down the aisle. Little rebel. I wonder who she takes after…

Acknowledgements

Firstly a massive thank you for buying my book – you keep my toddler in shoes! Thanks to all of my supporters; you guys have helped my dreams come true. Still feel like I'm going to wake up any moment!

Thanks to my family and friends for putting up with me. It can't be easy having a sleep deprived, day dreaming nutcase around. Special smoochy kisses to my husband Simon who makes me endless cups of tea and cooks continuous dinners so I can keep typing into the early hours. Also my two cheerleaders Mum and Mad; what would I do without your unconditional love and belief in me?! Huge shout out to the Colleran clan in both England and Ireland!

Big hugs to my friends Clare Pinkstone, Julie Wills and Nikki Chamberlain who are my trusted ladies to read the first draft and tell me all of the holes and inconsistencies in the plot. Without you nothing would make sense!

Thanks to Adam Wilson for showing me that Shift F7 gives me a shortcut to a thesaurus – endless hours saved!

Thanks to my Yorkshire friends Debbie Wilson, Laura Wilson and Natalie McMullen for answering all of my stupid questions ('do they say dickhead up there?' ha ha). Also shout out to the two Yorkshire men I met while drunk on the Euston to Watford train. I promised you a mention and I'll never forget your words of wisdom ☺

Major shout out to all of the many blogs that have helped spread the word about me. There are SO many, but a few I feel I'd like to mention are Island Lovelies, Two Ordinary Girls & their Books, A Reader's Review…my God, there's so many! If you're not mentioned please don't feel I don't love you any less. Without each and every one of you taking time out from your day to help spread the word of us Indie authors, we'd be nowhere!

Thanks to KMS Freelance Editing and Tara at Begmeforbeta (your comments always make me laugh and I know that you 'get' me).

Thanks to my new author friends who I badgered with endless stupid questions. Especially Dani Lovell and Yessi Smith.

Lightning Source UK Ltd.
Milton Keynes UK
UKOW04f0745250216

269080UK00002B/68/P